MW01231975

WARRIOR'S CROSS

MADELEINE URBAN
AND
ABIGAIL ROUX

Dreamspinner Press

Published by
Dreamspinner Press
4760 Preston Road
Suite 244-149
Frisco, TX 75034
http://www.dreamspinnerpress.com/

Cover Art by Anne Cain annecain.art@gmail.com
Cover Design by Mara McKennen

ISBN: 978-1-61581-029-1

Printed in the United States of America
First Edition
August, 2009

eBook edition available
eBook ISBN: 978-1-61581-030-7

To the mysteries in life.

CHAPTER I

"CAM? He's back."

The waiter looked up from the bottle of wine he was corking. "He?"

Miri Taylor rolled her expressive eyes and tipped her head to one side, sending the long blonde tail of hair off her shoulder. "Yes. *He*. You know; tall, dark, devastatingly handsome, always comes alone on Tuesday nights, always writing in the little notepad—"

"Always orders the special and no dessert. Yes, I remember," Cameron Jacobs answered hastily, going back to the bottle in an effort to hide the little jump in his nerves.

"Well, Mr. Nichols put him in your section again," Miri informed him with a smirk. "Did you ask for him to be seated in your section? That's like six times in a row!"

"Is it?" Cameron asked nonchalantly, although for the past month and a half he had looked forward to Tuesday nights like nothing else for that very reason. "I hadn't really thought about it," he lied. "I do work sixty-plus hours a week, you know," he reminded her. "I don't always remember everyone."

"Yes, you do," Miri argued.

Cameron gave her a sideways glance and tried not to smile.

"Well, you'd better get out there," she urged as she glanced through the slats of the fashionable wooden shutters that hid the service area from the rest of the restaurant. "That man is so fine," she muttered to herself.

Cameron stifled a laugh. He finished with the bottle and took a deep breath to calm the sudden racing of his heart. “Put this back in the cooler, would you?” he requested as he handed Miri the bottle and headed out to the floor.

Carefully recessed lights, candles on every table, and tiny, twinkling lights reflecting off the soaring glass ceiling lit the dining room. Large, clear windows along one wall offered a look at Chicago’s sparkling skyline, and tables dressed with fine linen, crystal, and china were spread about the ample space on varying levels. Soft jazz filled the air, just under the quiet buzz of voices highlighted by the clinks of utensils on plates and the scratch of chairs moving on the floor. Keri, the restaurant’s chief hostess, escorted a couple from the full waiting area to a solitary open table while many other patrons waited patiently, plied with champagne and light hors d’oeuvres.

Because at the four-star restaurant named Tuesdays, the food and service were said to be impeccable.

Cameron moved silently through the tables, his slight frame ghosting along in the all-black wait staff uniform. He wasn’t the type of man one tended to notice right off; he was trim and a little wiry, of average height and build, and he kept his brown hair cut short and neat. His quiet personality and tendency toward introversion made him naturally discreet while working, and his pleasant but unremarkable appearance made him perfect for scooting behind chairs and reaching around people with plates, coming and going without garnering attention or interrupting a patron’s meal.

He was perfect for what he did, and he enjoyed it. But tonight there was a little more to it.

Pausing near a burbling fountain, Cameron looked across the room at his goal: a quiet alcove for two, where one man sat alone.

He’d been coming to the restaurant sporadically since it had opened eight years ago, but in the past year or so he’d become a regular. Met at the door of Tuesdays by the restaurant’s owner every time he came to eat, he always sat at the same table. He was there once a week, always on a Tuesday, whether by design Cameron couldn’t have guessed. He always ordered the special—without looking at what it might be that day—and the house wine, but declined dessert.

Cameron knew these details like he knew hundreds of other tidbits about his regular patrons, people who frequented the fine restaurant and valued the renowned service. It was one of the many traits that made him excellent at his job.

His competence gave him confidence he wouldn't otherwise have had. Here at Tuesdays, he could handle these repeated encounters with the mysterious *him*.

Cameron came to a silent halt at the table and spoke softly. "Good evening, sir. The evening special and house wine?" he offered knowingly. It was the same thing he asked every week. He'd stopped introducing himself several months ago.

The dark man looked up at Cameron's approach and nodded wordlessly. Cameron bowed slightly and collected the untouched menu. The patron had always been this way. The first night Cameron had served him, a long finger had jabbed at the specials card and the house wine listing. He had never said a word then or since—at least not to Cameron—only nodding or shaking his head. Cameron never pressed him, and he'd started making an effort to ask questions in a way the man could answer without much trouble. He'd wondered more than once if the man could speak at all.

"Bring an extra glass, please," the man asked abruptly as Cameron turned away. His voice was barely there, much quieter than his large frame and dark, slightly ominous looks suggested it would be. It was as if it had wilted from disuse.

Cameron turned back, eyes a little wider than usual. "Of course," he said, hoping the surprise didn't show. "Anything else?" he asked before inwardly berating himself for sounding like an idiot as he stared at his normally silent customer.

The man shook his head curtly, the motion one sharp jerk of his chin to the left.

"Yes, sir," Cameron murmured, and he went on his way.

The man's voice, hoarse and raspy, echoed in his head. Cameron was sure he'd never forget the sound of it. And another glass? The enigmatic customer was one of the staff's favorite mysteries and thus a near endless source of gossip and intrigue. Each person had a theory, fantasy, or story about him. If anyone had seen the man speak to him, it would send the entire wait staff into a tizzy. Every little tidbit they could glean simply fueled their interest.

Cameron's heart beat a little faster as he thought about the extra glass, and he wasn't quite sure why. He collected the wine and the glasses from the bar, checked to make sure there were no smudges on the crystal, and returned to the table, the whole time telling himself to be cool. There was nothing to get excited about, he repeated silently as he deftly set down the glasses and started uncorking the wine.

The patron's eyes followed his movements unerringly. "I'll do that tonight," he said, his voice low, though a bit stronger than before. "Thank you," he added as he raised his head and looked at Cameron with dark, shadowed eyes. They reflected the candlelight like polished obsidian.

Cameron's hands stilled, and after a moment spent caught in the man's gaze, he offered the linen-wrapped bottle.

The man took it and nodded. "Thank you, Cameron," he said softly. There was a hint of a polite dismissal in the words.

Cameron stared for a moment before snapping out of it. "You're welcome," he said as he placed the corkscrew within reach before stepping away. Hearing his name on the man's lips made him shiver. It was… seductive. Without ever meaning to be, Cameron was sure.

The man waited until Cameron moved away before he deftly uncorked the bottle and poured himself an unseemly full glass. He looked up at the empty glass on the other side of the table for a long, motionless moment, then leaned over and poured a dainty glassful for the absent person who would sit across from him.

"Cam, what's he doing?" Miri demanded curiously as soon as Cameron returned to the service area.

Cameron deliberately avoided looking out into the dining area, instead going to work on filling a bread-basket. "What do you mean?" he asked, feigning ignorance in the hope that his own curiosity wouldn't show.

"He's got two glasses tonight. Is he meeting someone? Was he talking to you? What'd he say?" Miri asked excitedly.

"Don't you have work to do?" Cameron coaxed. He didn't want her to know that as soon as he'd heard the mystery man's voice, he'd fallen just a little more for him. It had been a long time coming, he knew. It was embarrassing enough to have a crush on a patron. It was worse to have a crush on someone who'd never actually spoken to you before.

Miri huffed and crossed her arms. "Well, it's a slow night. You *could* share a little, you know? That guy is the biggest mystery most of us have going! Let me live vicariously!"

Cameron wouldn't admit he felt the same way. He prided himself on his professionalism, and gossiping about patrons was not something he did or intended to start doing. "There's nothing to share," he insisted. "He asked for an extra glass; that's all."

Miri puffed her bottom lip out petulantly and turned to look out into the dining room. At the mostly hidden table for two in the far alcove, the mysterious man lifted his glass, toasted the one across from him, and then took a genteel sip of the expensive wine.

"That's really weird," Miri muttered as she watched.

"I've got work to do," Cameron said quickly before he could cave and go to look. He lifted a crystal water pitcher in one hand and the bread basket in the other and then fled the prep area to the floor, filling water glasses and making inquiries as he slowly worked his way toward the man who sat alone with his two glasses of wine.

Upon arrival, Cameron set down the basket and filled the water glasses. Both of them.

No matter how much he wanted to, Cameron couldn't come up with a question to ask in hopes the man would speak again. He'd seen other servers try to engage him in conversation, and it always made the dark man look annoyed or frustrated. Perhaps that was why he stayed in Cameron's sections now, because Cameron never pressed him.

Cameron turned to leave, giving the man his privacy once more.

"How long have you worked here?" the man asked suddenly.

Arrested, Cameron turned to face him, trying not to show his continuing surprise. "Since Tuesdays opened eight years ago," he replied warily, wondering why the man would ask.

The dark man looked at him steadily, his face expressionless and shadowed by the low mood lighting. "Do you enjoy what you do?" he asked.

Cameron felt unable to escape, pinned by those black eyes. He tried to avert his gaze by studying the man's face instead, something he had never allowed himself to do at such proximity. It was all hard lines: a high forehead, triangular jaw, sharp cheekbones. This close, he was even more handsome than Cameron had thought. His close-cropped dark hair was just barely graying at the temples, and his neatly trimmed mustache and beard were impeccable. He always wore dark clothing, blacks and charcoal grays, which did little to disguise his tall, muscular body once he shed his heavy winter coat. That color—or lack thereof—suited him in a way Cameron couldn't quite identify.

He was like a dark angel, to Cameron's mind.

After a moment, Cameron focused on answering the question. "Yes," he said. "I do enjoy it. Why else stay so long?"

The man's eyes slid away, and he turned to look back at the untouched wine glass. "Why, indeed," he agreed, the words clearly signaling the end of the conversation.

Cameron glanced to the second wine glass and back to the man. When dining here, the man had always been silent and polite, but surprisingly approachable in his own way, once Cameron got used to him. Tonight he just seemed… off. The fact he was speaking at all made this evening an unusual thrill. But the change in the man's routine also worried him.

"Are you… is everything all right?" Cameron ventured in a hushed voice.

The man looked back at him as if surprised to see Cameron still standing there. He answered with a curt nod and looked away once more. This time the dismissal was clear.

Disappointed but not offended, Cameron moved away, only casting one look over his shoulder as he stopped several tables away to fill more water glasses. The man in the alcove didn't look to have moved; he was still staring at the wine glass. The only movements he made were to bring his glass of wine to his lips and set it back down again. His eyes rarely strayed from the glass across from him as he waited for his dinner.

Cameron couldn't help but wonder about him. What was he doing? And more importantly, why was he doing it? What was different about tonight? It was obvious that no one would be joining him, so who was the glass for? With a quiet sigh, Cameron shrugged off the questions and headed to the kitchen to check on the special.

It was about ten minutes after leaving him that Cameron arrived back at the table with the tray, setting it on a stand and serving, trying not to let his eyes settle on the man despite the urge to study him up close again.

As Cameron placed the plate in front of him, the man's suit coat emitted a discreet dinging sound. He reached into his inner pocket and withdrew a cell phone, looked at the display briefly, and then looked up at Cameron.

"Could you bring the check, please?" he requested with a sigh of what might have been annoyance. It was, perhaps, the first hint of emotion he'd ever displayed to Cameron.

Cameron raised an eyebrow and nodded. "I can box this for you," he offered.

"No, thank you," the man responded as he replaced his phone. "Just the check. Quickly, please."

"Yes, sir," Cameron said, gathering the empty tray and leaving the dining room to fetch the requested item. He was back with it in only a few minutes, and he offered the black leather folder silently.

The glass across the table from the dark man sat undisturbed, a third full. His own glass was empty, and his food only slightly touched. He had obviously eaten what he could as he waited. He took the check with a nod.

Cameron stepped back to wait so he could complete the transaction as quickly as possible. He watched silently as the man reached into his suit jacket and removed a leather billfold. He withdrew three bills, slid them into the folder, and handed it back to Cameron.

"I won't be needing any change," he said. Cameron could barely hear his voice even though the background noise was slight. "Thank you for the advice," the man said as he stood and reached for his overcoat.

Cameron had never been this close to him when he was on his feet. He guessed the man was taller by at least four inches, perhaps even more. As he shrugged into his heavy overcoat, the black wool had the effect of making him appear even larger than he already was, and the overall impression was that he simply towered over Cameron.

Confused and slightly distracted by his physical presence, Cameron just nodded. He had no idea what advice he may have given the man, but he wasn't about to question him. He actually had to tip his head back a little to look up at him. "Have a good night," he offered. His voice was flustered.

The man gathered his belongings. He nodded at Cameron as he buttoned his overcoat. "Tuesdays are always good nights," he murmured.

Cameron tipped his head to one side, even more confused, but he knew better than to say anything else. He wasn't sure his tongue could actually form any more words anyway.

With a last nod, the man walked away from the table and Cameron, who watched until he was out the door.

Out of sorts, Cameron shook his head and cleared the table, the folder securely at the small of his back. Once he finished with the dishes, he went to settle the receipt and found three hundred dollars. One hundred would have covered the dinner, wine, and a pleasant tip. Cameron stood there looking at the money, wondering just what had happened tonight.

CAMERON spoke pleasantly with an older couple that dined at Tuesdays a few times a month before turning to head out of the dining room. The dinner crowd had thinned to almost nothing around nine, and business had slowed accordingly. Although the restaurant stayed open until midnight, Cameron knew it wouldn't pick up again. He had time now to work on his receipts. But that just meant he had time to think, as well.

It was Tuesday night, and he kept thinking about the Tuesday night two weeks ago that had rocked his world. He'd gone over it in his mind, closing his eyes to hear the dark rasp of the man's voice. When he hadn't come to dinner last week, breaking a months'-long streak, Cameron was terribly disappointed.

He still wondered what had happened to the mysterious patron and if he would see him again. All Cameron knew for sure was that he would've liked to have heard his voice again.

Now it seemed another Tuesday had passed without him.

Him. He of the tall, dark, and handsome variety, who stuck in Cameron's head like some sort of brooding fantasy. Cameron sighed. *Fantasy*. A man like that was certainly nothing but a fantasy to Cameron, someone who was too far out of his league in every way.

As he pondered, he heard Keri greet a new guest, followed instantly by the distinct voice of Blake Nichols, the owner of Tuesdays, greeting the same person warmly. When Cameron moved to peer through the fronds of the large plant next to him, he saw Blake shaking the guest's hand and directing Keri to lead him to an alcove table.

It took Cameron a long moment to actually realize who he was seeing. It was *him*.

Cameron stared for a long moment, unable to make himself move as his heart rate picked up. After a few frozen moments, he shook himself, entered the prep area, and picked up a bottle of house wine and a clean glass before moving to the table.

As he got closer, he could see that the man wasn't quite himself tonight. There was a tight line of stitches above his left eye and his right arm was in a sling. He was carefully shrugging out of the restrictive brace when Cameron approached the table.

Cameron took a few quicker steps and set down the bottle and glass. “Let me help,” he requested before thinking about it. He lifted the strap that was catching on the man’s jacket. He took a steady breath to ease his nerves over the liberties he was taking, and in so doing got a brief whiff of the man’s subtle cologne. He shivered and tried not to react to the intoxicating scent.

The man froze as Cameron touched him, but he relaxed quickly and lowered his head, allowing Cameron to help him out of the sling before he sat down. Cameron carefully pulled the fabric straps free and stepped back, simultaneously exhilarated by the contact and relieved to be moving away. He folded the sling and laid it in the chair opposite where the man settled.

The big man rolled his shoulder carefully and looked up at Cameron with dark, unreadable eyes. “Thank you,” he said. His voice was low again, the words barely audible.

Cameron’s polite reply was totally forgotten as he looked over the man’s face critically, taking in the stitches and fading bruises before meeting his eyes. “Are you okay?” he asked instead.

The man gave the customary jerk of his head in answer without moving his eyes from Cameron. Then he smiled slowly, one side of his mouth curling upward into a slight smirk. It made his face far less severe and foreboding, and if possible, even more handsome. “I’m fine,” he answered, sounding bemused. “Thank you,” he repeated.

Cameron nodded slowly, entranced by that slight curve of the man’s lips. “You’re welcome.” He blinked several times and finally recovered. “The evening special and house wine?” he asked awkwardly, gesturing to the bottle he’d set on the table.

“What do you recommend for dessert?” the man asked him in response.

Cameron’s brows jumped, and he had to grasp for something to say. He wasn’t accustomed to being so off-balance when taking someone’s order. The process was generally pretty cut and dry. “Ah. The praline cheesecake has been popular this evening,” he managed.

The man’s gaze didn’t waver. “What do *you* recommend?” he repeated slowly.

Cameron swallowed, feeling a little warm as the man kept his eyes and attention focused solely on him. "The pistachio crème brûlée." Why he was unnerved, he didn't know. He gave recommendations all night. But for this man to ask for his *own* favorite, it made his entire body warm.

"That's what I'll be having then," the man responded with a slight twitch of his lips that might have been another smile.

Cameron wondered if the man noticed how his waiter stared at him. Probably. He seemed like the type of man who noticed a lot. Cameron's cheeks heated, and he licked his lips nervously. "After dinner?" he asked.

"For dinner, if you please," the man answered with that ghost of a smile and even an amused light in his eyes. He obviously enjoyed how disconcerted Cameron was.

"Ah. Okay," Cameron said. He sighed as he realized the man knew he was embarrassed. "Do you want the wine?" he asked clumsily.

The man's black eyes drifted over the bottle and then back to Cameron slowly. "I do," he answered gently.

The nonthreatening tone helped Cameron find his composure, and he took shelter in the familiar movements, pulling the corkscrew out of his back pocket and picking up the bottle to open it. The man watched him the entire time, his eyes intent and shadowed. Cameron pulled the cork free and offered it to him, his other hand tight on the bottle. He felt the unusual nerves easing, and he was able to straighten his shoulders and recover his usual poise, even though he could feel those black eyes following his movements.

The man nodded at the cork and met Cameron's eyes. "Do you still enjoy what you do?" he asked out of the blue, his voice gruff and somehow intimate in the way he kept it at a whisper.

Cameron swallowed as the sound of it sent awareness zipping through him. Just like the first time, Cameron nodded. "Yes." But this time he asked, "Why?"

"Because you appear content," the man answered immediately.

Cameron blinked and then gave him an open and honest smile. "Yes. I suppose I am." He placed the cork on the table and poured a couple swallows into a glass for him to approve. "I'm good at it," he said with a shrug.

"Yes," the man murmured as he picked up the glass. He sampled the wine and nodded his head in approval. "Being good at what you do does help. Thank you, Cameron," he said softly.

"You're welcome," Cameron said. "Your dessert will be out shortly." He put down the bottle and left the table, taking the corkscrew with him and fighting back the fluttering in his chest.

"You know, I think he likes you," Miri asserted with a slight smile as soon as Cameron stepped into the service area.

"For God's sake, Miri," Cameron muttered as he blushed deeply.

"He likes you, and you are totally missing it. Would you even know what to do about it?" she challenged slyly.

Cameron made an aggravated sound and deliberately ignored her question. "How in the world is this either relevant or remotely appropriate? You're talking about a loyal customer, one who Blake always greets personally," he reminded pointedly.

Never mind that Cameron thought about him fairly frequently. Wondered about him. Even fantasized about him and that rough, quiet voice.

The waitress shook her head. "Wow, Cam," she said. "I bet if you made a move, he'd respond," she hinted.

"I don't want to make a move," Cameron insisted stubbornly.

"Why the hell not?" she asked in shock. "*I* would if I thought he'd go for it!" she claimed with a laugh. "No man who dresses that nice would be straight, though," she muttered. She peered through the blinds with an exaggerated sigh.

"If you're this bored, I'm sure we can find you something more to do," Cameron threatened as he glared at her.

She turned around and winked at him, patting him on the back. "Fine, Mr. Head Waiter, sir. I'll take his dessert out then," she taunted, swooping in to take the plate and ramekin that had just appeared, setting it on a small, linen-covered tray, and heading out to the dining room.

Cameron caught his objection at the last second and watched her go before he turned narrowed eyes on a couple of the other waitresses who huddled at the end of the bar. They scurried back to work with a flutter of giggles. Cameron groaned. This was all he needed. Miri and the other girls would pester him about it forever, never mind that he was technically their supervisor. He didn't know what Miri hoped to get out of this little interaction, but he hoped she was satisfied with whatever it was.

As much as he hated to, Cameron went to the slats and peered through, watching curiously.

Miri composed herself and approached the man's table. "Your dessert, sir," she offered as she presented the plate.

The man watched the plate as it was set in front of him. He slowly looked up at the waitress, his expression blank for a long moment before simply nodding his thanks.

Miri offered him a polite, charming smile. "May I bring you anything else?"

The man gave her his usual jerk of the head in answer as he placed a linen napkin in his lap with his good hand.

"Feel free to flag us down if you need anything," she told him happily, pausing for a few breaths before moving along to make her way back out of the dining room.

Once through the dark doors, she marched over to Cameron and waved her hand at the blinds. "See?" she said triumphantly.

"No, I don't," Cameron responded, looking up from the coffee service he was preparing. Yes, he'd given in to the urge to watch Miri talk to him, but *she* didn't need to know that.

"He was annoyed with me," she informed him with a smile. "He only wants you, Romeo," she crooned with a smile before heading off again.

Cameron stared after her before turning to check the dining room. He watched the man for a minute, examining the set of his shoulders and searching for signs of annoyance before frowning and shaking his head. Why would a man like that be interested in someone like him? First of all, he'd have to be into guys. And even if he was—which was a long shot in Cameron's opinion—why pick up a mere waiter? The man looked rich and successful and powerful. None of which Cameron was.

As he watched, Blake Nichols appeared and approached the table. The restaurant's owner stood for a long while as they talked, and then he sat on the edge of the chair across from the man, speaking with what was obviously concern. The patron's expression didn't change, but Cameron sensed he was speaking to Blake somewhat heatedly, if the motions of his uninjured hand were any indication.

The men were a study in opposites. The unnamed man had a tall, firm frame with tight muscles under his well-tailored clothing, jet black hair with those little hints of gray at the temples, his ever-present well-groomed beard and mustache. Blake Nichols, on the other hand, was clean-shaven with fine blond hair that always looked as if he'd been dragging his socks against the carpet. Fashionably messy. He wasn't as tall or as broad, but he was still trim and in very good shape.

Another difference between the two men: Blake wasn't shy about expressing himself verbally when his smooth, polished persona wasn't required on the dining floor. Cameron was extremely familiar with that. And Blake was a warm, friendly guy who tended to be easily distracted. In Cameron's experience, the patron had always been Blake's polar opposite, cold as ice and unflappable. But now Cameron was seeing true emotion, seeing the dark-haired man come alive, even if it was with some sort of frustration. And he was magnificent.

Cameron cursed under his breath. Now he'd never be able to get rid of the damn crush.

Soon enough, Blake stood and placed his hand on the dark man's uninjured shoulder before leaving him to his dessert. Cameron watched as the man sat silent and blank for a moment before pulling a small, beat-up moleskin notebook from his seemingly endless supply of pockets and placing it carefully beside his plate. He then extracted an expensive-looking pen and opened the notebook.

He ate his crème brûlée carefully with his injured right hand as he wrote in the notebook with his left. It was something he did often, writing in the little book while eating his dinner. Cameron had noticed that he used either hand to write, and he'd often wondered what the man was doing.

None of it was any of Cameron's business, and he realized that he was ignoring his responsibilities. He just couldn't help himself. Cameron scrubbed his hands over his face and pressed his lips together in resignation before lifting the tray and getting back to work. He served coffee to two tables that were finishing up, and he'd brought an extra cup, just in case. After a look toward the alcove, he took a deep breath to bolster his confidence and decided to go over.

"Would you care for some coffee?" he asked, pausing on his way past. He hoped he sounded calm and collected.

The man didn't look up from his writing. He gave a simple shake of his head in answer.

Put at ease by the more usual reaction, Cameron went on his way. He'd just let himself be distracted by attempting personal interaction when he was better served forgetting his silly fantasy and doing his job; that was all. Satisfied and back on balance, Cameron went to finish up the checks for the remaining tables.

Then Blake passed by the man's table on his usual rounds of the patrons. The man reached out without looking up and snagged Blake by the arm, stopping him without a word. He didn't even stop writing as he held onto Blake's wrist. Blake stood there for a moment as the man wrote. Then he gently extricated his arm and slid into the seat opposite the man.

Cameron wondered how it was that Blake knew him. Besides greeting him personally at the door like he did only a privileged few, Blake actually sat and talked with him. Cameron had never seen Blake do that with anyone else.

Blake said something more, and the man raised his head slightly, ran two fingers over his lower lip in thought, and then looked down at his book with a frown. Blake nodded and stood once more, strolling away from the table with a small smirk, one hand casually in a pocket, obviously pleased with whatever he'd said to make the dark man think.

Frowning, Cameron wondered what in the world was going on. He shook his head and told himself again it wasn't his business, no matter how gorgeous the guy was. He headed out to clear a vacated table, deliberately keeping himself from peeking back at the alcove.

When he did happen to glance over at the table, the man caught Cameron with his dark eyes and inclined his head slightly. Now this Cameron was used to.

"Are you from here in the city?" the man asked him when Cameron arrived at the table.

The question totally threw Cameron again. He'd been expecting a request for the check or perhaps more wine. "Yes," he answered tentatively.

"Do you know it well?" the man inquired, either not noticing or not caring about Cameron's discomfort.

"Yes, I think so," Cameron answered, slightly more confident.

"Do you know of a place called The Zenith?" the man asked, his voice holding a hint of barely hidden frustration to it. "Anywhere that could be called that? An establishment, a location, a landmark. Anything?"

Cameron's cheeks immediately darkened, and his eyes widened as the man spoke. Just when he thought this man couldn't surprise him anymore, he out and asked about something like the Zenith. Great. Was this what he and Blake had been discussing? Blake wouldn't know about a club like the Zenith, would he? Cameron blushed further and cleared his throat.

The man's observant eyes did notice his reaction this time, and he tilted his head inquiringly.

Cameron cleared his throat again, shocked by how uncomfortable one little question could make him. "That's the name of an exclusive club," he answered with a nervous smile. "Caters mostly to gay men, I believe," he hedged.

The man cocked his head and looked away thoughtfully. He pursed his lips and looked back down at his notebook. “Interesting,” he murmured to himself. “You can have the woman bring the check now,” he ordered without looking up again.

Cameron swallowed hard. “Yes, sir,” he practically whispered.

Once in the back, he stiffly set down his tray with a muted clatter and leaned his head against the wall. The man had asked a question, and he’d answered it. And for that he was not just dismissed, but replaced with another server?

Cameron rubbed at his eyes. What was it about this man that threw him so easily off kilter? With a sigh, he headed into the kitchen to find Miri.

The next time he looked out across the dining room, she was stepping back from the man’s table. She spoke and then turned smartly on one heel and walked away.

The man looked up quickly and narrowed his eyes, glancing around the restaurant slowly as if he were looking for someone. His eyes returned to the kitchen door where Cameron had disappeared and narrowed further.

Cameron, watching from the service area, fought not to shrink back from those piercing eyes. If he hadn’t known better, he would have sworn the man knew he was there behind the blinds.

The man removed a bill from his wallet and placed the money on the edge of the table without looking away from the blinds. Then he walked away with his coat over his arm, not bothering to struggle back into it despite the cold weather. Just before he got to the door, Blake emerged from the hallway that led to the private offices and stopped him for a few words.

The man towered over Blake, but Blake Nichols’ presence alone could overpower a room. Blake had been a medic in the Special Forces, though Cameron had never had the nerve to ask which branch or for how long. Blake carried himself like a capable soldier as well as the affluent businessman he had become. He was a hard man to outshine.

Cameron watched nervously, knowing his boss was asking the dark man about the service and what had happened. The man pointed at the slats with his good hand and spoke to Blake heatedly. To Cameron's horror, Blake actually laughed in response. Cameron stepped back so fast he almost knocked down another server. Jesus, what was he telling Blake to make him laugh like that?

He cautiously crept back to the shutters to try to see what was going on. The man said something else, and Blake laughed harder. He took the bigger man's arm and led him toward the door, helping him into his coat as they went. Surely if Blake were amused, it wasn't anything bad. Right? Cameron swallowed hard, replaying the evening in his head. There wasn't a single thing he could see that had been done wrong, aside from knowing the answer to that question. And Blake knew Cameron was gay, so that wouldn't come as a surprise to him or anyone else who knew Cameron even remotely well.

Blake actually walked out of the restaurant with the man into the lobby of the top floor of the building to the elevators. Cameron held his breath for a moment and let it out slowly to calm himself. It was okay, he told himself. Everything was okay. And he had work to do before he could go home and try not to dream about the man again.

Several minutes later, Cameron just happened to glance up while clearing a table, and he froze. He stood motionless, like a rabbit caught in the eyes of a cougar, as Blake moved toward him. No point in running, after all.

Blake went by the alcove table and swept his hand across the linen tablecloth as he made his way over to Cameron. "May I speak to you for a moment?" he asked politely as he passed Cameron by and crooked his finger, indicating he was to follow.

Cameron reminded himself this was just Blake. He was the restaurant owner and Cameron's boss, yes, but he'd also become a good friend over the years. He nodded and placed the used glasses back onto the table before following. They walked to the front of the restaurant and into the hallway off the front foyer, where Blake led Cameron into his private office. He ushered Cameron in.

"He wasn't upset with you, kiddo," he told Cameron as soon as the door closed.

Cameron blinked. "Excuse me?"

"He wasn't upset with you," Blake repeated slowly as he reached into his breast pocket. He handed Cameron a hundred-dollar bill and nodded at it. "Your tip."

"What?" Cameron looked at the folded bill in his hand. "I don't understand. He told me to…"

Blake smirked, obviously trying not to show his amusement. "He was trying to bring to your attention that he doesn't appreciate Miri waiting on him," he told Cameron with difficulty, since he was clearly trying not to laugh.

Speechless, Cameron stood there just looking at Blake. "I don't understand," he finally said. "Appreciate?"

Blake allowed himself to laugh softly. "He doesn't like Miri, kiddo," he told Cameron sympathetically. "Says she's too nosy. Don't let her bring his food again."

Cameron shrugged helplessly. "Okay?" He looked down at the money again. "He could have just said so. But there's only so many of us here who work the floor. He's bound to be put in her section sometime."

"No." Blake laughed as he opened the door for Cameron to shoo him out. "No, he's not."

Cameron wandered back out onto the floor, more confused than ever. He still held the money between his fingers and after a moment slid it into his pocket. Shaking his head to clear the daze, he went back to work. He'd have plenty of time to ponder the mystery of the dark man who came every Tuesday when he was done.

"HAPPY ANNIVERSARY," Cameron offered with a wide smile, placing the special dessert on the table in front of the wife's wide eyes. The husband smiled and nodded, and Cameron left them to the remainder of their romantic dinner.

It was a busy Saturday night, finally starting to wind down at almost eleven. The restaurant was running perfectly, and Cameron was in his element, mostly directing the wait staff and making certain the patrons enjoyed their dinners. On Saturday nights, there was enough staff working that Cameron didn't have to actually wait tables. Other duties required his attention on these busy nights, and he liked the variety.

He breezed through the service area in time to catch several of the bus-boys peering up at the television in the corner.

"What are you doing?" he asked them in annoyance. That TV wasn't even supposed to be on during service hours unless there was bad weather or a big game the patrons might inquire about.

They scrambled as the sportscaster finished up his spiel of NFL predictions for the next day's games. Cameron shook his head and looked around for the remote to turn it off.

"*And in local news*," the television droned on as he searched. "*The body of a man found in Lake Michigan this morning has been identified as Mr. Steven Bosley. Bosley disappeared roughly three weeks ago after a night out at the Zenith Club in downtown Chicago. The authorities initially thought Bosley left the country to avoid prosecution for his dealings with local organized crime syndicates, and police are calling his death a homicide. Speculation from an inside source claims his murder to be the result of a, professional hit.*"

Cameron clicked off the television, shaking his head. The mention of the Zenith Club immediately brought his obsession to mind. The mysterious man hadn't been spotted at the restaurant for nearly a month, and Cameron was certain he wasn't coming back. He'd almost gotten the handsome stranger off his mind—until now. Cameron sighed and gathered two wine bottles to take back out to the birthday party in the private room.

Several minutes later, Keri edged into the party room, got Cameron's attention, and pointed at a four-spot along the wall of windows. It had a lovely view of the snow-covered city from the restaurant's top-floor location, and a man sat there alone.

It was him. *Him.*

Cameron stood there for more than a minute, studying him. He wasn't at his usual table. He wasn't even anywhere near Cameron's usual section. But Cameron knew without asking that Blake had directed that he wait on this table, and he had a pretty good idea why. Cameron walked across the dining room slowly as he tried to suppress the nerves bubbling inside him.

"Good evening," he said once he stopped in front of the table.

The man tore his gaze away from the cityscape and looked up at Cameron, his eyes registering the briefest glimpse of surprise. When he turned, the lighting of the main floor highlighted fading bruises on his cheek and upper neck. They were different from the ones he sported before, and Cameron would have sworn the bruises above his throat were fingerprints. The cut over his eye that had been newly stitched the last time he'd come to Tuesdays was now a fading scar, barely visible. Whoever had done the stitching was very good.

Tipping his head to one side, Cameron looked over the man for just a moment. Perhaps he was a professional fighter of some sort? He had the size for it.

"The evening special and house wine?" Cameron asked instead of allowing himself to ponder. The time that had passed since the man's last visit to Tuesdays and the unpleasant way in which it had ended had helped alleviate the fixation he'd developed, and Cameron was easily able to keep his composure. For now, anyway.

The man nodded and tilted his head to the side discreetly, as if he were aware of the light hitting him and highlighting the bruising. Cameron acknowledged him silently and deliberately lowered his eyes; he didn't want to make the man uncomfortable. Apparently, they were back to the silent dance.

Cameron returned five minutes later with the bottle of wine and a crystal glass, setting them down along with the bread-basket from a tray he handed off to another server. He started working on uncorking the bottle, pausing to look out at the falling snow with a pleased smile before returning his attention to what he was doing.

The man watched him contemplatively, his expression giving away nothing else as he waited for Cameron to finish. Humming just slightly under his breath, Cameron looked up at him as he set the cork aside. The man had never examined it before, and Cameron didn't figure he would now, so he went ahead and poured a few blurbs into the glass.

"We'll be needing another," the man said to him as he poured, his voice barely above a whisper, as always.

Cameron's hand shook a little as he pulled the wine bottle back. "Of course, sir," he said. He wondered if the odd ritual from that night weeks ago would be repeated. He wasn't sure he wanted to see it; that was when his fascination had gone into overdrive. But if the man wasn't going to repeat that gesture, that meant he was actually meeting someone.

The dark man reached out and took the glass gently, his big hand cupping the crystal and bringing it to his lips without even disturbing the liquid inside. He tasted it slowly and nodded his approval as he set the glass down on the table.

Cameron's mouth curled up at one side. He would never tire of watching this man sample wine, he knew that much. He left the man sitting for a few moments before reappearing with the other glass, placing it carefully with the other place setting, and departing without comment.

The big man stood suddenly as Cameron moved away from the table. His eyes were on the entrance, and his fingers deftly buttoned his suit coat as he stood straight and tall. The movement nearly startled Cameron into turning toward him again, but he managed to keep moving as he glanced toward the entrance.

Keri was escorting a woman to the table. She was tall, blonde, and thin, pretty in a fake sort of way, her long legs accentuated by her stiletto heels and the high slit in her black dress. The man greeted her with a murmur of words and kissed her cheek as he pulled out her chair for her.

As soon as he reached the service area, Cameron had to hold himself back from darting to the shutters to try to see what was going on. He reminded himself to act properly, to be respectful of the customer and his privacy, and then he sighed, knowing it was a losing battle.

"That's the first time he's ever had someone with him," Miri said as she stopped next to him and peered through the shutters.

"Quit spying," Cameron chastised, even though that was exactly what he wanted to do. Miri looked at him with a raised eyebrow, and Cameron bit his lip as he looked at her. "What are they doing?" he asked, almost against his will.

"He's definitely talking to her," Miri answered with a wry smile as she turned back to watch some more.

Cameron sighed and picked up a water pitcher. If the man had someone at the table with him, then he needed to go check on them. It had never happened before, and it struck him that he might be slightly jealous. Cameron thought of the man's time at Tuesdays as his, no matter how unrealistic it was. And if it were a date, it was poking all kinds of holes in Miri's theory.

He unobtrusively approached the table, silently taking up first her water glass and filling it, then his.

"I received your offer this morning," the woman was saying in a low, pleasantly smoky voice as Cameron filled their glasses. "That's not the price we agreed on, Julian."

"It's the price, nonetheless," the man she addressed murmured as he leaned back and looked up at Cameron. He nodded his thanks.

Cameron swallowed hard on a knot of nervous excitement. *Julian.* That was the man's name. Finally, after all these months, he knew the man's name. It was such a rush and a relief. Why had he never thought to ask Blake?

"What's good here?" the woman asked as she picked up her menu. "I assume you're footing the bill?"

Julian merely nodded.

"The special tonight is braised boar marsala over creamed potatoes with baby peas," Cameron offered after clearing his throat. "The house favorites are vegetable penne in lemon sauce and marinated shrimp in champagne beurre blanc." Somewhere inside, he was turning over the man's name. Julian. Julian. The dark man looked like a Julian.

"Shrimp sounds wonderful," the woman responded with a smile that showed a glimpse of perfect teeth. She closed her menu and handed it to Cameron. "I'd also like a cosmo," she added. She looked at Julian and grinned mischievously. "You don't mind if I drink on the job, do you?" she teased.

Julian narrowed his eyes and cocked his head slightly. "If it will improve your performance," he responded with all seriousness.

Cameron pressed his lips together to keep from frowning. He took the menu with a soft murmur of acknowledgment and turned toward the bar. One cosmo, coming up. Surely to God the woman wasn't what she was talking like. She looked far too classy for that, and the man—Julian—certainly he'd never need to pay for companionship.

Cameron put in the woman's order and couldn't keep his eyes from straying to the mirror to watch them. They were obviously talking, the man still stoic as the woman waved one hand around lazily. Cameron's eyes widened as he saw the woman's foot rise and deliberately rub along the man's calf. Julian tilted his head and said something in response.

Coughing slightly, Cameron picked up the drink. He headed back over to the table, delivering it silently, trying not to listen to the end of their conversation and failing.

"Do I look like a whore?" the woman asked him before he could back away from the table. Cameron's eyes widened, and he could only blink at her.

Julian barked a laugh and shook his head. The sound sent a jolt through Cameron's gut, and he found himself flustered again despite telling himself he wouldn't be. Cameron glanced quickly to Julian, who was looking out the window, probably to hide his smile. It made him unbelievably gorgeous. His dark eyes watched Cameron's reaction in the reflection on the glass.

Despite his surprise and the sudden heat under his collar, Cameron tore his attention away from the man's transformed face, tipped his head, and answered with the first thing that came to mind. "If you are, ma'am, there's no way I could afford you." Cameron bowed slightly and turned away, hoping his haste wasn't overt as he fled the table. His heart pounded so hard that he felt lightheaded. He stopped at a nearby table of several people to answer questions.

"At least you're an expensive whore instead of a gold-digging married woman," Julian said to the woman with a smirk while Cameron was still within hearing range.

The woman sighed loudly and shook her head. "I thought they said you were professional about these things," she groused. Julian remained silent, merely raising an eyebrow in response. She sighed heavily again and began tapping her wedding ring against her glass nervously. "So, how do we go about this?" she asked.

"Leave that to me," Julian responded, his voice low and calm. "You've already done your part simply by coming here. As soon as I receive payment, we continue."

"And if I change my mind at the last moment?" she asked with a hint of uncertainty in her voice.

"Will you?" Julian asked her in that oddly calm, smooth voice.

She stared at him and then looked down at her drink with a frown. She inhaled deeply and then shook her head. "No," she answered. "No, I want to do this."

Julian nodded wordlessly. "Then enjoy your dinner," he suggested, "and stop worrying about what comes next."

Making his way back to the service area, Cameron didn't know what to think about what he had overheard. The woman was obviously joking about being a prostitute. There was no way she would advertise so blatantly if she really were one. He stepped through the doors and walked over to the counter, thinking that he certainly hoped it was a joke. Julian was too gorgeous a man to pay for sex. Then he stopped still, staring at the wall. What if Julian wasn't the one paying? That last snatch of conversation he'd heard certainly sounded incriminating.

"What's wrong with you?" Miri asked as she whisked by him.

Cameron shook himself. "Uh. Just thinking," he said weakly. "I'm okay."

Miri stopped and looked at him doubtfully. Cameron waved her off. "Just got too much going on," he said. "Go on."

"All right," she responded with a frown as she took her next tray of food and made her way back out into the dining room.

Fifteen minutes later, Cameron emerged with both dinners, setting the tray down expertly before moving to place their plates. He glanced between them to wait for their attention.

Julian watched him as he worked, his eyes following unerringly as his dinner mate looked out the window and rambled about how much she hated Chicago winters. As Cameron arranged the china, he noticed Julian watching him closely and raised an eyebrow in question.

"Thank you," Julian said to him, the soft words and intent look in his eyes making Cameron feel like the only person Julian saw at that moment was him.

Cameron straightened, smiled nervously, and nodded as he tried to tell himself that he was imagining these things and to calm down. "You're welcome," he murmured.

"Are you always this pleasant?" the woman asked Julian dryly.

"Not often," Julian answered without taking his eyes off Cameron.

Cameron stepped back with the tray, glancing to the woman before looking back at Julian. "Enjoy your meal," he said solely to the dark man, feeling a jump in his pulse at his own boldness. Then he edged back from the table.

Julian's black, unreadable eyes followed his movements, and Cameron paused for a moment, feeling that odd flutter strengthen; then the woman's chattering voice broke the moment, and he turned to leave.

"If you'll bring the check back with you," Julian requested softly.

Cameron looked back at Julian, nodded obediently, and departed; he didn't even realize he was smiling until he got into the back and one of his fellow waiters gave him a strange look. "What?" he asked suspiciously.

Charles shook his head and grinned impishly. "You're so completely screwed," he said with a laugh before moving on with his own tray of food.

Cameron sighed and rolled his eyes. Miri had obviously been talking. He got the check together as requested, despite several of the others chattering around him as they took advantage of a lull in the Saturday night crowd. He wasn't flustered, just... fascinated, right? Yes.

He sighed, forcing himself to be honest, at least with himself. He was infatuated. Maybe it was the voice; it was always low and husky, sometimes practically not there. And that one laugh he'd heard...

His mind wandered back to the thought that this Julian might be the "escort"—a crazy thought, for sure. But with looks like that, Cameron could imagine the man would command whatever money he wanted. It would explain why he was so well off but had to jump up and run at the ring of a cell phone.

Nose wrinkling, Cameron told himself to quit being silly. He put the check in the folder and headed back out, stopping at several tables along the way before heading toward the window table.

Both Julian and the woman were standing; he was helping her into her coat. She placed her scarf around her neck and gave him an improperly long farewell kiss, then whispered something into his ear as she slid her hand into the pocket of his suit coat and placed something inside it. She practically looked through Cameron as she turned away and walked toward the door. The heads of several men in the restaurant turned to watch her go.

The display didn't do too much for dispelling Cameron's little theory, even though he supposed if the woman were paying for sex, Julian would probably have left with her.

Julian waited until she left the restaurant before he returned to his seat, discreetly wiping her lipstick off his lips and cheek with his napkin. He reached into his pocket and extracted a piece of paper. He tilted his head as he read it, shook his head, and tossed it carelessly onto the table.

Cameron waited until he was done to approach with the check. He set the folder at Julian's elbow before silently picking up the woman's plate. He resisted the urge—only barely—to make eye contact again. Or to glance at the slip of paper.

"Would you do me a favor if I asked it of you?" Julian inquired quietly.

Now Cameron couldn't resist, and any unfounded thoughts about the man's profession melted into the background, overpowered by the man himself. He turned his chin to look at Julian as he straightened slowly. His answer wasn't the ready-to-please answer he'd usually give. It was simply, after studying Julian for a few breaths, "Maybe."

Julian produced a small electronic device, seemingly from nowhere, and he slid it onto the table, his palm on top of it as he looked up at Cameron. "Can you give this to Mr. Nichols after I'm gone?" he asked. "Without anyone seeing you do it?" he added pointedly.

It wasn't at all what Cameron expected to hear. His eyes flickered from Julian to his hand, flat on the table. Without speaking, he reached to take up Julian's plate with one hand, set it on top of the woman's plate already in his hand, and reached again to pick up the linen napkin, dragging the cloth over Julian's hand. "Let me just get this out of your way."

Julian watched him as their hands touched, and he nodded, his eyes as unreadable as ever. "Thank you," he murmured sincerely.

Cameron gathered the item in the napkin, holding it securely. "You're welcome," he offered, looking at Julian directly and enjoying the way it made him feel just to meet the man's eyes.

Julian reached under his jacket for his wallet and extracted several bills, never looking away. He slid them into the leather folder and offered it before Cameron could even turn away.

Cameron shoved the bunched-up napkin into his pocket and reached to take the folder. He finally dragged his eyes from Julian and noted the heavy falling snow outside the window. "Be careful out there," he said, knowing he meant more than one thing by it when he walked away.

IT WAS late before Cameron had time to seek out Blake Nichols in his office. The little recorder burned a hole in his pocket all evening, and despite pulling it out and studying it, wondering what it meant, Cameron hadn't found the nerve to turn it on. He turned the corner, stopped at the office door, and knocked quietly.

"Enter," Blake called from inside his office.

Cameron opened the door and stepped inside. "Evening, Blake," he greeted. Blake had threatened him into dropping the "Mr. Nichols" almost six years ago.

Blake looked up from the papers on his desk and smiled widely. "Good evening, Cameron," he greeted in the same friendly manner he always did. "What can I do for you? How's the night going?"

"Really well," Cameron said, smiling. "I think all three parties went off great, the people were happy… and they drank a lot of wine," he added with a knowing smile.

"Wonderful," Blake commented wryly. "The better the tips, right?" he joked as he picked up his pen and tapped it against the papers on his desk. "Was that all?" he asked, still friendly and open but obviously distracted.

Cameron hesitantly slid his hand into his pocket and took the three steps to Blake's desk. "He asked me to give this to you." He pulled out the recorder and set it down.

Blake looked down at the recorder, his body suddenly noticeably tense when he glanced back up at Cameron. "He?" he questioned softly without touching the recorder.

Cameron shifted uncomfortably. "Him. Julian."

One of Blake's eyebrows edged up, and he looked down at the recorder again. "Did you listen to it?" he asked evenly.

Cameron shook his head, looking at Blake steadily.

Blake hummed thoughtfully and picked up the recorder, turning it over to examine it before pressing the rewind button briefly and then hitting play. Julian's deceptively soft, deep voice filtered out of the tiny speaker almost immediately:

"I trust you know never to come back here."

"Of course. In twenty-four hours I'll be in the Caymans, mourning my dead husband. I have no reason to come back."

"Good. Finish your meal."

Blake cut off the recorder with a click and looked up at Cameron with a small smile. "Thank you, Cameron," he said in a pleased voice. "You didn't hear that," he instructed with a grin.

Cameron shrugged. "I don't hear a lot of things," he said with a small smile, though he thought the exchange exceedingly odd. A lot of people talked about delicate things at restaurants, forgetting the help that moved around them silently. He didn't know what was going on, and he didn't think he wanted to know.

"Well, you've done your good deed for the week, at any rate," Blake informed him as he picked up the phone at his elbow and dialed. "What did you think of the woman?" he asked slyly as he waited for an answer.

Cameron's lips twitched. "She asked me if she looked like a whore," he said significantly.

"She might as well be," Blake grumbled good-naturedly. "We'll see how she likes a nice eight-by-ten cell," he added with relish. "Don't put me on hold!" he shouted into the phone, and then he cursed under his breath and looked back up at Cameron. "Julian, huh?" he asked with a small, knowing smirk.

"That's what she called him," Cameron offered weakly. "You asked—"

"That is his name," Blake assured him. "What do you think of *him*?" he asked, the smirk growing into one of his signature mischievous grins.

"Think of *him*?" Cameron echoed with a slight crack to his voice. His mind raced as he tried to think of something appropriate. "Uh. He tips really well, and he doesn't ask for outlandish things. He's a good customer," he finally said, not sure what he could say without revealing how he felt.

"He certainly is," Blake agreed with a nod, though his smile didn't fade. "Did he say anything to you about this?" he asked as he waved at the recorder on the desk. "Or did he just thrust it at you and grunt like he usually does?"

Cameron thought about it, his eyes going out of focus. "He asked me if I would do him a favor if he asked. I said maybe." He shrugged again.

"Slightly foolhardy of you, considering the man asking the favor," Blake chastised as he tapped his pen impatiently, still holding the phone to one ear.

Cameron snapped out of it and answered without thinking it through. "What about him? It's not like I know him. I mean, if a gorgeous woman asked you for a favor, wouldn't you say yes?"

"Probably." Blake laughed softly. "Ha!" he exclaimed suddenly. "No no no; don't put me on hold," he growled into the phone. He looked up at Cameron and grinned wickedly. "Go ahead and take off, Cam," he advised with a jerk of his head. "Let the others clean up tonight."

"Okay," Cameron responded in amused confusion. Blake was obviously doing something he was enjoying immensely, and when Blake was enjoying himself, it was hard not to be amused.

He gave Blake one last look as the man turned away and started talking. At least Blake hadn't teased him after that "gorgeous" line. As he walked down the hall and toward the kitchen to get his coat, Cameron told himself to stop thinking about the man named Julian. He rolled his eyes. As if that would do any good now.

THE man known as Julian Cross paced restlessly as he waited for midnight. He held his phone in his hand, had been holding it long enough that it had grown warm, in fact, and he glanced at the time display every few seconds as the hour neared. Finally he allowed himself to dial Blake Nichols' number.

"I wondered how long you'd wait," Blake said in greeting.

"Shut up," Julian grumbled as he forced himself to stop pacing. "Did you get it?" he asked worriedly. He'd harbored doubts about using the waiter as a delivery service, but Blake had more than once assured him the man was reliable and discreet, and Julian's own slight infatuation had pushed him into being incautious. He'd been fretting over it ever since—something he wasn't prone to do.

"It's safe right here in my hot little hands," Blake answered. He paused. "Did you really think Cameron wouldn't bring it to me?"

"Hey," Julian grunted in annoyance. "When something leaves my hands, I worry, okay? That's what I do. I don't trust you or your harebrained ideas any farther than I can throw you."

Blake chuckled. "Well, you can stop worrying. Cameron delivered it just like he said he would. He didn't even listen to it first." He paused again. "Why'd you ask him? Why not bring it to me directly? You knew I was in my office."

Julian pressed his lips together and then pursed them thoughtfully. He thought about pointing out that there was always the possibility that he was being followed and traipsing back into the private offices to see Blake whenever he wanted probably wasn't a good idea. But Blake already knew that. He was simply poking at one of Julian's very few vulnerable spots. Blake knew Julian was interested in Cameron, and he just couldn't help himself from teasing Julian mercilessly about it.

"He's more fun to look at than you are," Julian finally answered instead of giving a more serious answer.

Blake's laugh rang out. "You're an ass," he responded delightedly. "Oh, by the way, did you know you're *gorgeous*?"

"Yes, I was aware," Julian answered without missing a beat. He waited a moment before he gave a suspicious, "Why?"

A snicker came across the line. "Never mind. I made the call, and they'll get this thing to the right people. Good job, by the way. She wasn't as smart as we gave her credit for, huh?"

"Not nearly." Julian groaned. "I'm almost embarrassed I put so much effort into her. Did you know she wrote me a fucking check? Talk about a paper trail."

"What'd you do with it?" Blake asked in amusement.

"Burned it when I got home."

"Well, lessons learned," Blake replied easily. "Will you be here next week? It's a holiday, you know. I'll be out of town."

"If you'll be out of town, why do you care where I'll be?" Julian countered.

"I don't want to think about you sitting in that mausoleum of a house alone on Christmas Eve," Blake answered sincerely.

"How sweet," Julian responded flatly. He sighed softly and looked out at the falling snow. "But since you won't be here, regardless, again I ask: what do you care?"

"Jackass," Blake accused fondly.

"Yeah. There's always Christmas Mass," Julian muttered.

"That doesn't count as company," Blake pointed out.

"Yes, well, it'll do," Julian assured him, thinking to himself that if he could muster the nerve, he could probably find himself some of Blake's brand of company. His mind turned again toward thoughts of a dark-haired, blue-eyed waiter.

"Take care of yourself, Julian," Blake advised knowingly. "Unless something breaks, you're free 'til Christmas. Good night."

"Sweet dreams, you bastard," Julian offered with a small smile.

"Of course they will be. Emily's back from Paris," Blake said with a laugh, and he hung up.

Julian smiled and shook his head. He folded his phone and tossed it onto the nearest piece of furniture, wondering what in the hell he was going to do with himself for the next several days without any jobs to work or research. He stared out at the snow, pondering the memory of the way the waiter's lips had curved into a smile when he'd watched the snow falling outside of Tuesdays.

He growled slightly, shaking his head in defeat. He thought about that man far too much for it to be healthy. He couldn't help but wonder, though, if Cameron would respond favorably if he made a move.

Julian cocked his head and stared out the window, letting himself wonder and think about a man he didn't really know.

CHAPTER 2

CAMERON stood at the greeting stand cleaning off the board that listed the evening special in artistically rendered colored chalk. Keri had begged off early so she could be at home with her kids on Christmas Eve, and he was the only one working the floor. After the two early evening parties cleared out, the restaurant remained deserted, and he'd sent everyone home but the sous chef and a couple other guys on the kitchen staff. Most people were at home with their families by now, and the weather didn't help business. It had snowed heavily all day.

He hummed along with the holiday string concerto playing in the foyer, not yet tired of the Christmas music that inundated people everywhere this time of year. Since he had plenty of time, he pulled out the wait staff list for the next week and started working on the schedule.

A slight whoosh of air warned him of someone coming in. Surprised, he shifted off the stool and stepped around the stand to see how many were in the party. He stopped still and stared for a moment before he could compose himself.

It was *Julian*.

The man stepped into the foyer, unwrapping the scarf from his neck as he looked around. When his eyes landed on Cameron, he stopped and cocked his head slightly to the side. "Merry Christmas," he greeted.

Cameron blinked stupidly in response. "Happy holidays," he answered finally. Was it Tuesday? Yes. Yes, it was.

Julian glanced around the restaurant and moved closer, appearing to glide as his long overcoat swirled around him. "Thank you for what you did," he said as he got closer.

Cameron knew exactly what Julian was talking about; he'd thought about it for the past several days, wondering what it was about and what had happened. "You're welcome. Did—" He paused, aware that he was about to be very rude. "Did you want dinner?" he improvised.

"It worked out fine," Julian answered without looking away.

Cameron suppressed a shiver, feeling those black eyes focus totally on him. He clasped his hands behind his back. "Good," he said quietly. "I… wondered," he said, shifting his eyes sideways before raising them to look at Julian.

Julian nodded, ducking his head as if trying to keep Cameron's eyes on him. "How much longer would I have to eat?" he asked.

Julian's eyes were so intent, Cameron tried not to shuffle under his gaze. He glanced at the elegant wrought-iron clock on the wall. "About an hour," he answered shakily. What would he do with no one in the restaurant but Julian?

"So you'll be free in an hour," Julian ventured as he tipped his head to one side. It seemed that he could never get enough power behind his voice to speak at volume. It was an intriguing trait in a man so big.

Cameron slid one hand into a pocket, trying to hide the slight tremble in his fingers. His pulse was already racing as he peered at the other man. "Yeah," he answered without even wondering about the purpose of the question. If he let himself wonder, he wouldn't be able to form coherent sentences. Then he tacked on, "I was actually getting ready to close early. You're the first customer in almost two hours."

Julian tilted his head the other way and then nodded curtly, letting his eyes travel over Cameron thoughtfully. "So if I were to leave, you could, in theory, meet me in the lobby in fifteen minutes," he surmised.

Subtle disbelief filtered into Cameron's eyes. "In theory," he agreed cautiously. Was the man coming on to him? How crazy was this?

Julian continued to look him directly in the eye for a long moment before nodding thoughtfully. "I'll wait twenty," he announced in a bare whisper.

What *was* this? Julian wanted to meet him for… what? A sizzling jolt shot through Cameron. His first impulse was to jump at the chance even though he knew absolutely nothing about the man or what he had planned. Was he really going to do this?

There was no question. Yes. Yes, he was going to do this even though it was insanely foolhardy. "I better get moving then," Cameron said, unable to tear his eyes away.

The corner of Julian's mouth twitched in what might have been a smile. He turned without another word and left, moving slowly and deliberately as he exited the restaurant. He always seemed to move in measured bursts like he was putting a lot of effort into reining in his stride.

Cameron wasted thirty seconds staring at the door and pondering the way Julian moved before he lurched to activate the locks and turn down the lights. He hurried through the restaurant and back into the kitchen, telling the sous chef to close up shop. By the time he'd finished locking up what needed to be secured, twelve minutes had passed. He swore, grabbed his heavy coat and scarf, and took off, pushing through the doors and loping toward the elevators.

Julian stood in the lobby, his big shoulders squared in his heavy wool overcoat as he stared out the glass front of the building and waited. The sound of the elevator as it arrived in the lobby was a tiny chime in the quiet of the marble floors and high ceilings. He glanced over his shoulder as Cameron stepped out of the elevator. Julian turned around and inclined his chin, visibly surprised that Cameron had actually come.

Cameron shrugged into his long, charcoal-gray coat and pulled the scarf slung over his arm around his neck, licking his lips nervously. Had the man not expected him to show up? Then why even ask?

Julian began walking slowly toward him. "Do you have someone to get home to on Christmas Eve?" the big man asked as he moved closer, his low voice carrying across the marble.

Cameron's hands stopped on the coat buttons as he watched the other man approach, and he spoke before thinking it through. "No. That's why I always volunteer to work."

It had already occurred to him that Julian might be dangerous. But leaving alone with him, late at night, and admitting no one was waiting for him? It was not a very good idea at all.

"I wouldn't want to keep you," Julian murmured as he stopped several feet away. It was as if he could sense Cameron's sudden unease and was trying not to alarm him by being too close or too loud.

Cameron was torn between a silent wave of longing and a tingle of apprehension. He waited until he was sure what he wanted to say would be what actually came out of his mouth, unconsciously licking his lower lip. "No one's waiting."

Julian nodded slightly. "I was going to suggest we talk while we walk, but it's begun snowing again," he said as he glanced at the window. "Do you mind?"

Cameron couldn't stop the smile. "I love the snow."

Julian smiled slightly and held his hand out toward the door, inviting Cameron to lead the way. Moving ahead, Cameron walked out into the snow, immediately stopping and grinning as he lifted his face to the big, fluffy flakes for a long moment before turning to move down the street. The snow was almost two inches deep, and he left tracks behind as he trekked through it.

Julian was soon beside him, walking with his head down. "She was trying to have her husband killed."

Cameron glanced at Julian in surprise as they made their way down the sidewalk. He had no idea what to say to that. Should he ask? Was it appropriate? "And you…" he ventured after several yards.

"Had been hired by her husband," Julian answered, his frozen breath billowing out in front of him. "For a slightly different purpose."

"To keep him alive, I'm guessing," Cameron said.

Julian shrugged noncommittally and turned slightly to look behind them. "I do this and that," he finally answered. "I'm sorry I involved you."

Cameron's mind started racing, his imagination shifting into overdrive. He'd been hired to do this and that… maybe something that would get the wife mad enough to want to kill her husband? Remembering the conversation between the woman and Julian, he wondered if Julian had been catering to the husband instead of the wife. His cheeks heated a little at the thought, and he pushed the idea aside.

"Why *did* you involve me?" he asked curiously.

"Because I trust you," Julian answered bluntly. "And I couldn't do it myself."

"How can you trust me?" Cameron asked in surprise. "You don't even know me."

"I consider myself a decent judge of character," Julian answered as he lowered his head, watching where his footsteps fell.

Would this man never stop surprising him? Cameron mused over a reply. "Thank you," he murmured.

"That's an odd thing to thank someone for," Julian observed.

Cameron stuck his hands in his pockets and shrugged. "You complimented me, didn't you?"

Julian finally turned his head to look at Cameron. "I suppose I did."

Cameron gave another shrug. "Then it's not odd at all."

"What do you think of me?" Julian asked him, changing the direction of their conversation without warning.

Blake had asked him the same thing. It was a question Cameron still had no idea how to answer. Julian seemed to do that to him a lot: ask something, say something, whatever something knocked Cameron off balance. He thought back over the months of seeing Julian in the restaurant, wondering if he'd ever truly drawn any conclusions.

"I think you're mysterious," he admitted haltingly.

Julian started in obvious surprise. "Really?" he asked, the first word he'd spoken that didn't seem measured.

"Yeah," Cameron said with a shrug as they paused on the street corner. "Ten minutes total of near-silent interaction a week doesn't offer a lot of information," he pointed out. "So. Mysterious."

Julian turned to face him as the snow began to fall harder. "Is that all you think of me then?"

The tone of Julian's voice made Cameron shift to look at him. The other man had several inches on him, and Cameron remembered the shift and pull of muscles under expensive shirts and jackets, the black of his eyes as they focused on nothing but him. "No," he murmured distractedly. "I think…"

Julian raised an eyebrow as Cameron trailed off. "I ask because I think of you," he told Cameron quietly. "Quite a lot."

A look of complete shock covered Cameron's face, and he blinked stupidly as they stood on the street corner. He'd *never* expected to hear that. Hadn't even dreamed it. "You think of *me*?" he asked with a near squeak. "Why?"

Julian merely tilted his head and smiled as he watched Cameron.

Cameron stuttered a few incoherent words and then swallowed. "I did think about you," he admitted after regaining some of his composure. "Especially after the first time you missed dinner. I mean, that first time you talked to me and then didn't come back the next week."

"You're talking about the night I was hurt," Julian supplied with an easy smile as they crossed the street and got to walking again.

"Oh. Well, I hope it wasn't bad," Cameron said awkwardly, remembering the sling Julian had worn.

"It's always bad," Julian said as he looked away, peering up into the falling snow.

Cameron's brow furrowed. "I'm sorry. I didn't mean to pry. It's just that I wondered where you were that week when you didn't come to the restaurant." He paused. "It's not my business though."

Julian lowered his head, staring at the sidewalk for a moment before he looked back up at Cameron. "Do you really want to know?" he asked dubiously, coming to a halt on the snow-covered walkway.

Cameron stopped too. He knew to say yes would be admitting more than he wanted. But he was here, wasn't he? He'd already forfeited any pride in the matter. "Yes?" he ventured, expecting to be rebuffed.

Julian stared at him for a long moment, his eyes raking over Cameron's features and obviously contemplating him. "Would you believe me if I told you I was shot?" he finally asked with a mischievous glint in his black eyes.

Cameron stared at him. "Shot? Like, *shot*? By a gun?"

Julian tilted his head and nodded. "It's hard to be shot with a knife."

"So you'd been shot the week before, but you still came to dinner at Tuesdays?" Cameron looked doubtful.

"Two weeks before, actually," Julian corrected. "I missed a week."

"Didn't it still hurt?" Cameron asked incredulously. "A lot?"

"Yes," Julian admitted. "And it made me cranky," he added with a slight reddening of his cheeks that wasn't because of the freezing temperature outside.

"That was the night you asked for Miri," Cameron remembered. "'Tell the woman to bring the check'," he repeated flatly.

Julian lowered his head silently. "I owe you an apology for that," he finally stated.

Cameron shook his head, though Julian wouldn't see it. "It's okay. Blake explained. Sort of."

It registered suddenly that Blake *knew* this man. Julian couldn't be all that bad if Blake knew him, could he? Surely Cameron was safe with him. He stood there pondering, slightly dragging one foot back and forth, making a furrow in the snow as it fell between the towering concrete and glass buildings and onto the lit streets all around them.

Julian shook his head in return and gave Cameron a small, embarrassed smile. "My own time is very limited," he explained. "I'm jealous of the time spent at the restaurant," he said candidly.

"Jealous?" Cameron was at a loss. "I don't understand. The food's not *that* good," he said.

"But the service is extraordinary," Julian said softly.

There wasn't any breath left in Cameron's chest after Julian's explanation, so he couldn't even start to answer. He could only stand there as the sparkling flakes fell silently and thick around them, staring at the man he'd been fantasizing about for months. He finally shrugged helplessly, unable to think of anything else to do.

Julian shook his head again and smiled as he looked at Cameron. "I look forward to seeing you," he explained. "Whether it's bringing me my meal or waiting on the table next to mine. I don't want someone else doing it."

"All I do is serve the food."

"And all I do is sit there and watch you," Julian countered.

Cameron's gut clenched and his breath caught. After several heartbeats, he blurted, "I watch you too."

Julian's face broke into a wide smile. It completely changed the way he looked, and even the way it felt to be around him. The apprehension that had tightened Cameron's chest eased up somewhat, and he found himself staring raptly. Dark and brooding, Julian was sinfully handsome. But when he smiled, he was absolutely devastating, and Cameron didn't think he'd be able to move from that very spot anytime soon. Not as long as Julian was smiling at him.

"I know," Julian said simply.

"You… How?" Cameron asked. He did almost all his watching from the safety of the service area.

Julian looked at him silently for a moment and then smiled again and looked behind them. The snow had already blotted out their footprints. "Midnight Mass will start soon. I'll let you go," he finally murmured, not answering the question in the least. "I merely needed to tell you."

Cameron couldn't drag his eyes away. "Julian?" The word came out deep and slightly breathless. It was the first time he'd spoken it aloud.

"Yes?" Julian responded calmly in turn as he looked back at him.

For a wild, insane second, Cameron wished it were in him to do something brash. While working, he knew exactly what to do in almost every situation. Outside of work, it was decidedly the opposite. But right now he wished he had the nerve to ask this man, practically a stranger, to come home with him. He felt sure he wouldn't get another chance. But he simply couldn't force the words between his lips.

"How's your arm now?" he asked weakly.

"It's doing well," Julian answered with another bemused smile. "Thank you for asking."

Nodding, Cameron took a step back, telling himself to quit babbling and leave with a hint of dignity intact. "I'm this way," he said, gesturing to the right.

Julian glanced in that direction and tilted his head like he wanted to say or do something but was uncertain. The quiet, frozen surroundings and Julian's indecision stirred something unusual in Cameron, and from far away he heard himself ask, "Do you have someone to get home to on Christmas Eve?"

Julian looked at him closely as the snow began to fall even harder. It made it difficult to see, even though they stood only a few feet apart. He looked off in the direction of Holy Name Cathedral before returning his piercing gaze to Cameron and stepping closer. He shook his head, looking down at Cameron's upturned face. "No one."

The snow was getting so heavy it was catching on Cameron's eyelashes, and he had to keep blinking. When he heard Julian's reply, he steeled himself for what had to be the craziest thing he'd ever done in his life.

He held out his hand.

Julian looked down at it as if he wasn't quite certain what it was and then back to Cameron in surprise. He reached out slowly and slid his fingers over Cameron's trembling palm. The soft leather of his glove was cool, but warmer than Cameron's chilled hand. Cameron closed his fingers around Julian's, and after a moment, tugged lightly. Julian allowed himself to be led across the deserted street.

If Cameron let himself think about it, he knew he'd start to freak out. So he carefully didn't think about *anything* but the next step: get home. He just kept walking, leading Julian along the sidewalk, through the piled snow that was getting deeper by the minute. Three blocks later he came to a stop in front of an older warehouse building that had been converted into condos, where he chanced a look at the other man.

Julian was studying the building with a frown. "I find myself wanting to caution you against trusting people like myself," he murmured to Cameron as he looked down at him. "I would still order the special if you sent me home right now."

"People like yourself?" Cameron prodded.

"People who find themselves shot while working," Julian provided as he stepped closer and enveloped Cameron's cold hand in his own.

"Maybe you need taking care of?" Cameron responded uncertainly.

Julian's eyes met Cameron's with new intensity. "What would you propose?" he asked hoarsely.

Cameron knew without a doubt that this would be his only chance, and the fear of never having another stirred him where desire would not. His heart pounded as he shifted his weight onto his toes, lifted his chin, and lightly brushed his cold lips against Julian's.

Cameron's eyes were closed when he pulled back, and he reopened them when he realized it. He was looking right up into the other man's black eyes, no more than a foot away, and Julian was staring at him with what he could only describe as open longing. Cameron's breath caught. He didn't think he'd *ever* been the focus of a look like that.

Julian breathed out heavily when Cameron moved away; the frosty air swirled around Cameron and caressed his face before dissipating.

"Come on," Cameron whispered, tugging lightly again. Julian's grip tightened on Cameron's hand and he followed obediently.

Cameron quickly led him into the building before he could lose his nerve. He bypassed the elevator for the stairs—he was just one flight up, and the climb would give him less time to think through what he was doing. When they reached the landing, he was still determined to take this stranger into his apartment, and probably his bed, without further internal debate. He stopped in front of his door and dug out his keys, fumbling with them since his fingers were almost frozen.

Julian watched for a moment before reaching out and gently taking Cameron's hand. He cupped it with his own, raised it to his lips, and breathed on it, trying to warm the skin as he kept his eyes on Cameron's.

If his heart beat any harder, Cameron was sure Julian would be able to hear it. The slightest brush of those lips against his fingers was enough to send Cameron's brain into lockdown, and he was mesmerized. It took long moments of just staring before Cameron pulled his chilled fingers away so he could unlock the door.

Julian smiled slightly, obviously enjoying the effect he was having on Cameron, who blinked hard and started to open the door, remembering at nearly the last second to say, "I hope you're not allergic to dogs."

"Only their teeth," Julian answered flatly.

"Don't worry. They don't bite too hard." Cameron cracked the door open, and there was a sudden cacophony of yapping and scraping as little feet came rushing across the hardwood when Cameron entered.

Julian stayed behind Cameron and kept his fingertips on Cameron's hips from behind, using him as a shield as they watched the clown parade. Four tiny white puppies skidded at their feet and began jumping and yipping happily. Julian stared at them for a moment before turning his attention back to Cameron. He didn't appear to be nearly as composed as usual, but Cameron wondered if it was more than simply nerves. Julian's next question answered that for him.

"Will they take exception if they see me touching you?" he asked as he let his hands slide off Cameron's hips.

Cameron's stomach flipped the second Julian pulled his hands away, and he wished all of a sudden the other man would stay close. He looked down at the little group of fuzzy puppies that barely stood as tall as his ankles. "I'll hazard a guess and say you're safe," he said with a smile as he shut the door behind them. "Just don't step on one, please."

Julian nodded obediently, looking down at the four puppies with complete seriousness. As soon as the door was shut, though, he took Cameron by the elbow and, very gently, pressed him back against the door as he stepped closer. Cameron inhaled sharply as heat rushed through him. This was crazy, absolutely crazy, but he didn't care. He wanted very much to feel Julian against him.

Julian waited to give him a chance to change his mind or protest, but when Cameron did nothing of the sort, Julian leaned in and kissed him slowly.

Cameron could feel himself trembling, and his eyes fell shut as Julian's lips touched his. He couldn't catch his breath, and his heart raced as he tried not to gasp. He dared set his hand lightly on Julian's broad shoulder, and when he made contact Julian immediately wrapped his arms around him and pushed closer.

The kiss became more heated, and with it came a thread of desire as the chill was chased away. God… Julian was kissing him silly. His body was as solid as it looked, and it felt good pressed against Cameron's. Cameron curled his hand around Julian's shoulder to make it feel more real.

Finally, Julian pulled back and rested his hands on the door by either side of Cameron's head, trapping him there. "I can't tell you how long I've wanted to do that," he breathed in a slightly relieved voice.

Cameron pulled his eyes open, still feeling the pressure of Julian's lips against his own. "Why not?" he asked without thinking.

"Because I fear you would think me a stalker and make me go home," Julian admitted wryly, his mouth curving into a smile.

Cameron laid his head back against the door and met Julian's eyes. "Bit late for that now, don't you think?" He slowly let his hand slide from Julian's shoulder and down his coat lapel.

"It's never too late for stalking," Julian practically purred as he pressed his body against Cameron's.

A breath shuddered out of Cameron, and he gasped for another. "I thought you'd never speak to me," Cameron admitted as he grew more accustomed to Julian's body against his.

"I didn't want to bother you while you worked," Julian murmured as he ducked his head and slowly ran the tip of his nose along Cameron's cheek.

Cameron's eyelids fluttered down as he felt Julian's breath on his chin and throat. "So bother me now," he whispered shakily.

Julian kissed him again, hard this time. His fingers gripped Cameron's biceps and pressed into him hungrily. Giving in to the onslaught with a soft moan that disappeared into Julian's mouth, Cameron scrabbled to hang onto Julian's shoulders as the kiss lit a fire inside him. The sensations swamped him and all he could think was that if he could speak, he'd mewl for more.

Julian pulled back abruptly, as if just realizing what he was doing. "I'm sorry," he said breathlessly as he leaned his forehead against Cameron's.

Cameron's dazed eyes blinked at him. "Sorry?" he rasped.

Julian looked down to where his fingers still gripped Cameron's arms and nodded as he brushed his lips over Cameron's again and slowly relaxed his grasp. "Usually, I'm more restrained."

Cameron smiled slowly, though he still felt more than a little off-balance. "I'll take that as another compliment."

Julian nodded jerkily and kissed him again, the impulsive movement hard enough to lift and pin Cameron against the door. Groaning against Julian's mouth, Cameron curled one hand around Julian's neck. He felt like he was burning up under all the layers of clothes and Julian's body, and Cameron welcomed the feeling.

"This isn't why I came to see you tonight," Julian insisted against Cameron's lips even as he continued to kiss him hungrily.

Cameron made a weak inquisitive sound as he reveled in the onslaught of Julian's attention. Julian's lips were hot and moist and surprisingly soft, an odd counterpoint to the prickle of his beard. Julian finally broke the kiss and shook his head as he let Cameron settle on his feet. "I just wanted to see you," he whispered.

Cameron gazed at him, distantly aware of how vulnerable Julian suddenly looked. He didn't get it. He knew why he thought about Julian, why he was infatuated with him. He just didn't get how someone like Julian, a man who obviously had looks and money and adventure to spare, could possibly be interested in him. He was just an average guy, nothing spectacular.

"Yet another compliment. But why?" Cameron asked softly.

Julian narrowed his eyes and tipped his head to the side slightly, his brow furrowing in thought. "You're happy," he said. "And I look forward to seeing it every week."

Those little furrows appeared between Cameron's brows again. That was it? Because he was happy? He searched Julian's face, seeing nothing that would make him think it was a line. "I'm sorry. I just don't…"

Julian took a slight step back and placed his gloved hands on either side of Cameron's face, looking down at him intently as he waited patiently for Cameron to continue.

Cameron swallowed with difficulty. "You look at me like there's nothing else in the world," he whispered to Julian nervously.

"There's not right now," Julian answered immediately. "It's Tuesday."

Cameron couldn't speak for a long moment as he wondered about the implications of those words. "I missed you those weeks you were gone," he admitted. "I wondered where you were."

Julian blinked in something like surprise, and he licked his lips. "I was working."

"What's that look for?" Cameron asked when he saw Julian's reaction. "Didn't you believe me when I said I thought about you?"

"I don't know," Julian answered, displaying another hint of uncertainty about what he was doing.

Cameron frowned slightly and pulled back a bit, feeling unaccountably disappointed. "I don't just do this sort of thing… on a whim," he warned, shaking his head.

Julian smiled suddenly, his leather-covered fingers sliding down Cameron's cheeks to rest on his jaw. "Neither do I," he murmured in response.

He seemed sincere, but Cameron committed Julian's face to memory all the same, just in case this never happened again. He didn't figure it would, despite Julian's provocative admissions. At this point, he wondered if it really mattered. This night was looking to turn into one of his fantasies. Could he really pass that up just because he knew the man wouldn't call later? The longing in him made his hands clench tighter on Julian's arms.

Julian looked down at the fingers that gripped him and then back up to meet Cameron's eyes questioningly. "I would never come here without the intention of trying to come back," Julian assured him with a small smirk as he leaned closer and let his hands slide down the sides of Cameron's body to rest on his hips.

"So now what?" Cameron asked as he relaxed a little.

"You kiss me again," Julian answered in a soft, confident voice.

Given that direction, Cameron didn't wait. He lifted his chin and pressed his lips to Julian's. Julian pulled him closer and growled softly, deep in his throat. His hands began to unravel Cameron's scarf carefully, trying not to break their kiss or strangle him in the process.

The scratchy wool sliding against his skin got a tiny bit of Cameron's attention, just enough for him to lift his head away from the door so Julian could remove it more easily. Julian yanked the scarf away and dropped it. He pulled back, unwound his own scarf effortlessly, and let it fall as he slid his hands under Cameron's heavy coat.

"This is so much easier to do in summer," he muttered.

"I'm not sure I'd have had the courage then," Cameron told him breathlessly, referring to the many months ago when Julian had started sitting in his section like clockwork every Tuesday.

"Why?" Julian asked as he continued to attempt to tug at clothing.

At a loss, Cameron made a noise of self-deprecation and shrugged slightly.

"Were you frightened of me?" Julian asked with an audible frown, though his hands didn't stop their actions, nor did his lips stop moving against Cameron's skin.

Cameron shook his head. "No," he said, voice sure.

"Then why?" Julian asked, even as he pushed Cameron's coat off his shoulders and tugged it down his arms.

Cameron shrugged and shook off the coat so that it fell to the floor in a quiet thump of heavy fabric. "Why would you be interested in me?" he asked logically as Julian nipped at his neck. "I'm just a waiter."

"That's what you do," Julian whispered into Cameron's ear before he straightened. "That's not who you are."

Shaking his head slightly, Cameron shrugged again. He was okay to look at and could usually find someone to fool around with for a while when he wanted more than a friend. But it gave him a real thrill to know Julian obviously liked what he saw. He reached for Julian's coat, sliding his hands under the shoulders to push it away. His fingers moved under Julian's suit jacket as well, but caught on something hard at Julian's hip. Cameron drew his hand back, unsure of what to do.

"Sorry," Julian murmured. He shrugged out of his overcoat, and it fell to the floor. He reached under his suit jacket and undid his belt, then pulled a holster and gun off it, sliding it loose and holding it up to let Cameron see it. He set it carefully on the floor beside them, and then he met Cameron's eyes carefully.

"What's that for?" Cameron blurted, shocked, looking from bottomless dark eyes to the gun and back. For the first time, he felt a flash of fear.

Julian pressed his lips tightly together and looked down at the gun. "It's so I don't get shot as often as I would," he murmured.

"What kind of job do you have that you get shot at so much you need to carry your own gun?" Cameron asked as his mind whirred, and he tried to tamp down the worry. "Are you a detective of some kind?"

Julian licked his lips and tilted his head slightly. "Of some kind," he answered vaguely.

Cameron still felt very uneasy. A stranger was high enough on his danger list. But a stranger with a gun? But really, he reminded himself, how much of a stranger *was* Julian? Blake knew him. Cameron tried to focus on that. "Is it… safe?" he asked hesitantly, trying to convince himself it was okay. That Julian was okay, even if the gun wasn't.

Julian looked from Cameron to the gun and back again. "It's loaded," he answered, obviously worried that Cameron would send him away. "Safety's on."

"You do realize how scary that thing makes this?" Cameron asked, voice a little higher. "I've just let a stranger into my apartment with a gun."

Julian lowered his head slightly and took a small step back, his palms on the door behind Cameron's head.

Cameron let his own hands drop, his arms crossing in front of him. "What am I supposed to think?" he asked shakily.

"That if I were a psychotic killer, I would use a knife?" Julian answered hopefully as he met Cameron's eyes.

"That's not really funny," Cameron pointed out.

"Do you think I'm going to hurt you?" Julian asked calmly.

Cameron blinked in confusion and looked down. He didn't feel threatened, despite Julian's larger size and his dark, mysterious demeanor. If anything, he felt safe in the other man's arms, which was distracting in itself. Cameron slowly shook his head as he made his decision. "You don't scare me," he murmured. The gun, yes. Julian? No.

"Good," Julian murmured. He looked down at Cameron's hands and flexed his own against the door, obviously wanting to touch him again but restraining himself. Cameron saw the twitch of Julian's fingers, and he slowly reached out to slide their hands together.

"I'm sorry," Cameron said as he took the tiny step to bring him right up against Julian again.

Julian shook his head and pulled Cameron to him. "It's good to be careful."

"Okay," Cameron said. He looked at the gun. "Want to put it on the table so the dogs don't try to play with it?" He inclined his head down to where the four little white puppies quietly swarmed Julian's expensive overcoat, sniffing and pawing at it. Julian nodded and obediently picked the weapon back up, then carefully set it on the little table beside the door, sidestepping the dogs with extreme care.

Cameron watched and nodded when Julian turned back to him. He felt tongue-tied, and he waited to see what Julian would do next. Cameron wanted to touch him again. Kiss him again. He wanted more, despite the gun's appearance. Irresponsible, probably. Foolhardy, almost certainly. But honestly, it wasn't like Julian would need a gun to hurt him if he planned to. He wouldn't need the knife he joked about, either.

Julian removed his gloves slowly and placed them on the table, revealing his knuckles, covered with cuts and bruises. He removed his suit jacket as well and reached up to loosen his tie as he moved back toward Cameron.

Cameron watched as one of his favorite dreams about this man came to life in front of him. It was intoxicating, and whatever dull fear he felt about the gun began to fade. His fingers reached out to brush gently over the abused knuckles. Julian caught his hand and used it to pull him closer, kissing the inside of his wrist gently as he did so.

Cameron's pulse fluttered at the tender gesture, and he moved forward slowly until he was practically glued to Julian's chest. Julian leaned to kiss at his neck and began undoing the buttons of Cameron's shirt with one hand as he held him close. He was remarkably good at it.

He tugged at Cameron's shirt, pulling it out of his waistband and unbuttoning it the rest of the way before he slid both of his cool hands along Cameron's warm torso. Cameron sucked in a quiet breath as Julian touched him. He shuddered and leaned closer, eyes falling mostly closed as his lips parted on a breath. Julian brushed his mouth over Cameron's teasingly and gently pushed the shirt off his shoulders. He let his fingers drag across Cameron's skin as he kissed along his jaw.

It was the simplest, most intoxicating seduction Cameron had ever been exposed to.

He was dizzy in Julian's arms as the other man held him close, taking pleasure in the mere touch of their bodies. When Cameron's grip tightened on him, Julian growled low in his throat and picked him up easily, taking a few steps to press him none too gently against the door again. His shoes barely brushed the floor as Julian's body supported him.

Choking back his surprise, Cameron held on tight, even as his back hit the wood. He knew he was smaller and lighter than Julian, but… *damn*.

His hands finally began to move slowly, carefully over Julian's shoulders, arms, and back, feeling the muscles under the dress shirt bunch as they worked. Julian kissed him demandingly, and Cameron gave in easily, wallowing in the way he felt devoured and wanted. He tugged where Julian's shirt was tucked into his trousers, just below the small of his back. Julian reached between them with one hand just long enough to undo the top button of his pants, and then his hand returned to the back of Cameron's thigh to support his weight. He hefted Cameron higher against the door.

Gasping, Cameron sought Julian's lips once more as he pulled the shirt free and slid his hands under it to stroke smooth, warm skin that bunched under his palms.

Julian groaned softly into the kiss and pressed closer. "Can we take this somewhere that doesn't involve gravity?" he panted finally.

Cameron nodded jerkily. "Bed," he rasped.

Julian let him slide slowly to the ground without backing up any more than he needed to. Cameron couldn't even take a breath as his aroused body dragged against Julian's, and his eyes flickered toward the other man's to check his reaction. Julian's eyes never left Cameron's face, and far from their usual masked black, they seemed to spark with outright desire.

Cameron curled one hand around Julian's. "Come on," he urged breathlessly.

He stepped away and around Julian's coat, where the dogs curled in a pile, sleeping soundly. A few steps later, the condo opened up to a large room with a twelve-foot ceiling. It was furnished comfortably, the big space divided into a living room, a dining area near the kitchen, and a bedroom sectioned off by tall decorative screens. Cameron got halfway across the living room before stopping to look back at Julian, then at the set of panels that hid the bedroom. He felt like he needed to give Julian a chance to change his mind.

Julian followed, glancing back at his coat when Cameron stopped. "I may need some duct tape for that," he muttered as he turned back around to look at Cameron.

The odd comment struck Cameron as funny. He snorted as he tried not to laugh. "Don't worry. I've got about a hundred lint rollers. I wear black to work, remember?" He gestured to his mussed clothes.

"You look good in it," Julian assured him in a low voice as he let his eyes travel over Cameron's body. His lips quirked into an uncharacteristically playful smirk and he added, "You look good out of it too."

Cameron's cheeks flushed, and he dropped his gaze as he plucked at his unbuttoned shirt, pulling it slightly back up over one shoulder. Julian's frank regard was scorching, and Cameron wasn't used to it. He indulged in the occasional casual roll in the sheets with someone who turned him on, yeah. But it was never like this.

Julian prowled closer to him, moving fluidly with a sort of catlike grace Cameron had only caught glimpses of before now. The movement caught his eye and fascinated him. He didn't want to—

couldn't—look away. Julian caught him up in his arms and yanked the shirt the rest of the way off. His hands traveled over Cameron's skin, dipping beneath his trousers teasingly as he toed off his own shoes and kicked them away.

At that point, Cameron didn't even care about the shirt; he wanted more of Julian touching him, and he started pawing at what remained of Julian's clothing to help him along. Julian's pants clung precariously to his hips, but as he moved they came closer and closer to falling. Finally, he shoved at them and stepped out of them as they fell. He stood unselfconsciously in his steel-gray shirt and black briefs and socks, hands working at Cameron's belt.

Cameron was far too distracted by Julian's mouth, and it took a lot of willpower to keep working on Julian's shirt without just ripping the buttons off. Finally, he pushed it off Julian's shoulders, his fingers brushing over a thin chain around the other man's neck. He took a moment to look at the pendant curiously before he was distracted by the jerk of his belt, how it pinched slightly at his waist as Julian tugged on it. He moaned in encouragement and closed his eyes.

Julian didn't even bother yanking the belt off when he finally got it loose. He just unbuttoned Cameron's pants and pushed them down while kissing Cameron's neck possessively.

The clinging boxers under Cameron's pants did nothing to hide how aroused he was. His cheeks heated again as he got his shoes off and stepped out of his trousers. He swallowed hard to make himself focus—Julian's fingers were very, very distracting.

"Bed's there," Cameron announced in a hoarse voice, tilting his head toward the screens.

Julian nodded without looking. He slid his hands further under the warm material of Cameron's boxers and buried his face against his neck. "Nice place," he murmured against Cameron's skin.

"Thanks," Cameron managed, putting his hands on Julian's shoulders, unable to resist touching the moving muscles again. He'd never had a size kink before, but he was starting to see the appeal.

Julian pushed Cameron's boxers down his hips before sliding his hands back up and placing his palms flat against his back. It seemed to

Cameron that Julian could *feel* the uncertainty in him, and it caused his actions to be more hesitant than perhaps they normally would have been. But Cameron wanted nothing more than for him to take the lead and do what he wanted. He took Julian's face in his hands and kissed him boldly, hoping to urge him along.

Julian reacted accordingly, groaning softly into the kiss as he dragged Cameron toward the gap between the panels.

Cameron gave a pitifully grateful thought of thanks as Julian moved them both. They stumbled through the dividing screens, Cameron turning in Julian's arms to rub against all that warm skin.

Julian groaned again and let his hands roam freely over Cameron's body. He picked him up again without warning, carrying him the short distance to the bed and dropping him down on it. Cameron gulped as he went from vertical by the screens to horizontal on the bed with no effort or warning. Muscles, indeed. He looked up at Julian, for the moment more hungry than nervous as he dragged his eyes down Julian's body.

"Sorry," Julian offered insincerely as he bent over him and began kissing his way down Cameron's body.

Cameron groaned, arching up against his mouth. "Yeah, right."

Julian slid his hands up Cameron's sides, holding him there like a large cat would a meal, and he nipped at the tender skin of Cameron's hip before dragging his nose along his abdomen. Cameron closed his eyes as he let his body move. He pulled up a knee and sank long fingers into Julian's hair as the other hand gripped the quilt.

Julian slid one hand under his body and lifted him slightly. He propped himself on that elbow and looked up at Cameron admiringly before lowering his head and licking at Cameron's cock slowly. He swirled his tongue around the head and used his arm to pull Cameron's hips upward, forcing him up into his mouth.

Cameron tensed and bit his lip against a soft cry, his fingers flexing against Julian's scalp as his cock sank into the wet heat of Julian's mouth. He opened his eyes to look and practically whimpered at the sight. That certainly wasn't what he'd been expecting. A man like Julian had Alpha Dog written all over him.

But Julian bent all his considerable attention toward sucking Cameron off for several glorious moments as Cameron tried and failed to form a cohesive thought. Julian's hand urged Cameron to thrust up, and his tongue swirled and teased expertly. Finally he looked up, let Cameron slide out of his mouth, and grinned.

Cameron watched him with heated, glazed eyes while he gasped for air. "Jesus Christ, Julian," he hissed. He was shaking all over.

Julian didn't waste any time in bowing his head once more and taking Cameron into his mouth again. He raised Cameron's hips until he had to arch his back, and Julian began sucking with the sole apparent purpose of hearing Cameron scream. It didn't take long. Not long at all.

All the excitement of the evening's rendezvous had already put Cameron on a hair trigger. His breath hitched as he croaked out the other man's name, pushing ineffectively at strong shoulders as he was about to lose it. But Julian's grip tightened and he redoubled his efforts.

Cameron sucked in a deep breath and gritted his teeth against the wild yell he wanted to loose as he came hard, right against Julian's moving tongue, more and more until he couldn't stop a near-sobbing cry from breaking free.

Julian swallowed with a muffled moan, his fingers digging into Cameron's skin. He continued sucking until Cameron flinched and writhed beneath him. Then he looked up at Cameron with dark, hungry eyes.

After a whole-body shudder, Cameron felt those predatory eyes focused on him. Despite the strong orgasm, desire cramped in his belly. He whispered Julian's name in invitation, enjoying the fact that he could do so freely.

"Do you have condoms?" Julian asked in a low, heated growl.

Cameron dragged in a breath and nodded, extending his arm to gesture to the top drawer of a nearby dresser. Julian's eyes followed the point, and as he moved he once again reminded Cameron of a large, predatory cat—long, smooth body lines, rippling muscles. There was no longer any restraint in the power or speed of his movements. He rolled off the bed and went to the drawer, rummaging hastily through it to find the supplies he needed.

Cameron kept his eyes on him the whole time. He was well beyond infatuated at this point, and he knew this had been both a brilliant idea and a horrible mistake. It had all the hallmarks of ending badly, but he had no chance in hell of pulling back now. The thought of what was coming made all that seem insignificant, anyway.

Julian pushed his own briefs down and kicked out of them as he tossed a bottle of lubricant onto the bed. Finally, he found a foil packet, and he tore it open as he turned to openly admire Cameron on the bed. His eyes didn't leave Cameron's as he slowly rolled the condom on. Cameron was more than half-hard again as he watched Julian handle himself.

Julian reached across the bed and grabbed Cameron by the backs of his knees, pulling him across the quilt, tugging him until he lay on his back in front of where Julian stood by the side of the tall bed. He placed Cameron's legs around his hips and ran his hands down Cameron's thighs without breaking eye contact.

Cameron could barely breathe as Julian manhandled him. Julian bent and reached for the tube of lubricant, letting his cock slide against Cameron's thighs as he did so. "You tell me if I hurt you," he ordered sternly, his voice low and hoarse with desire.

Cameron groaned and nodded again, reaching to touch what he could of the other man's body.

Julian rested a knee on the mattress, bending over Cameron to kiss him. He pushed one of Cameron's legs back as he did so, easing it up onto his shoulder as he licked at Cameron's lips. He teased with one lubricated finger, mimicking the motion with his tongue.

Cameron slid his arms around Julian's neck as they kissed, and the now-familiar taste mingled with his own helped him relax. He wanted this more than he would have imagined. Soon, Julian had two fingers inside him, twisting and stretching intently. The bigger man trembled with restraint, but his movements were becoming more hurried and less gentle.

Cameron loved it. Groans growing louder, he shifted to wrap his other leg around Julian's calves to tug him forward. "More," he rasped, making eye contact in the dim light. "C'mon."

And that was apparently all Julian needed. He jerked his head to the side and growled wordlessly, then removed his fingers and quickly covered himself with a generous amount of lubricant. He gripped Cameron's hip with one hand and propped his weight up with the other as he bent over Cameron again.

Julian kissed him hungrily as he pushed into him.

Cameron gasped the pain out into Julian's mouth—he couldn't help his body's natural reaction to tense, especially considering Julian's size—but as for what he really wanted, that he could do. He pushed back as hard as he could, and he was rewarded by the singularly incredible feeling of Julian boring deep into him, making that connection Cameron craved. Julian gasped as well, panting against Cameron's mouth as he rolled his hips and sank deeper. He muttered incoherently and tightened his grip on Cameron's thigh as he began rocking against him.

Cameron murmured encouragement, his body bowing up into Julian's as the drag of their skin slowly drove him insane. It was incredible to witness such a normally detached, undemonstrative man like Julian become unraveled and passionate because of him. He was certainly spoiled forever, now. After this little adventure, nothing would be the same.

Julian gasped for breath against Cameron's ear. "Okay?" he managed to ask.

Cameron moaned aloud. "Yes. Oh, yes," he whispered, clutching Julian as close as he could. "Don't stop."

"Hold on," Julian gasped as his hips moved in a slow, languorous rhythm.

Cameron moaned again and hitched himself closer to Julian's hip to rub his cock against heated skin. The sensations arched through him, along with every slide of Julian inside him. Julian lowered himself more, giving Cameron more friction, and he gasped as the angle of his thrusts changed. He cursed under his breath and twisted his fingers in Cameron's hair as he kissed him hard.

Cameron lifted his hips mindlessly, over and over, falling deep into the pleasure and ache. Playing into the tight, strung-out wire that yanked at his insides. Julian's thrusts were hard and rhythmic, starting out slow to enjoy the slide of their bodies, but soon becoming less controlled.

Cameron held on just like he'd been instructed, wrapping his legs tight around Julian's waist. Julian clenched his hands, holding Cameron down as he writhed. Suddenly, Julian called out plaintively, lowering his head and pounding into Cameron brutally as he rode out his orgasm. Cameron's eyes rolled back into his head as Julian took him hard and fast, and he reveled in it along with his own smaller climax, soaking in the feeling of being able to make this man lose control even this little bit.

Julian trembled and panted as he gripped Cameron's hips. He kissed him one last time as he carefully pulled out, and Cameron collapsed into a mess on the sheets, arms and legs quivering as he tried to catch his breath.

"Are you okay?" Julian gasped as he slowly slid to his knees at the side of the bed.

Pushing himself to his elbows, Cameron dragged his eyes open to look at Julian's flushed face. "Yes," he said between jerky breaths.

Julian nodded and exhaled slowly, then pulled himself up and crawled onto the bed to flop down beside Cameron, who rolled to his side and pillowed his head on his own outstretched arm. His panting slowing, Cameron quietly watched Julian move and settle, admiring his body, wondering what in the world was in the man's head to give him the thought to hook up with someone like himself.

Julian returned the look admiringly. "That was fun," he murmured finally.

Cameron smiled. "Yeah?"

Julian mirrored the smile and nodded. He reached out and gently ran his fingers over Cameron's face, and they lay there quietly for long minutes, enjoying the comfortable silence. Finally, Julian glanced around the room as he pushed himself up. "Washroom" he asked softly.

Cameron pointed across the room to a door hidden in the shadows, too tired to get up and show Julian the way. The room was mostly dark, lit by subtle lights Cameron left on in the other room for the dogs, but his eyes had adjusted enough that he could see Julian quite well. He was sitting up in the bed, rolling his shoulders back and forth and stretching out hard, toned muscles.

"Be right back," he murmured to Cameron before reaching out and snagging Cameron's hand. He kissed the inside of his wrist again and then hefted himself off the bed to disappear into the bathroom.

Once Julian was gone, Cameron covered his face with both hands and sighed softly. He let them fall to the side and stared blindly up at the ceiling, noting faintly how the light spilled through the dividing screens to fall over the bed in odd shapes. He couldn't remember the last time he'd turned on a light in the bedroom, since he usually got home and simply crashed every night. Sighing, he rolled to pull a pillow against his chest and face, feeling the ache when he shifted his hips. His entire body felt languid and sated, and sleep called to him. But he hated to sleep when he had Julian here in his apartment for perhaps the one and only time.

After a couple minutes, the bathroom door opened, and Cameron heard Julian's footsteps on the wood floor halt several steps away from the bed. He looked up to see Julian stopped short, looking around the room uncertainly. Cameron watched him admiringly for a long moment. Then the awkwardness seemed to seep back into him as he realized that the passion of the moment was spent and now they would actually have to speak to each other.

"Do you want…?" Cameron stopped and bit his lip.

Julian moved to the bed and slowly crawled onto it, his eyes never leaving Cameron's as he prowled closer. "Do I want what?" he prodded as he moved closer.

Watching Julian move so sinuously made Cameron's eyes glaze again. "Do you want to stay?"

"Yes," Julian answered. "Will it make you uncomfortable?" he asked bluntly.

Cameron took a long moment to sort out what he was feeling. Warm and satisfied. More than a little surprised that Julian was here at all. A bit of residual apprehension from the weapon out in the front room. "Yes," he admitted. "But I want you to stay anyway."

Julian's brow furrowed briefly before the unreadable mask returned, and he nodded. Then his lips twitched and he nodded again. "Well, then. I'm going to need a razor," he whispered as he drew close enough to kiss Cameron gently.

After the light kiss, Cameron nodded. "I've got an extra toothbrush too."

"That may come in handy," Julian growled playfully as he gathered Cameron up in his arms and dragged him to the head of the bed. "I'll be taking advantage of you at least twice more tonight," he claimed as he did so.

A surprised laugh bubbled up as Julian held him close and pulled him bodily up to the pillows. Cameron had expected Julian to be somber and serious after the passion cooled, just like he was at the restaurant, not playful and genuine.

"I've never heard you laugh," Julian observed with a smile as he nuzzled Cameron's neck.

"Before tonight we've never been together more than five minutes at a time, if that long," Cameron pointed out.

Julian shoved the covers aside and pulled them over their bodies as he clasped Cameron close. "I have watched you, though," he admitted.

Cameron turned onto his side within the circle of Julian's arms so he could prop his head on the pillow and look at the other man. "Yeah? At the restaurant?"

A tiny smile ghosted across Julian's lips. "If I said no, it would worry you," he said wryly.

Both Cameron's brows raised. "Really? Are we back to the stalking thing again?"

"I wouldn't call it stalking," Julian responded, his voice just a bit defensive. "It was only one night," he admitted. "The first time I was at your table. It was late. I didn't intend to follow you," he insisted. "We were merely going the same way. You were almost mugged that night; you didn't even know it. That's what caught my attention. You were… oblivious to your impending doom," he said with a teasing smile.

Cameron gave a slight start. "I was?" His eyes narrowed. "You stopped it?"

Julian gave a slight shrug of his shoulder and flushed in the low light.

Cameron reached up to stroke the blush under the short beard. At the same time he felt the tiny sting of whisker burn across his lips, cheeks, and neck, only just now noticing it.

"I'm not the type of person who enjoys seeing violence just for the hell of it," Julian murmured seriously.

Cameron nodded, trying to reconcile that statement with the fact that Julian carried a gun and sported an impressive array of injuries. If it was true, it meant whatever violence Julian was seeing, it wasn't by choice. After several moments' thought, he leaned forward and kissed Julian chastely. "Thank you."

Julian blinked rapidly at him and then stared at him as if he wasn't sure what to do. "Don't mention it," he whispered finally.

"Not really good at taking compliments or thanks, are you?" Cameron ventured.

"Not really," Julian answered with a small smile as he closed his eyes.

Cameron smiled and yawned as the drowsiness dragged him down. He shifted closer against Julian's body, unable to say anything more as he sank into the unexpected comfort of a stranger's embrace.

THE sound of running water was unusual enough that Cameron woke to lift his head sleepily and look around. Early morning light streamed through the windows, and the bedroom was cold. He was sprawled on his belly and had to shift to reach for the sheets—and the night came back to him as he felt the ache. Julian had been true to his word, and over the course of the night and early morning he'd taken Cameron twice more, each time slower and longer and more mind-blowing than the last.

Cameron would be sore for days, but it had been worth it. Blinking away the sleepiness, he sat up, looking at the closed door to the bathroom.

Julian. He was still here.

Cameron shivered. He'd get to kiss him goodbye. And despite the man's claim, Cameron couldn't bring himself to believe this would happen again. His chest ached as he wondered if Julian would come back to Tuesdays anymore after this. He closed his eyes and rubbed his torso, trying to ease the uncomfortable tightness there.

Julian opened the bathroom door and leaned against the frame as he wiped his hair with a towel. He stopped, tilted his head, and watched Cameron for a long moment. "Merry Christmas," he finally offered in a soft, hoarse voice.

Cameron was taken aback for a moment. "Yeah, it is," he said as he continued to rub at his chest.

"You feel okay?" Julian asked with a slight frown.

Cameron dropped his eyes to take stock of himself and soon nodded. "Yes. You?"

Julian nodded wordlessly and walked toward the bed, his dark eyes intent on Cameron. Swallowing, Cameron tried to look his fill, though he suspected he'd never get tired of the sight.

"I feel like I should be thanking you," Julian admitted.

Cameron blinked and looked up at him. "Thank me?" he echoed cautiously. He wasn't sure he liked how that sounded.

"For trusting me," Julian provided.

Cameron relaxed and studied Julian's face. "You said you trusted *me*," he countered. It probably made him seem really naïve, but Cameron couldn't be anyone but who he was.

Julian's eyes narrowed thoughtfully and he sat on the edge of the bed, his back to Cameron. In the daylight it was easy to see the chaos of bruises on his back and ribs. He had obviously been in some sort of accident or fight recently. There was also an array of scars, including one on the meat of his arm that looked to be recent.

Looking over the damage to Julian's body made protectiveness and worry swell in Cameron—things he knew he had no business feeling. Still, he reached forward and lightly brushed his fingers down Julian's spine. He might as well take advantage of this stolen time to touch and store away the memories.

Julian shivered violently with the caress, and he glanced over his shoulder with a smile. "They're just on the surface," he assured Cameron. "Workplace hazards."

Cameron heard, but still he felt moved to lean forward and smooth his lips over some of the bruises. It hurt him to even see them, and he wished he could make them disappear. He couldn't imagine how Julian moved so smoothly with his body so beat up. Cameron wasn't sure he believed that Julian was what he said he was, but whatever he did, it was brutal.

Julian reached back and ran his fingers through Cameron's hair. It was comforting. "What do you have planned today?" he asked.

Cameron shook his head and shrugged off the slightly dark thoughts. "Lazy day. Restaurant's closed." He settled his hand at the base of Julian's spine, lightly stroking.

Julian nodded and looked back at the wall opposite where he sat. "Sounds delightful," he murmured.

It was a little easier now to be daring, since he was still naked in a bed that smelled of Julian and sex. "Want to join me?" Cameron asked.

"I would love to," Julian answered, his voice a soft, regretful murmur. "But I can't."

It was the answer Cameron had expected, but it didn't make the pang in his chest any easier to feel. "I understand." And he did. He'd brought someone he barely knew home for sex; he couldn't expect the man to come back for conversation.

Julian turned around and examined him closely. "I should be free by four," he told Cameron evenly. "I've got a last-minute client to take care of first."

Client. Julian had a client. Cameron's mind flashed through all sorts of different meanings that could have. What if he himself was just a client, being given a credit because Julian liked the way he looked? Did he want more if that was the case? How would he pay for it later? In heartbreak? Cameron pushed away those disjointed thoughts and swallowed on a sickened twist in his belly.

"You could come by. If you wanted," he hurried to respond, determined not to worry about what might come and to take full advantage of anything he could.

"I will certainly try," Julian promised as he turned and stretched to kiss Cameron's neck.

Cameron closed his eyes and turned his chin as Julian's lips met his skin. Try. He'd accept it gracefully and save the disappointment for when Julian was gone. He almost wished it were a regular day so he had the comfortable routine of work to escape to. Instead, he had long, lonely, empty hours ahead of him. And Julian would be working, whatever that entailed.

"You'll be careful?" Cameron blurted before thinking about it, and he colored brightly in embarrassment.

"I'm always careful," Julian assured him.

Offering him a smile, Cameron nodded and slowly lay back, giving Julian space to do as he liked.

Julian watched him and narrowed his eyes. "I'd better be going," he whispered finally. "Thank you," he repeated, "for last night. And for getting that tape to Blake. And for every Tuesday," he added with a small smile.

"Tuesdays," Cameron murmured, not looking away from Julian. "The good days." It was what Julian had said.

"Yeah," Julian affirmed with a nod and a wistful smile.

"Do you come on Tuesdays because of the name of the restaurant?" Cameron found himself asking.

Julian lips quirked slowly. "No," he answered. "But I know why the restaurant is called Tuesdays," he offered in amusement.

"Really?" Cameron asked curiously. It had always seemed such a random thing to call a four-star restaurant. He'd often wondered why Blake had chosen it.

Julian hummed and tilted his head. "Ask Blake about the god of war," he advised mischievously. "He'll tell you the story."

Cameron merely nodded in confusion, not even sure if he wanted to know what that meant. "Give me another kiss?" he asked softly.

Julian raised an eyebrow and smiled wryly. He turned and crawled closer, kissing Cameron roughly.

Cameron gasped under the unexpected onslaught, grasped at Julian's arms, and held on tight as he gave into the swirling heat of the other man's mouth. His body responded right away, and he arched up against Julian instinctively.

Julian grinned against the kiss, extending it well past the time of propriety. Finally, he growled softly and pushed up onto his hands and knees. "You could get a man fired, you know that?" he muttered in frustration as he looked down at Cameron.

A silly smile curled Cameron's lips. "Another compliment?"

"I would think so," Julian murmured, "considering I'm self-employed." He hesitated, looking down at Cameron. "I'm sorry," he said with a pained wince. "But I do have to go."

Feeling a little better seeing that Julian didn't look happy to have to leave, Cameron scooted to the edge of the bed, let the sheet slide down his body, and climbed out of bed. As Julian sat back on the edge of the bed, rubbing at his neck and looking around for his clothing,

Cameron padded into the bathroom, cleaned up a little, and pulled on shorts and a T-shirt.

He ran the water to brush his teeth and get a cool drink, and afterward he looked at himself in the mirror for a long moment, seeing the resignation in his own eyes. He didn't want to think anything about Julian right now; he just wanted to live the moment while it lasted. He took a long drink before heading back out to the bedroom.

"Will you be here?" Julian asked him when he reappeared. He was already half-dressed. There was a pile of his clothing on the bed behind him, as well as the gun he'd shed the night before.

Cameron stopped in the doorway and leaned against the frame, folding his arms. "Yes," he answered, lifting a foot just enough to brush it back and forth over the threshold.

Julian watched him for a long moment and then nodded. He stood and pulled his pants up, buttoning and zipping before he walked over to Cameron, his shirt still partially unbuttoned even though he'd tucked it in. He stopped just in front of Cameron, who straightened nervously and waited, fingers gripping the wood of the doorframe.

Julian tilted his head and reached out slowly to take Cameron's hand, keeping his eyes on Cameron's as he raised his hand and kissed the inside of his wrist gently. It was becoming obvious that the gesture was a habit. Eyes widening, Cameron watched the man's lips slide against his skin, and he shivered before looking back up at Julian. That touch made him melt inside. This whole encounter had been disconcertingly tender, and it left Cameron aching for more.

Julian released his hand and backed away, buttoning his shirt up. "Do you have one of those lint rollers you mentioned?" he asked.

Cameron swallowed heavily and nodded. That was easy enough. "Sure. Out in the main room," he murmured. "I'll get one for you. Need to feed the pups, anyway." He stepped around Julian slowly before tearing his eyes away and moving around the screen. Soon, a soft pitter-patter followed him, along with some excited yips.

When Julian stepped out of the bedroom, his overcoat and scarf were draped over his arm and he was fussing with his tie. Cameron stood at the kitchen bar across the room. Little white puppies bopped around his feet, and he ignored them as he looked through a stack of mail. There was a lint roller waiting at his elbow, and when he heard Julian's soft footsteps, he looked up. So did the four puppies, who all immediately charged across the floor to bounce off Julian's ankles.

Julian picked up one foot as one of the puppies latched onto his pants leg and began pulling and growling, trying to carry him away toward the playpen in the corner. "Ambitious, are we?" Julian said softly to the tiny puppy.

Chuckling, Cameron walked over with the lint brush. "Ever optimistic," he corrected. He pushed Julian's hands away from his uncooperative tie, handed him the lint roller, unwrapped the mangled fabric, and started over with it.

Julian held his hands away and focused on Cameron. The puppies continued to tug at him unnoticed as Cameron drew all his considerable attention. Cameron messed with the tie for a moment before realizing that he couldn't tie one if he was facing it, so he moved self-consciously around Julian and reached around his broad shoulders from behind. He couldn't help but to press his nose against the back of Julian's shoulder as he tied the tie, and he inhaled the man's scent with a small smile. Julian stood motionlessly, letting him do as he pleased.

He moved back to stand in front of Julian and checked the tie to make certain it was straight, and he smoothed Julian's collar down before glancing up and seeing the man's pinning gaze. He colored a little and stepped back, then cleared his throat.

"What needs help?" he asked, reaching to take back the roller.

"Just my coat," Julian murmured without looking away from him. He moved deliberately as he shrugged into the heavy wool, his eyes never leaving Cameron's. He held out his arms for inspection.

Glad for a reason to escape that intent gaze, Cameron moved around him slowly again, making sure to get all the fine white hairs he could see with the roller. He finished in front of Julian once more. "All done," he murmured before looking down at the puppies still climbing over their feet. "Pants legs?" he asked, not wanting to look up just yet.

Julian ducked his head, trying to catch Cameron's eyes. "Please," he answered evenly.

"Just a sec," Cameron murmured. He leaned over to gather the four wiggling puppies and carried them over to the playpen tucked unobtrusively in the corner. He set them inside and plaintive yapping followed him back to Julian, where Cameron knelt down on one knee to run the roller over Julian's calves. Even though he made sure to avoid the other man's eyes the whole time, he could feel Julian's piercing gaze on him. Julian always watched him so closely; he couldn't imagine how he had never felt those eyes on him in the restaurant. Warmth swamped his entire body.

Several more swipes and Cameron was done. He climbed back to his feet and finally offered Julian a crooked, nervous smile. "All presentable now."

"Thank you," Julian said to him softly. He opened his mouth to say more, but closed it again without saying anything. He tilted his head to the side and gave a small, almost embarrassed smile as he wrapped his scarf around his neck. It occurred to Cameron that Julian often dipped his head to one side or the other, or even ducked his chin as he spoke, and it was clearly because he was so tall. It was the only way to keep eye contact with someone so much shorter than he.

Cameron put his hands behind his back, fingers worrying at the roller as he watched Julian get ready to go. He had no idea what to say. Nothing sounded right. Instead, he skimmed over Julian's body one last time, trying to commit it and the feel of it against him to memory. As Cameron watched him, Julian lowered his head and began to walk slowly toward the door.

Then he stopped suddenly, turned around, and moved quickly toward Cameron to roughly pull him close and kiss him.

Cameron almost choked as he was grabbed and kissed within an inch of his life, and he held on tight for the length of the moment, savoring it, soaking it in. Julian held him so tightly that Cameron thought he might have bruises when it was over.

Julian detached himself just as suddenly as he'd moved before. "I hope to see you tonight," he murmured as he backed away. "Merry Christmas," he offered before turning and heading for the door on those silent cat's feet.

"Merry Christmas," Cameron echoed as Julian exited the apartment without looking back.

Cameron stood there for long minutes, staring at the door after Julian left before wrapping his arms around himself and turning in place, feeling lost and overwhelmed. Finally, he went over to the playpen, liberated the puppies, and sat down on the floor, letting them cavort around him while he reflected on what had been an odd, amazing night.

CHAPTER 3

THE snow falling heavily outside almost obscured Cameron's view of the street and the city beyond. A few candles filled the apartment with a popular scent of the season, and he had switched on the tiny twinkle lights he'd hung in the windows. His favorite Internet radio station played jazz holiday tunes, and he felt that was about all he needed for the holiday mood this year.

The afternoon and early evening had come and gone without so much as a hint of Julian's return, and Cameron had convinced himself that it was what he'd expected, trying to ignore the disappointment.

He'd abandoned his book on the couch in favor of fixing himself dinner, using a recipe from Jean-Michel, the chef at the restaurant. It wasn't exactly Christmasy: a thick, meaty lasagna with several layers that had required Cameron to search out a kitchen store the week before to buy extra-deep lasagna pans. He chopped and grated and cooked ingredients for almost an hour; one pan of lasagna was done and had been in the oven about two hours. Now he was putting the second together to freeze for another time.

Washing his hands for the umpteenth time, he paused to finish his glass of wine and refill it, grunting in surprise to find he'd somehow managed to finish the entire bottle. Shrugging, he set it aside and pulled another bottle off the rack. No reason not to get more than tipsy tonight, he thought wryly. No work tomorrow, no one to be presentable for, nowhere to go. He looked down at the huge lasagna and smiled. And he'd have food for days. Weeks, maybe.

Without warning, the puppies started yapping hysterically and ran for the front door. Cameron looked after them in surprise. He hadn't heard the bell ring or buzzed anyone into the building. Frowning, he glanced at the clock. Seven-thirty. With a soft harrumph he rounded the bar to walk toward the door, carefully shooing the puppies away with his feet before peering through the peep-hole.

He jerked back in surprise and allowed himself a moment to quietly panic before he pulled off the chain and opened the door.

"Hello, Cameron," Julian greeted in a soft voice. "May I come in?" he requested.

Blinking several times, Cameron stared for a long moment before shaking himself and stepping back. He thought vaguely that he should ask how Julian had gotten into the building, but when Julian spoke, the thought totally disappeared from his head.

"Thank you," Julian murmured. When he stepped into the apartment, his dark clothing glistened slightly; it was soaked through and flecked with ice crystals.

Cameron closed the door behind him after counting the puppies now flopping around Julian's feet, and his eyes moved upward over Julian's clinging clothing. "You're all wet," he observed stupidly. "I'll get you a towel," he added, blushing slightly as he turned to head toward the bathroom.

"A towel won't do me much good," Julian answered with a wry smile as his hair dripped and rivulets of melted snow ran down his face, catching in his beard.

Stopping, Cameron looked at him more closely and stifled a laugh. "What'd you do? Snow angels?"

Julian gave him a self-deprecating smile and lowered his head to run his hand through his wet hair. "Well, I considered one, but at the time I still had a dry sock to consider," he joked. "I was walking. I had to leave my car because of the blizzard. You were much closer than home," he admitted, looking slightly abashed. "I'm sorry," he offered.

Cameron frowned. "Leave your car?" he repeated dubiously. On the well-snowplowed Chicago streets?

Julian pursed his lips. "You really want to know?" he asked, repeating himself from the night before.

"I think so," Cameron answered before considering it.

"I hit an ice sheet," Julian said right away. "The car was pretty much done for the night after that."

Cameron cocked his head and looked Julian up and down, not seeing any injuries. "Are you okay?" he asked as worry flared.

"I'm not hurt," Julian assured him quickly. "I may be sore tomorrow," he added as he pointed to his chest and rubbed it. "Safety belt," he explained.

Still concerned, Cameron nodded toward the bathroom. "There's towels in the basket if you want to shower. You must be freezing. It's like ten degrees outside even without the wind."

Julian nodded and watched Cameron with a curious expression. "Do you mind?" he asked seriously. "I can call for a ride and go."

"Of course I don't mind!" Cameron said in surprise. "I wouldn't turn you out soaking wet." He pointed at the bathroom. "Go," he said firmly.

Julian's lips twitched in amusement, and he nodded obediently as he began to loosen his tie. "Yes, sir," he drawled in a soft, low voice.

Cameron raised an eyebrow and crossed his arms, watching in interest. Every time they spoke, a little more of Julian's personality seemed to creep forth. It was anything but cold and foreboding. There was actually humor buried under there somewhere.

Julian removed his coat as Cameron watched, hanging it carefully on the coatrack beside the door. He turned and considered Cameron's gaze. "Did you want to help me?" he asked in amusement.

Reaching out to touch Julian's hand, Cameron could tell he was nearly frozen. "If that's what it takes to thaw you out," he said frankly. "I'm surprised you're not blue. Get moving. I'll try to find you something dry to wear."

"Thank you," Julian murmured before turning and heading for the bedroom, undressing as he went.

Cameron followed along behind, taking the wet clothes as Julian pulled them off. Once in the bedroom, he slung them over a chair and went digging in his dresser. It would be a neat trick to find anything to fit Julian, but Cameron thought he had a couple oversized pairs of sweatpants and T-shirts that might work. For all that Julian was tall and broad-shouldered, he was very trim through the middle.

Cameron couldn't dry Julian's clothes for him; it was all high-class, dry-clean-only stuff. He cringed as he looked at the expensive labels. He couldn't afford to breathe the air in those stores. Not many people could.

Julian made short work of showering, apparently just getting reasonably warm. He re-entered the bedroom with a towel around his waist, but water still ran down his chest and shoulders in thin streams.

Cameron glanced up from where he knelt in front of the fireplace beside the bed, having set it to burning. He stood and gestured to the clothes spread out on the foot of the bed before walking over with a frown. "If you don't dry off, you'll be right back where you started," he scolded.

Julian smiled. "At least I'll already be out of the wet clothes." He licked his lips as he looked at Cameron fondly. "You've been drinking, haven't you?"

Cameron narrowed his eyes. "What makes you ask that?"

"Because you're a little less… twitchy," Julian pointed out with a cock of his head.

The huff that was Cameron's reply didn't do anything to counter Julian's statement. Neither did Cameron reaching out to yank the towel from the other man's hips and tossing it over his head to roughly dry his dripping hair. Julian grunted in surprise and lowered his head obligingly. Cameron continued rubbing until he thought Julian's hair might be sufficiently dry, and then he pulled the towel away and slid his hand into the damp hair to check. Julian watched him from under lowered lashes, his dark eyes shining.

Appeased, Cameron took the towel and dried Julian's neck, shoulders, and chest before stepping back and pointing at the clothes expectantly.

Julian gave him an amused smile.

"I might have had some wine," Cameron said reluctantly.

"No kidding." Julian laughed.

Cameron turned up his nose. "Fine then," he said, letting the towel drape around Julian's neck and shifting his weight to step back.

Julian snagged him and pulled him closer, kissing him with a small snicker. "I quite like you like this."

Smiling again, Cameron curled his arm around Julian's neck. "Don't do it often," he admitted. "Usually working." He ran his lips along Julian's jaw and down the side of his neck, humming softly as he breathed in the other man's scent.

"How much have you had?" Julian asked in interest.

Cameron flushed and hid his face in the crook of Julian's neck. His answer was muffled in warm skin.

Julian laughed harder as he wrapped his still-damp arms around Cameron and hugged him. "That much, huh?" he prodded.

Cameron pulled back, looking obstinate. "Some. A bottle. Maybe."

"Uh-huh," Julian responded. "Well, come on; give me some," he invited with a smile as he turned Cameron around and began pushing him out toward the kitchen, heedless of the fact that he was still nude.

Clearly, Julian was a man who was either used to being naked or was very comfortable with his body. Possibly both, Cameron speculated. He laughed as Julian urged him along. "I was getting ready to open the next bottle when you knocked," he explained. "I'm making lasagna!" he claimed, as if that justified it.

"Sounds like a drinking task to me," Julian affirmed with a sage nod.

"You're humoring me," Cameron accused as Julian pushed him into the kitchen.

"Yes," Julian answered with a laugh.

Cameron stopped at the bar. "You're laughing at me too."

"Only a little," Julian insisted with sincerity.

Cameron reached out to snag the corkscrew and slid around the bar that separated the living room and the kitchen, putting it between him and Julian. "No wine for you," he muttered.

Julian snorted and turned his head a bit when the sound of tiny feet came stampeding around the corner toward them. "Oh, fun," he commented as the puppies lobbed themselves at his bare ankles.

Cameron snickered at the look on Julian's face. He set the corkscrew on the bar and walked over to the lasagna fixings. "How was work?" he asked.

Julian looked up at him, a hint of the guarded mask appearing before he looked back down and gently lifted his foot, trying to shake off a puppy without booting it across the floor. "It was… predictable," he answered vaguely.

"Predictable," Cameron commented. "Sounds… exciting. Although, I guess you would think my job is predictable."

"I waited tables once," Julian told him. "*Once*, as in *one* night," he was quick to clarify. "Nothing predictable about that. I'm much better off doing what I do, thank you."

Cameron looked over his shoulder, grinning. "I can't see you as a waiter," he agreed. "You sort of have to talk to people, you know?" He turned back to the pan and finished layering the second lasagna.

"I talk," Julian responded, sounding affronted by the implication that he didn't.

Cameron wiped his hands off on a dish towel and covered the deep pan with aluminum foil. "Uh-huh. And just *how many* dinners at Tuesdays did it take before you said word one to me?" He glanced to Julian as he carried the pan over to the freezer.

"I was nervous," Julian offered lamely.

Cameron shook his head in disbelief as he shut the freezer door and turned around. "Then why sit in my section every Tuesday for who knows how many months?"

Julian grinned and finally wrapped the towel around his waist again after wresting it from two growling dogs. "Ten. Because I liked to watch you."

Cameron blinked. Ten months. Wow. That long? "Watch me, but not speak to me."

Julian sighed as his smile fell, and he lowered his head for a moment. "I was afraid I would say something out of line," he said seriously.

Cameron's brow furrowed. "Out of line?" He tipped his head to one side as he walked back to the bar and started opening the bottle of wine.

"Blake Nichols is a very good friend of mine, as well as a business partner," Julian explained softly. "It wouldn't do to get on my knees in the middle of his restaurant and beg you to come home with me."

Cameron fumbled with the corkscrew while he blinked in shock that was aided by too much wine. His mouth dropped open as he tried to say something, but nothing came out; he could do nothing but stare at Julian with wide blue eyes.

Julian returned the look earnestly, waiting.

"Would you really have done that?" Cameron finally managed to ask.

"Probably," Julian answered with a nod. "Blake told me I couldn't," he added in what was nearly a sulk.

Cameron's eyes widened again. "Probably?" he repeated weakly.

"I would have been subtle," Julian insisted with a straight face.

Cameron was completely bowled over. "Subtle? How is getting down on your knees and begging *subtle*?"

"I could make it subtle," Julian insisted under his breath as he waded through the puppies and around the bar to join Cameron. He took the wine cork with one hand and Cameron's hand with the other before he gracefully dropped to his knees in front of him and looked up at him with impish dark eyes.

Cameron had not one single idea what to do. All he could do was stare down at the gorgeous sight in front of him. That glittering gaze held him mesmerized as he tightened his fingers around Julian's.

"See?" Julian asked innocently. "It's less subtle when I'm naked, but you get the point," he said in a low voice, obviously trying not to smile as he released Cameron's hand and slid his hands up the backs of Cameron's calves. It was obvious he was enjoying himself, but Cameron wasn't quite getting the joke.

Cameron waffled a little and finally lifted his free hand to ghost over Julian's short hair. He thought about it for a long moment before finally murmuring, "Point taken."

Julian grinned up at him and let his hands move up over the backs of Cameron's thighs. "Were you cooking?" he asked.

"Cooking?" Cameron repeated in a daze, hand still moving lightly over Julian's head to curl down and coast over his ear and cheek.

Julian laughed softly, seeing the effect his actions were having.

Cameron shook his head to clear it and dipped it to one side. "I would have said yes," he whispered.

Julian gave that a genuine smile that warmed his eyes to a deep brown. "That's good to know."

Cameron felt a flash of panic. "You're not going to try it, are you?"

As he put a hand to his heart, Julian gave him the most angelic face Cameron had ever seen. "Try what?" he asked.

Visibly worried, Cameron reached down to tug at Julian's hand, urging him to stand. "Not that I would mind the effort," he clarified as Julian grunted and got back to his feet slowly. Cameron looked up at him. "C'mon; I'll feed you," he said abruptly, trying to dispel the sudden tightness in his chest. "But you'd better get dressed or I'll get distracted again."

Julian smirked as he looked down at his towel. He watched Cameron moving toward the oven for a moment before turning on silent feet and padding across the main room to disappear behind the screen. Cameron's eyes lifted to watch him the whole way, and he slowly licked his bottom lip. Once the man disappeared behind the dividing screens, he let out a shuddering sigh and practically collapsed against the counter.

Julian had wanted to beg him. *Beg him.* The concept literally took Cameron's breath away. For his own reasons, Julian wanted him. Badly. And in no way would Cameron put any sort of stop to it.

Cameron took a long, shaky breath. He could very easily love this man. That was far scarier than any gun or ambiguous job.

Julian was frowning and rubbing at his chest when he stepped back out into the outer room, wearing one of Cameron's T-shirts and a pair of sweats that didn't quite reach his ankles.

"How are you?" he asked Cameron abruptly.

Cameron looked up from the heated lasagna he was pulling out of the oven when Julian spoke from across the room. He really had no idea how to answer that question, given the last half-hour. He settled on the easier answer. "Hungry." He nodded down to the hot dish. "This just needs to set up some, and I'll get some French bread and salad out."

Julian came closer carefully. "It smells wonderful."

Nodding, Cameron unwrapped the bread with only slightly shaky hands and turned back around to look at Julian and grasp for something to say. "Wine?" he asked after his eyes cast over the newly opened bottle.

Julian looked down at the bottle and smirked. "No, thank you," he responded. "Am I making you uncomfortable?" he asked, his voice low and calm once more. "I can go," he offered.

Cameron glanced at him and just as quickly looked away. "I just don't know what to say," he said. "No one's ever said something like that to me before. I don't want you to go," he managed to get out as he stared at the wine bottle. "Why did you come back?" he asked starkly.

"I promised I would," Julian answered in surprise. "I intended to get here earlier, but I tend to drive faster than I can walk."

"I didn't expect to see you again," Cameron told him. "Like I said earlier, you'd never spoken much to me at all."

"You didn't think I'd come back?" Julian asked in a hurt voice.

"I don't know you," Cameron answered defensively. "Not really. And for the most part, anybody I get involved with isn't interested in sticking around," he added.

Julian stared at him in open shock. "Then you've been fucking the wrong people," he finally said with absolute certainty.

Cameron's head snapped up, and he boggled. "I have?" he said, voice cracking a little.

"Of course," Julian responded with a nod of his head. "Someone would have to be out of their mind not to come back to you. I walked through a blizzard to get here."

Cameron met Julian's eyes. "I've never met anyone like you before," he said in quiet amazement. "You make me feel…"

Julian raised an eyebrow and rubbed his chest distractedly, waiting.

"Special," Cameron supplied, barely audible. "Wanted."

Julian grinned widely. "Good," he said matter-of-factly.

"And confused," Cameron added with a sigh of resignation. "Why is that good? Strokes your ego?"

Julian pressed his hand over his heart as if he'd been hurt. "Ouch," he responded with a slight huff. "No," he added as he leaned his elbows on the counter. "Because that's exactly how I want you feeling."

"Oh." Cameron just looked at him in wonder. "I just might have to kiss you now," he warned.

"Well then, just let me move closer," Julian drawled cheekily as he glided around the counter and stopped next to Cameron. He wrapped an arm around Cameron's waist carefully and leaned down to give him a chaste kiss on the corner of his mouth.

As soon as Julian came close, Cameron lost his hold on his worries, and they melted into the background. Instead, he turned into the heat of the other man's body, lightly bumping Julian's lips against his again. He drew a shaking breath and tilted his head back to kiss Julian gently.

"Maybe I need some more wine," Cameron whispered.

"No, you don't," Julian assured him, tugging him closer and kissing him hungrily, cradling his head in one large hand as he did so.

It was easy to relax against Julian's chest and be kissed, and Cameron reveled in it, feeling the heat spark between them just like it had the night before. Just like that morning. Just like he hoped, at that very moment, it would for more time to come.

Julian hummed contentedly and smiled as he pulled back from the kiss. "Thank you for letting me stay," he whispered against Cameron's lips.

"Any time," Cameron murmured without thinking, raising his eyes to meet Julian's. Somehow, being in Julian's arms soothed the nerves and worry of the unknown.

"I could grow used to this," Julian said.

Cameron let his eyes move over Julian's face. "Okay," he said softly.

"Okay?" Julian echoed.

Cameron nodded solemnly. "I'd like it," he clarified, "if you grew used to this." He held his breath as he waited for Julian to answer.

Julian smiled slowly—a real, honest smile that seemed to melt away his hardened exterior. "Good," he responded as he slid his hands into the rear pockets of Cameron's jeans possessively.

Cameron released his breath and smiled as he gulped for another one. He shifted and hooked his wrists behind Julian's neck. "You might change your mind once you get to know me. I'm awfully boring."

"So am I," Julian retorted with a spark of mischief in his eyes.

"I really don't see how that's possible," Cameron said dryly. "The man who would get on his knees in the middle of a four-star restaurant to beg a waiter to go home with him?"

"That's not interesting. It's just being smitten," Julian corrected.

"Smitten? With me?" Cameron asked with a disbelieving laugh.

"You think I get on my knees for just anyone?" Julian asked with another playful sparkle in his eyes, as if sharing a private joke with himself.

"Had I not seen it with my own eyes, I would bet you got down on your knees for *no one*," Cameron said with absolute surety.

Julian lifted an eyebrow. "Well. You were mistaken," he chastised gently. His eyes flicked around the kitchen. "What shall we do for the few minutes it takes for dinner to finish?" he asked softly.

Both Cameron's brows rose as he considered the question and grasped for some sort of answer. "Roast chestnuts?" he threw out.

"Is that what you call them?" Julian asked innocently as he turned and looked at the herd of tussling puppies. Cameron's jaw dropped, and he rapped Julian on the chest with his knuckles. Julian gasped and pressed his hand to his sore chest, backing away. "Ow," he protested, though he still laughed.

Cameron turned up his nose. "Love me, love my dogs," he said snootily, trying to make a joke.

Julian tried to suppress a smile as he looked at the puppies again. "Well," he sighed with regret. "I suppose I could learn."

Cameron wondered about that answer. Learn to love the dogs? Or learn to love *him*? He edged slightly closer to the other man again. It was a weakness of Cameron's, something the majority of men he met didn't like: he thrived on physical contact. He loved the simplicity of touching. He craved it even more than the thrill of hot sex. So he stole the opportunity to lean his temple against Julian's shoulder for just a moment and press his nose to the warm skin of Julian's throat.

Julian wound his arms around him, and he dropped his chin and kissed Cameron impulsively before he let loose a long, growling sigh. Cameron stiffened slightly and pulled back, thinking Julian was reluctantly humoring his stolen moment of cuddling.

"What?"

"I wish I'd known I'd be here for Christmas," Julian answered while tightening his arms around Cameron's waist to stop him from moving away. "I would have… gotten something," he finished uncertainly.

"Gotten something? Like a present?" Cameron asked.

"Yeah," Julian answered with a nod, and his cheeks flushed.

Cameron gazed at him for a long moment. "You're more than enough of a present," he finally said.

Julian raised a wry eyebrow. "You got coal in your stocking as a kid, didn't you?" he asked flatly.

Cameron thumped Julian's chest again. "You've already told me how you'd embarrass yourself in front of an entire restaurant to try to get me to go home with you, and you think you can come up with a better present than that?"

"I can't help it if your standards are low." Julian laughed as he pulled Cameron even closer and trapped his arms to protect his sore chest.

"See if you get laid tonight!" Cameron told him with a huff.

"Is that a challenge?" Julian asked as interest sparked in his dark eyes.

Cameron narrowed his eyes. "Challenge? Are you gonna get on your knees again?"

"If that's what I need to do," Julian purred as he kissed gently behind Cameron's ear, holding him as if they were slow-dancing.

"And the challenge would be resisting you?" Cameron asked, sighing softly as Julian nuzzled the tender skin.

Julian hummed in the affirmative and nipped at Cameron's neck.

Cameron moaned and tilted his head back. "For how long?" he asked hoarsely. His jeans were already getting tight across the front, damn it.

"You said tonight," Julian reminded in a murmur as he slid his hands under Cameron's shirt.

Cameron whined softly. “Did I?”

Julian lifted his head and sniffed the air pointedly. “Smells like dinner,” he announced with an evil grin as he began to pull away.

Cameron growled and yanked him close. “One more kiss,” he demanded. Julian grinned just before it was snuffed out by the meeting of their lips.

“All right,” Cameron said reluctantly as he finally let Julian go. “Dinner.” Then he got a crafty look in his eyes. “Can’t have you weak and hungry before bedtime.”

“That’s right.” Julian grinned happily as he rubbed his hands together in exaggerated anticipation.

Cameron shook his head slowly. “You just amaze me, you know that? Sometimes I don’t know what to say.”

Julian watched him with an unreadable expression before lowering his head slightly.

Using hot pads, Cameron carefully lifted the lasagna from the stovetop and set it on the trivet.

Julian chewed on his bottom lip, for once not making eye contact as he frowned thoughtfully. “I suppose it’s hard to find common ground with a man you don’t know,” he offered.

Cameron nodded slowly. “Is there… is there something beyond the fact that you liked to watch me?”

Julian raised his head and met Cameron’s eyes again. “At first?” he asked. “No. You *were* fun to look at,” he admitted with a smile that said he might still be fun to look at.

Cameron’s eyebrow jumped, although Julian had already said something along those lines earlier. “And then?” he prodded.

“You weren’t afraid of me,” Julian said promptly.

Confusion crossed Cameron’s face. “Afraid of you? Why would I be afraid of you?”

Julian shrugged slightly. “Some people are,” he admitted.

Cameron considered that, tipping his head as he recalled Julian dressed all in black and towering over him. And the gun. "I guess I can see that," he admitted. "You could look sort of intimidating, if I'd met you somewhere else, maybe. Hadn't occurred to me, though. Not in the restaurant. I mean, in general, like leaving with a stranger after admitting no one was waiting for me, and then the gun, yeah. That's scary. But not you specifically."

Julian smiled weakly and nodded.

Concerned, Cameron set down the spatula and leaned one elbow on the counter, peering at Julian. "It hurts you," he said in realization.

"What does?" Julian asked as he unconsciously placed his hand on his chest again.

"People being afraid of you. Maybe even… lovers being afraid of you?" Cameron asked softly.

Julian raised his eyes and met Cameron's with what might have been hints of surprise and sadness. They were gone just as quickly as they had come. "Maybe," he acknowledged at a whisper.

"Have any of them *not* been afraid of you?" Cameron asked, meaning the lovers. His heart hurt for him.

Julian studied him searchingly for a long moment. "Can I include you in that answer?"

Cameron swallowed. "I *am* a person," he said.

Julian smiled slightly and nodded. "You are," he affirmed as he continued to look into Cameron's eyes. "Then just the one," he added in answer to the question.

"Person?"

"Lover," Julian corrected.

Cameron blinked, amazed he'd pried that answer out of Julian, but the implication really bothered him. "I'm your only lover who's not been afraid of you?"

Julian nodded silently and shrugged. Cameron frowned in sympathy. How could anyone be afraid of a man who had turned out to be so gentle? Was Cameron just missing something? Was there another part of Julian he hadn't yet seen? Was it the gun people couldn't get past? He couldn't believe that.

"How do you stand it?" he whispered. "Don't you have anyone?"

Julian gave his head a slight jerk in answer and smiled. "A few people."

Cameron relaxed a bit and nodded. "Good," he said as he stepped over to the refrigerator to pull out a bowl of tossed salad and a bottle of dressing. "Everyone should have someone."

Julian gave a small smile and shrugged in embarrassment.

Cameron frowned. "What about the restaurant?"

"I go there to see Blake, not eat the food," Julian admitted. "And then it became to see you. Because I don't like the cranky bastard all that much," he added with a laugh.

Cameron's jaw dropped. "You don't like the food? But why eat? Why not just see Blake and leave?"

"I didn't say I didn't like it," Julian pointed out. "It's…." He trailed off and shrugged. "The scenery is much better."

Cameron colored a little and smiled shyly. "How about dinner now?" he asked as he slid the bottle and bowl onto the bar.

"Sounds good," Julian agreed.

Cameron nodded and turned away to start scooping thick, sauce-dripping pieces onto cobalt-blue stoneware plates. "So, now what?" he asked. He had no idea where they would go from here, besides to bed.

"Well. Logic tells us that perhaps we need to get to know one another," Julian pointed out as he watched Cameron work on the lasagna.

Cameron's lips twitched. "Yeah, that would make sense," he commented. He pushed one filled plate toward Julian. "We've already skipped ahead several steps to the sex."

"Better to get that out of the way first to make sure we're not wasting our time," Julian deadpanned as he moved to stand behind Cameron. He tugged at Cameron's hip to turn him around and then stepped back to put a little space between them and held out his hand. “Julian Cross,” he offered with a twitch of his lips.

Cameron reached out automatically and slid their hands together, stifling a chuckle. “Cameron Jacobs,” he answered. His lips curled into a true smile. “Pleased to meet you.”

“Oh, no, no,” Julian murmured in a low voice as he held onto Cameron’s hand and slid his other hand up Cameron’s arm. “The pleasure’s all mine, I assure you,” he drawled with a smirk.

Cameron laughed softly. “Debatable,” he replied. He looked down at the lasagna and glanced back to Julian. “Um. Would you like to have dinner with me? Tonight?” he managed to get out, the oddness of the fact he was asking at all, much less in these circumstances, making him nervous once more.

Julian looked down at the lasagna and then back up at Cameron with a brilliant smile. “As long as it comes with dessert.”

Cameron raised an exaggerated eyebrow. “I thought you didn’t like desserts. To my knowledge, you’ve only ever ordered one.”

“Ah, but it was a good one,” Julian affirmed with a wicked smile.

CAMERON popped open what must have been the twentieth bottle of champagne for the night. It was a little past ten, and the restaurant was in full swing, filled to capacity. New Year’s Eve was always a crazy, busy night. He’d been going full steam since before noon. He broke free of the table of twelve he was helping and headed to the service area while all his tables were safely occupied with the festivities.

Miri thumped her tray down next to him. “Geez, I’m tired. New Year’s is always a madhouse,” she muttered.

“A very good-paying madhouse,” Cameron reminded her absently as he punched numbers into the register.

“Well, yeah,” Miri said drolly. “I make more tonight than I do in a month. And you working all day when you don’t have to? You’ll be able to retire soon.”

Cameron shrugged. "What else am I going to do? Sit at home by myself and watch the ball drop on Times Square? I'd rather be here with you, gorgeous." He leaned over and kissed her cheek.

Miri swatted at him playfully. "Get back to work, Romeo."

Cameron nodded as she moved off and hit the button to review the next order, tapping his finger on the counter. Once done, he took a breath and glanced at the small clock. Ten twenty-four. On a Tuesday night.

Since Julian had left his place the morning after Christmas, Cameron had heard nothing from the man. He didn't have a phone number to try calling. And tonight should have been the night when Julian returned to the restaurant, but he had yet to show. It was far past his usual time, and Cameron was telling himself a lot of things to keep from getting depressed about it all. It was New Year's Eve, after all. The restaurant had been booked weeks in advance, and even a regular customer like Julian couldn't just walk in. Or maybe he had prior plans for tonight and couldn't change them.

Maybe he'd had to work.

Cameron closed his eyes for a moment and sighed. Julian hadn't asked for Cameron's phone number to get in touch with him, much less offered one. He'd merely left the next morning with a farewell kiss. It didn't bode well for any future between them.

Cameron was relieved when the soft bell signaling a ready order sounded so he could go back to work and stop thinking about it. He'd been delivering appetizers in the party room for about fifteen minutes when he glanced up from taking orders to find himself looking straight at Julian. Julian's eyes were on him, and when Cameron looked at him, the big man smiled slightly.

Cameron blinked a few times and then returned the smile brilliantly. He nodded ever so slightly and went on his way back to the service area, tempted the whole time to look over his shoulder. When he got back there, Miri was waiting, arms crossed, a smile on her face.

"Trade you tables," she offered. Cameron flushed, and she laughed lightly, patted him on the shoulder, and handed him a table chit.

"Happy New Year." Then she was out the door, moving toward the party room.

Cameron stood and looked at the chit before he shook his head and grinned. He snagged a bottle of wine and a glass and headed out to greet Julian.

Julian looked up from his examination of his little notebook, and he smiled discreetly as Cameron neared him. Cameron expected to be nervous when he saw Julian again. But he wasn't; not really. He set down the wine-glass and tried not to grin. "Good evening," he greeted, eyes sparkling and a soft smile curving his lips.

"Happy New Year," Julian murmured to him.

"Not quite," Cameron responded, pulling the corkscrew out of his pocket. "About an hour yet." He worked the tool into the cork. "But if you order all the courses, you'll be here at midnight."

"That's what I'm counting on," Julian told him in a low voice, his eyes not leaving Cameron's.

It was a long moment later when Cameron realized he was just standing there with his hands on the wine bottle, looking back at Julian. He shook himself slightly as his cheeks flushed, and he pulled the cork. "Good thing your back is to a wall," he murmured. No one could see the silly look on his face except Julian.

Julian raised an eyebrow and glanced around before looking back up at Cameron. "You like my back against a wall?" he asked in a suggestive manner.

Cameron's cheeks darkened more, and he offered a flustered murmur as flashes of Christmas evening came back to him. More wine had certainly made Cameron more adventuresome than usual, and Julian had taken full advantage.

"I'll take that as a 'yes, thank you, I'd like some more'," Julian drawled with a barely restrained smirk.

Picking up the wine-glass, Cameron bit his lip and then smiled ruefully as he poured. "You're quite a bit like this wine," he finally said as he sat the half-filled glass down in front of Julian.

"What, not drunk yet?" Julian asked as he fiddled with his notebook.

Cameron shook his head as he pocketed the corkscrew and deliberately met Julian's eyes. "Intoxicating," he explained breathlessly. After two heartbeats, he escaped, heading for the service area to get the water pitcher and a bread basket.

His cheeks were still burning when he got there. After placing the basket and pitcher on a small, cloth-draped tray, Cameron took a few deep breaths to settle his heart rate before he headed back out the door. Lord knew what Julian would say next or how he'd react to it. Julian was right; he could easily bother Cameron at work just by being there. He stopped in front of the table and waited for Julian to look up.

Julian finished writing and set his pen down, looking up deliberately and meeting Cameron's eyes.

"Are you ready to order?" Cameron asked as he set the basket on the table.

"How long are you here?" Julian asked him, so softly that only Cameron could hear.

Cameron shrugged. "Restaurant's open until everyone leaves. I came in at ten this morning for prep, and usually I stick around and help out. But you're my only table now."

"So," Julian posed thoughtfully, "if I were to have my food boxed up and paid my check, you would be free to go?"

Cameron looked at him in surprise and tried to keep calm. "Ah, yeah, I guess I would," he said, starting to smile. "But you haven't ordered yet, except for the wine."

Julian's smile was slow and crooked, giving his normally serious face a mischievous light. "Check, please," he requested.

Both Cameron's eyebrows rose, and then he nodded. "Yes, sir," he replied before leaving the table to do just what Julian proposed.

Cameron arrived back at the table in fifteen minutes with his coat over one arm and a large, heavy paper sack with handles in his hand. There was no sign of a check. "Ready to go?" he asked.

Julian stood gracefully, buttoning his jacket as he did so. He took up his coat and scarf and draped them over his arm. “Ready,” he murmured with a smile.

Cameron led the way to the foyer, where he set down the bag long enough to pull on his coat and scarf before they rode down the elevator and walked out onto the cold street. There were only flurries tonight, but snow still covered the sidewalks, and Cameron’s breath came out frosty white. He turned his chin to look at Julian, wondering what would come next.

“Busy weekend,” Julian said to him vaguely. Cameron was uncertain whether it was a question or a statement.

Nodding slowly, Cameron watched the other man as they walked. After a quiet minute, he said, “I thought about you.”

“Did you, now?” Julian drawled with a pleased smile, his hands in the pockets of his heavy coat and his head down, seemingly watching his steps.

Cameron sucked his bottom lip between his teeth, just answering with a quiet hum.

“I thought about you as well,” Julian admitted freely.

Cameron looked over to him, a happy smile on his face. “Really?”

“Of course,” Julian stated as he looked over at Cameron and smiled. “I have something for you,” he added as he reached into his coat pocket.

Stopping in front of a holiday window display that cast multicolored light on the white-coated walkway, Cameron frowned slightly. “What is it? Christmas was last week.”

“Yes, and I felt badly for having nothing for you,” Julian reminded him as he reached into his pocket and withdrew a small box. It was wrapped in plain gold paper. He handed it to Cameron and smiled at him. “Please don’t feel obligated to accept.”

Cameron looked at the little box amazement. “Do you… do you want me to open it now?”

“As you like,” Julian answered with a lopsided shrug.

Cameron blinked at the gold paper for a moment before holding out the heavy bag to Julian so he could have both hands free. Without a word, Julian took it while he watched Cameron's face intently.

Turning the box over in his hands, Cameron chanced another look at Julian before running a finger under the seam of the paper to unwrap the box. It came off in no time. Julian smiled, but he looked unsure as Cameron opened the box. Intrigued by Julian's uncertainty, he pulled the top off and peered inside the box.

Inside was a flat disc of battered gold with a single garnet in the center melded to a chain so it could be worn around the neck.

Cameron stared at the glinting gold, highlighted by a flash of deep, dark red, before he glanced up at Julian with wide eyes. "This is like yours," he said, a smile curving his lips as he dipped a finger into the box to touch the pendant. He remembered dragging his fingers over it and the feel of body-warmed metal sliding over his chest as Julian moved against him.

"It *was* mine," Julian told him with a smile. "One of a kind. Now it's yours, if you'll have it."

Looking up in surprise, Cameron searched Julian's face for some clue about the meaning of the gift. Julian obviously wasn't the type who needed to recycle things as gifts to save money, so the necklace must have some sort of significance. Cameron stroked the gold again. "Is it important to you?" he asked.

"It has meaning," Julian answered. "And it's important in that I want you to have it."

Cameron nodded slowly. "Thank you," he said solemnly. "I'd like to put it on, but I think my fingers are already frozen," he said with a shiver. "I guess I ought to get some gloves."

"Don't be silly; it's only Chicago in winter," Julian scoffed sarcastically as he set the bag down. "Why would you need gloves when you can have frostbite?" he asked logically, smiling slightly as he reached out to take the pendant. He unhooked the clasp and stepped closer, sliding his arms around Cameron's neck slowly and fastening it before letting the pendant fall a few inches below the hollow of his throat. He tilted his head as he looked into Cameron's eyes. "It's called a warrior's cross. The garnet and the gold symbolize the Roman god Mars," he explained quietly. "The god of war."

"God of war," Cameron repeated slowly. "Like the one I'm supposed to ask Blake about?"

"The very same," Julian assured him. "The thinking is it gives you strength and protection."

Cameron held still as the cool metal settled against his skin inside the collar of his shirt, and he lifted his free hand to touch it. "Do I need protection?" he asked softly, not looking away.

Julian's eyes flickered briefly. "I know I would if I lived with your four savage beasts," he finally answered just before kissing Cameron chastely on the very corner of his mouth.

Unable to hold back the smile, Cameron lifted his chin to accept the kiss, and he wished it had lasted longer. "Thank you for the gift," he murmured while Julian's lips were still close.

"You're most welcome," Julian whispered in response before taking a step back.

After a few moments, Cameron realized they were standing there silently, staring at each other in the cold. "C'mon," he said, sliding the box and paper into his coat pocket. "We don't want dinner to get cold."

"No; that would be tragic," Julian murmured in earnest.

"Yes, it would. Now, come on." Cameron grabbed Julian's hand and started pulling him along the sidewalk at a faster clip.

Julian just barely managed to snag the bag of food he'd set down before Cameron yanked him along. "Is there a reason we're expending unnecessary energy?" he asked.

"You'll get plenty back with all this food," Cameron promised as they turned the last corner heading to his apartment building. "And I've got dessert too."

"Oh, yeah?" Julian drawled. "What'd you get?"

Cameron stopped in front of his building's door. "It's not in the bag," he said, eyes dancing.

Julian let his eyes rake over Cameron from head to toe and back again, and he raised an eyebrow in interest. "I'm listening," he assured him intently.

Cameron bit his bottom lip again and his cheeks flushed from more than just the cold. "You should be watching," he said as he used the key card to open the door so they could enter the building.

"I'm fascinated," Julian admitted in an amused voice. "And wondering whether I should be as turned on as I am right now."

Reaching out to grab Julian's arm and pull him inside, Cameron said, "Oh, I certainly think so."

Julian growled softly, and the look in his eyes turned slightly predatory as he was pulled along. They clattered up the stairs and stopped at Cameron's door long enough for him to get it open and pull Julian inside. He shut the door quickly before the snowball parade could sneak out.

"Little angels," Julian murmured to them as they came thundering toward the door. He extracted four tiny puppy treats from his pocket and tossed them with a flick of his wrist. The stampede of puppies immediately veered away as they charged the treats, and Cameron fell back against the door laughing.

"Never met a dog I couldn't distract," Julian murmured with a self-satisfied smirk.

Cameron grinned and pulled off his coat, hanging it on the hooks beside the door. Julian had planned to be here tonight, or soon, since he had those treats in his pocket. That simple act reassured Cameron a lot. "Give me your coat so we won't have to lint roller it this time."

"I enjoyed the last lint roller experience," Julian argued as he shrugged out of his coat.

Cameron wrinkled his nose as he took Julian's coat and hung it up. "Enjoyed it?"

Julian reached out and snagged him by his shirt-front, pulling him closer with a slow smile. Without the coat, Cameron only wore the black trousers and the pressed, button-down black shirt, open at the collar. The top of the gold amulet peeked out, glinting a bit in the light as Julian's fingers gripped the material.

"Anything that gets you on your knees is an enjoyable experience," Julian murmured.

Blue eyes widened as Cameron let himself be maneuvered. "Me on my knees?" he echoed, licking his lower lip as Julian's voice deepened. "In front of you?" he added, looking up at the taller man.

"You were," Julian confirmed with a nod and something like a low purr. He pulled Cameron closer and kissed him gently.

After the soft kiss, Cameron leaned back a bit to study Julian's face. "You liked that, hmm? I certainly liked seeing *you* on *your* knees."

"I would be lying if I tried to be a gentleman and said I didn't enjoy either experience immensely," Julian drawled.

Cameron hummed softly and laid his forehead against Julian's cheek as he pressed their bodies close together. "I don't want a gentleman. I'd rather have you," he murmured.

Julian barked a laugh and turned his head to kiss Cameron's cheek sloppily. "Well, that's a relief."

Cameron chuckled and wiped at his cheek with the back of his hand. "How about some dinner? I slaved over it all day," he joked as he stepped back and picked up the bag.

"Sounds fabulous," Julian answered cheekily.

Rolling his eyes, Cameron led the way to the kitchen. He started unloading the bag, pulling out all sorts of little boxes and a taller one that held a bottle of wine. Julian stepped up behind him as he worked and slowly slid his arms around him, watching over his shoulder. Cameron sighed and relaxed back against Julian's chest, savoring the feeling of it. "Doesn't feel like we've only known each other for a week," he said.

"It doesn't," Julian agreed as he rested his chin on Cameron's shoulder.

Cameron hummed contentedly, then crossed his arms and laid his hands over Julian's as he closed his eyes to enjoy the feel of him so close. "I was hoping you'd be there tonight."

"I wouldn't have missed it," Julian assured him in a whisper.

Cameron unconsciously stroked the back of Julian's hand. "But you could have," Cameron murmured. "You chose to come back."

Julian closed his eyes and let his lips drift slowly over the warm skin of Cameron's neck. "Yes," he affirmed softly.

Cameron sighed as his eyes slid closed. "To… me?"

"I think we established that the food's not *that* good."

Cameron grinned and shifted to the side so he could turn his head, tip it back, and kiss Julian longingly. Julian's hand came up to hold the side of his face as his other arm wrapped around him, preventing him from turning around all the way. The kiss grew hungrier as he trapped Cameron against him.

"I say we just skip to dessert," Julian growled finally.

Cameron licked the dampness off his lower lip. "The customer's always right," he agreed, his voice husky.

"Damn straight," Julian growled as his arm tightened around Cameron. He pushed him slightly until he was pressed against the counter.

Hands falling to curl against the rounded edge of the countertop, Cameron arched back against the hard, warm body behind him as his belly pressed against the Formica. "Julian," he breathed.

Julian hummed in response as he kissed behind Cameron's ear and began to make his way slowly to his neck. His other hand came up and pulled Cameron's shirt out of the way to reveal the chain of the gold necklace and more skin for him to nip at. Cameron's fingers clawed up his shirt to unbutton it so Julian could pull the collar further open, and he hummed in approval when he felt the edge of Julian's teeth. Julian growled softly in response to the sounds and pressed himself against Cameron, making the smaller man moan raggedly.

Julian grinned and backed away slowly, gently urging Cameron to turn around in his arms. Cameron did, setting his hands on Julian's chest and sliding them up and down, humming in pleasure as his fingers slid over hard muscles and soft material. He felt dazed when he looked up, and he bit his abused lower lip. "I like… to touch," Cameron murmured thoughtlessly, cheeks flushing.

"Well, lucky me," Julian murmured with a smile.

Cameron blinked. "I mean… not just sex. Sometimes more than sex. Or without sex," he rambled. Despite the embarrassment of what he was saying, he was determined to say it. Cameron wanted to know now if he needed to curb his natural tendencies in order to keep Julian coming back.

"You say this as if I may have a problem with it," Julian responded in confusion.

"I… some men don't like… to be petted. It's not manly, I guess." Cameron shrugged slightly.

Julian raised an eyebrow and slid his hands deliberately up Cameron's arms. "You think I'm not manly?" he teased.

Cameron's eyes widened in panic, and his mind raced to come up with an answer. Julian laughed softly and placed his hands on either side of Cameron's face, grinning widely.

Cameron sulked. "You're making fun of me."

"No, I'm not," Julian soothed as he pulled Cameron closer. Cameron laid his forehead against Julian's cheek. "Now," Julian sighed contentedly. "Tell me about dessert."

Cameron chuckled. "I was talking about me," he admitted.

"I know," Julian crooned. He pushed Cameron away and held him by his shoulders, tilting his head sideways to study him up and down. "It'll do," he finally announced as he wrapped his arm around Cameron's chest and pulled him against him. Julian dragged him out of the kitchen and into the living room, narrowly avoiding the white swarm at their feet.

Cameron laughed aloud and clung to him. "But I'm hungry!" he sort-of-protested. "I've not eaten since three o'clock!"

"You should really learn to plan better," Julian chastised as he stopped pulling and released him with a sniff.

"Uh-huh. When was the last time you ate? You worked today, didn't you?"

"Maybe," Julian answered carefully, pursing his lips and tilting his head in thought. "I ate lunch."

Cameron crossed his arms. "Told you that you needed taking care of."

"You were right," Julian conceded obediently with a bowed head.

"You remember that. It doesn't happen often," Cameron warned. He pushed himself onto his toes to kiss Julian's forehead, wondering again exactly what it was Julian did. He suspected now that it had something to do with the police or private detective work, but either Julian couldn't tell him or didn't want to scare him. Both of which Cameron could appreciate, but it didn't assuage the curiosity—or the concern. At least now he was fairly certain Julian wasn't a male escort or something more sinister.

Cameron pointed to the bedroom. "Go start a fire and pull the quilts onto the floor. We'll have a gourmet picnic, how about?"

"You don't want to watch the ball drop?" Julian asked with a raised eyebrow.

Surprised, Cameron looked over to the clock at the desk. One minute until midnight. "I forgot," he said. "But I'd rather watch you," he added frankly. Julian didn't seem to mind him being blunt and forward. In fact, he seemed to enjoy it.

"You'd rather watch *me* drop?" Julian teased as he reached out and snagged Cameron by his shirt again.

"It's a gorgeous sight, you on your knees," Cameron said, his voice going a little hoarse.

Julian gave a quirk of his eyebrow and his lips twitched slightly. "I find myself fascinated by you," he admitted in a low voice as he stood in front of Cameron.

"*I* fascinate *you*?" Cameron asked incredulously. "I thought it was the other way around." He opened his mouth to say something more, but the clock he kept on the mantel next to the bedroom began chiming softly. "It's midnight," he stated needlessly.

Julian glanced toward the bedroom and then back at Cameron wordlessly so that their eyes locked on each other. Long seconds went by as the clock chimed. He stepped closer fluidly as the clock rang twelve and slid his arms around Cameron's waist. "Happy New Year," he offered quietly.

"Happy New Year," Cameron responded, wrapping his arms around Julian's neck and pressing their mouths together again.

Julian returned the kiss, keeping it gentle. "I was always told that whatever you did on New Year's Day, you were going to do all year," he whispered to Cameron when they parted.

Cameron gazed up at him. He wondered again if this were just a dream, because it had been a dream come true so far. "So what are you doing today?" he asked hesitantly.

Julian smiled widely. It made him look five years younger and not nearly as serious. "You," he answered mischievously.

Cameron couldn't help but grin in response. "You've got twenty-three hours and fifty-nine minutes."

"You really want dinner that badly?" Julian rasped.

"I'll eat tomorrow," Cameron assured him. "Maybe you can fix me breakfast."

"Oh, love, you don't want me to cook!" Julian laughed. "You pack that food up," he added in a more serious voice. "We'll eat after dessert."

Cameron warmed at hearing the endearment, and his body flushed at the thought of what was to come. "All right. Be right there." He moved over to the bar and started packing the boxes back into the bag, well aware that Julian watched him for a moment before turning on his heel and heading for the bedroom.

After refilling the bag and stashing it in the refrigerator, Cameron gathered up the puppies, petting each of them a little before putting them in the playpen with some toys. When he finally turned to the bedroom, his heart was thrumming. He knew he shouldn't be nervous after the couple of nights they'd spent together the week before, but he couldn't help the feelings Julian caused in him. He didn't really want to.

All year, Julian had said. Cameron walked over and stopped between the screens, watching Julian fuss with the covers of the bed and wondering how this would turn out. He wasn't sure he believed in happy endings, no matter how much of a prince Julian seemed to be. He figured his heart would be broken no matter what happened. But seeing the man before him, his lover, he also knew it would be worth it.

As he watched, Julian seemed to sense his presence and he turned to look at him. For the first time, Cameron didn't blush under his intense gaze. "I could get used to this," he murmured as they looked at each other.

"Good," Julian returned bluntly as he let his eyes drift over Cameron's body in frank appraisal.

Cameron straightened his shirt and felt the necklace move against his skin. He lifted a hand to touch the gold disc, and his fingers stroked along the edge. Julian watched the movement, his black eyes flashing with a sudden concentrated interest. He moved suddenly, swooping in on Cameron and pulling him off his feet and against his chest.

A soft sigh was Cameron's answer as he set a hand on each of Julian's shoulders. He turned his chin to kiss Julian's temple. "Do you like seeing me wear it?"

"I do," Julian whispered as he allowed Cameron to slide down his body to place his feet on the floor. Cameron reached for one of Julian's hands and lifted it to press long fingers to the pendant. Julian's eyes met Cameron's as he let the gold sit against his fingertips. They were dark and unreadable.

Cameron kept his eyes trained on Julian's, though it was difficult. He wasn't one for being so forward, and this was everything he had always avoided, this singular focus Julian seemed to have. He'd always imagined finding someone comfortable and easygoing, much like himself. Julian was a totally new type of lover: intense, dramatic, and highly unpredictable.

He moved Julian's hand slightly, dragging it across his sternum and throat, and then he sighed soundlessly. Julian's grip tightened around Cameron's neck, and he lunged forward and kissed him hungrily.

Gasping, Cameron grabbed hold of Julian's shoulders to keep from pitching backward. He moaned as their lips met; he could almost feel Julian's desire as a tangible thing, a thing that Cameron evoked. He shivered all over. Julian pushed him back hard, pinning him to the wall beside the bathroom door with the weight of his body, holding him by his throat.

A soft cry tore out of Cameron as his back hit the wall; his eyes widened as he lifted one hand to cover Julian's at his throat and the other to grip at Julian's side. Then he realized he could still breathe with no problem. Groaning, Cameron shifted his hips against Julian's weight, trying to get some friction even though he was unsteady on his tiptoes, caught in Julian's arms. He'd already been hard just from the anticipation of the coming rendezvous; now he was almost painfully so. The aggression from Julian hit a hot button Cameron hadn't known he possessed.

Julian pushed away from him with one last growl and let his fingers around Cameron's throat loosen slowly. He was breathing hard as he looked down at Cameron. "I'm sorry," he panted.

Breathing brokenly, Cameron didn't think. He reached out to catch the hand that had been at his throat, and he grasped Julian's arm. "Don't… don't go," he rasped.

Julian licked his lips as he looked at him uncertainly. Cameron wavered between giving in and letting him move away and asking him again to continue. "Julian. I want you. And if that's part of you," he said with a gesture to his throat, "that's what I want. You didn't hurt me, and you're not gonna break me!"

Julian lowered his head with a pained wince and shook it once. "You shouldn't see that part yet," he told Cameron as he took a deep, calming breath.

It was one thing to be cared for and protected. It was another to be denied without an explanation, and after his willingness to accept and go along with anything Julian threw at him, it was frustrating to be turned down. Cameron grunted and pushed at Julian's chest as hard as he could. Julian stumbled back and watched Cameron with a slightly wounded expression.

"Don't give me that look," Cameron complained. "What do you mean, 'yet'? I realize you're a very private man, Julian. You don't share a lot about yourself. But how do you know you're not exactly what I want?"

Julian stared at him, dumbstruck.

Cameron cocked his head, getting more upset as the other man didn't answer. "Julian?" he asked plaintively.

"I don't want to hurt you," Julian answered.

"You won't," Cameron said firmly. "Not on purpose. Or are we back to you thinking I shouldn't trust you?" He rubbed his throat unconsciously. He could still feel Julian's hand there. He wanted it there again; he wanted to feel possessed, knowing Julian wanted him that much.

The wounded look flitted across Julian's eyes again. Cameron flinched and dropped his eyes, unable to keep eye contact any longer. He'd tried. Cameron sighed and shifted away from the wall.

Julian's hand shot out and grabbed him before he could move. "Don't," he whispered. Cameron swallowed and stopped moving, but he didn't look up. "I don't want to scare you," Julian told him calmly.

Forcing himself to look up, Cameron nodded slowly. "I understand," he said. "But I wasn't scared."

"Yet," Julian corrected quietly, but he didn't look away. "I'm sorry," he offered.

Cameron sighed. Julian had contradicted him again. He closed his arms around himself. "Me too," he said. "I guess I shouldn't have pushed."

"It's okay to push," Julian said softly. Then his lips quirked into a smile, and he gave Cameron's shoulder a shove.

Cameron flailed as his back hit the wall again, and he looked up in surprise to see a mischievous light back in Julian's black eyes. "You could try the patience of a saint, you know that?" he claimed in annoyance.

"But it's worth it," Julian purred as he moved closer and pressed himself against Cameron once more, gently this time. "Thank you for letting me come back," he whispered into Cameron's ear.

Cameron opened his mouth to say the same in return, but realized he'd already said it more than once. So instead he nodded once, meeting Julian's eyes as the man pulled away from him.

"Would you care for dessert?" Julian asked him, holding out his hand to escort Cameron to the bed.

When Cameron slid his hand into Julian's, he knew this was only the beginning of what was sure to be a hell of a roller-coaster ride.

CHAPTER 4

JULIAN CROSS pushed the heavy door open and stepped into the men's room on the lowest level of the Field Museum of Natural History. He stood motionless, looking around at the seemingly deserted space as the door swung shut behind him with a slight creak and a deep whoosh of air.

Emergency lights that ran at night after the museum closed lit the room. One of them flickered occasionally. A faucet dripped somewhere to his right. A toilet ran on the far left wall. The heating grate in the ceiling rattled as if it had recently been dislodged somehow. And a large metal trashcan lay on its side with trash spilled out across the tile.

That was the sound Julian had heard: the crash of the metal trashcan.

His black eyes lifted upward, narrowing at the grate in the ceiling. In newer buildings, the heating ducts were only eighteen inches across: much too small for a grown man to squeeze through. But in the basement of the nearly ninety-year-old Field Museum, it was probably possible for his quarry to climb up there and crawl through the ductwork like an idiot, looking for a way out.

He lowered his gaze to look once more at the stalls on the far side of the bathroom. There were really only so many options in a room like this, and he knew the man he was after wasn't exactly the type who could think on his feet. The mere fact that he'd ducked into the bathroom rather than trying for the emergency stairs or even the bank of glass windows in the McDonald's on the opposite side of the museum was evidence of that. He'd probably *tried* to use the trash can to climb into the heating grate, fallen on his ass, and when that had failed…

He'd only had roughly thirty seconds to get away from the bathroom once Julian was alerted to his location. Julian knew he would have seen or at least heard the man if he'd made a run for it as he approached the bathrooms.

Which meant he was still in here. Hiding.

Julian moved slowly, his expensive shoes making a hollow, foreboding sound on the echoing tile as he walked. He pushed his heavy coat aside, pulling his weapon from his holster and slowly screwing a silencer onto the end of it as he moved.

He got to the first stall and pushed it open gently, holding his gun close to his face with one hand as he peered into the stall. The corner of his mouth twitched when he found it empty, and he moved on.

He skipped the second and third stalls, enjoying the knowledge that with every second that passed, his target was suffering from the tension.

It was painfully difficult, knowing you were about to die.

Sometimes the mere stress of waiting made people simply give up when they were finally found. It was always easier that way. The ones who fought back were the ones that left Julian bruised and battered.

He moved slowly, reaching the fifth stall with a heavy step. He cocked his head, listening, and then he smiled slowly. He turned, shoved at the stall door just hard enough to break the flimsy lock and pointed his silenced gun at the man cowering on the toilet within.

"Hello, Ted," he murmured casually.

"Please, don't kill me!" the man blurted as he held his hands in front of his face and turned away as if Julian were a light too bright for his eyes. "I have copies of the research! I'll give it all to you, I swear! You can't do this!"

"You had your chance," Julian told him calmly. He pulled the trigger three times, barely blinking as the gun popped in his hand.

Then he turned and walked away, leaving the restroom and heading out into the empty hallway. Across from him was a large, enclosed cafeteria area for school trips, and Julian knew on either side of him there were stairs leading up to the main floor. Why the man hadn't tried for them, Julian couldn't guess. People did odd things when they ran for their lives. They also did stupid things when they were stupid people, but that was just Julian's personal opinion.

He also knew that on the other side of that bank of windows in the McDonald's on the far end of the museum was an outdoor courtyard surrounded by a brick wall that would be easy to scale. He headed there, not yet hurrying. He hopped over the barriers, grabbed a heavy metal trashcan, and broke the lock of the gate that was supposed to keep people out of the fast food restaurant when it was closed. He wasn't worried about cameras; he'd already taken care of those.

He kicked the gates open and headed for the wall of windows, dragging the can behind him. The snow fell in the darkness outside, melting as soon as it hit the ground, creating a peaceful scene in the brick courtyard on the other side of the tinted windows, but not one that would hinder his plans. He couldn't have investigators finding any tracks in the snow. Or lack thereof. Julian cocked his head, reared back, and chucked the trashcan through the nearest window.

Alarms began to blare as the glass shattered, and Julian turned on his heel and ran back into the belly of the museum, heading for the nearest stairwell and losing himself in the maze on the floor above that made up the Africa and animal exhibits.

He turned one corner, then another, and yet another as he heard the commotion behind him. The noise emanated from the lower floor, where he had just been, and Julian slowed as he walked around glass cases of preserved animals. He had all the time in the world since he'd mangled the museum's security system to the point that it wouldn't be up and running for quite a while.

They would find the body soon enough and call the police, and the museum would be almost as crowded with investigators and forensics people as it was during the day with tourists. It would be simple for him to use one of his fake "official" identifications to slip out through the chaos. Hanging around and waiting was so much easier than running like a criminal through the darkened alleyways of the city.

He stopped at a case near the far wall of the exhibit, his breathing and pulse slow and even as he unscrewed the silencer from his gun and replaced both pieces under the folds of his heavy coat. He pulled off the black gloves he wore and stepped closer to the glass case to study the lions inside.

He'd seen the Lions of Tsavo many times during his years in Chicago, but he was always compelled to come back. They were much smaller now than they'd been when they lived, their hides having suffered maltreatment over the years before they found their home at the Field Museum. The lions weren't really all that impressive if you knew nothing about them. They were positioned like tame housecats, looking out at passersby with mere curiosity. The Maneater of Mfuwe on the floor below was much more physically striking.

But some people claimed the eyes of the Tsavo lions followed them when they walked by. Julian had never seen that. To him they seemed timid and conquered, held in this glass case for eternity as punishment for their sins. But underneath that, the Tsavo lions had a *feel* to them, one Julian knew all too well.

They were simply evil.

They had killed more than one hundred and forty men during the latter part of the nineteenth century in Africa, and that was just the men the British railway had counted. No one knew how many undocumented African and Indian workers had lost their lives to these two animals. It was far too great a number in far too short a time to have been from hunger or even territorial protection. Julian tended not to listen to the various and sundry scientific theories of why these two male lions had gone rogue and killed men together. He had his own theory.

They simply enjoyed what they did.

Julian sighed softly, cocking his head as the commotion in the far reaches of the museum died down. By his count, his tally was almost even with the lions now.

CAMERON bent over, laughing so hard that he could barely stand up. Every time he tried to stop, he'd snort and start laughing again. "God. I wish I had a camera!"

"Shut up," Julian mumbled at him as he struggled with the four tumbling puppies. Every time he extracted one from his long, flowing scarf, another would take her place and begin tugging again. The scarf was hopelessly wrapped around the legs of one of the puppies, who was upside down and struggling to turn over, and Julian was so obviously uncomfortable with the tiny animals anyway that he could barely touch them to untangle them as his scarf choked him.

Snickering, Cameron finally dragged himself away from the door to help. "You have no idea how adorable you are right now with that look on your face."

"They're so little!" Julian insisted in frustration. He picked one up to demonstrate, holding it in the palm of one large hand as the puppy's tiny tail wagged between his fingers. "How can they be so little and so mean at the same time?"

The earnest question set Cameron off into peals of laughter again. "They're little, yes, but they make up for their size with their attitude," he managed to respond. "And Westies aren't mean. They're tenacious." He stooped over to unwrap Scarlet from Julian's scarf.

"Why do you have four of them, anyway?" Julian asked grumpily as he bent to carefully set the puppy down again. "And why the hell do they like me so much?"

Cameron swiped at Julian's scarf and wound it around his hand, pulling it over the other man's head before yet another puppy could latch onto it. "Well, originally I was going to get two so they'd be company for each other," he said. "When I contacted the owner, she had a litter of three. I didn't want to leave one alone. So I got Cobalt, Scarlet, and Saffron. A few weeks later a friend of mine saw Snowflake at the Humane Society shelter. I figured one more wouldn't make much difference." He chuckled and picked up Saffron and Snowflake. "And they like you because you're so very likable," he said with a grin, leaning to steal a kiss.

"Fascinating," Julian grumbled as he looked down at the pandering puppies in distaste and then reached to pet each of them on the head daintily.

Cameron smiled warmly. "Thank you," he said. "Now get Cobalt and Scarlet, and we'll put them in the playpen with some snacks so you can have some peace," he teased.

Julian looked down at the other two puppies. He frowned, bent over, and picked them up carefully. He carried them over to the playpen and knelt to place them inside. Cameron knew he was afraid he would drop them if he tried it any other way.

Biting his lip, Cameron watched Julian being so careful, finding it endearing and hilarious at the same time. "They *will* get bigger. They're just babies right now."

"They're *evil*," Julian announced with certainty as he looked down at them.

Cameron snickered again and set the other two in the playpen. "Yes, we're planning to take over the world."

Julian muttered under his breath and shrugged out of his coat.

Cameron raised an eyebrow. "What was that?"

"Nothing," Julian answered as he tossed his coat on the back of the couch and turned to face Cameron with a small frown.

"Right. Sure you don't want to share? I can always let them out again," Cameron mentioned.

"No, that's okay," Julian said quickly.

Cameron laughed and walked over to stand a foot away, hands on his hips. "You know, if you're so uncomfortable around the dogs, we could go somewhere else."

Julian inclined his head slightly, a hint of discomfort showing in his eyes. "I don't mind the dogs," he finally responded.

"If you change your mind, we can always go out," Cameron said, shrugging. "I don't mean to trap you here," he said, his voice and manner obviously reluctant.

"Do you want to go out?" Julian asked uncertainly.

Cameron met Julian's eyes and shook his head. "I want you to myself," he admitted.

Julian smiled widely and nodded. "Good," he responded softly.

Cameron took that last half-step and slid his arms around Julian's neck. "Good," he whispered just before pulling Julian down for a kiss.

Julian hummed happily and wound his arms around Cameron's waist. "I love Tuesdays," he murmured against Cameron's lips.

Cameron smiled. "Me too."

Julian grinned and gave Cameron's ass a pinch.

"Ow!" Cameron yelped. "What'd you do that for?"

"Because it's fun," Julian answered enthusiastically.

"For you, maybe!" Cameron objected. "Ow!"

Julian snorted and easily picked Cameron up so his toes dangled above the ground and gave him a little kiss. Cameron laughed and set his hands on Julian's shoulders. "Okay, I cannot tell you how much I like it when you do this."

"Oh, really?" Julian asked with a smirk.

Cameron grinned and kicked his feet gently, but couldn't get any footing on the hardwood floor. Julian tightened his grip and kissed him slowly. Cameron sighed against his lips and opened his mouth to invite a deeper kiss.

"Would you care to do anything before I take you to bed?" Julian asked in a low voice.

"Um. Not that I'm not *really* interested, but I have something for you first," Cameron answered as he was held suspended.

Julian blinked in surprise, but then he smiled slightly. "It better be damn good," he whispered teasingly.

Cameron didn't smile; he was suddenly nervous. "You'll have to tell me, I guess," he said.

Julian's smile fell as he saw that his teasing had fallen flat, and he slowly released Cameron and nodded obediently.

Biting his lip slightly, Cameron backed away once he was solidly on his feet. "Why don't you go ahead to the bedroom, and I'll bring it in there?"

Julian looked at him curiously and nodded again, moving slowly.

Cameron watched him until he disappeared into the darkness behind the screens. He walked over to the desk and slid open a drawer so he could pull out an envelope. He'd prepared it over the weekend, and he'd wondered ever since if it was the right thing to do. He held the envelope in his hand for a moment as he doubted himself. What if it was too fast, too much, too soon? What if he scared Julian off? It had only been a month or so…

But he'd already told Julian he had something to give him. He couldn't back out now.

After another few moments' waffling, Cameron grew annoyed by his indecision. He turned on his heel and walked between the screens to join Julian. He approached the bed where Julian sat and held out the envelope. Although he wasn't shaking, he was afraid his voice would crack if he tried to speak.

Julian looked down at the envelope and then up to meet Cameron's eyes questioningly.

Cameron's lips pressed together for a moment. "It's for you," he said shakily. "Don't… " He gave a short, nervous laugh. "Don't feel obligated to accept."

Julian took the envelope without looking away from Cameron. He smiled at him affectionately and carefully slid his finger under the flap of the envelope as he looked down at it. He glanced up at Cameron one more time and then peered into the envelope. It held a keycard and a key, both strung on a simple black woven key chain. Julian blinked down at it before looking up at Cameron in surprise.

"I said any time," Cameron said, not mentioning the fact that Julian already seemed to be able to get into the building without the card. "I meant it. I want you to know you're welcome here."

"I don't know what to say," Julian said candidly. "Thank you, Cameron."

"You're welcome," Cameron answered as he watched Julian carefully.

Julian stood and picked Cameron up again with a smile. "I'm thrilled," he whispered.

Cameron gasped softly in relief as he braced one hand on Julian's shoulder. "I'm glad I made you happy."

"Well, it's Tuesday," Julian murmured with a smile as he slowly turned them in a circle. "You always make me happy on Tuesdays."

"Technically, it's Wednesday," Cameron corrected.

Julian hummed in acknowledgment. "Spoilsport," he accused softly.

Cameron's smile was unrivaled. "But you've been with me all the Tuesday nights and Wednesday mornings lately," he pointed out.

"That's true," Julian acknowledged with a grin as he set Cameron on his feet again. "Perhaps we've earned ourselves another day."

"Yeah?" Cameron asked hopefully. He'd love to see Julian more than one night a week. He'd wondered sometimes why Julian couldn't be here more often, besides the obvious explanation of work. Julian had to sleep at some point, didn't he? Why couldn't he do it here? But Cameron kept those questions to himself. They'd almost argued once over Cameron pushing for information, for explanations. He didn't want to risk it happening again.

"I've seen you at the restaurant every Tuesday for months," Julian was saying as Cameron thought about the situation. He looked down at Cameron curiously. "Christmas Eve, New Year's Eve… Do you ever *not* work?"

Cameron gave him an amused smile. "I guess we have that in common, don't we?"

Julian shrugged. "Do you work so much because you like it or because of the money?"

"I do like it a lot," Cameron admitted as he slid his hands into his pockets. "And the money's nice, but I inherited the condo, and I've got more than enough money saved up for just me and the dogs that I wouldn't have to work for awhile if I didn't want to. Mostly it's because I don't have anything else to do."

"I'd like to see you more," Julian told him bluntly. "Perhaps we could both pick a day to be free?" he asked. "Then you could have something else to do."

Happiness clutched at Cameron's chest. His joy at that idea was clear on his face. "I'd really like that."

Julian grinned widely and nodded. "Good. Is it easy for you to get nights off?"

"It's my job to make the schedule," Cameron answered with a small smile.

"Any night but Sunday and Monday," Julian told him with a smirk.

"Damn." Cameron huffed. "The restaurant's closed on Mondays; that would have worked well," he told Julian with a frown.

"The restaurant's closed on Mondays because Blake is busy with his other business responsibilities," Julian answered vaguely, smiling slightly.

"Oh. Well, will we still have Tuesday nights?" Cameron chanced, knowing better than to delve further into that little tidbit of information.

"I wouldn't miss them," Julian answered.

"How about Fridays for a regular day off? For all I know, you look different by sunlight," Cameron prodded.

"I'm actually a blond," Julian deadpanned. Then he smiled crookedly. "I like it."

Cameron chuckled over the joke and then hummed agreeably, closing his arms around Julian's middle and hugging him close. "You mentioned taking me to bed?"

"Yes, I did." Julian picked Cameron up completely and turned fluidly, tossing him onto the bed without the slightest effort.

Cameron yelped in surprise and laughed as he bounced on the mattress and looked up at Julian. "You enjoy that, don't you?"

"Immensely," Julian growled with an evil smirk as he crawled onto the bed.

BLAKE NICHOLS sat in his office, tapping his pen against the desk as he watched the little television in the corner. Cameron sat across from him, patiently waiting until the news story ended before he spoke.

"Authorities are still baffled by the murder of Theodore Young," the news anchor said. "Young, a research assistant at Chicago's Field Museum, was found Thursday night in the men's room in the Museum's basement after an alarm alerted museum security to a break-in. He was shot three times in the chest. While the Chicago PD is remaining silent in regards to the circumstances of the murder, an insider claims the killing looks to be a, professional hit. The thirty-eight-year-old Young was said to be assisting on—"

Blake reached over and turned off the television before the anchor could drone on. "Some people just have no luck, hmm?" he said to Cameron with a wry smile. "Can't even take a piss without getting it," he mumbled as he fiddled with some papers on his desk and then looked up at Cameron again. "Now, what was it you needed?"

Cameron shifted forward now that he had Blake's attention. "You wanted the comparisons on the wine vendors? The house wine supplier jumped the price per bottle by twenty dollars?"

"Right, right," Blake responded with a nod. He leaned back and laced his fingers behind his head. "Switch to someone cheaper; call their bluff."

Cameron winced. "We don't want to piss the supplier off. We have a lot of regulars who drink the house wine every time they come in."

Blake smiled slowly. "Anyone in particular you're thinking of?" he asked.

Cameron blinked several times. “Particular?” he echoed. “Uh. Well… I guess so,” he admitted as his cheeks colored. “But a lot of other customers really do drink it too.”

Blake continued to smile, watching Cameron and waiting for him to say what he really wanted to say.

“Blake, I… I have a question, but I don’t… I don’t want to pry, you know, too much,” Cameron waffled.

“So I’ll tell you when you cross a line,” Blake invited with a wave of his hand.

Cameron screwed up his courage. He’d come this far; he might as well ask. “Julian said that he’d do something here in the restaurant—about me—but that you told him he couldn’t,” he said in a rush.

Blake stared at him blankly for a moment before frowning slightly. “Remind me,” he requested finally.

“He said… he said he’d wanted to get down on his knees and beg me to go home with him.” Cameron winced once the words were out. It sounded silly now, but he was having a really difficult time absorbing it. He hoped Blake would be able to confirm Julian’s sincerity.

Blake laughed, quickly covering his smile with his hand as he turned in his chair. “Did you want me to let him?” he asked in amusement.

Cameron’s eyes widened. “It’s true? Really?”

“Well, he did say it,” Blake affirmed with a nod, still smirking. “Whether he’d really do it, I don’t know,” he added. “But I’ve learned to anticipate him.”

“Anticipation denotes expectation based on previous performance,” Cameron said weakly, leaning back in his chair, flustered.

Blake continued to smile as he looked Cameron over. “What’s brought this on, Cam?” he asked with a hint of concern.

“It just surprised me,” Cameron admitted. “I mean, really surprised me. No one’s ever—”

"Cameron, back up," Blake said softly. "Pretend that I have no idea what you're talking about, okay? When did Julian tell you this? Have you become seriously involved with him?" he asked in surprise.

"He told me a few weeks, ah, well, a month ago or so. And as to serious? I'm not quite sure," Cameron said as his brow furrowed.

Blake cocked his head and pursed his lips thoughtfully. "You've been seeing him for over a month?" he asked finally.

Cameron nodded slowly. "Sort of," he murmured.

"He must be pretty serious about you," Blake murmured as he continued to look at Cameron thoughtfully.

"What?" Cameron asked. "Is that a surprise?" Now he wondered just how good of friends Blake and Julian really were.

"Honestly?" Blake said as he leaned forward and frowned. "Yeah, it is." He looked at Cameron as if just realizing what he'd said, and he held out a hand. "I mean, not because it's you," he said quickly. "Jules just isn't the long-term type, usually."

Cameron managed a half-hearted smile, though Blake's words echoed in his ears. Jules? He couldn't imagine anyone calling Julian that. "A month is hardly long term," he argued weakly.

"Then you still have a lot to learn about Julian Cross," Blake advised with a kind smile.

"Believe me, I know that," Cameron murmured.

"You want to talk about it?" Blake asked carefully.

"Yes, but I'm not going to," Cameron answered, shifting his weight to stand. "If he wants me to know something, he'll tell me." He hoped.

Blake rested his chin in his hand and raised an eyebrow at him. Cameron crossed his arms and tried not to shuffle, but it didn't take long for him to relent. "Okay, so he won't. But he won't appreciate me asking you instead of him."

"Asking me what?" Blake asked nonchalantly.

"Anything remotely personal," Cameron replied.

"I wouldn't answer anything he wouldn't want me telling," Blake offered, his brow furrowing worriedly. "Are you afraid of him?" he asked.

Cameron's shoulders immediately straightened. "No, I'm not. He asked me that too," he said. "Why do you ask that?"

"A lot of people are," Blake answered carelessly.

Cameron gave Blake an obstinate glare. Blake looked back at him in surprise, and Cameron's eyebrow jutted up in response. "And?" Cameron asked.

Blake shrugged, his eyes straying to the silent television briefly. "*Most* people are," he corrected, watching Cameron carefully.

Cameron's shoulder edged up. "Well, I'm not," he stated.

Blake nodded and then smiled widely. "Good. So why does it bother you that he wanted to make a fool of himself in public for you?" he asked in an entirely different tone. An amused tone.

"But that's—that's crazy!" Cameron exclaimed. "Not only crazy, but it would get him, and me, all sorts of attention. I don't want to sha—" He cut himself off with a surprised blink. Where did that come from?

"I'm sorry. Don't want to what?" Blake asked.

Cameron flushed and sank back into the chair. "Shit, I've got it bad," he murmured.

"I can see that," Blake agreed with a laugh. His smile faded, and he leaned back in his chair again, bringing his hands together against his stomach as he looked at Cameron thoughtfully. "Try to fall slower," he advised, that tone now serious.

Cameron went still. "Are you going to tell me why you say that?" he asked, meeting Blake's eyes.

Blake tapped his finger against the back of his hand. "You told me you didn't want to know," he pointed out.

After a long moment of quiet, Cameron nodded and stood. "Yeah. I did." He moved to the door.

"Cameron?" Blake said softly.

Cameron turned his chin to look over his shoulder as he paused with his hand on the doorknob.

"I hear there's been trouble with the vineyards this year," Blake said to him. "Keep the house wine. We'll stick with them for a bit longer."

The corner of Cameron's mouth turned up. "Good night, Blake."

"Sleep well, Cam," Blake responded with a sigh.

Cameron nodded and stepped out into the hall, pulling the door shut behind him. He stood there a moment, then opened the door again and stuck his head back in. Blake hadn't moved. He still sat there looking at Cameron expectantly.

"What does the name of the restaurant have to do with the god of war?" Cameron asked him curiously.

Blake snorted. "Google it, Cam," he advised with a smirk. "Good night."

Cameron grunted in annoyance and closed the door again. He dropped his head back against the door and decided it was time to go home.

AS THE weeks passed, Julian spent Tuesday nights after the restaurant closed at Cameron's, and he showed up every Friday morning like clockwork, staying as long as he was able. Sometimes it was early Saturday morning before he left.

Now, another Tuesday had come around, and it was two nights before Valentine's Day.

The restaurant's décor was classy, as always, but now fresh roses in a myriad of reds, pinks and whites filled vases around the floor, and all the ladies took a few home with them. The dessert menu featured triple the number of items, strolling violinists promoted the romantic atmosphere, and the staff had a hard time keeping champagne cold because the bottles were going out so fast. Tuesdays was booked to capacity with a waiting list every day of the week.

When Julian stepped into the restaurant, he lost his usual air of mystery for a brief moment as he looked around at his surroundings with wide eyes. He hadn't expected the restaurant to be decked out like it was. He recovered quickly, though, and schooled his face back to its polite mask.

Keri, well used to seeing him, greeted him with a smile and invited him in, leading him to one of the quieter alcoves. Julian was silent as he followed, and he reached out discreetly to snag one of the roses from a vase as he passed. As Keri showed him his table, he produced it out of the folds of his coat as if by magic and handed it to her with a small smile.

She smiled widely and thanked him before telling him Miri would be right with him, and then she took up the extra place setting and was on her way. Julian watched her go before he shifted to steal another rose and seated himself. He couldn't help but be disappointed that he wasn't in Cameron's section, but sometimes it was fun to watch him from afar. He supposed he could live with the nosy waitress for tonight. Perhaps she'd be too busy to pry. Julian was feeling very amenable tonight.

It wasn't long before Miri appeared. "Good evening, sir. Your regular?" she asked.

"If you please," Julian answered with a nod. He produced the rose he'd hidden with a flourish and handed it to her with a tiny smile. "Thank you."

"Oh, thank you," she said, smiling a little more than usual. "I'll be back with your wine in a bit." As she walked toward the service area, she passed Blake, who said a few words to her. She nodded in response and went on her way, and Blake made his way to Julian's table, pulled out the opposite chair, and sat down heavily.

"Damn Valentine's crap," Blake muttered to Julian as soon as he was seated.

Julian raised an eyebrow and cocked his head. "Scrooge," he accused softly.

Blakc turned up his nose. "Christmas is my kind of holiday. Valentine's? I'm running out of creative jewelry to buy, you know?" he said defensively. "And the goddamned violinists are giving me a migraine," he went on grumpily. "Unfortunately, I make enough money on a single holiday to carry me through at least a month, if not more."

"Yeah," Julian murmured. "Me too." He sighed as he looked away. He couldn't remember the last time he hadn't worked on a holiday. Holidays made people careless; they thought everyone took a break. Julian found a tiny, perverse bit of pleasure in proving them wrong.

Blake sniffed and sprawled back in his chair. "However, *you* have a reason to like holidays now, don't you?" he murmured, his twinkling eyes belying the disgruntled face. "Someone to spend them with?"

Julian looked back at Blake carefully and grunted at him. "I'm going to steal him away from you," he threatened under his breath, an impossible promise, he knew, even as he joked about it.

Blake actually chuckled. "He'd probably go too," he allowed.

A smile flickered across Julian's lips, but he didn't say anything in response. "Do I need to give you a rose, as well?" he finally teased.

"That would go over well," Blake said, leaning forward. "About as well as you getting down on your knees here in the restaurant to declare your undying devotion to my best waiter."

Julian glared at his friend in warning. "He's been talking, has he?" he asked softly.

"Just to me," Blake admitted. "You really shook him up with that, you know? I wasn't sure he was taking it that well."

Julian narrowed his eyes and then looked away. He'd wondered that himself at the time. Cameron had been really surprised. He hadn't taken it as the lighthearted joke it was meant to be.

Blake tipped his head to one side, the teasing light fading from his eyes and his tone. When he spoke, his voice was low and serious. "Why did you tell him that, Julian? Trying to get him into bed?"

"You know me better than that," Julian chastised sharply, his focus snapping back to Blake.

Blake raised an eyebrow in question. "Don't fuck around with him if you're not serious, Julian. He's too good a man to deserve what'll happen if you have to dump him and take off. You know how realistic that scenario is."

Julian looked back at him with a momentary surge of anger, an emotion that seeped out of his black eyes almost immediately. He looked down at the table sadly. He couldn't be mad at Blake for pointing out what was simple reality. He knew better than to think he could have Cameron in his life without it causing problems, but…

Julian frowned. He'd lost his appetite along with his good mood.

"Julian, come on. Don't give me that kicked puppy look. I'm just looking out for both of you. You *can* make it work. Lord knows, if anybody deserves some happiness, it's you. Just… be careful. Please," Blake implored quietly.

Julian pressed his lips together tightly and looked back up at Blake. "I don't think I'll be eating tonight," he murmured. "Can you get Cameron for me? I'd like to say hello before I go."

Blake frowned. "Cameron's not here."

Julian didn't even twitch in response. He merely looked at Blake without blinking for a moment. "Where is he?" he asked softly, searching his memory to find if Cameron had mentioned anything unusual the last time they were together.

"He's at home, I assume. He called in sick all weekend and today," Blake said. "When was the last time you saw him? Didn't you know he was sick?"

"Friday afternoon," Julian answered hoarsely. "He was fine." He stared at Blake intently and asked, "Are you sure he's sick?" His pulse began to pick up as a nameless dread stirred in his gut.

"I sort of thought maybe he was shacked up with you somewhere and just didn't want to tell me," Blake admitted. He looked up to see Miri approaching with a bottle of wine. "Miri, have you heard from Cameron?"

"Not since Sunday morning," she answered as she pulled out a corkscrew. "He called and left me a message, asked me to pick up his dogs." She glanced up at Blake and then over to Julian. "Why?"

"Did you see him?" Julian demanded of her. Now his mind was starting to conjure scenarios he really, truly didn't want to imagine Cameron being involved in.

Miri looked to Blake in concern, but answered Julian. "No, he wasn't there when I stopped by. I just took the dogs and left."

"He was too sick to care for his dogs, but he went out?" Julian asked in a low voice.

"He didn't sound well on the phone," Miri said with a shrug. "He sounded exhausted, and his voice was hoarse. I figured he went to the doctor or the drugstore or something. He left the door unlocked for me."

Julian looked away from her to stare at the linen tablecloth. His mind raced, trying to remember how Cameron had been the previous Friday and fighting down the panic that leading his life could create. Had someone found out about Cameron? Was he hurt?

Blake looked at Julian hard for a moment. "Thank you, Miri. I'll pour the wine," he said pleasantly.

She left the bottle and went off to another table after casting another curious glance Julian's way.

"You think he's not sick?" Blake asked.

"I think I need to go," Julian answered as he stood abruptly, unable to sit still any longer.

Blake stayed seated casually, but he watched Julian with a sincere worry in his eyes. "Call me," he requested simply.

But Julian was already moving calmly toward the door. He kept his head down, but stayed alert to his surroundings as he went. If anyone followed him, he would know it. He waited until he was outside the building before he broke into a run.

EVEN as fit as he was, he found himself out of breath when he reached Cameron's building, darting in through the entryway as a woman exited. Sprinting up the stairs didn't help, and by the time he found himself at Cameron's door he was fighting back the very real urge to panic. He banged on the door as calmly as he was able.

There was no answer.

Julian waited three breaths and then banged again, looking up and down the hallway carefully.

Still no answer.

He dug in his pocket for the small leather case he always kept with him. He opened it hastily and extracted two small utensils from the lock-pick set before remembering he actually had a key. He shoved the set back in his pocket and searched for the key with a quiet curse. After a brief moment of fumbling, he had the door unlocked, and he pushed it open carefully, practically vibrating with the urge to throw caution out the window and storm into the apartment.

But Julian was nothing if not cautious. He drew his gun.

He carefully surveyed the interior before entering. The main room was lit with only one lamp, and the kitchen was dark. The large space was very obviously empty. It was odd walking into Cameron's apartment without being barraged by little white fluffy things. And it was cold. Very cold.

A survey of the room showed that all the windows were shut. But the window near the fire escape in the bedroom wasn't. It was open a few inches, letting in the frigid winter air. Julian's blood ran just as cold, and he moved through the apartment with even more care, searching the shadows for anything untoward before he closed and locked the window.

The bedroom was dark and empty except for a little spill of light coming from the bathroom door in the corner. The room behind the screens was heavily shadowed, what with the blinds drawn and the fireplace cold. Clothes lay scattered messily across the floor rather than neatly tucked away as usual, and pillows and quilts sagged off the end and sides of the mussed, empty bed. All that was very unlike the normally tidy Cameron. Julian headed for the light, investigating quickly as he moved toward the bathroom.

"Cameron!" Julian finally called out as he pushed open the bathroom door.

His lover sat on the floor, crumpled against the wall, a fever-flushed cheek pressed against the decorative tile. Each breath rattled as he pulled in air and caught on a thick rasp as he exhaled. There were several prescription bottles on the counter, a couple knocked over into the sink, along with an open bottle of codeine cough syrup and a sticky spoon.

"Jesus," Julian breathed as he lunged toward the man and took his face in his hands. An odd mixture of intense relief and increased worry struck Julian hard. "Cameron?" he whispered. "Can you hear me?" he asked as his cold hands burned where they met Cameron's skin.

Cameron gave a weak whimper and blindly leaned against the cool skin that touched his cheeks.

"Did you take all this medicine?" Julian asked as he set his gun on the tile floor and reached into his jacket to grab his phone.

Dragging his bloodshot eyes open, Cameron looked around dazedly, drawn from his fevered sleep by the voice. "Julian?" His voice was mangled and hoarse, and the words came out broken. "You're here?"

"I was worried," Julian answered as he dialed the phone. "I'm taking you to the hospital," he told Cameron firmly.

"Doctor said I'm sick," Cameron rasped weakly, slumping against the wall. "Gave me medicine."

"Your doctor should be shot," Julian spat angrily. He held the phone to his ear and spoke Cameron's address curtly before hanging up. "Come on," he urged as he tried to help Cameron to his feet.

"Where're we going? I'm too tired," Cameron protested helplessly. "Can't breathe."

"Hospital," Julian murmured.

Cameron wavered for a moment before he moved. He was part-way up when his breath caught, starting a terrible coughing fit, and his legs gave out under him as he tried to clear his lungs and throat. Julian caught him and held him as the coughs wracked his body. Once the fit ebbed, Julian hefted him up into his arms, carrying him out of the bathroom.

Although Cameron was smaller, it still wasn't easy for Julian to carry him out of the apartment and down the stairs. Julian was certain it was adrenaline that made it possible; he could feel it coursing through him as he moved. While it would have been easier, a fireman's carry would surely have made Cameron's condition worse, and Julian couldn't bear the thought of tossing Cameron over his shoulder like that.

When the sharp cold outside struck them, Cameron flinched in his arms and tried to suck in a breath, moaning aloud. The chill against his hot skin must have been painful, because he started shivering violently, and Julian wanted nothing more than to hold him close and keep him warm.

A sleek black Lexus pulled up in front of the building just as they exited, and Julian carried Cameron to it. A thin, light-haired man jumped out of the driver's door and hurried to help him.

"Closest hospital, Preston," Julian ordered quietly as they struggled to get Cameron into the back-seat quickly. The driver nodded and hurried back to slip behind the steering wheel. Julian shut the back door and pulled Cameron to him, cradling his head in his lap and struggling to get out of his heavy coat so he could cover Cameron with it.

Cameron opened his glazed eyes again. "Julian?" he asked, like he didn't remember that they'd just spoken a few minutes ago. He stopped to fight his way through a couple breaths. "Is it Tuesday?"

"It is," Julian answered gently.

"Couldn't call," Cameron rasped as his head lolled in Julian's lap. "No number."

Julian's apology was an agonized whisper.

One of Cameron's hands crept up to press lightly against Julian's chest, and he lapsed back into a fitful doze.

Julian covered him with his coat and rubbed at his shoulders as the car whipped through the city at worrying speeds. He paid it no mind. Preston was a professional. The only thing Julian worried about was Cameron.

CHAPTER 5

IT WAS quiet in the hospital room now that the doctors and nurses had come and gone. Tucked into the bed, Cameron looked pale and even smaller than usual with the oxygen tube set in his nose and the IV in his arm. He was out cold, drugged to the gills—both to counteract the drugs he'd been given by the Convenient Care doctor and to treat what was really wrong.

Pneumonia, the doctors said, and a really bad case of it.

X-rays confirmed the fluid filling Cameron's lungs, and it had worried the doctors enough that he had been admitted immediately. They'd even considered a breathing tube. Now, with Cameron settled, Julian paced restlessly in the hospital room, his overcoat and scarf trailing behind him like a supervillain's cape as he prowled.

Long minutes passed before a nurse came in to check Cameron's vitals again. She paused just inside the door, surprised to see the dark-clad man there. "Hello?"

"How is he?" Julian asked in a voice barely above a whisper.

The nurse gave him a look and went to check the machines hooked up to Cameron. "He's just fine," she told him. "Reacting well to the medicine and resting easy." She looked back at Julian in slight annoyance but then seemed to notice the tension in him. "You don't have to stay. I promise we'll take good care of him," she offered.

"I have nothing more important to do," Julian responded without tearing his eyes away from Cameron.

Her expression softened. "You may be more comfortable in the chair," she said. "There's a cafeteria downstairs; it's open twenty-four hours. Don't you get sick too," she scolded gently as she left the room.

Julian meant to murmur a thank-you as she left the room, but his attention was all on Cameron. He moved closer, his mouth dry and his chest tight. Cameron's face was still, drawn, and shadowed. Even asleep, he looked exhausted. Julian reached to touch him but stopped before his fingers made contact. It wouldn't do to wake him.

He examined Cameron carefully, feeling sick over just the thought of what *might* have happened. He moved impulsively and this time ran his fingers gently through Cameron's hair. Heat still radiated from him, despite how pale he looked. Deep in the drug-induced sleep, he was totally relaxed against the mattress.

"Don't you do this to me again," Julian whispered to him. He'd faced many things in his life that most people never faced, but he was not immune to terror. He'd discovered tonight that being scared for someone you cared about was an entirely different animal from simply fearing for your own life and limb.

He turned slightly when he felt someone else enter the room. "Shall I park in the overnight lot, sir?" Preston asked him in the same soft tone Julian usually used.

"No," Julian answered with a shake of his head. "You may go for the night, Preston. Thank you for your speed."

"Yes, sir," the man murmured with a nod of his head. "Will he be okay?"

Julian simply nodded and turned back around.

Soft footsteps shifted a little outside the door, and the nurse re-entered just after Preston departed. She looked at Julian sympathetically as she moved closer and changed one of Cameron's IV bags.

"You're Mr…?"

"Bailey," Julian answered softly as he watched her hands move. He'd slipped enough bags of tainted saline past hospital security to know how it was done, and he found he couldn't quite bring himself to trust anyone completely. Definitely not with Cameron's health and safety.

"Mr. Bailey. Visiting hours are over at eight for non-family members," she said. "So from now on, you're his brother," she advised.

"Thank you," Julian said to her sincerely as he looked back at Cameron and chewed worriedly on his lower lip.

"I'll be in every couple hours to check on him. He should sleep well into tomorrow." She gave him another smile and left just as quietly as she'd come.

Julian stood for several more moments before he gently took Cameron's hand and sank into the chair beside the bed to wait.

The night passed mostly undisturbed, and although the noise around them picked up come morning, the closed door to the room kept most of it out as the sun reached the angle to shine in the window and fall across the blanket that covered Cameron.

Julian slumped in the chair next to the bed, finally having fallen asleep just thirty minutes before sunrise. He jerked awake and sat up as the sun hit him, blinking away the grogginess as he looked around. When he relaxed and looked back down, Cameron was watching him.

"Hi," Julian greeted in surprise.

Cameron's mouth opened just enough that he could moisten his lower lip with his tongue. His reply was barely audible. "Hi."

"You scared me," Julian whispered immediately, unable to think of anything else to say.

Cameron's eyes widened slightly. "Sorry," he whispered, fingers tightening on the blanket.

Julian reached up and ran his fingers through Cameron's hair. "Go back to sleep," he urged softly.

Eyes fluttering, Cameron turned his head just slightly against Julian's fingers. He pulled in a very slow breath, his lungs still clogged with fluid. "Okay," he managed in a thread of his normal voice before dropping off quickly.

Julian watched him silently as he felt the minutes ticking by, knowing he needed to leave very soon. Finally, he stood up and turned around to find Preston standing silently in the doorway.

"Your appointment, sir," the man reminded. Julian nodded.

Cameron slept peacefully, half in the sunshine. He was still pale and very ill, but something about him looked better. Julian watched him longingly for a moment, and then he swept out of the room with Preston at his heels.

JULIAN rested his head against the damp brick wall behind him and closed his eyes. Preston stood beside him, calmly loading a spare clip as they waited.

"I'm certain you could postpone your appointment until tomorrow, sir," Preston said softly as the clink of each round snapping into the clip echoed through the early morning.

"We know where he is right now," Julian argued without opening his eyes. "We won't tomorrow."

"We'll know again soon," Preston pointed out confidently.

Julian opened his eyes and turned his head slightly to look at his companion. The man's icy blue eyes were as emotionless as ever, but Julian knew him well enough to see a hint of worry in his expression.

"You're tired," Preston observed as he pushed the last round into the clip and slid it into his pocket. "Mistakes could be made."

Julian nodded distractedly. He was thinking more of Cameron lying unconscious in the hospital than about the job at hand. Which was bad, to say the least.

The man they targeted wasn't atypical, as far as Julian's targets went. He was crooked and probably skimming off the wrong people. He'd definitely pissed *someone* off. He was nervous and paranoid. He had bodyguards. He had security coming out his ass. He took a different route to work every morning, and he split his nights between four different condos throughout the city.

Julian didn't know what he did or why he needed to be confronted. His job today was not to kill the man. They were there to scare him and drive him further into his shell. From the little Julian had observed of him, they were probably going to cause a nervous breakdown. But mental defects as the end result of his work were not his problem. Whether the man ended up six feet under or in therapy was not his concern unless his orders specifically said to put him there.

"Sir?" Preston prodded gently.

Julian nodded and rubbed his tired eyes, trying to banish the vision of Cameron from them so he could focus on work. "You know the plan?" he asked hoarsely.

"Yes, sir. It's not a very good one," Preston observed neutrally.

"We're taking a few shots at him to scare him. It takes more skill to miss intentionally than it does to hit the target," Julian reminded.

"If we're attempting to make ourselves look second-rate then why not simply lob a bottle of flaming vodka at his car and run away?" Preston asked in a flat voice.

"Because with my luck, we'd actually kill the bastard," Julian answered grimly. He checked his weapon, a hot automatic he'd bought off a jittery man in the back of a stolen van several nights before. Anything they could do with this job to make it look amateur, they had done. "Ready?" he asked his companion.

"Yes, sir, by all means," Preston drawled as he pulled a black ski mask over his head. "Let's go get shot at."

CAMERON stuck his thumb in the book and closed it as he reached out to pick up the glass of ice water and take a careful swallow. He set it down with a wince and let his head fall back against the raised mattress behind him, surprised at how tired even that simple action made him.

He felt better even though he was still weak, and his chest still hurt so badly. Miri had come by to catch him up on what was going on at the restaurant and with the dogs. He caught her looking at him funny a few times, but she never said anything. He was too tired to try to figure out why. She'd brought him a few books, a top-secret ramekin of crème brûlée from the pastry chef, and a promise to visit again very soon.

So he'd slept and then slept some more. He'd read a little bit and even managed to get some food down since the nurses wanted to take out the IV line sooner rather than later. He grimaced. It just hurt so much to swallow. He sighed and looked out the window at the cityscape, his mind wandering.

When he turned his attention back to the room, Julian's large shadow darkened the doorway. Cameron's breath caught, and he swallowed on the cough that threatened. "Hey," he managed to rasp.

"Hello," Julian returned as he cocked his head in familiar fashion and looked around the room warily. His cheekbone was badly scuffed, and his eyes appeared shadowed and dark. He looked exhausted. "How are you?" he asked.

"A little better," Cameron said in his ruin of a voice. He peered at Julian, seeing the marks on his face and the slump of his broad shoulders. "Are you okay?" He gestured to his own eye to echo what he saw on Julian.

"Better now," Julian answered quietly as he moved into the room, a slight limp slowing him. He didn't otherwise outwardly acknowledge the purpose of the question.

Cameron didn't move. He simply tracked Julian's movement with his eyes and frowned slightly. Julian was hurt; that much was obvious. "Better?" He sounded like he didn't quite believe him.

"Seeing you," Julian clarified. "I worried for you."

The corner of Cameron's mouth quirked up. "Sorry," he mumbled. "Didn't exactly plan on getting sick."

Julian shook his head as he took Cameron's hand and sat on the edge of the bed. "When do you get to go home?"

Cameron curled his fingers through Julian's. "Couple days, maybe," he said. "Nurse says I'm doing good." He swallowed hard, but had to cough. It was still a hacking, painful sound.

Julian scowled and nodded, looking around the room again. "I see you've had visitors," he observed.

Cameron's free fingers brushed over the book. "Blake came by this morning. And Miri too."

"She may well have saved you," Julian informed him.

"She got me here?" Cameron asked, not remembering much of anything from the past couple days.

Julian looked down at the floor sadly and then up at Cameron with a weak smile. "In a way."

Cameron shook his head slightly. "In a way? She did or didn't. Don't remember, but I thought I was carried." He looked at Julian speculatively. "Miri couldn't do that."

"No," Julian agreed readily.

Cameron turned his head against the pillow so he could see Julian better. "You can," he whispered.

Julian leaned forward, letting his thumb slide against the inside of Cameron's wrist. "I can," he confirmed.

"You did. Carried me down," Cameron said in broken sentences to save his throat. "Oh God, Julian, what if you fell?"

"Then I'd have called an ambulance," Julian responded calmly. "And cried."

Cameron sighed, trying not to laugh. His eyes didn't waver from Julian's face. "My hero," he rasped.

"At your service," Julian murmured with a hint of a smile, though it was tempered by the worry in his dark eyes as he stared down at their linked fingers. He looked up at Cameron and met his eyes. "I've not been that terrified in quite some time," he whispered, unashamed.

Cameron's chest ached with more feeling than pain, but he couldn't name it. He turned his free hand to press his palm to Julian's cheek. "I'm okay," he said softly.

Julian looked down and nodded jerkily.

Cameron gazed at him, stroking his cheek. He was content just having Julian there. "I feel better already."

"We need to talk," Julian told him abruptly.

Cameron's body grew cold with dread, but he licked his parched lips and nodded. "Okay."

"I was afraid… I feared you'd been hurt because of me," Julian told him, his words measured.

Cameron frowned, not trying to hide his confusion. "What do you mean 'because of you'?"

Julian broke the eye contact again with a sigh.

Cameron frowned. "Julian?" he prodded.

"What do you think I do, Cameron?" Julian asked, not looking up.

Letting his head turn to the side against the pillows, Cameron thought about it. "I guess a detective of some sort. I don't know. Some investigative kind of job." He shrugged. "At one time I thought you might be a male escort," he added with a soft laugh.

Julian looked up quickly in surprise. "A what?" His voice edged up into a near squeak.

"Just that one night, when the woman came into the restaurant and made the joke about being a prostitute," Cameron admitted, trying not to smile at Julian's reaction. "I didn't know anything about you, and some of the things you said…" He flushed and shook his head. "I didn't seriously think that," he said as he backpedaled.

Julian blinked at him, mulling that over. "That'd make a pretty good cover," he muttered to himself finally.

Cameron stifled a laugh, and it came out as a snort. "You could certainly pull it off," he said.

"Shut up," Julian said with a soft laugh.

Smiling, Cameron reached out and slid his fingers along Julian's cheek. "Who could resist you?"

Julian pursed his lips and lowered his head so Cameron wouldn't have to shift to touch him. "I deal with some dangerous people," he said as his eyes darted to the door of the hospital room. "I was afraid someone had found out about you."

Cameron watched Julian's face, something he'd taken to doing to try to learn to read the other man, who wasn't exactly forthcoming with information, much less many emotions. Hearing him say something so specific was unnerving. "Which would put me in danger?" he asked awkwardly. He wasn't sure he wanted to know the answer.

"Yes," Julian whispered without looking up.

Cameron could tell Julian was serious. Very much so. He forced himself to swallow and flinched when it hurt. "What kind of danger?"

"Are there different kinds?" Julian asked.

Cameron tensed. "I suppose there's getting-hurt danger, and then there's the end-up-dead kind of danger," he said shakily.

Julian was silent, his head still lowered as if he was afraid to look up.

Cameron drew his hand back, watching it tremble. "Is this… this fear, is it what you deal with every day?" It hurt. It scared him to think that Julian might live in fear day in and day out.

"Every day but Friday," Julian answered without pause.

Cameron pressed his lips together, at this point hurting and more afraid for his lover than for himself. "Julian, please look at me."

Julian winced and looked up slowly, meeting Cameron's eyes regretfully.

Cameron had a difficult time understanding the conflict in those black eyes. He'd never seen the emotion there before. But then, he'd never seen Julian afraid before. "Is it worth it? Spending time with me?"

Julian winced again and shook his head disbelievingly. "You're asking me if spending time with you is worth you getting hurt?" he asked.

"You already made that decision. Didn't you?" Cameron pointed out evenly, although his heart was pounding anxiously. "Just by asking me to take a walk in the snow on Christmas Eve."

Julian pulled away as if Cameron had smacked him, and he sat back in the chair in a daze.

Cameron watched his reaction solemnly. "I wouldn't change it," he said. "Not for anything. I hoped… you felt the same."

"I can't say that I do," Julian breathed in an offended voice. "I wouldn't have you hurt."

A no-win situation, for sure. Cameron's breath caught painfully, and he had to look away to blink through the upset as he tried to draw in air without coughing. When he thought he had it under control, he spoke. "So now what?" came out in a clogged rasp. It wasn't logical that he would choose Julian over his own safety, Cameron knew. He would, though, and logic be damned.

"I should have told you from the beginning," Julian told him softly. "I should have let you know the danger, and I'm sorry for not doing it. I can't make your choices for you, though."

Cameron would have laughed if he could have gotten enough air to do it. Julian was talking himself in circles, obviously struggling with the topic just as much as he was. "No, you can't," he said weakly before finally having to cough hard as Julian watched him helplessly. Gasping for breath, Cameron closed his eyes after the effort. "I wouldn't change it," he whispered, opening watery eyes to look at Julian. "Please don't make me."

Julian lowered his head to try to hide the relief in his eyes. "I won't," he promised with difficulty.

Struggling through several shortened breaths, Cameron curled his hands into the sheets and tried to relax again. He could feel the threat of tears, which was the last thing he wanted or needed, so instead he let the choppy breaths take his energy.

"What if something happens to you?" Julian asked suddenly, obviously unable to let the topic go just yet.

Letting out a shaky breath as fear of the unknown clutched at his throat, Cameron realized he had no answer. "I don't know," he responded bluntly. "What if something happens to you?"

Julian blinked in surprise. "To me?" he asked.

Cameron exhaled in disbelief. "Yes, Julian. What if something happens to *you*?"

"Nothing will happen to me," Julian assured him softly, seeming to fall back into his natural confidence.

Cameron raised an eyebrow disbelievingly and looked at the scrapes on Julian's cheek pointedly. "You asked 'what if' first." He sighed heavily. "You'll just have to protect me, won't you?" he finally said, lifting his hand to his bare throat where the necklace usually hung. He'd taken it off days ago when applying copious amounts of Vicks and hadn't put it back on.

The motion drew Julian's eyes, and he stared at the spot where the warrior's cross should have been for a long moment of silence. Finally his lips twitched slightly. "Does that mean I have to protect your dogs as well?" he asked as he looked back up to meet Cameron's eyes.

Biting his lip on a laugh, Cameron tried to look appropriately sober. "I don't know. They're awfully ferocious on their own." He couldn't help the heartfelt desire in his eyes from showing. He wanted to be with Julian, no matter the risk of some nebulous danger that might not ever happen. He'd found someone he wanted, and that someone wanted him in return. Cameron wouldn't give that up without a fight.

Julian leaned forward again and ran his fingers along Cameron's cheek. He stared for a long moment, and then he stood and bent over him to kiss his temple carefully. "I have to go," he said regretfully.

Cameron covered Julian's hand, and his eyes fell shut as he felt Julian's lips. "I'll be here."

"Take care of yourself," Julian whispered into his ear.

Opening his eyes just in time to see Julian pass through the door, Cameron sighed shakily. "You do the same," he said to the empty room.

"SO WHAT have we learned from this little escapade?" Julian asked as he broke the bag inside his instant ice pack and shook it angrily.

"Down doesn't always mean dead, sir," Preston answered obediently.

"And if the mark is wearing body armor?" Julian asked irritably as he pressed the ice to his temple and closed his eyes.

"Always take the head shot, sir," Preston rattled off, obviously trying to hide the fact that he was smiling as he drove.

"Of course it's funny," Julian snapped. "You're not the one who got tackled by fucking Lazarus!"

"Twice, sir."

"Twice!"

"He certainly had an impressive ability to get back up, sir," Preston pointed out.

"You think maybe you just missed him the first two times you shot at him?" Julian asked as he pressed the ice pack harder against his head.

"I don't miss, sir," Preston assured him confidently as he took the turn into Blake's driveway. "I do, however, sincerely apologize for the failure, sir," he added with as much sincerity as Preston's flat delivery was able to convey. "It's my job to deal with any protection detail, and—"

"Preston?" Julian interrupted tiredly as he saw Blake standing out on the stone steps of his house, waiting for them.

"Yes, sir?"

"Don't ever apologize to me again," Julian ordered with a small smile.

"Yes, sir. Terribly sorry, sir," Preston responded with a straight face as he put the car in park and got out. "Won't happen again, sir," he called just before shutting the door.

"What have you done to yourselves this time?" Blake called from the front door of his house.

"We're just making sure you stay in practice," Julian claimed as he started toward Blake. He stopped as his head began to spin, and his balance faltered.

Preston was at his side in an instant, supporting him easily and helping him the short distance into the house.

"Come on then," Blake muttered. "I've got the medical kit and the Valium all ready."

"I don't need any Valium," Julian told him as he held the ice pack to his head.

"It's not for you," Blake responded with a smirk as he led them to his study, where he always stitched them up when they ran into trouble. He walked straight to the sideboard and opened a bottle. "You're the most god-awful patient known to man. Your doctor gets the Valium. So does the nurse. Preston?" he offered cheekily.

"Thank you, sir," Preston responded, managing to keep a straight face as he took the glass of whiskey Blake handed him.

"I hate you both," Julian muttered as he covered his eyes with his icepack.

CHAPTER 6

CAMERON sat on a quilt on the floor, grinning as the four puppies tumbled all around and over his legs, each vying for his attention. He laughed at their antics; it was a warmer and healthier sound, if still a bit garbled. He'd just gotten home, courtesy of Miri, who'd picked him up at the hospital and shuttled him and the dogs home.

"Do you have any idea how much of a mess these little monsters make?" Miri asked grudgingly. "I can't tell you how much hair is all over my apartment."

"I told you that you had to brush them." Cameron laughed again as the dogs cavorted. "But they're worth it. Did you ever remember their names?"

Miri rolled her eyes. "No. I called the yellow one No, the red one Bad Dog, the white one Get Off That, and the blue one Stop It," she said drolly, referring to the colors of their tiny woven collars.

"That'll do," Cameron said as he picked up Saffron and cuddled her close.

"All right. Lunch," Miri said to change the subject. "I brought several dinners from Jean-Michel, and he said if you want anything specific, anything at all, just call the restaurant, and he'll send it over."

"You all take such good care of me," Cameron told her, preoccupied by being made into terrain by sixteen tiny feet. Miri smiled from where she stood at the bar and started unpacking the bags.

Cameron ran his fingers through the puppies' soft coats as he leaned back against the couch, taking it easy. He was tired after the trip home. He could tell he was much improved, but he was under doctor's orders to stay at home at least another week. He wondered what he'd do, besides Tuesday night and Friday.

That turned his mind to Julian. What Julian had said at the hospital bothered Cameron. He was concerned and a little afraid of the hints at some mysterious danger. It was so much easier to remain ignorant of what Julian did when he wasn't around. Because when Cameron began wondering and asking questions, even if he never actually voiced them out loud, he grew tense and worried. Sometimes, though, he couldn't help himself. What if what Julian did was illegal? Cameron already knew his job was dangerous, despite Julian's assurances that he would be okay. And every time he saw Julian hurt, Cameron got a little more scared for his lover. And now, perhaps the smallest bit for himself. Julian seemed fearless. If he was frightened for Cameron, shouldn't Cameron be afraid as well?

He snapped out of his thoughts when the phone rang. The handset was just within reach, so he waved Miri off and stretched out to pick it up. "Hello?"

"How are you?" Julian's soft voice questioned.

Cameron's eyes flew across the room to check on Miri. She was busy in the kitchen, unwrapping things.

"I'm doing better now. Still taking it slow, though." His voice warmed as he spoke. He'd missed Julian since their last visit in the hospital, where he'd ended up staying for a total of four days. Julian hadn't come back to visit him, even on Friday, and Cameron had tried not to worry.

"That's good. What are you doing right now?"

"Playing with the puppies while Miri fixes me some lunch. Jean-Michel sent over all my favorites, enough food for an army."

The line was silent for some time. "She's treating you well?"

While Cameron was mostly used to Julian's long pauses, he was also accustomed to having Julian in front of him when they occurred. It was hard enough to decipher Julian's emotions in person. On the phone, it was virtually impossible. So the pause and the question caught Cameron off guard.

"Yeah, she's great," he answered sincerely. "I could probably even get her to do my laundry."

"Good." The word had so many meanings when Julian said it, depending on the way he said it or the look in his eyes. Cameron realized this was the first time he'd ever spoken to his lover on the phone. He wasn't sure he liked it.

"Uh-huh," Cameron responded, shaking his head a little. "Any particular reason you ask?" he asked carefully.

Another quiet spell met Cameron's query. "I'm afraid to tell you," Julian mumbled.

"Why?" Cameron asked slowly. Their last conversation had been very emotional, something unusual for Julian, and Cameron still thought about it with some shiver of foreboding. He found himself wary of asking questions now, and when he did, more and more hesitant to ask anything that Julian might not answer.

"Because you'll laugh at me," Julian told him with a slight huff. "I'm jealous," he admitted. "I can make soup," he muttered. He sounded uncharacteristically cranky.

Cameron stayed quiet for a long moment as he reveled in the happiness those words gave him. Julian didn't talk about himself much at all, and he rarely, if ever, admitted to many emotions or faults. "I'm not laughing," he said gently.

"Yeah, you are," Julian grumbled. "You sound better," he added. Cameron thought a smile was evident in his voice.

"I feel better," Cameron agreed. "Except—"

"What?" Julian asked.

"I miss you," Cameron said. "This is the longest I've gone without seeing you in months."

"I miss you too," Julian responded immediately, though he didn't offer an excuse for his absence.

Cameron smiled happily. "Two more days to get through until Tuesday."

The silence stretched on. Then finally, "I've got to go out of town Monday. I may not be back."

The disappointment hit Cameron hard, like a physical blow. "As long as you mean may not be back by Tuesday rather than may not be back at all," he said, a quiver in his voice.

"Of course," Julian affirmed hastily. "I'm going to try, but… it could be very late."

"Just be careful. Please. Better late than never, right?" Cameron said in a hushed voice as he gripped the handset.

"Of course," Julian repeated. "Cameron," he added hesitantly. "What I do… I'm not the one in danger, usually," he informed him softly. "You know that, right?"

Cameron closed his eyes, some little frightened part of him inside easing its grip around his heart. "I'd hoped so," he whispered. "Didn't know for sure."

Again, Julian fell silent. It was frustrating, wondering what he might be thinking as the line buzzed with dead air.

"You tell Miri to take care," Julian finally said. "And you. Be healthy when I get back."

"I haven't told her about you," Cameron said reluctantly.

"Do you want to?"

Cameron looked up and across the room to where she puttered in the kitchen as the microwave hummed. He sighed. "I don't know. I know you very much value your privacy."

"My privacy is nothing to your happiness. If you want to tell your friend, do it," Julian told him firmly. "All I ask is that you tell her I deal in antiques, if she asks."

Cameron closed his free arm around himself, shifting uncomfortably. "I understand."

"Do you?" Julian asked carefully.

"As much as I can, I guess," Cameron said in resignation. "Can't really give away something I don't know."

"Cameron," Julian said quietly. "Are you okay with this?"

"Okay with what? Doing what I can to keep you safe?"

Julian was silent for another uncomfortably long moment. "I have to go," he finally said regretfully. "Take care of yourself."

"I'll be thinking about you," Cameron murmured.

"See you soon, love," Julian said, and the line went dead.

Cameron's breath caught when he heard the endearment. It had stopped sounding out of place when Julian said it, but it still made his pulse flutter. He sat there staring at the wall for a long time, only jumping slightly when the phone started beeping at him to remind him he hadn't hung up. He thumbed off the handset, closed his eyes, and sighed.

He wanted Julian here now, not later. It wasn't fair to have only two days a week to begin with. To have one taken away made it even worse.

"Cameron?"

He looked up to see Miri waiting with a tray.

"Is it ready?" he asked uncomfortably, hoping he hadn't looked too distraught.

"Yeah, I heated up the goose. Something nice and fattening for you. You lost weight in the hospital." She poked his arm as she sat down and handed him one of the two plates.

"Yeah, a little," Cameron acknowledged softly.

They ate quietly for a few minutes. "So. Who was that on the phone that put that look on your face?" Miri finally asked.

Cameron looked up at her, trying to decide what—if anything—to say.

JULIAN stood on the sidewalk, ignoring the snow flurries and staring up at the window he knew looked into Cameron's apartment. It was late, well past midnight. And it was no longer Tuesday. He wrestled with the fact that he was here at all. It would be all too easy for Cameron to get hurt because of him.

It still bothered him that Cameron discounted his warnings so quickly. Julian didn't know what he could tell him to impress the seriousness of the situation upon him without telling him the cold, hard truth. And that would certainly drive him away. But as much as he wanted Cameron with him, Julian couldn't bear the thought of seeing his lover hurt because of him.

He wouldn't let himself think about how he would feel if Cameron actually agreed with him and ended their relationship. It was a hard place to find himself, trying to do the honorable thing while at the same time hoping it wouldn't work.

Julian peered up and down the street indecisively and then slowly made his way toward the entrance to the building. When he got upstairs to Cameron's condo, he knocked gently.

When Cameron threw open the door several moments later, Julian stood in the hallway, hulking and covered with melting snow, expression blank as he tried to hide the nerves that surfaced. What if Cameron had changed his mind and didn't want to see him? He wouldn't blame the man for it.

But Julian broke into a smile as soon as he saw Cameron. It was obvious he'd been waiting up. "Sorry I'm late," he offered.

Reaching out to grab Julian's arm, Cameron practically yanked him inside the apartment so he could shut and lock the door behind them. Then he turned and threw his arms around Julian's neck, hugging him close without saying a word.

Julian wrapped his arms around him and held him tightly. He rested his chin on top of Cameron's head and closed his eyes. "You look better," he finally murmured.

Cameron pulled back just enough to look up at Julian's face. "You look tired," he said as he pressed his palm lightly against Julian's cheek.

"Well…"

Cameron shook his head ever so slightly. "We'll talk later. Bed. Sleep." He stepped back, pushing Julian's coat off his shoulders. It fell with a soft whoosh to the floor, covering three of the four puppies, who continued to yip and romp playfully beneath the expensive material as the fourth sat and looked at the coat with her head tilted to the side.

Julian stood motionless, paying the dogs no attention. He met Cameron's eyes seriously. "I've had a hard night," he admitted.

Leaving the coat, Cameron looked Julian up and down, and Julian knew he was looking for any telltale signs of injuries. When he didn't find any, he visibly screwed up his courage and said, "If you want to talk, I'll listen."

Julian was silent, frowning heavily. Finally, he gave a slight shake of his head. Cameron didn't need to hear about any of the things that bothered him. He didn't need to hear about how even Julian suffered from a guilty conscience occasionally. He didn't need to hear about how handlers and assets were turning up dead left and right in other major cities. He didn't need to hear that word was getting around that someone who knew the way the game was played had suddenly changed the rules. He didn't need to hear about how it might very well be every man for himself soon enough.

"Bed sounds wonderful," Julian said instead.

"C'mon," Cameron said softly, taking Julian's hand and leading him toward the bedroom.

Julian was tired, more so than usual after an out-of-town job. The job was hard enough when things went to plan. When they didn't, innocent people got hurt, assets got exposed, things caught fire and occasionally blew up… It got messy. Julian wanted nothing more than to sink into bed next to Cameron and forget it all for a while.

"Did you tell your friend?" he asked softly as he dragged behind Cameron obediently.

Cameron looked over his shoulder as they passed the dividers. "Yeah," he answered. "A little bit, anyway."

"How'd that go?" Julian asked wryly.

"Not so well," Cameron admitted with a wince. "I wouldn't tell her near what she wanted to know." He stopped at the foot of the bed and started undoing Julian's tie.

Julian placed his hands on Cameron's hips and watched him ardently as Cameron fussed with his tie. If he had his choice, he'd never look away. "I'm sorry," he finally whispered.

Pulling the tie free of Julian's collar, Cameron started on the buttons of his shirt without saying anything. He glanced up at Julian and bit his lip. "You're more important to me."

Julian didn't respond as he watched Cameron undress him. He wasn't really sure what kind of declaration would pour out of him if he opened his mouth.

Cameron finished with his shirt buttons and took up one hand to unfasten Julian's cuff. "She'd pretty much guessed it was you," he said.

"It?" Julian asked with a raised eyebrow as he waited for Cameron to continue.

Cameron smiled. "What's been making me so happy."

Julian blinked at him in surprise and then smiled weakly. Happy. If only for a little while, anyway.

Cameron raised an eyebrow. "What? It's true."

"Good," Julian murmured.

Cameron's brighter smile and gleaming eyes transformed him, putting some more color in his pale cheeks, and he pressed himself as close as he could get to Julian, curling one arm around his neck, the other around his waist. It had taken Julian a little time to get used to the random and sudden hugs Cameron liked to steal, but he had grown to enjoy them quite a bit.

He slid his arms around Cameron and held him close, resting his chin on Cameron's head again. "Some nights," he said, "all I can think about is being here and holding you."

"Nights you're not with me," Cameron whispered. "Too many nights," he added sadly.

"Yes," Julian breathed, regret tightening his chest. "I'm sorry." He hated saying those words; he seemed to say them to Cameron all the time. But he couldn't risk being here more than he already was. It might already be too much. Having a routine was a dangerous thing. Tuesdays at the restaurant were already a dangerous game he played. Soon enough, someone would uncover where to find him on Fridays as well. But to do it any differently would be to risk his carefully constructed house of cards to chaos.

Cameron pulled back enough to kiss him longingly as he pulled Julian's shirt from his waistband. There was no point in saying anything else, and they both knew it. Julian was the only one who could change the way things were, and he wasn't willing to do that. Yet.

He reached for Cameron's hands as they brushed along his back and stilled them gently. "I have… I have a slight injury," he admitted softly.

"Injury?" Cameron asked worriedly, pulling his hands away.

"Just a pulled muscle, I think," Julian told him. "My back. Missed a step in the dark," he admitted with a slight blush. It had been a really long step, actually, with a very sudden stop. But Cameron didn't need to know that either. "As long as you're careful."

Some of the tension invested in Cameron's shoulders relaxed. "Better than being shot," he muttered, taking the time to push Julian's shirt over his shoulders.

Julian smiled slightly. "I rarely get shot while dealing antiques," he said, barely restraining a snicker.

Cameron rolled his eyes. "Antiques. How in the world did you come up with that? Is it even remotely close to what you do?" He moved around Julian, helping him remove the shirt so he wouldn't have to twist.

"Remotely," Julian answered defensively.

Cameron snorted and knelt down to start unlacing Julian's shoes. "Remotely," he repeated with a shake of his head.

“I deal with… old… things. Sometimes. I have an old gun,” Julian offered hopefully.

“Is the old gun a collector’s item?” Cameron asked cheekily.

Julian watched him raptly, his body tensing pleasantly as Cameron knelt at his feet. “No,” he answered gruffly as he lifted first one foot and then the other obediently. “Just old.”

Pulling off Julian’s Italian loafers and socks, Cameron knelt back on his heels and looked up at him.

“I don’t know that I have the energy to do to you what I want to,” Julian muttered with a frown.

Cameron slid his hands up Julian’s calves to settle behind his knees. “Which would be?”

“Unseemly, I’m sure,” Julian murmured in a slightly more hoarse voice.

“Why don’t you let me be the judge of that?” Cameron slid his hands slowly to coast up the fronts of Julian’s thighs.

Julian closed his eyes and raised his chin, breathing out slowly as if trying to retain control. Usually, when Julian came home this tired, Cameron gave in gracefully and quite happily curled up in his arms and slept. But he’d obviously been starving to touch and be touched. Julian didn’t blame him; he felt the same way even with the extreme fatigue. He shuddered as Cameron’s hands kept moving, just coasting over the fine fabric of Julian’s tailored trousers.

Julian’s hand slid into Cameron’s hair gently, almost unconsciously. He opened his eyes again and looked down at him, torn between wanting to touch him and simply wanting to collapse onto the bed.

Cameron seemed to sense it, though, and his hands went still. Slowly, Cameron leaned forward and set his cheek against the juncture of Julian’s hip and thigh.

Julian ran his hand gently over the top of Cameron’s head as he looked down at him. It felt odd, standing there with the other man on his knees and hugging him. It also felt good, for a variety of reasons.

Julian felt like he was somehow protecting Cameron, even though there was no immediate danger. Julian rarely got to feel like that in other aspects of his life. It was one of the reasons he found being with Cameron so appealing.

After a minute, Cameron sighed and moved, scooting back and getting to his feet. His hands moved to unfasten Julian's pants efficiently, this time with the simple goal of removing them. Julian still watched him unerringly. His dark eyes showed a whisper of arousal, but it was overpowered by exhaustion.

"C'mon," Cameron said softly as soon as he had Julian suitably undressed, taking his hand and leading him over to the bed.

Julian's fingers squeezed at Cameron's. He didn't know what to say, and he couldn't let out the words that threatened. At this point they wouldn't be very believable, no matter how true he himself believed the sentiment to be. They barely knew each other, but the connection between them, Julian believed, was real.

Stopping at the bedside, Cameron pulled down the quilts and sheet and shifted to urge Julian to lie down.

Julian stopped him and held his hand tightly, looking down at the bed as he tried to convince himself that he wasn't mentally prepared to do what he wanted to do. That Cameron wasn't prepared to hear it.

"Fuck it," Julian finally breathed in annoyance. He reached for Cameron's other hand and pulled until Cameron was facing him. "I believe I may be in love with you," he blurted.

Cameron blinked at him several times—clearly surprised—too stunned to respond.

"I just… needed to say that," Julian went on as he released one of Cameron's hands and waved at his own head. "Outside of my head."

"You think you might be in love with me?" Cameron repeated. "And you've been thinking it… already? Before now?"

"I've been thinking it since I first saw you," Julian admitted softly. "But now I'm actually sober, and I'm fairly certain," he added as he felt his face flushing slightly.

"But… but when you first saw me, that was almost a year ago," Cameron whispered.

"I can be a little slow," Julian joked as he blushed further.

Cameron reached up to lightly touch Julian's reddening cheek, his fingers brushing through the finely trimmed beard. "That's astounding," he said shakily.

"It really is," Julian agreed. "Considering I've never thought it before."

"Never?"

"I had a thing for my first-year maths teacher," Julian answered with a straight face.

Cameron slapped lightly at Julian's belly. "Goofball."

Julian grunted and shuffled slightly, pleased that Cameron was comfortable enough with him to tease.

"You make me very happy," Cameron said, leaning in to cuddle close against him.

"I'm glad." Julian rested his chin against Cameron's temple.

It was another quiet minute before Cameron whispered against Julian's shirt. "I know I love you. It's crazy. And you…. I didn't think you'd ever…"

The words zinged through Julian's chest, and he held Cameron closer as he tried not to grin. He ducked his head and kissed Cameron's neck possessively. Whatever happened tomorrow would be okay, because they had this tonight.

IT WAS just before seven on a Friday night. Spring was taking root in the city and the sun was setting, sending shimmers of light through the windows. Decorations glittered all over Tuesdays; it was decked out for a private party that was to start at any moment, and the place buzzed with preparations. Metal detectors guarded the doors and large security officers stood around the room. There were men in tuxedos and women in fur lining up to be checked against the exclusive guest list.

The restaurant closed like this for private parties several times a year because of its excellent reputation for discretion, respect, and elegance, its secure upstairs location, and particularly because of Blake Nichols' extensive connections. There were a lot of big names in the restaurant tonight. Celebrities, politicians, high-powered businessmen, professional athletes, society debutantes. It was a mishmash of powerful people and their lackeys.

Nights like this always proved to be interesting. And profitable, if there was enough booze. And Blake always made *sure* there was enough booze.

In the lobby outside the restaurant entrance, Julian raised his hands and watched the burly security guard carefully as he was patted down. When the man was done, he stood once more and nodded at Julian. "Have a good evening, sir."

"And you," Julian responded softly as he stepped through the doors and gave a name to the hostess. It wasn't *his* name, but it was a name nonetheless. And lucky him, it wasn't Keri monitoring the guest list.

The woman gestured for him to enter after checking her list. He nodded to her politely, and soon he was into the party and gritting his teeth against the urge to groan. Julian hated crowds. They made him paranoid and edgy. Especially crowds like this, where trouble was likely to come from someone who knew how to make it. Guests milled about on the cleared front floor, where servers moved with silver trays of champagne and tiny hors d'oeuvres.

Julian made his way through the crowd gracefully, nodding politely to those who greeted him and sipping at his own glass of champagne. Blake had a client in the crowd, one who would be drawing the proverbial bull's-eye on someone's back as soon as Julian found him. Fridays were normally reserved for Cameron, but with a party like this, Cameron had been assigned to work anyway. Julian had thought he would be forced to sit at home and stare at the walls all night, but the unexpected need for his presence had been sudden. He'd had very little forewarning, not even enough to call Cameron and warn him that he'd be here.

But when Blake called, Julian had to move. It was the only reason he was here and not at home, catching up on his sleep.

"CAMERON," Miri whispered when she returned to the service area to fill her tray. "Julian's here."

He glanced up from the champagne he was pouring and smiled. "Really? I didn't know he'd be here."

"Why not?" she questioned incredulously.

"I don't ask where he is every minute of the day," Cameron said as he set aside the bottle.

"So, he knew you'd be working a party he was attending, and he didn't tell you?" Miri asked dubiously.

Cameron frowned a little. "He would have mentioned it, so he must not have known until the last minute."

Miri raised an eyebrow and looked at him. "You going to go out and see him?" she asked curiously.

Cameron shifted his weight, but stopped and thought about it for a long moment, the smile fading a little. "If he's here, he's probably working," he said slowly. "I wouldn't want to bother him." The thought that Julian might be "working" at Tuesdays sent a bolt of uneasiness through him. He still wasn't quite sure what Julian did, but he knew it wasn't necessarily… good.

"Working?" Miri echoed.

"Yeah," Cameron said, trying not to wince. "He's an antiques dealer, remember? He travels a lot looking for things for people. Usually rich people," he improvised. "Probably lots of them here tonight. Clients and contacts and… stuff."

Miri stared at him for a moment and then smiled slightly. "You're both so weird," she muttered as she moved away.

Cameron watched her go before shaking his head. "You have no idea," he murmured. He picked up the tray of filled champagne flutes and headed out to the floor.

JULIAN glanced toward the back of the restaurant briefly before his attention was drawn to a man beckoning him. He cut his way through the growing crowd easily and greeted the man and his companion.

"I'd like you to meet an associate of mine," the man said to Julian pointedly. "Ronald, this is the man I was telling you about."

"An honor to meet you, sir," the stranger offered as he shook Julian's hand. "Gary tells me you found him several rare books in the last year."

"Nothing that couldn't be found on eBay these days," Julian assured the man cheekily.

The target laughed and nodded. "I'm in the market for Middle Eastern antiquities," he told Julian. "I hear they're going cheap now that the whole damn place is blowing up. That something you might be able to help me with?"

"I'm sure it is," Julian assured him.

"Well, then I look forward to doing business with you," the man said with a smile that Julian didn't like at all.

"Likewise," Julian murmured with a crooked smile of his own. It was always easier when the target was a bit of a jackass to begin with.

He looked away, trying not to sigh heavily, and he caught sight of Cameron as he emerged from the back. Julian's stomach flipped uncomfortably, and he averted his eyes quickly, trying to pay attention to the conversation around him. Cameron's movements repeatedly drew his attention, though, and so Julian kept track in an effort to avoid him. He didn't trust himself or Cameron not to react in a manner that was too familiar when Cameron got close. Julian never knew who was watching at things like this.

He was going to kill Blake for talking him into this. What the hell had he been thinking? He could easily have caught up to this guy elsewhere. He wasn't exactly the most careful sort, standing in the middle of a crowded party chatting up a stranger about stolen antiquities.

Cameron moved around the room smoothly, offering the tray to various guests. Julian could see his professional façade and silent manner firmly in place, but he could also see the man unobtrusively scanning the crowd. Someone had obviously told him he was here. Julian's lips compressed, and he mentally cursed. He should have let Cameron know he'd be here somehow. The decision to attend had been last minute, but he still could have attempted to call the restaurant and explain. He should have at least tried.

He was going to buy Cameron a cell phone, right after he throttled Blake.

It took most of a round of the room before Cameron entered the area where Julian stood, speaking with a man he was pretty sure was the center fielder for the Chicago White Sox. The waiter stopped several times along the way as guests lifted tidbits from his tray. It was while glancing over a woman's shoulder that Cameron finally caught sight of him. He paused just a few seconds longer than he normally would have before silently turning away from the first group of party-goers and approaching the cluster of people surrounding Julian.

He looked uncertain and a little nervous. Julian hated seeing that look on Cameron's face, knowing he was the cause. He hated even more what he knew he was going to have to do.

He watched Cameron's approach discreetly, and when he finally caught Cameron's eye he shook his head minutely and pointedly looked away from him, turning his attention back to the man speaking to him.

The motion visibly took Cameron aback for a moment, but his innate skills smoothly moved him to a group to the side, neatly sidestepping where Julian stood. Julian glanced to the side guiltily and watched him walk away. He felt like a complete bastard, but he couldn't have the wrong people knowing he knew Cameron at all, much less that he was involved with him.

"Are you all right, son?" the deputy mayor asked him with a frown.

"Of course, sir," Julian answered in a low, smooth voice as he returned his attention to the conversation at hand.

"So, tell me," the man's wife asked Julian with a smile. "How does one become so successful when dealing antiques? You seem to know everyone here!"

"Word of mouth, ma'am," Julian answered with a smile as he took another flute of champagne from a passing waiter and gulped it down.

CAMERON got back to the service area and set down his tray before taking a deep, steadying breath. He rubbed his hands over his eyes as he headed back to the kitchen to switch jobs with the expediter. There was no way he wanted to put Julian—or himself—in that position again. He didn't know what was going on, but he had to trust that Julian had his reasons. But why couldn't he even nod hello, like so many other strangers in the room?

Before too long, Miri entered the kitchen. "What's wrong?" she asked him in concern as soon as she caught sight of him.

Cameron sighed. "Nothing."

"You look like someone kicked your puppy," Miri observed. "Did you get to talk to Julian?"

"He's busy," Cameron answered with a quick shake of his head. "I couldn't bring myself to interrupt."

Miri raised one eyebrow and looked at him dubiously. "You sure you're okay?" she asked again.

Cameron shrugged. "Just hard, you know? Reminds me that I'm just a waiter, and he's someone important."

Miri stopped what she was doing and stared at him. "He tells you that?" she asked in horror.

Cameron flinched, realizing how that sounded. "No!" he insisted, turning to look at her. "No, he doesn't. He's never even hinted at something like that. It's just what *I* think sometimes, is all."

She looked over him, brow furrowing in worried sympathy. "Are you two… okay?" she asked gently.

Cameron worried at his bottom lip and looked over at her again. Julian worked with Blake. This party had been in the works for weeks. If Julian were meant to be here, Blake would have told Julian that some time ago. So why hadn't Julian told Cameron?

"I guess so," he answered finally. "I don't know."

Miri's eyebrows climbed in surprise. "Why? What's going on?" she asked. "You seem so happy."

Cameron frowned a little. "I just get nervous. I don't want to mess it up. It just… scares me sometimes."

"Scares you?" Miri prodded carefully as someone called for her.

Cameron's shoulder edged up. Despite Julian's admission that he loved him, Cameron feared something would happen to make Julian leave. Being summarily turned away out there on the floor rocked Cameron's confidence. Not being sure of his place in the relationship both scared and frustrated him.

"Are you going to be okay?" Miri asked him worriedly.

Cameron nodded distractedly, and Miri reluctantly left the kitchen. He had the feeling it was going to be a long night, and suddenly he was very glad he'd switched jobs to work back in the kitchen. He didn't think he could wait a table where Julian was sitting, smoothly conversing with other people, and have the man ignore him.

Or worse, have Julian treat him like a complete stranger.

He tried to swallow on a little frisson of anger. It shouldn't have to be this way.

OUT on the floor, Julian broke away from the little group that had monopolized his time the past hour and began moving slowly through the crowd toward the back. He'd thought he would at least be able to get through the night, maybe get some good intel about the asshole he was supposed to follow home, but all he could think about was the look in Cameron's eyes when he'd turned away. He needed to talk to Cameron and explain or he was going to make a serious mental misstep out here. He avoided anyone he knew and anyone who looked like they knew him, aiming for the service entrance.

Julian stepped through the doors into the back, looking around for Cameron, just as Miri backed into the service area from the kitchen and almost ran into him as he stood there.

She recovered quickly, apologizing and backing away from him.

"I need to speak to Cameron," Julian told her softly.

Miri looked unsure as she glanced around. "Perhaps that could wait?" she said uncertainly. "He's occupied with preparations for the dinner service right now."

"I'll find him myself," Julian murmured as he started toward the kitchen.

Miri gave a little squeak of surprise. "Wait," she tried as she reached for his sleeve. "That area's not open to guests, sir. If you go back there you could get us all in a lot of trouble. Including Cameron."

"Then get him for me," Julian suggested.

His voice was low and even, but forceful nonetheless. The tone obviously affected Miri. It sent a shiver through her, and she took a tiny step back. Her voice wavered a little when she spoke. "Please… let him be, just for tonight. He seems upset enough as it is."

Julian closed his eyes and jerked his chin to the side, visibly expressing his disbelief. He'd known when he got the call this would be a bad idea, coming to Tuesdays tonight. He backed away from her in annoyance, then turned and strode to the doors, pushing through them and disappearing into the crowd again without another word.

CAMERON moved through the restaurant in an exhausted daze, musing over the deflated, disorganized air about the restaurant as the staff cleaned up. These parties always ended with everything in disarray. People always moved chairs, shoved together tables, and left dirty plates and half-full glasses in odd places.

He didn't even want to begin thinking about the bathrooms. Someone always found at least one pair of lacy underwear. Blake kept them in a drawer in his office labeled "Lost and Found."

Cameron wondered about Blake's sense of humor sometimes.

Miri broke through his fatigued mental ramblings when she approached him. "Tell me who he really is," she demanded.

Cameron's back stiffened immediately. "What do you mean?"

"Julian," Miri hissed at him. "Who is he, really?" she asked him with a frown, her hands on her hips as she looked at him. "He won't speak to you in public and he's… he's all mysterious and silent and… scary," she stammered.

"Scary?" Cameron asked, turning to look at her, surprise on his face. "Why would you think that?"

"He was back in the service area tonight, demanding to see you," Miri told him as she folded her arms around herself. "He didn't even raise his voice at me, but…"

Cameron swallowed hard. He knew Julian could seem intimidating — tall and dark and hulking, his stoic expression rarely changing and his voice rarely above a whisper. "But?" he pushed.

"He frightened me," Miri answered quietly. "He *growled* at me. Does he… is he like that with you? Does he, like… threaten you?"

"Threaten me? No!" Cameron exclaimed, horrified. Why would Julian act like that toward Miri—toward Cameron's friend? "He's… quiet. And gentle, usually."

Miri looked at him dubiously and shook her head. "What does he do?" she asked. "Why was he here tonight but ignoring you? Is he some closeted politician or a criminal or something? Is he married?"

Cameron's mouth worked but nothing came out. All of his own unanswered questions started crowding his mind. "I told you. He's an antiques dealer," he managed to answer. He took a breath, trying not to overreact. Married? She thought Julian might be married? He quailed at the thought. He really didn't know, but surely to God the answer was no, right?

"So why not speak to you?" Miri reasoned.

Cameron curled his fingers into his pants legs and shrugged. "I told you. He was working," he insisted. "Besides, he *tried* to speak to me, but apparently *you* kept him away."

Miri stepped back, looking hurt. "I couldn't let him back there," she said defensively.

Cameron merely rolled his eyes and shook his head. He turned away to start sorting the plates into stacks to be picked up and taken to the kitchen.

"Hey, did you guys hear about the guy that got dead after the party tonight?" Charles asked them as he walked by with an armload of dirty dishes.

"What? No! What happened?" Miri asked in surprise.

"Somebody said he had too much to drink, stepped in front of a cab or something. It broke his neck," Charles answered with the sort of morbid glee that could only come from talking about the odd or gruesome death of someone you hadn't known.

"Jesus!" Miri exclaimed in horror.

"Yeah. They said one minute the dude was standing there waiting for a cab, the next this big guy next to him is grabbing for him, trying to catch him as he fell. That's got to stick with you for a while, huh?" Charles said as he filled up on more plates and kept walking toward the kitchen.

"Wow," Miri murmured, still staring at Charles as he walked away. "Talk about a rough night," she muttered as she looked back at Cameron. "What was I saying?" Miri asked.

"You were talking about leaving me alone," Cameron tried.

"Is Julian dangerous?" she asked him suddenly.

Cameron's sight blurred as he stared at the tablecloth, trying to keep himself under control. "Why would you think that?" he asked softly.

"It was just a feeling he gave off," Miri murmured after a moment of thought. "Like he was… capable."

Cameron glanced over his shoulder at her. "I can't think of him that way," he answered.

Miri sighed. "Just promise me you'll be careful."

Tilting his head, he turned and stepped to give her shoulder a gentle squeeze. "I will," he assured her with a small smile, while inwardly all the lingering worry and sudden upset mixed with the little bit of blossoming anger threatened to make him ill.

It was after two in the morning before Cameron finally left the restaurant, having overseen the entire clean-up and prep for the next day. All who worked the party had Saturday off with pay as a thank-you for a job well done. Cameron had an extra day, just because. Despite his argument, Blake had insisted.

And for the first time, he found himself relieved that Julian wouldn't be with him.

It was Saturday morning now, past Julian's scheduled Friday visit, and Cameron would have the whole day as well as Sunday and Monday to himself to rest and think before going back to work on Tuesday, although he really didn't want to think at all. He knew he'd been lying to himself all this time, but he'd ignored it, hoping he'd give Julian no reason to change his mind about loving him. He would tell Cameron what he needed to know, wouldn't he? What bothered Cameron most was that he still knew next to nothing about Julian, even after four months of being lovers.

It all ate at him, making him tired and depressed. And right now, Cameron was forcing himself to ignore the fact that he wanted nothing more than to be in Julian's arms.

Cameron walked distractedly down the deserted sidewalk. He stopped briefly at the street corner, glancing each way before hurrying across the road and heading down the sidewalk toward his building, still stuck in confused, swirling thoughts, pretty much oblivious to everything around him. A couple blocks later, keycard in hand, Cameron stopped to open the door.

A hulking shadow stepped away from the building on the other side of the street and cleared his throat. Cameron's chin snapped around to look in the direction of the noise as he jumped in alarm. He didn't relax when he saw it was Julian.

"Are you okay?" Julian asked him without crossing the street. His voice carried in the cold night.

Cameron nodded slowly as he watched Julian, all of his worries echoing in his head as he found himself unable to relax. In the dark, lit only by a few harsh streetlights, Julian *did* look dangerous. Cameron realized now that he just hadn't let himself see it. "Tired," he finally answered hoarsely.

"I'm sorry I didn't give you warning," Julian told him as he stepped into the street. "I didn't know I was needed at the party until tonight."

Cameron nodded again, at war with himself. He believed in Julian, but his own insecurities ate at him. It made him mad that he wasn't brave enough to ask the questions he wanted answered so he could feel better about their relationship. And Miri's questions invested him with enough tension that he hesitated, unable to think of anything to say in response to Julian's apology.

Julian must have been able to see the tension in him, because he stopped in the middle of the street, looking at Cameron with a blank expression. "May I come by tomorrow?" he asked, oddly polite. The air in front of him frosted over as he spoke.

Unable to read Julian's face or his tone, Cameron hesitated. He'd hoped to have more time to think things over and come to terms with what bothered him. "Tomorrow meaning later today or actually tomorrow?"

"Tomorrow," Julian answered as a siren began to blare in the distance.

The sound startled Cameron, and he glanced toward where it was coming from. Julian didn't bother to turn his head, now standing in the middle of the street and waiting for his answer.

Cameron looked back at him. "I thought Sundays weren't available?" he asked uncertainly.

"I'm off this weekend," Julian told him flatly.

Cameron stared at him and nodded, the yearning to be with him almost outweighing what he hoped was merely irrational fear. "Okay," he agreed softly, knowing that if Julian had requested to come upstairs now, he would have agreed.

Julian nodded and smiled slightly. "Sleep well, Cameron," he said in a louder voice as the siren got closer. The fire truck appeared around the corner several blocks away and blared its horn. Julian glanced at it and began slowly backing out of the road. The fire engine roared down the street and by them, its sirens deafening as the lights spun.

Cameron watched it as it sped past. When it turned the next corner and disappeared from view, the street in front of him was empty.

Left standing alone, Cameron looked up and down the street for Julian, not seeing anything moving or any sign of the man at all. It spooked him, and he turned and quickly entered the building. He didn't breathe easily again until he was up in his apartment with the door shut and locked behind him.

BLAKE grumbled as he clomped down the stairs from his bedroom in his robe. It was well past midnight, and there was only one person who would be banging on the knocker at this time of night.

"What have you done now? You're not even working a job tonight!" he asked tiredly as he swung the door open, expecting to see Julian hanging onto Preston as he bled on the doorstep like usual.

But Julian was alone, standing up on his own, dressed casually in a pair of faded jeans and a fleece pullover. He'd shaved off his beard sometime recently, but tonight he was scruffy. Somehow, the bastard still managed to look high-class.

The look in his eyes, however, spoke of utter defeat.

"You look like hell," Blake blurted without thinking. "What happened?" he demanded.

Julian returned his frank appraisal with a wry nod of his head, and then he lifted a bottle of single malt Irish whiskey and shook it enticingly.

"A Bushmills night," Blake observed with a slight frown. "Come in, then," he added with a sigh as he turned slightly and waved Julian into the house. "Let me go put my pants on," he muttered as Julian stepped past him unsteadily. "How'd you get here?" he asked suspiciously as he realized Julian wasn't exactly sober.

"Preston dropped me off," Julian answered as he looked around the large entry foyer. "Said he'd pick me up in the morning."

Blake barked a laugh and shook his head. "He's just pawning you off on me," he said accusingly as he relaxed a little. "What's the problem then? It's not tactical or he'd be all over it."

"I think I'm losing him," Julian answered softly as he turned and met Blake's eyes.

"Preston?" Blake asked in shock. Julian and Preston had worked together for longer than Blake had known either of them—and that was no short time itself.

Julian shook his head and looked away. "Cameron," he answered in a voice that was barely a whisper. "He's starting to get scared. I can feel it in the way he looks at me."

Blake stared at Julian, worried and dumbstruck. He licked his lips and moved closer to his friend, taking his elbow gently and guiding him toward the study. "I'll put pants on later," he mumbled as they walked through the silent house.

Julian flopped into one of the heavy leather armchairs standing beside the cold fireplace, and Blake knelt to start the gas logs as Julian began struggling to open the bottle of whiskey. Blake sat down opposite him, crossed his legs, and watched him, knowing that when Julian wanted to talk, he would. Especially since he'd already been into the bottle. The problem, in the end, would be shutting him up.

Finally, Julian handed the bottle wordlessly to Blake for him to open it, and he slumped back into his chair and stared up at the dark ceiling. "He's asking questions I'm afraid to answer," he started abruptly. "If I lie, I lose him. If I tell him the truth, I lose him *and* risk him being hurt."

"Jules," Blake said softly as he carefully set the bottle of whiskey on the floor beside his chair, hoping Julian would forget it. "Can I ask you a question?"

"No," Julian groaned with a shake of his head.

Blake ignored him. "What do you see in him?" he asked curiously.

Julian stared at Blake with wide eyes. "What the hell kind of a question is that?"

"An honest one," Blake answered. "Don't get me wrong. I adore Cameron. He's a great guy. I've known him almost as long as I've known you. But he's not exactly… your type," he explained carefully.

"And my type is…"

"The type you never see again," Blake answered wryly. "Or the type who's likely to try to kill you afterward," he added thoughtfully. "Of which Cameron is neither," he clarified.

"Jesus, Blake," Julian muttered, rubbing his eyes tiredly.

"It's not pretty, Jules, but it's true. Cameron's not like us. And quite honestly, I can't imagine how he keeps your interest. And it wouldn't surprise me to find out he thinks the same."

Julian sneered at that and shook his head. "I love him," he stated angrily.

"I know you do," Blake assured him. "But why?" he prodded.

"There's no answer to that," Julian protested in annoyance that was obviously heightened by the alcohol he'd already consumed. Blake actually preferred dealing with Julian when he was drunk. It was almost like dealing with a normal person, one who let his emotions show. "I don't know *why*," Julian went on in frustration. "I just…" He closed his eyes and turned his head, and the fire cast shadows over his drawn face. "When I'm with him I feel like one of the good guys," he tried to explain.

"You're not one of the good guys," Blake reminded.

"Shut up," Julian grumbled. "I just… I feel normal with him."

"You hate feeling normal," Blake argued. He ignored Julian's grunt of protest and continued, leaning forward as he did so. "And how can you call what you have with him normal?" he asked in annoyance. "You see him, what, not even two days a week? Less than forty-eight hours? And you probably spend most of that screwing and sleeping. You don't know him, not really, because you've not spent any real time with him. And he certainly doesn't know *you*. It's not a relationship when all you do is fuck him and leave."

"Fuck you," Julian said in a surprised voice.

"No, fuck *you*, Julian," Blake responded calmly. "What you have is nothing near a normal relationship. Take him out somewhere."

"You know I can't risk that," Julian argued.

"And so does he, doesn't he?" Blake pointed out. "You've told him that much. So of course he's going to get scared. He's *not* stupid."

"I know he's not stupid," Julian whispered in a stricken voice. "He's not… he's not one of us, just like you said. He's the kind of man who if you gave him a gun and told him he had two choices—"shoot one of your dogs or shoot yourself in the head"—he'd put the gun to his ear and pull the trigger."

"Hell, Jules, you'd do the same thing if someone did that to you and your goddamned cats," Blake said in amusement.

"No," Julian murmured with a shake of his head. "No, there's a third option. People like us, we're third-option people. We take the gun, stuff it in the person's mouth, and eliminate the problem. Walk off into the sunset with our kitty."

Blake had to press his lips together tightly in order not to smile or laugh. That was such a Julian thing to say. He wondered if he'd opened up to Cameron enough to let the other man see his odd sense of humor.

"But Cameron," Julian continued with a wave of his hand for emphasis. "He doesn't know there's a third option." He shook his head and sighed softly.

"So… you love him, partly because he's never been exposed to that third option," Blake surmised with a small frown. "But just by being near him, you're exposing him to it."

"I love him because he's him. I don't want to change him and lose him," Julian argued.

"Then don't," Blake advised with a shrug. "I've never seen you truly happy before this past year. It's him doing it. I don't know why or how. Hell, *you* don't know how. But love is a funny thing, and when you find it, you have to hold on tight. Tell him what he needs to hear. Give him what he thinks he wants."

Julian sighed heavily and closed his eyes. "If I tell him what I am, I'll lose him," he said in a hoarse voice.

"I didn't say tell him the truth," Blake said. "Tell him what he *needs* to hear," he repeated slowly. "If it's what it takes to keep you both happy and him safe, do it."

Julian stared at him for a long moment, nodding slightly. "And hope he never finds out?" he finally asked.

Blake shrugged in answer. "Hope he doesn't, hope he does… Cameron might surprise you. Or he might kick you to the curb and run like hell. I know him pretty well, but I wouldn't hazard a guess when it comes to this. It's pretty serious, you know, if he loves you too."

Julian grunted unhappily and continued to look at Blake as the firelight warmed the dark room.

Blake smiled slightly and shrugged. "Me, I'd run like hell from you," he admitted freely.

Julian blinked slowly and a wicked smile began to form on his lips. "That's because you know I top," he responded mischievously.

Blake groaned, waved his hands through the air, and stood up, walking away from the fire and his friend. "Way too much information," he mumbled as he left the room.

CHAPTER 7

CAMERON lay on his side on the couch, staring out the window at the night, though he wasn't really seeing anything. He'd been lazy all day Saturday, and most of today as well, preoccupied with his thoughts of Julian. With his fears and questions and nerves.

With his wants.

Something about Julian made him want to just curl up in his lover's arms and ignore the unspoken truth, whatever the truth might be, soaking in nothing but the warmth and acceptance and safety.

But he'd made himself face reality the past couple days. He truly knew next to nothing about Julian: Where he lived. What his real job was. If he had family. Why he only stayed one night and one day a week. Where he spent his time away from him. Why they never went out in public. If he were married.

Cameron made himself calm down after working himself into a tizzy. There was no reason to think Julian wasn't on the up-and-up. Julian had never tried to sidestep a direct question. He had merely refused to answer some of them. That wasn't lying.

He'd not actually asked Julian where he lived. Julian admitted to having a dangerous job—one that might be dangerous to Cameron as well—and he'd even hinted that he might leave Cameron rather than see him hurt. He'd never mentioned family or friends, besides Blake. Julian never offered excuses for why he couldn't see Cameron more often, and he actually had asked Cameron once if he wanted to go out somewhere. And he didn't wear a wedding ring.

Then there was Julian himself—tall, dark, mysterious. Devastatingly handsome and as passionate in bed as he was controlled on the streets. The whole cliché. Dangerous. To others, surely, Julian had as much as told him that. But to Cameron? He didn't think so. Julian had never done anything to threaten or scare him, and he had even apologized on the rare occasion when he got rough, despite the fact Cameron had assured him he was enjoying it.

No, he was not afraid of Julian.

Cameron just didn't know what to think about the rest. He wanted to believe in Julian. He loved him—desperately so. He'd just found him a handful of months ago, and this had all happened so fast. He didn't want to let him go or be let go.

If Cameron asked more questions, asked for more explanations, would Julian change his mind and leave? Would he give him that same, lifeless look he'd given him at the party and then turn away from him? Cameron didn't think he could handle that.

Whether he could live and love in the dark of the truth remained to be seen.

A quiet knock on the door jostled him out of his thoughts.

Cameron's eyes slowly slid to the door before he pushed up from the couch. The dogs were already yapping and jumping up and down. He had to push them out of the way when he got there before he could check the peephole.

Julian stood calmly in the hallway with his head bowed, waiting. It surprised Cameron again that Julian had shaved his beard off; he'd barely noticed at the party before he'd fled to the kitchen, and then he'd forgotten. Julian still looked good. Too good. It just wasn't fair how good-looking the man was.

Cameron swallowed and took stock of his emotions. He felt relatively calm. He was a little apprehensive, but no more nervous than usual, he supposed. He unlocked the door and opened it.

Julian looked up when the lock sounded, and he smiled tentatively when he met Cameron's eyes. That smile helped put Cameron at ease. He couldn't think of Julian as a man who got nervous, but he *had* seen glimpses of nerves in the other man, hadn't he? Like that smile. It seemed so normal. He smiled in return and opened the door further, enough that the dogs swarmed Julian's feet.

Julian watched them with something like affectionate resignation. The first step he took dragged two playfully growling dogs along with it.

Cameron chuckled and bent over to pick up Saffron and Snowflake. The fact that the dogs were so enamored of Julian was another balm. Animals were good judges of character, weren't they?

"It's good to see I was missed," Julian murmured as he bent to pick up the other two dogs and stepped into the apartment.

Cameron stepped around and shut the door behind them. "You were," he confirmed.

Julian set the dogs down and met Cameron's eyes carefully. "Yeah?" he asked tentatively.

Holding the dogs to his chest, Cameron nodded, not looking away as he leaned back against the door.

Julian stared at him for a moment. "I'm sorry about the party," he said quietly, without looking away from Cameron's face.

Cameron dropped his eyes and shifted his weight uneasily. "You were working."

"I would have warned you, if I could have," Julian insisted. "Blake wasn't thinking. Those people… right now I'm an unknown to them. But in a year, or a month, or a week, that might change. I can't have them knowing how to hurt me."

"I don't understand," Cameron admitted. "How could they hurt you? You said you're not the one usually in danger."

"They could hurt *you*," Julian answered bluntly.

Cameron's heart was suddenly beating hard enough to make him light-headed. "How?"

Julian cocked his head and shrugged slightly, looking away as he thought about the question. "Foreclose on the condo. Make your tax records disappear and cause an audit. Implicate you in something that could send you to jail," he murmured finally. "Someone less… principled may go so far as to physically attack you, if they wanted to send me a message."

Cameron remembered what Julian had said about danger, but he hadn't had any context before now. The implications of what Julian was saying made Cameron tremble and tighten his arms, enough so that one of the dogs gave a soft yelp. He flinched and squatted to set them on the floor; he stayed there, shocked.

Julian watched him helplessly. "I'm sorry," he finally said again.

Cameron closed his arms around himself as he forced himself to stand up, but he couldn't stop the shivers. "You knew," he said shakily. "You knew, when we met, when we got together, that this might happen, that I might actually get hurt by someone else because of you. But you never told me this before? Why?"

Julian closed his eyes and bowed his head, unable to answer.

"Julian?" Cameron pushed. "If you knew… then why? Why would you do that?"

"I was selfish," Julian answered calmly. He looked back up and met Cameron's eyes again. "And perhaps overconfident. I wanted you. I thought I could protect you."

Cameron swallowed hard as he tried to order his thoughts. "I didn't want to ask for more explanations," he said. "I knew… you didn't want to tell me. And I didn't want you to leave."

The words made Julian flinch slightly, and he gave an offended grunt. "I wouldn't leave you for asking questions," he said in a horrified voice as he focused on Cameron's face.

Cameron felt very small as they stood opposite each other. "I didn't want to risk it. You seemed so sure about walking away that night in the hospital, remember?"

Julian winced again and looked away, seemingly oblivious of the tiny dogs struggling to climb up his legs. He looked back at Cameron and shook his head. "I'm sorry," he repeated regretfully. "I'd hoped that I could shield you from my life. That you understood the implications of being involved with me, what the consequences might be. I thought I could protect you. I made a mistake."

They stood silent for long moments before Cameron spoke. "Do I need protecting?"

"Not now," Julian answered confidently. "Not yet. That's why I had to behave as if I didn't know you, to keep it that way."

Cameron's fingers reached up to his own throat, to finger the chain of the necklace hanging there, just under his shirt collar. The warrior's cross, meant to protect the wearer. Julian sounded certain about what he was saying, and it eased Cameron's fears a little. "So you were protecting me," he said slowly.

Julian's eyes drifted down to the necklace, and then he looked back up and met Cameron's eyes silently, not answering.

Cameron studied him as he slowly calmed down. "There's so much I don't know about you," he pointed out almost accusingly.

Julian pressed his lips together, and he nodded again. "I'll tell you almost anything you want to know," he offered resignedly. "But you've got to be aware of the danger in knowing."

"Danger? There's always danger, Julian," Cameron responded, his voice sad and resigned. "Even if you're a normal, unremarkable waiter like me. You can be mugged at gunpoint. You can catch pneumonia and die. You can be hit by a bus on your way to buy groceries. Lately, I've thought the worst danger would be having my heart broken."

Julian was silent for a moment. "Ouch," he finally observed in a hurt voice.

Cameron rubbed his eyes and abruptly turned and walked toward the kitchen, where he pulled out a bottle of wine and two glasses, setting them apart from each other. He braced his hands on the bar for a long moment before he opened the bottle with jerky movements and filled the glasses.

"Cameron," Julian murmured worriedly as he followed hesitantly.

The glass tipped back for a small swallow, and Cameron's gaze returned to Julian. He had to ask. He had to know. "Do you love me, Julian?"

Julian's eyes flickered as he watched Cameron. "Yes," he said with certainty.

Cameron's eyes didn't move. "Are you going to leave me because loving me is dangerous?"

Julian blinked rapidly and visibly fought the urge to shuffle his feet. "No," he answered. "Not unless you ask me to," he amended softly.

Cameron watched him speculatively before he set down his glass and gestured to the other one. "Then take off your coat and have some wine."

Julian watched him carefully and then slowly began to move. He shrugged out of his coat, draped it over the back of a chair, and walked to the kitchen to look at Cameron across the bar. "I don't really need anything to drink tonight," he said with a wince.

"Had a bad night, did you?" Cameron asked in a hard voice.

Julian raised his head and met Cameron's eyes, not answering with words or his expression.

Cameron snorted at him. "Why'd you shave?" he asked with a wave of the bottle as he started to refill his own glass.

Julian licked his lips thoughtfully and then looked down at the counter. "Just time for a change," he answered softly. "Do you want me to grow it back?" he asked as he looked back up.

Cameron tipped his head to one side, focusing on the man across from him. "I'll think about it," he said. "What's your favorite color?"

"You," Julian answered immediately.

Cameron's brows jerked up. "What?"

Julian smiled and lowered his head. "Green," he answered seriously.

Cameron smiled a little. "Where are you from?"

"Just outside of Topeka," Julian answered without hesitation. "Kansas."

Cameron nodded and took another sip of wine. That explained Julian's complete lack of any accent. It also probably meant that all the culture and polish he exuded was self-taught. Cameron found himself impressed just by that little fact. He searched for more questions to ask. "Did you go to college?"

"Several," Julian answered with a growing smirk.

Cameron smiled wryly. "Yeah, I figured." He paused. Now that Julian was actually answering his questions, he couldn't seem to come up with any to ask. "Do you really not like my dogs?"

Julian huffed softly and looked away, watching as the dogs romped. "I… They're always a welcome sight."

Cameron's nose wrinkled. "I think you might be stretching the truth there a little."

"Yes," Julian admitted with a nod.

"But you'll tolerate them."

"Yes," Julian agreed with a suddenly tentative smile.

"They won't get much bigger. A couple pounds, maybe," Cameron explained. "Eight each, tops."

"Projectile size," Julian murmured with a glance at the dogs again. Cameron's eyes narrowed in warning, but Julian just smiled at him innocently. "I would never projectile your dogs," he promised. "Not on purpose, anyway," he amended.

Cameron snorted softly and took another sip of wine. "Are you always so soft-spoken because of your work?"

Julian blinked at him in confusion. "I… I don't think so," he stammered.

"What? You didn't realize?" Cameron asked with an amused smile. "You're so quiet most of the time, even when you're talking to me. The loudest I hear you is when you're fucking me as hard as you can."

Julian actually blushed and looked away. It was much more obvious now that he was clean-shaven. He cleared his throat. "I've never really thought about it," he admitted with an embarrassed shrug.

Cameron watched him for a long moment, taking a couple long swallows of wine. "Do you like your job?" It was an echo of the question Julian had asked him months ago.

Julian hesitated only briefly before nodding. "I'm good at it," he claimed in a voice that was barely there.

"What are you always writing in that notebook of yours?" Cameron asked, not allowing himself to linger on what being good at Julian's job entailed.

"Notes," Julian answered vaguely. "Notes for jobs and assignments," he clarified as he dug out the little moleskin notebook from an inner pocket and set it on the counter between them. He left his fingers resting on top of it. "Sometimes I work things out better if I put them in front of me, instead of letting them rattle around in my head."

Cameron looked down at the notebook, then up at Julian warily.

"You can read it, if you want," Julian offered quietly, and he slid the notebook across the counter and removed his hand. "There are things you may not want to see."

Cameron shook his head and gently pushed the notebook back toward Julian, who picked it up and slid it under his lapel into the pocket once more. Cameron argued with himself about the next question, but asked anyway. "Do you know things about me that I haven't told you?"

Julian looked at him thoughtfully for a long time. "That's a hard question to answer," he murmured finally.

Cameron suddenly felt very uncomfortable. What if there was something about *him* in that notebook? "Hard because you can't? Or hard because you won't?" he asked, one hand gripping the edge of the counter.

"Hard because if I say no, I'd be lying, and if I tell you yes, you'll assume the worst," Julian answered bluntly. "I know that you tug at your ear when you're nervous. I know that you talk in your sleep. I know that you like to fix my tie for me, even though you fuss about it. I know a lot of things about you that you haven't told me."

Cameron kept his hand clamped on the counter to keep from lifting it to tug at his ear just as Julian said he would. He looked at his lover evenly, a little annoyance creeping into his eyes. “That’s a lovely, roundabout sort-of answer,” he said before sniffing. “I talk in my sleep?” he asked hesitantly.

Julian lowered his head. Disappointed that Cameron hadn’t reacted better to what he’d hoped would be something sort of romantic? Cameron couldn’t tell. Then Julian sighed and looked back up, nodding.

Cameron glanced at the ceiling. “I’m not so sure I like that,” he muttered. “There’s no telling what I’m saying to you.” Then he stiffened. God, all the things he worried about happening to Julian, wondering what he would do if Julian didn’t come back, what he could do to keep the other man’s attention… did he voice those worries at night?

“Mostly you try to take my order and tell me to clear tables,” Julian told him, trying not to smile.

Head snapping up, Cameron looked at his lover, appalled. “No, I do *not*!”

Julian smiled and shrugged lopsidedly. “I’ve heard worse.”

Cameron narrowed his eyes, realizing he’d been pulled off track. He sighed and filled up his glass, though Julian’s still stood untouched. Julian was obviously a lot better at talking around things than he himself was. If he wanted to hide something from Cameron, he could probably do it without Cameron ever knowing. It was a sobering, depressing thought.

“What’s my favorite color?” he asked.

Julian gave a slight smile and glanced at the puppies. “Green?” he guessed as he studied them.

Cameron followed Julian’s gaze and smiled slightly as he shook his head. It was a valid guess, he supposed. The dog’s collars were blue, yellow, red, and white. No green to be found. Cameron figured a man like Julian wouldn’t be able to pick a particular dog to name after his favorite color, so he wouldn’t use that color at all. Julian was using that logic and applying it to Cameron. It was sweet, in a way, and Cameron had to fight not to kiss him for it.

"Where do you live?" he asked instead. "When you're not here with me?"

"At home," Julian answered as he looked back at Cameron. "What *is* your favorite color?" he asked curiously.

"I don't ask very good questions, do I?" Cameron muttered after drinking down almost half his glass again. He looked back up at Julian. In answer to his question, Cameron pulled open the collar of his shirt with one hand and brushed his fingers over the garnet stone in the pendant.

Julian's eyes followed the movement and then drifted back up to Cameron's in surprise. "You just need to be more specific," he murmured in answer to the question Cameron had posed.

Cameron wondered why Julian looked mildly shocked, and he kept his fingers on the pendant, stroking the stone warmed by his skin. His brow wrinkled as he tried to frame his next question. "More specific," he murmured. He raised speculative eyes to Julian's. "Will you take me home with you someday?"

Julian blinked at him and hesitated. "You'd want to see where I live?" he asked uncertainly.

"Yes," Cameron answered, tilting his head as he looked at him. "Is that a problem?" Julian looked down, obviously trying to think it through or stall before giving an answer. Brows raising, Cameron took another big drink of wine and set down the mostly empty glass with a clink to fill it back up. Julian's pause was not reassuring. "Is there someone else living there?" he asked, his confidence bolstered by the wine and growing unease. "Boyfriend? Girlfriend? Wife?" he asked pointedly.

Julian looked up quickly. "What?" he asked in shock.

Cameron took his time filling up his glass yet again. "It's a yes-or-no question, Julian. Actually, they both are. Pretty specific ones," he rambled a little before unconsciously raising a hand to squeeze the back of his neck and pull at his ear.

"You think I'm married?" Julian asked, his voice rising unusually high.

"Right now I don't know what to think. But I do know you well enough to know that if you were going to say no, you'd have said it immediately," Cameron claimed, waiting to see if Julian contradicted him.

Julian stared at him incredulously. "What, you think just because you hit someone with a hammer, they're going to immediately say 'ow'?" he asked.

"I need more wine," Cameron muttered, filling up his half-empty glass. "You act like two totally different people sometimes, you know that?"

"What?" Julian repeated helplessly.

"All right." Cameron said sharply, setting down his glass. "Set my mind at ease, one way or the other. Do you live with anyone else besides me on a regular basis?"

"No," Julian answered with obvious pain in his voice. He stopped suddenly and his brow furrowed as he looked down. "Unless you count Preston," he corrected.

"Preston? Who's Preston?"

"My driver," Julian said as he looked back up at Cameron almost pleadingly, the hurt still showing in the set of his shoulders. "What sort of person do you think I am?" he asked.

Cameron slumped and leaned over to hide his head in his arms on the bar. "You're upset with me," came out muffled.

"How long have you wondered if I was married?" Julian asked without responding to the statement. "First I was some sort of… man-whore; now I'm some asshole cheating on his wife? What else do you think of me, Cameron?"

Head snapping up, Cameron decided he was angry more than anything else. "I don't know what I think of you, Julian! You never talk about yourself! I can't do anything but guess!" His wine-fueled bravado suddenly waned, and he just stopped talking. "I've had too much to drink," he mumbled, pushing the glass away and moving to cork the bottle.

Julian stood at the counter, staring at him and waffling between appearing angry and hurt. "Fine," he breathed after a few tense moments of silence. "Get your fucking coat on," he ordered as he reached into his pocket for his phone.

Cameron looked up from the bottle. Resignation was clear on his face; he knew he'd not just upset Julian. He'd made him angry. One part of him was amazed to get a new reaction out of his lover. He'd never seen him truly angry before. The rest of him just hurt and ached and sort of wanted to cry. "Why?" he found himself asking.

"Because I fucking told you to," Julian snapped as he held the phone to his ear. He barked Cameron's address and then jabbed the phone off angrily.

Cameron blinked in surprise at Julian for a few heartbeats before thoughtlessly moving to obey. He scooted around the bar and out into the living room to get his coat. Julian muttered to himself as Cameron moved and then began stalking toward the door.

"Make sure the dogs have food," Julian said as he yanked the door open.

Cameron did what he was told quickly as Julian, practically vibrating with anger, waited silently. Cameron thought he might understand how Julian scared Miri, but despite how angry Julian looked and acted, Cameron didn't feel threatened. More upset with himself and ashamed than anything. He swiped his keys off the small table at the door and stopped an arm's length away from the other man.

Julian stared at him without saying a word. Finally, he let his eyes travel up and down Cameron and then met his eyes. "Ready?" he asked in the same low, quiet voice he always used at the restaurant. He seemed deceptively calm again.

Frowning a little, Cameron wondered where all the anger had gone so quickly. "Yes," he murmured. Julian reached out and took his upper arm, his fingers digging into the muscle as he ushered Cameron out into the hall and closed the door with a bang behind him. He pulled him toward the stairs without another word.

Cameron didn't resist as he shuffled along beside Julian, except to crane his neck back to make sure there wasn't a white puffball trailing along behind them in the hallway. He realized that the anger wasn't gone; it was just expertly masked. The fact that Julian could veil it so well bothered him more than Julian being angry in the first place. How many other times had Julian been feeling some emotion that he had suppressed and so easily hidden? The thought was disconcerting.

They stepped out of the building into the cold night just as a black Lexus pulled up in front of the building. Julian gestured to it with a low growl and moved Cameron toward the back door. Cameron glanced from Julian to the car and back, nearly stumbling into the side of the Lexus as Julian directed him along with the hand clamped around his upper arm.

Julian yanked open the back door before the driver could even get out of the car, and the blond man quietly sank back into the driver's seat after one look at Julian. Julian growled at him and shoved Cameron into the back-seat roughly, climbing in beside him and pulling the door shut with an unsatisfying muffled thump.

"Home," he ordered curtly, and the car pulled away from the curb.

Knowing better than to open his mouth, Cameron glanced from Julian to the driver—Preston?—and then out the window. He knew without a doubt that he didn't want to make Julian any angrier than he already was. As much control as Julian had over his emotions, he had to be furious to be displaying even this much. Cameron wasn't sure what he thought about the fact that it had taken getting Julian this angry to find out something concrete about him.

The city flew by in the night, eventually thinning into an old neighborhood full of refurbished turn-of-the-century mansions. The car turned into a hidden drive protected by a great stone archway and iron gate, and Preston reached out the window and slid a card past a sensor discreetly positioned near the shrubbery. The gate swung open on well-oiled hinges, and the silent driver pulled the car through and drove up to the front of the house. The Tudor house at the head of the circular drive wasn't large by the standards of the neighborhood, but it looked somehow foreboding. It was the house on the block that kids skipped at Halloween.

Julian sat with his head bowed and his eyes closed. After a few moments of idling in the driveway, he raised his head and stared directly ahead. "Home," he announced to Cameron quietly.

Cameron had already been staring out the window with wide eyes, which he now turned on Julian. No wonder the other man stayed with him only one or occasionally two nights a week. With this incredible house to come back to, why stay in an old, converted warehouse condo? Cameron suddenly felt his simple, lower-class lifestyle very keenly.

Julian glanced over at him carefully, almost visibly forcing the anger away. "Do you want to come in?" he asked softly.

Cameron turned his chin to look out the window at the imposing house again. His hands clenched in his coat pockets, and he shook his head jerkily. "I… I don't belong here," he whispered, feeling very uncomfortable.

"Does it matter to you that I love you?" Julian asked as he looked away and up at the house.

Cameron stared at Julian, wishing he could see his lover's eyes. "It's the most precious thing in my world," he answered brokenly.

"Then why can't you believe the same of me?" Julian asked softly.

Pain cut through Cameron deeply enough that he flinched and had to look out the other window to blink away the wet in his eyes. "I'm sorry," he whispered. "I just have a hard time understanding what someone with a life like this," he nodded out the window, "could see in someone like me."

"You were happier when it was just me and you in your condo," Julian murmured with a nod as he looked up at the house sadly.

Cameron grunted in frustration. "You knew I'd feel this way," he realized out loud. "You always know," he said bitterly as he kept his eyes trained on the house. "You know me better than I know myself. Am I really so predictable?" he asked plaintively.

"You're anything but predictable," Julian muttered irritably.

Cameron couldn't help but look back at Julian as one of his hands flew to cover his mouth and muffle a strained laugh.

"See?" Julian groaned and rubbed his eyes.

Cameron's answer was muffled until he moved his hand and repeated himself. "See what?" He glanced out the window yet again. "I feel like Little Orphan Annie," he muttered under his breath.

"Shut the hell up and get out of the car," Julian grumbled as he pulled the handle and pushed open his door.

Cameron bit his lip and followed, stopping once he was standing to let his eyes track all the way up the façade of the house. "You live here alone? In this huge house?"

"The wife and kids live in that wing," Julian deadpanned as he waved his arm carelessly to the left.

Cameron blinked at him, taken aback until Julian rolled his eyes and shook his head impatiently as he turned to start up the steps.

"I deserved that," Cameron muttered as he walked up the stairs next to Julian.

"Yes," Julian agreed coldly as he stopped at the front door and fished out his keys.

Cameron shifted his weight nervously from foot to foot, especially once Preston drove the car away. In the dark, Julian almost looked like a stranger, and Cameron wanted very much to touch him, to reassure himself that this was his lover, the man who held him at night, and not some angry shadow of a man he didn't recognize.

Julian unlocked the large front door and pushed it open, turning to look back at Cameron in the welcoming light that streamed out of the foyer. He was quiet for a long moment, and then said, "You wanted me to take you home," he murmured to him. "So… come home with me."

Tipping his head, Cameron looked at him intently before one corner of his mouth curled up. "I thought you were going to get on your knees and beg me there for a minute." He took a half-step toward the threshold.

Julian growled and reached out, grabbing him with the same force he'd used earlier and yanking him into the house before slamming the door closed behind them. He kissed Cameron hard in the middle of the massive foyer, holding him tightly so he couldn't get away.

Cameron gasped against Julian's lips and clutched at his shoulders as he was overwhelmed. Julian had brought all his strength to bear upon him and he couldn't resist. He draped himself against his lover, trying to kiss him back, to take part in the consuming kiss.

When Julian released him, Cameron allowed himself to look around dazedly. He jumped slightly when he noticed a nondescript man in a dark suit standing unobtrusively at the base of the staircase, his hands behind his back.

"Will that be all, sir?" the man asked Julian.

Julian didn't tear his eyes from Cameron's face as he waved the man off.

"Very well, sir," the man drawled. Cameron could see the amusement in the butler's expression as he turned and quietly disappeared into the inner reaches of the house.

Cameron opened his mouth to speak, but Julian kissed him again and cut off his words. Seconds later, Julian pulled away from him and met his eyes intently for a few moments, then began heading for the stairs, Cameron's elbow firmly in his grasp. Cameron followed obediently, trying not to gape at his surroundings. Julian took him up to the first landing, where a hallway broke off and led them to a pair of double doors. Beyond was a relatively small bedroom that took up one of the house's turrets.

Julian pulled Cameron inside and flipped on the lights. It was simple and sparse with nothing but a four-poster canopy bed against one wall and a sitting area in a bay window that curved in the turret's shape. A flat-screen television hung on another wall, and there were two very large, long-haired orange cats sitting side by side on the bed staring at them with matching green eyes.

Cameron cast his gaze around the room and came to settle on the two cats. "You *do* live with somebody. Somebodies!" he said in mock accusation.

Julian cleared his throat as one of the cats stood and stretched languidly, then fluffed his long fur and jumped off the bed with an audible thump before prowling toward them. "That's Wesson," Julian muttered with a point of his finger. He nodded at the cat still on the bed and said, "And that's Smith."

Cameron stifled a laugh and watched them guardedly as Wesson stalked toward them. They were perhaps the largest cats Cameron had ever seen. They had to have been half-lion. He edged slightly behind Julian. "They look—" He cleared his throat. "Um. Not very friendly?"

"No, no. They're completely evil," Julian assured him as he bent and picked up the cat that was winding around his ankles. The cat was massive. Cameron thought it had to weigh at least twenty pounds, and then the long fur made it look twice its already impressive size. It hung over Julian's large shoulder, making the big man look like a child trying to drag an oversized teddy bear. It was purring so loudly Cameron could hear it just fine without moving closer, and it stared at Cameron with the same blank, knowing expression its master always had. More than ever before, Julian's mannerisms struck Cameron as being like those of a very large cat. Perhaps he spent too much time with these two beasts.

Julian gave Wesson a squeeze, and the cat let out a low, throaty meow of complaint before Julian snickered and set the cat down again.

"You live with these two monsters, and you can't like my *little bitty* dogs?" Cameron asked incredulously.

"My cats would turn your dogs into hairballs," Julian scoffed affectionately.

Cameron crossed his arms. It seemed his easy-going lover was back… for the moment. "Well, you've got four dogs at my place who are head over heels in love with you. And these… cats. And they are the only ones I'm willing to share with," he said seriously.

"You think I might have someone else?" Julian asked in a hard voice as the cat jumped back up onto the bed and turned to watch them. "You think I lied when I told you I loved you?"

Cameron studied Julian's face. He could clearly see the frustration there. He shook his head. "I don't think so," he said. Then his own frustration broke free. "But can't you understand where I'm coming from? You never show me anything! Tonight is the first time I've seen you angry, for God's sake!"

Julian's jaw clenched. "You've not seen me angry," he said in a low, calm voice.

Cameron's lips compressed, and as he shook his head, he held out both hands in a sharp movement, as if to say, '*Well, see?*' "Why is pulling information out of you like pulling teeth?" he asked in frustration.

"Cameron, what will it take for you to realize I'm trying to keep you away from something ugly?" Julian asked quietly as he lifted one hand to take Cameron's chin. "I don't want you to see the world like I see it. What is it that you want so badly?"

"I want to know you," Cameron answered, a little desperation in his voice. "I want to *know* you," he whispered as the upset choked him and threatened to spill over.

Julian's expression softened, and he moved the two steps to close his arms around Cameron and pull him close. Cameron clutched at his arms with trembling hands as his heart pounded with fear—fear that the time had come and Julian would put him aside.

But the large arms surrounding him didn't move, and then he felt Julian press a kiss to the side of his head. Cameron closed his eyes and held on tight. "I love you, Julian," he said clearly.

"I know."

THE knock came at Cameron's door early one Friday morning. Earlier than usual, but Julian was nothing if not unpredictable when he wanted to be. The puppy procession made its noisy way to the door, hopping and jumping like crazed dust mops. Cameron shook his head and shooed them out of the way so he could look out the peephole. He opened the door in surprise.

"Preston?" he asked tentatively.

"Good morning, sir," the man greeted with a slight nod of his head. He was dressed in his usual well-tailored suit, just like his boss always was, and his closely cropped white-blond hair was sprinkled with snowflakes that hadn't quite melted yet. He didn't seem to notice them.

"Would you be so kind as to come with me, sir?" he asked Cameron politely.

"Come with you?" Cameron tipped his head to one side. It had to have something to do with Julian. A niggle of fear mixed with curiosity began to grow in his chest. "Ah, sure," he said anyway, knowing any questions he had wouldn't be answered even if he voiced them. "I just need to get some shoes and a jacket," he said as he kept blocking the puppies with one foot. "Do you want to come in?"

"Thank you, sir. I'll wait here," Preston assured him with another tip of his head and a neutral smile.

Cameron nodded slowly. "Sure. I'll be right back." He pushed the door shut and got his coat and running shoes. He was already in jeans and a sweatshirt; they would do. Julian seemed to prefer him in such everyday clothes. He had yet to figure out why, but he suspected it had something to do with Julian almost always having to wear such formal, expensive clothing.

He checked the dogs' food bowls, gave them treats, and grabbed his keys as he reopened the door. "Okay, I'm ready."

Preston didn't say another word. He merely nodded and turned on his heel, looking disturbingly military when he did it, and led the way down the stairs to the car that waited. He opened the rear door for Cameron and stood rigidly beside it.

Cameron paused for a moment, but shrugged off the weird feeling and climbed in. "Thank you," he said, wondering what was going on. Julian wasn't in the car like Cameron had expected him to be, and Preston offered no explanation as he slid into the driver's seat and started the car. As he pulled out into the heavy traffic, his ice-blue eyes slid sideways to check Cameron in the rearview mirror, and he gave him what could have been meant to be a reassuring smile.

The driver reminded Cameron a lot of Julian. They looked nothing alike, obviously. Where Julian was large and bulky, Preston was wiry and hard-looking. Where Julian was dark and warm, Preston was pale and cool. But they had the same capable, unflappable air to them. Cameron was almost certain, as he watched Preston, that there was some sort of military training behind it. He knew Blake had been a medic in some branch of the military years ago. Perhaps that was how they all knew one another. He would have to come up with the nerve to ask Julian.

Relaxing a bit into the luxurious seat, Cameron turned his eyes to watch the city pass by. It wasn't long before the built-up areas began to fade away, replaced by the large old homes Cameron remembered from his last trip in Julian's Lexus.

This time, in the daylight, he could see more, and the sight was even more impressive. He'd never seen houses like this in his life, even on television. It occurred to him that Julian must not be just well-off, but extremely wealthy. Just the property taxes on these places would drain most people's bank accounts in no time, Cameron was sure. He shook his head. It just didn't seem like Julian to be… posh. He wasn't. He was just Julian.

Soon enough, Preston pulled up to the iron gate that protected Julian's driveway. He rolled down the window, letting in some chilly morning air and a few stray snowflakes as he swiped the card that sent the gate sliding open. When he pulled up to the front of the house, he hopped out quickly and came around to open Cameron's door wordlessly.

Cameron climbed out and stood quietly as Preston shut the door and started up the steps. He figured he'd better follow, and he had to hop quickly to catch up. Preston ushered him into the large foyer, and the door shut behind them with a foreboding echo.

"This way, please," Preston requested, and he made his way toward the massive staircase.

On more familiar ground, Cameron followed him up the stairs and down the hall to Julian's little suite of rooms, brow furrowing along the way. "Preston, what's—"

"He doesn't exactly know I went to get you, sir," Preston answered with a twitch of his lips that betrayed some amusement. "I'm not even sure he's aware today is Friday," he confided as they got to the set of closed heavy double doors of Julian's bedroom.

Cameron's eyes widened. "Aware… What's going on? What happened?"

Preston actually smirked, a reaction he obviously tried to suppress. He reached over and shoved the doors open, and he waved Cameron into the room.

The curtains in Julian's bedroom were drawn, and the little bit of dull morning sunlight managing to leak around the edges was the only light in the room. It was still easy enough to make out the two huge cats on the bed, their tails flipping in annoyance at the disturbance. Beneath them, under a quilt and several pillows, was a lump that had to be Julian, curled on his side and unmoving.

"Is… is he okay?" Cameron asked shakily, trying very hard not to run right to the bed.

In response, Preston cleared his throat against a slight laugh. The figure in the bed groaned and shifted just enough to disturb the cats, who both meowed plaintively as their tails twitched harder.

"Preston," Julian's hoarse voice said from under one of the pillows. "Please kill me," he requested miserably.

"I'm sorry, sir, but that will have to wait. You have a visitor," Preston responded with a grin at Cameron. He nodded his head, urging him to go further into the room.

The unusual humor from Preston got a half-smile out of Cameron, and he shook his head as he walked over to the bed and sat on the edge, trying not to disturb the nearby cats. "Julian?"

Julian shifted slightly under the quilt, and his hand moved slowly to push the edge of a pillow up to reveal one dark eye blinking up at Cameron blearily.

"Cameron?" he asked in confusion, his voice almost comically muffled by his quilt.

"Yeah," Cameron said quietly, reaching to pull the quilt down slightly. He pushed the pillow away from Julian's head and smoothed back his hair. He was pale under the flush of what was probably a fever. "What's wrong?" Cameron asked worriedly.

Julian answered with a plaintive groan and closed his eyes. "I'm dying," he answered, his voice just on the verge of a whine. "What are you doing here?" he asked with the oddest hint of hope in his voice.

"Ah, I'm not really sure?" Cameron tried, glancing to Preston.

"You asked me to bring him, sir," Preston offered helpfully. "Don't you remember?" he asked, barely restraining a laugh as he turned and left the room, closing the doors behind him.

"I did?" Julian asked Cameron as he opened his eyes again and blinked slowly. At the end of the bed, one of the cats stood and stretched languidly before it began stalking his way slowly toward Cameron.

"Julian—" Cameron looked from the door to the cat to his lover and back to the cat, just in case. He had only had one experience with the two animals, but he had seen just how mean and possessive they actually were. He thought he'd be safe as long as he didn't move closer to Julian. "What's wrong?" he asked. "Are you sick?" He laid a hand against Julian's forehead. He felt fevered as well as looking it, and Cameron frowned harder.

"They shot me," Julian answered, his voice actually cracking and ending in a squeak.

Cameron blinked. "Shot? Again?"

Julian shook his head and groaned, beginning to struggle to drag the quilt off his shoulders. When he pulled it all the way down, Cameron could see his bare shoulder and chest were clearly bruised and battered, with several red welts that looked like scratches that hadn't quite broken the skin. His forearms were bandaged heavily and his hands were bruised and badly scratched. On the upper part of his right arm was a single Care Bears Band-Aid, and he pointed at it petulantly with the other hand.

"Shot," he spat as he pointed at it again emphatically.

Cameron stared at the Band-Aid for a long moment and then bit his bottom lip. Now, he knew why Preston was trying so hard not to laugh. “That’s just… terrible,” he managed to get out before he had to clamp his lips shut again.

The cat began to walk his way up Julian’s body, crouching on his master’s hip as Julian waved his hand. His tail twitched back and forth, sliding against Cameron’s arm as it did so.

“It’s not funny,” Julian insisted miserably. “Bad kitty!” he shouted suddenly, just before the cat pounced on him, batting at the whites of the bandages on Julian’s waving fingers and then attacking his face and biting Julian’s chin before hopping to the other side of the bed to lick himself clean.

Cameron couldn’t help it. His laughter rang out, and he almost fell off the bed as Julian burrowed back under his bedcovers for protection. There was another tussle as the other cat joined in, pouncing on Julian’s feet as he moved beneath the covers.

“Bad kitties,” Julian muttered pitifully.

Smiling, Cameron watched his normally stoic lover so helpless and pitiful, and he found it oddly endearing. He savored it. “You’re not feeling that bad,” he remarked. “Not if you’re wrestling with those monsters.”

“They’re evil,” Julian insisted as he tucked his toes under Wesson’s loudly purring body, causing the cat to give a throaty meow of complaint.

“But you love them,” Cameron pointed out in amusement.

Julian sighed tiredly and closed his eyes, his body relaxing and going limp in the bed. “How can two tiny little shots make your entire body so bloody sore?” he asked Cameron miserably as his words slurred together.

Cameron bit his lip. “What sort of shots did they give you?” he asked in a voice that wavered with amusement.

“Tetanus and rabies,” Julian answered grumpily. His accent began to morph into something that sounded almost foreign. As if there was a hint of New England to it, maybe. "Fucking rabies. Like I'm a fucking dog."

Cameron bit his lips hard to keep from laughing. "Anything I can do to help?" he asked after he was sure he could form the words.

"No," Julian groaned. "My arm hurts. My leg hurts. My head hurts. My ass hurts," he rattled off in complaint as he fussed with his pillow and wallowed miserably.

Shaking his head tolerantly, Cameron reached out to comb his fingers through Julian's hair. "Poor baby. Your ass hurts, and I didn't even get to contribute."

"I can't believe he brought you here," Julian grumbled against his pillow.

Cameron frowned. "He said you asked him to."

"He's a lying bastard," Julian claimed grumpily. "Why would I want you to see me like this?" he asked as he finally looked up at Cameron with glazed black eyes.

"Why wouldn't you? You've seen me a hell of a lot worse," Cameron said, frowning slightly. He leaned over to kiss the corner of Julian's eye. "You don't have to be Mr. Tough Guy all the time."

"Yes, but…" Julian groaned softly and shifted in bed. "I'm cranky," he admitted. "And drugged," he added with a point of one long, scarred finger toward a bottle of painkillers on the bedside table.

"You're allowed," Cameron said as he cocked his head at the bottle. He shifted slightly. "You really want me to go?"

Julian looked up at him again and pursed his lips, frowning. "Not really," he answered finally. "If you lift my arm for me I might hug you," he added with a small smile.

Cameron stood up, kicked off his shoes, and climbed onto the bed next to Julian. He stayed sitting up and leaned against the headboard. "C'mere and let me hold you," he suggested. "I promise I won't tell."

Julian looked around warily as if not quite trusting the situation. Cameron didn't imagine Julian got many offers of comfort when he was miserable like this. He struggled to push himself up from the mattress, the muscles in his back and left arm bunching with the extra effort, and he held his right arm to his body protectively as he slid a little on the bed. When he moved, the sheets fell down even more, revealing a large piece of gauze taped to his lower thigh, just above his knee. It was stark white against his skin, with a hint of red spreading through the center. He lowered himself slowly and laid his cheek on Cameron's thigh with a sound that was nearly a whimper.

Cameron sighed and shook his head slightly as he rubbed one hand up and down Julian's back slowly, the other beginning to twirl through his hair. "You're bleeding," he murmured sadly. "What really happened, Julian?"

"There wasn't supposed to be a dog," Julian insisted gruffly.

"A dog?" Cameron looked at the bandages and then at Julian's arm. "You got attacked by a dog? Seriously? Was it Cujo?"

"It was a big dog," Julian insisted. He pointed at his bite wound and displayed the defensive marks on his arms. The teeth appeared to have sunk into the muscle of his quad and taken out a chunk of it before the dog went for his throat. He'd gotten his arms up in time, and they'd taken the punishment meant for his jugular. "He didn't even have to stand on his tip-toes," he insisted as his eyes seemed to close against his will.

Cameron petted him soothingly. "I'm sure he was very big. And scary," he murmured. It was on the tip of his tongue to question Julian further, but he couldn't do it. Not when Julian was so obviously not in control of his senses.

"There wasn't supposed to be a dog," Julian repeated slowly. "They had to know there was a dog," he muttered to himself. "That's something you're supposed to tell people."

Cameron had no idea what to say, and none of what Julian was telling him was making much sense to him. "Shhhh," he urged softly. "Sleep." He kept petting gently.

"I think they tried to kill me, Cam," Julian mumbled, using Cameron's nickname for the first time that Cameron had ever heard. "Death by dog. Big-ass fucking dog."

Both Cameron's brows rose, and he chewed his lip again. Julian had to be talking about work. Nothing else made sense. "Who would think that would kill you, Julian? You're better than any dog." Okay, so, he had no idea what he was talking about. But he believed in Julian's skill, nonetheless.

"He was like Rin Tin Tin on speed," Julian said, his words running even more. "Preston wouldn't shoot him."

"Well," Cameron said, face screwing up, "I'm not sure I could shoot a dog either."

"He was eating me!" Julian insisted pitifully. "I had to get a shot! Two shots! And I have to go back for more rabies shots! I'm probably going to wake up with fur," he claimed, his oddly accented words beginning to truly slur with exhaustion and misery on top of the effects of the medication.

"So did you shoot him?" Cameron asked awkwardly before running his fingers across Julian's cheek.

"No," Julian answered grudgingly. "He was just doing his job," he sighed, as if that was the only thing he could say to console himself for not killing the animal that mauled him. "Preston fired into the air, and it scared him. The dog, not Preston. And then he ran off to go find Blake and left me there. Bleeding. Preston did. Not the dog," he told Cameron very seriously. "And then Blake laughed at me."

Cameron covered his mouth, shaking with silent laughter.

"I think they set me up," Julian said suddenly. He opened his eyes and blinked rapidly. "There was nothing there but a dog."

Cameron frowned, his laughter dying. "Julian?" His lover didn't talk about his work except in the vaguest of terms with him. He didn't want Julian to be angry later because he'd allowed him to ramble like this.

"Hmm?" Julian responded dazedly.

"Do you know what you're talking about?" Cameron asked tentatively.

"Usually," Julian answered in an innocent voice.

Cameron snorted. “What about now?”

“I’m pretty sure. There was nothing but a dog,” Julian answered in the same tone.

“Right.” Cameron shook his head. Cameron knew Julian wouldn’t want him to hear him like this. “All right. Time to sleep, lover,” he murmured.

Julian’s eyes closed obediently, and his fingers tightened against the fabric of Cameron’s jeans. “It’s changing, Cameron,” he murmured. “They’re starting to eat their own.”

Cameron really hoped Julian wasn’t talking about dogs. “Just be careful,” he whispered, starting to pet Julian’s hair again. It sounded like Julian was being threatened, and that hit Cameron in the gut.

Julian was silent, his breathing even and steady for several minutes. He opened his eyes again slowly. “Would you ever leave Chicago?” he asked softly. His words were still slow, but he was obviously putting more effort into making sense.

“Never really thought about it,” Cameron admitted as he peered down at Julian. He’d thought the other man had finally fallen asleep. “I’ve lived here all my life, and I’ve had no reason to leave. Why?”

Julian stared off into the distance for a long, silent moment before closing his eyes again. “My arm hurts,” he finally murmured in place of an answer.

Confused, Cameron let it go, instead shushing him gently again. “Go to sleep. It’ll be better in the morning.”

“No, it won’t,” Julian practically whined. “They hurt for fucking days.”

Cameron sighed. “I guess you’ve had a tetanus shot before, huh? Are you sure I can’t get you anything to help?”

“They gave me painkillers,” Julian answered slowly, as if measuring his words now to keep from slurring. He’d apparently forgotten he’d already told Cameron that. “Preston left an hour ago to get me ice,” he added. “Ice!” he suddenly shouted accusingly at the closed double doors, and then he buried his face against Cameron's thigh and groaned miserably.

"Were you this cranky when you really got shot?" Cameron asked, amusement tinting his voice.

"I really got shot this time," Julian insisted, his voice muffled.

"I mean shot-shot. With the gun," Cameron corrected patiently.

"Getting shot with a gun is easier," Julian claimed.

"Easier?" Cameron exclaimed in disbelief.

"People don't laugh at you when you get shot-shot," Julian spat as he raised his head.

"Julian," Cameron said quietly. "I don't want you hurt at all. I don't care if it's a gunshot wound or a paper cut."

"Paper cuts hurt too," Julian pointed out as his eyes closed once more.

"Yeah, I know," Cameron murmured, resigning himself to holding Julian for however long it took for him to get to sleep. "You going to rest or should I get Preston to bring you some ice?"

"Rest," Julian repeated obediently. "Cameron?" he added in a near whisper, his voice going hoarse in a manner reminiscent of the way he had spoken when he'd first said anything to him.

"Yeah?" Cameron brushed his fingers lightly over Julian's cheek.

"If I had to pick up and leave," Julian said in a hushed voice, "would you go with me?"

Cameron's pulse sped, and he had to draw in a long breath as several thoughts buzzed through his mind. But what it boiled down to was… he loved Julian. "Yeah. I think I would."

Julian's body seemed to relax slightly, and he sighed loudly. "Next time someone tries to kill me with a dog," he muttered.

Cameron smiled tremulously, glad Julian couldn't see it. "Okay," he breathed agreeably.

CAMERON took a couple vacation days from work and stayed at Julian's house most of that weekend, venturing out only to return to his place and feed the puppies. He found himself spending most of the time trying desperately not to laugh about how miserable Julian was because of his shots and the dog bites. There was something so wrong yet so funny about such a large, stoic man whimpering about being drugged and sore.

While Julian slept off the misery, Cameron spent the rest of his time trying not to piss off Smith and Wesson, trying to get Preston to say more than a few words at a time, and trying not to worry about the things Julian had said when he'd been suffering from the effects of the painkillers.

He'd also explored Julian's house a little, feeling almost like a small child who was up past his bedtime and snooping. He discovered there were a total of four people on staff at the house: Preston, the butler, a maid, and a cook. They were all friendly, if reserved.

On Monday Julian was up and about but doing nothing more intense than showing Cameron a secret passage that went from the study to the kitchen. It had made him laugh like a little kid as he showed Cameron how to get in and out of it.

They'd spoken no angry words, they'd not dealt with secrets or mysteries, and the most stressful thing they'd done was play with Smith and Wesson, an activity that often included screaming at the top of your lungs when one of the cats got tired of being poked and latched onto a toe or other suitably tender area.

It had been fun, spending time with Julian somewhere different but still *safe*. Thinking that, Cameron found himself more disturbed than ever.

BACK to work, Cameron smoothly delivered dinner to a couple dining out on a quiet Tuesday night, answering their questions about the gourmet selections and promising to check on them soon. When he returned to the service area, Miri was waiting for him. It was her first night back after a week off to visit her family.

"How was your weekend?" she asked him pointedly.

Cameron peered at her, wondering where the attitude was coming from. "It was fine. Quiet. I took the weekend off. How was your visit home?"

"Cam," she said in a low, serious voice. "Don't avoid the subject I'm tactfully trying to address, okay? Did you talk with him?"

"A little," Cameron admitted. Although he'd never minded Miri's curiosity before, now he was uneasy. Julian had been right all those months ago; she was damn nosy.

"And?" she prodded

"Look, I appreciate that you're concerned," Cameron said to her in growing annoyance. He'd just gotten comfortable with Julian again. He didn't need Miri bringing up more tricky questions. "But it's really not any of your business who he is or what he does."

Miri narrowed her eyes and looked at him closely. "Did you even ask him who he is?" she asked after a moment of studying him.

"I know who he is," Cameron said quietly. "He's my lover, and that's enough for me."

Miri sighed and closed her eyes as another waiter brushed past them carrying a large tray. She waited until they were alone once more and stepped closer to Cameron. "Is he married?" she asked worriedly.

"No!" Cameron said. "He's not married, he's not closeted, he's not a crook, and he's not a danger to me," he told her, repeating himself diligently.

"He broke his arm that one time and gets all those bruises from dealing antiques?" Miri asked flatly.

"He kickboxes," Cameron told her, shocking himself with the lie that came so quickly to his lips. "Look, just drop it, okay?" he asked in a pained voice as he threw down his towel in frustration. "I'm happy right now. Can't you be satisfied with that?"

She winced and reached out and took his hand gently. "I want you to be happy," she insisted. "But what sort of relationship can you possibly have if you know nothing about him?" she asked. "He's the big, bad rich guy, and you're the poor little waiter he keeps on the side?"

Cameron sighed in exasperation and turned away from her. Every time she questioned him, all his insecurities and worries flooded back, no matter how much he tried to remember Julian's soft words and reassurances. He stalked toward the employee workroom, knowing without a doubt that Miri would follow him.

She did, hustling after him and talking as she followed. "So far all I've seen is that he comes here every week and barely speaks to you, and when he was with people he knew, high-class type people, he *told* you not to speak to him, like he's embarrassed to be with you," she rambled. "Plus, you don't even know how to get in touch with him! You were at death's door, you were so sick that one time, and he didn't even know it!"

"He was out of town—" Cameron began to explain, but what Miri said was true. Julian hadn't ever offered a phone number, and Cameron knew why, at least vaguely. Julian was trying to protect him. Right?

"He wasn't out of town when you were sick," Miri muttered. "He was here, eating dinner with Blake. Another one of his high-class friends."

Cameron refused to answer until they were in the workroom with the door shut firmly behind them. "That's not how it is," he insisted. His voice was stronger now as he felt a flare of anger. He was angry because, deep down, he wasn't certain of anything he was defending. And he was scared. Scared of the secrets. Scared of what might happen. He wasn't even sure what else.

He'd seen Julian's temper. He'd seen Julian's strength; the quick bursts of speed and power he used to manhandle Cameron. And Cameron didn't even want to delve into the issue of how used to being in control Julian was. Cameron had never tried to take the reins, but would Julian even allow it if he did? To this point Cameron had never been afraid of Julian. But knowing the little he did now, he had to admit it would be easy to be scared.

Miri met his eyes worriedly. "I know you're head over heels, Cam," she said gently. "But can you really handle him?" she asked doubtfully. "I mean…"

Cameron practically sagged in front of her and leaned back against the wall, distraught. What little Julian had told him about what might happen swirled in his mind. He knew, without a doubt, that Julian would never hurt him physically. But mentally? Emotionally?

"I don't know," he whispered with a helpless shrug. "But I'm sure as hell going to try."

Miri sighed softly and shook her head, the corner of her mouth twitching with a slight smile. "You're in love," she announced, as if just discovering the fact. "I'm happy for you, Cam. Just don't get your heart broken, okay?" she requested softly as she turned to go.

Cameron slowly leaned against the wall as Miri walked away, frustration and helplessness swirling around him. He was certainly in love. And he was afraid, the way he'd been feeling lately, that his heart was breaking anyway.

Nearly ten minutes later, the door opened slightly and Miri stuck her head back in. "It's Tuesday," she reminded him softly. "He's here."

Cameron shuddered. He couldn't go out there and face Julian tonight. He couldn't go out there and look Julian in the eye and be able to tell him that he was okay when he really wasn't. Julian could see through him like glass. Just last night, he'd been fine. And now…

He tried to pull himself together, rubbing his face with the heels of his hands until his eyes were red from the abuse. He didn't even notice when someone else entered the workroom a couple of minutes later.

"Cam?"

He looked up to see one of his fellow waiters standing there, looking at him in concern.

"Are you okay?" Charles asked.

Rubbing at his face with his hand again, Cameron shook his head. "I… I'm just not feeling right," he stuttered, trying to stall and decide whether to go out and alert Julian to the problem or just hide back here like a coward. He liked the sound of cowardice tonight.

"You don't look good. Why don't you go home? I'll take care of your tables," Charles offered.

Cameron nodded slowly, mulling it over. "I think I might just do that," he croaked. "Thanks, Charles."

Charles frowned worriedly but nodded, then turned to go, closing the door quietly behind him. Cameron took in a shuddering breath.

He knew if he came back at Julian with yet more worries and insecurities so soon after their last discussion, Julian would be irritated. More than irritated. He could almost see the exasperation that would be on his lover's face.

He needed to talk to Julian, but he needed to do it when he had all his ducks in a row. Right now, his ducks were all over the fucking pond.

CAMERON sat in the workroom for longer than he'd intended. He finally realized that if he didn't do something soon, either Blake or Julian would find him. He left without speaking to anyone, got his jacket, and fled quietly out the service entrance.

It was late, far later than he'd realized, and he was utterly exhausted. He feared it wouldn't take but one look at Julian to send him into another fit of uncertainty, and he hated that. Cameron knew Julian didn't like his insecurities, and he wondered how long his lover would be so understanding of them before he got fed up. He rubbed at his eyes as he walked down the street, not really paying much attention to where he was walking.

"Do I scare you?" Julian's voice asked out of the darkness of the alley Cameron was passing.

That Cameron actually jumped in fright didn't help. He stood gasping before he could turn and look for Julian in the shadows. "Julian?" he hissed. "What the hell kind of question is that to ask out of the dark? You just scared the shit out of me. And how'd you even know I was here?" he demanded.

"It's what I do. Do I scare you when I'm not lurking in alleyways?" Julian posed seriously as he stepped out into the light, not even bothering to apologize.

Cameron swallowed hard. He couldn't get any words past his lips. He truly believed it wasn't Julian that scared him, but the entire situation. The secrecy and the obvious danger. Everything that surrounded the other man. And then there was the question of whether Julian was even one of the "good guys." But how was Cameron supposed to separate the man from his life?

Julian stepped closer and cocked his head, peering at Cameron through the gloom. "I do, don't I?" he asked sadly, wincing visibly at the realization.

Cameron couldn't do anything but look at Julian miserably. He remembered the first time they'd talked about this, how Julian had claimed he'd never been with someone who hadn't, at some point, been frightened of him. It made his heart ache to see Julian react to him now.

"I… I don't know," Cameron stuttered, trying to be honest with himself and with Julian despite how much it might hurt them both. "I don't think you do, but then something happens, and—"

"Something happens to make you question me," Julian observed as neutrally as possible.

Cameron could almost see him internally trying to come to terms with this new turn of events. He bit his lip to keep from trying to apologize. He had to be honest now if they were ever going to resolve this. "Maybe," he answered regretfully. "I wait for you every night, counting the days 'til I get my damn turn with you, scared to death that you won't be coming back. What sort of life is that?"

Julian pulled back and looked at him with a hurt frown. "I've been doing everything I can to protect you," he insisted.

"But are you doing everything you can to protect yourself?" Cameron demanded.

"Of course!" Julian snapped in frustration.

Cameron's shoulders hunched. "I still worry about you. Wonder if you'll be back. Wonder if you'll be killed or hurt somewhere where I can't get to you. Wonder if something will go wrong and you'll have to just… disappear. I love you, Julian, but every thought like that is so painful I can hardly stand it. And apparently everyone I know is scared of you!"

"What the hell does that matter?" Julian asked in frustration.

"It matters to me!" Cameron insisted.

"You can't have it both ways!" Julian hissed. "I can't be this nonthreatening entity you and your friends seem to want me to be and still be the type of person able to protect myself and you like I have to!"

"What is it about your life that's so dangerous that makes you feel I can't handle knowing about it?" Cameron blurted. The fear of what he was doing actually clawed at his throat. "It's not so dangerous that it keeps you from coming back week after week."

Julian took a step back as if Cameron had actually slapped him. Cameron couldn't see any emotion in Julian's black eyes, but he knew he'd hurt him.

"That's because I'm fucking good at what I do," Julian snarled after a moment. "I can come back because I *am* fucking dangerous," he said in a low, angry voice. "It's what I do!"

Cameron tried to hold back the tightness gathering in his throat. "What you do—what you do? I don't know what that is, except it means you get hurt and shot at and beat up and maybe even killed," he said. "If that's your job, I'll never stop being scared. I'll never stop hurting."

Julian stared at him, visibly stricken by the implication. "Do I hurt you, Cameron?" he asked suddenly. "Do I abuse you in some fashion? Do I leave you with any doubts whatsoever that I love you and I'm doing everything in my power to be with you?"

"I'll never believe that you would hurt me physically," Cameron answered confidently.

"Physically," Julian echoed. "If not that, then what?"

"How about emotionally?" Now that Cameron was on this road, he had to get all the doubts out there or they'd eat him up inside.

Julian stared at him in disbelief, for once his emotions playing clearly across his face. "This is what you think of me?"

"I love you more than anything. I can live with not knowing the details. But you tell me how I'm supposed to live like this and not be scared," Cameron choked out. "Live with you not even two days a week, not knowing where you are or what you're doing or if you're coming back. How long will this go on? Do people like you retire? Is there anything in the future but a funeral? You haven't told me anything!"

Julian brought his hand up to push against his stomach as if he might be ill. He looked away and actually groaned softly. "Are you telling me it's all or nothing?" he asked with difficulty, unable to look back at Cameron just yet. "You or my job?" he breathed as he finally forced himself to look at Cameron and meet his eyes.

A tear escaped to trail down Cameron's cheek. He found it within himself to straighten up and look clearly at the man he loved. If Julian had taught him anything, it was to stand up for himself. "I can't live like this, always scared, never knowing if you're okay or if you're coming back."

Julian's stricken black eyes searched Cameron's for long moments of tense, painful silence. Finally, he lowered his head and nodded, not saying a word in response. He turned silently and began walking back toward the shadows.

Cameron was so stunned that he couldn't even breathe, much less call out to stop him, and the tears spilled free as the darkness swallowed Julian up.

CHAPTER 8

MIRI stood quietly at the counter, organizing the early evening's tickets. It kept her mind busy on the slow nights, especially when she didn't want to get stuck with bathroom duty. She turned up her nose slightly as she punched numbers into the register.

Movement caught her eye, and she glanced up to idly watch Blake as the man walked slowly across the floor to the bar area, where a stranger in a black pea-coat sat hunched over on the end stool. Blake walked up to him and actually sat down beside him. They sat side by side for several minutes, neither man moving or speaking. Finally, Blake said something to him, stood back up, and gestured to the door.

Miri frowned. She'd never seen Blake tell someone to leave the restaurant before, and she wondered what in the world the man could have done or said. The man turned on his stool, staring at Blake for a long moment before he stood, picked up his heavy glass with a smirk, and walked out with it. Blake didn't even try to stop him from taking the glass with him.

Miri's brow furrowed as she caught sight of the man moving, almost prowling, out the door. It was a little creepy, truth be told, and after seeing that, she was happy Blake had asked the man to leave.

After a moment of watching the man in the pea-coat walk away, Blake moved and disappeared into the back. Concerned, Miri set her checks aside and followed Blake, intending to ask him if everything was okay. She followed him to his office; he hadn't even bothered to close the door entirely before he picked up the phone and dialed.

Miri stopped short at the half-open door when she caught some of his words.

"Julian," Blake greeted in a low voice. "I thought you might like to know I had a visitor tonight."

Miri glanced around and took a slight step closer to the office door, straining her hearing.

After a moment Blake said, "Lancaster's in town. No, he was just here… I don't fucking know, but you need to watch your back, friend."

Miri looked blankly at the door for a split second before backing away slowly, hoping he wouldn't hear her. She needed to find Cameron.

He was in the service area, showing a new waitress how to properly prepare a full coffee service. He sent her off with instructions to keep smiling just as Miri entered the area. He glanced at her and raised an eyebrow at the look on her face.

"You know that Julian and Blake are friends, right?" she asked him without preamble.

Cameron's shoulders stiffened, but his hands kept moving. "Yes," he said, turning away from her.

"Blake's on the phone with him," Miri told him, an odd chill bothering her. "He told him to watch his back; that someone named Lancaster was in town. Watch his back, Cameron! That's not something you say to an antiques dealer!"

Cameron showed an unusual fit of temper, throwing down his towel in frustration. "What's your point, Miri?" he asked, refusing to look up at her.

"What do you mean?" Miri asked in confusion.

"Julian is no longer any of my business," Cameron told her in a harsh whisper, turning back to wiping down the counters. His shoulders hunched, and he'd dropped his head.

Miri took another slight step back and watched Cameron, sadness written across her face. "I'm sorry, Cam," she offered lamely, wanting to ask what had happened but knowing not to push. "But… aren't you just a little… worried, though?"

"I was always worried, Miri," Cameron said quietly. "That was the problem." He left the counter, pushed past her, and disappeared into the kitchen.

"ARE you sure it was him?" Julian demanded as he gripped the phone tight in his hand.

"I'm getting old, Jules, but I'm not senile," Blake snapped in return.

"He came to the restaurant," Julian murmured as his mind raced. Blake hummed in affirmation, and Julian closed his eyes and shook his head. "That means he's identified you as my handler," he said with a wince. Unless Lancaster was there looking for someone else. Julian pushed that thought away.

"Or at least thinks he has," Blake agreed.

"We have to move you," Julian told him with a hint of shock in his voice. They'd planned for this contingency, but he'd never actually expected to need to use it. He'd always assumed that he would be the one found first.

"And just how do you propose we do that?" Blake asked with a disbelieving laugh.

"Very quickly," Julian answered grimly.

"Fuck, Julian," Blake muttered in disgust.

"We'll start tomorrow."

"Us and what army?" Blake asked incredulously. "Emily won't let me leave all her shit behind, you know. We can't hire a moving company; he'll be able to trace it."

"Be creative, Blake," Julian told him impatiently. "Send Emily off to wherever, and tonight I'll find somewhere to move you. I'll be at your house at five in the morning to start. Don't be sleeping, and make damn sure you have help, because Preston and I aren't lifting your goddamned furniture alone," he snapped before ending the call and stalking out onto the landing of the massive staircase. "Preston!" he bellowed into the darkened house. "We have problems!" he shouted as he started down the steps two at a time.

IT WASN'T unusual for Blake to call his wait staff into the back rooms of the restaurant and have meetings every now and then, but tonight it was obvious that this meeting was totally unplanned. The floor full of diners was completely unstaffed, and prepared dishes waited to be taken out. It was unprecedented.

Blake stood in front of the group of gathered servers and didn't wait for the chatter to die. "Ladies and gentlemen," he started, his commanding voice immediately silencing the room. "The restaurant will be closed tomorrow. You'll all be paid overtime for the inconvenience. Those of you wishing to take the day off, I hope the weather is nice for you," he said with a smile, but there was no humor in his voice or in his eyes as he spoke. "But anyone wanting to make a little extra cash in exchange for some heavy lifting, please come talk to me in my office at some point before you take off tonight. That's all," he finished, not even attempting to end his announcement with something clever like he usually did.

He turned and left the prep area, head down as he made his way back to his office.

Standing with a gaggle of waitresses who immediately began talking excitedly about the unexpected day off, Cameron frowned, wondering what was going on. Heavy lifting? He shooed the others back to work and corralled the hostesses to help deliver waiting meals as he pushed his curiosity aside.

But hours later, once most of the staff was gone, Cameron set his jacket aside on the bar and ventured down the hallway to Blake's office, where he rapped lightly on the door.

"Enter," Blake's distracted voice called through the closed door.

Cameron pushed the door open and stepped part-way inside. "Blake?"

Blake's eyes were wide, reflecting surprise at seeing Cameron. He reached over to the phone on the corner of his desk and said, "I'll call you back," before hitting a button on the speakerphone to end the call. "Are you here for heavy lifting or is there something else?" he asked Cameron curiously.

"Both, I guess. To offer help and ask if everything's okay," Cameron said, studying the older man.

"Everything is not, in fact, okay," Blake answered with a hint of humor. He gave Cameron a small smile. "I have to move, you see. Very sudden thing. And I need help with all that damn antique furniture," he grumbled.

Cameron raised an eyebrow. "Thus the need for heavy lifting," he commented. Then he shrugged. "I'm happy to help."

Blake looked at him dubiously. "Do you need the extra money?" he asked.

"Not hardly," Cameron answered. Then he frowned. "Have you got enough help already?"

"Not hardly," Blake answered wryly. "We're starting at six a.m., but you're welcome to get there any time you like. I can send a driver for you so you don't have to catch a cab," he offered.

"Yeah, getting a cab at six a.m. would be a pain in the ass," Cameron agreed. "So a ride would be great." He studied Blake. The other man looked worn out and worried. "Are you okay?"

Blake ran his hand through his hair and gave Cameron a small smile. "Not at the moment," he answered truthfully. "But I will be, as soon as Julian gets this shit straightened out."

Cameron stiffened, unable to return that smile. He settled on a jerky nod.

Blake didn't seem to notice his sudden discomfort, and he picked up a piece of paper and turned it around and around on the desk, fiddling with it to dispel some nervous energy. It was the first time Cameron had ever seen him fidget. "So," he said as he folded the paper in half and tapped it on the desk. "You call me when you're ready for the car to get you. I'm providing breakfast, lunch, and dinner, if needed. There will be copious amounts of alcohol if we finish by nightfall," he rambled.

"In a hurry, huh?" Cameron said quietly. "I'll call," he said.

"In a very big hurry," Blake muttered with a nod of his head. "Thank you, Cameron," he added as he reached over and picked up the phone again. "You have a good night."

Uneasy, Cameron nodded and stepped out, pulling the door shut behind him. He should have known he wouldn't completely get away from reminders of Julian. Shaking his head, he headed back to the bar for his jacket. It would be a quiet walk home with his memories.

"WHAT the hell, Blake?" Julian muttered as he sat on one of the counter stools in Blake's gourmet kitchen. Preston sat beside him, sipping from a mug of coffee.

"What?" Blake asked defensively. "I have Irish crème," he offered with a grin as he held up the coffee-pot.

"I told you to be ready at five a.m., not wandering aimlessly in your boxers and a robe," Julian said.

"You know, I read a study that said wandering aimlessly for an hour fulfilled a percentage of your daily exercise regimen," Blake told them as he poured his own mug of coffee and sat opposite them. "You should wander aimlessly more often," he advised seriously before taking a small sip of the steaming liquid.

"If I had the fucking time to wander anywhere, I would," Julian snapped, his impatience growing as he thought about the large house full of large furniture they would need to move before nightfall.

"Technically, sir, you have quite a lot of time. You just can't wander," Preston pointed out quietly, hiding his smirk behind his coffee mug.

Julian turned his chin slightly to glare at the man. "You jump from a fucking twenty-foot brick wall and see how daintily you land," he challenged. "And stop calling me sir, goddamnit," he added crankily.

He tried to stand from the counter stool, but the unwieldy walking boot on his newly broken left foot got caught in the bottom rung, and he had to kick at the stool and curse before he was free.

Neither Preston nor Blake laughed as he struggled. They knew better.

"When is your fucking help getting here?" Julian demanded as he thumped away from the center island and looked out the large bay window of the breakfast room.

"He's cranky, is he?" Blake asked Preston in a low voice.

Julian turned in time to see Preston merely raise one eyebrow and take another conveniently timed sip of coffee.

Blake's smile faded as he glanced at Julian and met his eyes. Julian knew the man well enough to know that he wasn't as cheerful or as cheeky as he seemed this morning. They were preparing to uproot his entire life. It was a heavy day in more ways than one.

Julian sighed softly and reminded himself to go easy on his friend. It wasn't going to be fun.

"I have a list of addresses," Blake told them as he pushed a piece of paper across the counter and slid it in front of Preston. "You can take my Escalade. Less trips," he added as he placed the keys next to the paper.

"Yes, sir," Preston acknowledged with a nod as he glanced over the list and then folded it into his pocket. He looked over to Julian as he stood, then back at Blake before turning and heading toward the foyer.

Julian frowned, wondering what the odd look had been for. He shrugged it off, though. "Where are we starting?" he asked Blake softly.

"Bottom floor, I guess," Blake answered with a sigh. "We need to find creative places to hide shit. Just in case."

Julian nodded and cleared his throat. "You may want to get dressed first," he reminded as he turned back around and looked out at the misty morning.

THE buzzer rang at almost exactly the time Blake warned Cameron it would. He shoved his wallet into his jeans and grabbed his keys, and then he was out the door, leaving behind forlorn yips and yaps as he hurried down the stairs.

He stopped still at the glass door when he saw Preston outside, surprised and confused to see the man. He pushed through the door. "Preston?"

"Good morning, sir," Preston greeted as he stepped slightly to the side and waved his hand at the huge black SUV parked at the curb.

Cameron glanced to the truck and saw Charles wave at him from the back. He shot another look at Preston. If Julian's driver was going to be at Blake's, that meant—

"We have several more stops to make, sir," Preston said to him pointedly. He walked swiftly to the back door of the Escalade and opened it for him.

Swallowing hard, Cameron shoved his hands in his pockets and followed, climbing into the truck with no comment, instead nodding to the others Preston had already picked up, all of whom were in various stages of wakefulness. When Preston closed the door, it echoed in Cameron's ears. He closed his eyes.

He had a sudden feeling that today was going to very uncomfortable.

The rest of the ride to pick up the other volunteers and take them to Blake's house was a quiet, unsettling one, but Blake was waiting on the great stone steps of his home to greet them when the car pulled up in his driveway.

"Good morning!" he called cheerfully. "I have coffee and breakfast of sorts in the kitchen," he offered as he shook each of their hands in turn. "Morning, Cam," he said with a smile as he took Cameron's hand. "Thank you for coming."

Cameron nodded slowly and studied Blake. It occurred to him that Blake might not know he and Julian had broken it off. Surely if he'd known, and if Julian really was here, Blake wouldn't have put Cameron in this situation. Right? He offered half a smile and followed the rest inside. His stomach was already churning.

As they walked through the house, it became obvious that a little work had already been done. There were bare spots on the walls where paintings had hung, shelves where knickknacks might once have sat. The formal rooms near the front of the home looked as if a herd of elephants had tried to play chess with the furniture, but nothing appeared to have been moved out of any of them yet.

As they neared the kitchen, a repetitive banging echoed in an adjoining room. As Blake passed by he began to snicker, and he stood at the doorway to the kitchen and ushered everyone by while looking past them toward the noise.

"Come eat breakfast, Jules. Those things can wait," he called out.

Cameron stopped so suddenly in the doorway to the kitchen that Keri ran into him and squeaked. He turned to the side, apologizing as the others laughed and paused in the hallway, teasing him about still being asleep.

"It's not breakfast when you've been up all fucking night, Blake," Julian's voice answered as soon as the banging stopped. "Did you find the painter's tape?" he asked in an annoyed voice as he leaned out of the doorway, just ten feet away from Cameron. His eyes were on Blake as he spoke, but when he saw Cameron he seemed to jerk slightly, blinking at him in stunned silence before recovering and moving his eyes back to Blake without any other reaction to Cameron's presence.

All discussion died off as Julian appeared, drawing everyone's eyes.

Blake grunted at him and nodded, reaching into his back pocket to extract a roll of blue tape. He tossed it at Julian, muttering about breakfast as he turned and walked into the kitchen, obviously expecting to be followed.

Keri cleared her throat first, being the most accustomed to seeing Julian—besides Cameron, of course. "Good morning," she greeted him. The other staff members raggedly joined in with a variety of comments along the same line. All except Cameron, who was looking at anything except Julian.

Julian merely nodded to return their greetings and then disappeared back into the room.

"C'mon, Cam," Charles said, pulling at his arm. "Let's get something to eat before Blake works us like dogs."

"Like usual," Keri added playfully.

Cameron let them pull him along, making himself look toward the kitchen and not back at Julian. Just that one look at him had set his heart pounding hard enough to make him breathless, and he could feel the pendant under his shirt heavy and warm against his skin.

Blake stood at the end of the large center island, eating a doughnut and scowling at them. "I wouldn't work my dogs like I work you people," he told them with a small smile.

Dragging his attention to the bar, Cameron picked through the pastries. "Do you actually have dogs?" he asked distractedly, looking around at the fancy kitchen.

"Only if you count Julian and Preston," Blake joked with a wink as he poured himself more coffee.

Cameron cleared his throat and reached for the juice as the other restaurant staff started talking and wandering around the house to gawk while they had the chance. He stayed right there. Cameron hadn't seen Julian even once since that very painful night—not once in three weeks. He squeezed his eyes shut for a short moment. He didn't want to dwell on how much he was hurting.

"Cameron?" Blake asked softly as soon as the others had begun to wander. "Are you okay?"

"I… I didn't know he'd be here," Cameron said softly, not looking up from his juice.

"Who?" Blake asked in confusion.

"Julian."

Blake glanced at the kitchen door with a frown. Just beyond, the banging started again, perhaps a little louder now than it had been. "I don't understand," Blake admitted as he looked back at Cameron.

Cameron swallowed. Obviously Julian hadn't said anything to Blake. "We're not… together anymore," he murmured, poking at the half doughnut in front of him.

Blake inclined his chin and gave a small, "Oh." He was silent for a moment before shaking his head. "I'm sorry. He hadn't said anything to me," he offered. "I wouldn't have accepted your offer to help if I'd known." He hesitated for a moment, something Blake wasn't apt to do. "Would you like Preston to take you home?" he asked uncertainly.

Tilting his head toward the continued banging, Cameron sighed and shook his head. "No. He knows I'm here. I expect we'll do fine avoiding each other." He picked up his juice. "Especially if he keeps banging on the wall like that."

"That's not the wall," Blake responded with a wince. "That's my ten-thousand-dollar billiards table," he explained.

Cameron's head jerked up and his eyes widened. "Uh." He glanced in that direction. He'd seen Julian lose his temper only once, and even then the man had regained it with remarkable speed. What in God's name was he *doing* in there? "Would *you* like Preston to take me home?" he asked awkwardly.

Blake smiled and shook his head. "I need all the help I can get. Besides," he sighed regretfully, "he's not abusing the furniture because of you." He gave Cameron a sad shake of his head. "He's just trying to take the damn thing apart."

Cameron bit his tongue to keep from asking the most obvious question; why did taking it apart require quite such vehemence? But Julian's state of mind wasn't his business anymore. "What will we start with?" he asked instead, gesturing around.

"We cleared the front rooms earlier; we start there," Blake answered in a slightly more businesslike tone as he gestured for Cameron to follow him out of the kitchen toward the front of the house again. "We're three rooms behind you, Cross," he called into the game room as he passed. "Double time it!"

"I'm going to find creative things to do with this boot if you don't shut up," Julian responded calmly from where he sat under the pool table. He was taking it apart, piece by piece, and there were envelopes full of documents scattered around he seemed to be placing inside the table itself before patching it back up.

Cameron tried to ignore what looked like a very suspicious scene and instead glanced to Blake, mouthing a questioning, "Boot?"

Blake pointed to his own foot and shook his head. "Broke his foot," he explained almost silently.

Raising one brow, Cameron almost looked back into the room before he stopped himself. Shaking his head slightly, he started walking again. Not his business. How Julian might have broken his foot was not his business, nor was the fact that he seemed to be hiding Blake's important documents inside a piece of furniture. None of it was his business.

And that was his own fault.

"Mr. Cross is cataloguing my artwork and antiques in case anything gets damaged in the move," Blake explained to Cameron and several of the others who had rejoined them. "If he tells you to do something, you do it, and you do it fast. Otherwise, just stay out of his way," he advised. "If you have a question, ask Preston or myself. Stay out of Mr. Cross' way," he reiterated slowly.

The staff members buzzed quietly over "Mr. Cross" and all the gossip he represented as Cameron drew in a long, slow breath, trying to settle the nerves that still plagued him. He followed Blake to the front, where his boss began collecting the volunteers and telling them just exactly what they would be doing. Heavy lifting, mostly. And a lot of it.

What surprised Cameron was that apparently Julian really was there to take care of the antiques and artwork, because as it turned out, he seemed to know what he was talking about. More than once Cameron heard his ex-lover's voice rattling off the details of the provenance of some random bit of artwork or an antique piece for whoever was writing it down. Why had Cameron never known that about him? Frowning, Cameron told himself to stop thinking about it and just do what he was told.

They worked in groups of three and four to move the solid furniture. There was a lot of moaning and groaning, but the morning was uneventful except for Charles smashing his thumb in a cabinet door that hadn't been secured.

By the time noon came around, Cameron had almost convinced himself that Julian wasn't there. Almost. It was about that time when Preston came through with a pad of paper, taking lunch orders.

"Where are you going?" Blake asked the quiet driver as he stretched his back.

"Mr. Cross said to tell you that you could have Wendy's," Preston answered evenly.

Cameron and those within hearing distance paused and turned to stare. Blake Nichols owned a four-star restaurant. He didn't frequent fast food drive-thrus. Blake muttered, but to everyone's surprise, he gave Preston his order and returned to work without a word of argument.

Cameron listened as the others made their requests, and when Preston approached he just shook his head. "No, thank you," he murmured. His stomach was still churning, and he didn't want to risk actually being ill.

"Are you certain, sir?" Preston asked with raised eyebrows. "I'm afraid there won't be more food until nightfall," he warned.

Wrinkling his nose, Cameron sighed. "Get me one of those salad bowls, please," he requested. He would just stick it into a cooler with the drinks in case he wanted it later.

"Very well, sir," Preston responded as he wrote down the order and turned away. He stopped at Blake's side as he left and turned to him, lowering his voice as he spoke. Cameron wasn't able to hear what he said.

"Where's he taking it?" Blake asked, loud enough for Cameron to hear.

"He hasn't said, sir," Preston answered in a low voice that just barely carried to Cameron.

"You don't know?" Blake asked incredulously.

"You know how he is, sir. He insisted on going alone," Preston answered with a shrug. He slid his pad of paper into a pocket. "And he wants to make the first trip himself to make certain it's safe before anyone else accompanies him to help."

"You're not going with him?"

"He insisted."

Blake sighed heavily but nodded in agreement, and Preston left without looking back.

Cameron frowned. Something was odd, and he couldn't quite put his finger on it. Blake was the one moving, and he and Julian both had repeatedly alluded to the fact that Blake was somehow in charge of things, but today Julian sure seemed to be calling the shots. Cameron had never known Blake to give in so quietly to anyone under any circumstance. Perhaps Julian and Blake were closer friends than he knew.

Shaking his head, he turned from the almost-empty room and walked out into the hallway, heading for the downstairs powder room.

When he looked up from his feet, Julian stood with a large parcel in his hands directly in front of him at the other end of the hall. The package was obviously a painting or something similar; it was wrapped in brown paper and secured with blue tape. Julian knelt down, the action awkward and difficult with the unwieldy boot on his foot, and he leaned the package against the wall to join several others. When he heard Cameron approaching, he turned his head slightly and then looked quickly away, down at the wrapped painting once more.

He shook his head as he reached into his breast pocket for a large permanent marker. "Hello, Cameron," he greeted softly without looking up.

Cameron stopped in place, eyes settling on the man who had been his lover. "Hello, Julian," he answered faintly. He licked his bottom lip nervously. He'd have to move past Julian on his way to the bathroom. He didn't know if he could physically do it. He scrambled for something else to say. "Ah. Blake said you broke your foot?"

"Several times," Julian answered in the soft, formal voice Cameron knew so well as he wrote on the brown paper, labeling the painting. He didn't look over at Cameron, and he seemed to be concentrating very hard on not doing so.

Cameron nodded, feeling the awkward tension crank up. He wanted to stand and look at Julian, to look his fill and listen to that gentle, barely there voice say anything at all, but he couldn't stand it. It caused too much pain for him to stand still. "Excuse me," he whispered as he brushed past to flee toward the bathroom.

Julian didn't respond. He didn't even stand until Cameron had moved well past him. As soon as Cameron reached the bathroom door, though, Julian stood and turned away, calling out, "Preston! Get it in gear!"

Cameron closed himself inside the powder room and leaned back against the door, wrapping his arms around his middle and hanging his head. God. He missed the man so, so badly. He hadn't realized how much until just now.

"Are you coming with me, sir?" Preston's voice responded from somewhere close. "Well, shake a leg, sir. We're running behind schedule and it won't do to be sitting down on the job," he drawled.

"I swear to God, Preston…" Julian sounded supremely annoyed.

"Oh, I have more, sir," Preston assured him. "I know how you appreciate variety." Cameron could hear their footsteps moving away.

"I appreciate silence more," Julian responded irritably before they were out of earshot.

After they were gone, Cameron could still hear Julian's voice echoing in his head, this time speaking tender words he'd once spoken; could still smell him, even if it was just his imagination. And all his reasons for driving Julian away seemed all of a sudden so useless and silly. Closing his eyes, Cameron sighed shakily, trying to convince himself that he hadn't made a mistake.

BLAKE watched through the windows as Julian stepped down from the moving van and made certain his booted foot was on the ground before he put any weight on it. He'd tripped and fallen so many times in the past week that Blake had lost count. He almost felt sorry for his friend, but he knew Julian had dealt with worse, and it was funny watching him struggle with the heavy walking boot. Blake could really use the amusement right now.

Over the course of the day, they'd made several trips to the safehouse Julian had found for Blake, but because they were trying to keep the amount of exposure to a minimum, none of the volunteers accompanied them to the new house, and Julian and Preston unloaded the majority of the heavy furniture by themselves.

All of the hard labor made both of the men slightly cranky. Actually, it had made them both downright bitchy, and Blake was careful not to laugh at them every time they returned from a trip, bickering with each other in the most polite of ways. It was hard to respond to an insult that had "sir" tacked onto the end, which he knew frustrated Julian to no end.

They were back from their last run, accompanied by another order of food to hand out to the volunteers before they were taken home. The volunteers scattered on the front lawn with their meals, enjoying the mellow weather and in some cases dozing off.

Blake watched Julian and Preston as they approached the house, bypassing the others. He winced as he saw Cameron glance at Julian but just as quickly look away. Julian didn't return the glance, keeping his head down as he made sure of his fatigued steps.

Preston walked ahead of Julian, carrying three McDonald's bags as Julian limped behind him. He appeared to be muttering to himself, but then Preston would mutter back to him. Blake lifted the window to hear what they were saying.

"I'm going to kill Blake when this is over," Julian was telling Preston through gritted teeth.

"You should have done that before we moved everything, sir," Preston responded without missing a beat. "It would have saved us quite a lot of trouble."

"Smartass," Julian muttered under his breath. "And stop calling me sir!"

"Of course, sir," Preston responded with an obvious smile as he walked through the open front door.

"Are you two still bitching?" Blake called out as he moved away from the window. "Bring me my dinner!"

Julian caught up to Preston and dug into one of the bags as the other man held it patiently and tried not to smirk. He pulled out a cheeseburger wrapped in yellow paper, walked into the room where Blake was working, and chucked the burger at him.

Luckily, Blake looked up just in time, and he caught the burger against his chest. "Thank you, Julian," he drew out as he sat down on a box. "Feeling any better?" he asked pointedly.

"Do I look like I'm feeling better?" Julian demanded. "Do I *seem* to be in a better mood?" he asked sarcastically. "Preston!" he shouted suddenly. "Give me my fucking nuggets," he demanded as he turned, only to find Preston standing behind him with a box of chicken in his hand. "Goddammit," Julian offered before snatching the box and stalking out of the room with his food.

"I'll just be taking the others home then, sir," Preston said to him, and Blake knew the man was trying desperately not to laugh. Julian didn't respond other than to growl something unsavory as he disappeared deeper into the house.

Blake sighed. He knew exactly what was making it so bad. "I didn't know, Preston," he murmured, referring to the young man standing outside with the rest of his remaining volunteer moving company.

"How could you, sir?" Preston asked with a cock of his head.

"I'd have thought that he *would have told me…*" Blake's voice rose toward the end of the sentence. He stopped and shook his head. "Doesn't matter. The day's done, and they both suffered, from what I saw. Spilled milk. Go ahead, Preston. And thanks for your help."

Preston remained where he was, still managing to look oddly dignified as he held several bags of fast food in his arms. He looked like he was about to say something, but finally he nodded in response and turned to leave.

"Preston?" Blake asked, having caught the other man's hesitation.

"Yes, sir?" Preston answered as he turned obediently.

Blake frowned. "What were you going to say?"

Preston was silent as he met Blake's eyes. "Mr. Cross has become quite reckless," he finally said softly. "I believe sharing the news was the last of his concerns."

Blake's eyes went hard. "Reckless," he stated. "Do you feel he's… purposely endangering himself?"

Preston pursed his lips and shook his head. "No, sir," he answered curtly. "Perhaps what I meant to say was he's not exactly a master of his emotions like he once was. He tends to… throw cheeseburgers."

"I see." Blake relaxed a little, and he nodded. "All right. Thank you, Preston."

"My pleasure, sir," Preston offered with a little bow, and he turned on his heel and left the room.

Blake sat there thinking as he unwrapped his cheeseburger, and then got up to go find Julian. "Cross! Where'd you go?" he yelled out.

He found Julian sitting at the counter in the kitchen, shoulders slightly hunched as he ate his McNuggets. The man looked so odd eating out of a cardboard box that Blake had to stop and just stare at him for a moment.

When he forced himself to move again, Blake snagged two cold bottles of Coca-Cola out of a cooler and set one on the counter in front of Julian. He waited several minutes, until it was clear Julian wasn't going to say anything.

"Why didn't you tell me, Jules?" he asked.

"What was there to tell?" Julian asked softly, looking up to meet Blake's eyes.

"Well, how about, 'Blake, I'm not seeing Cameron anymore, just so you know'," Blake posed.

"I didn't know the issue would become a problem," Julian responded icily.

"It wasn't." Blake paused significantly. "For *me*."

Julian's chin jerked slightly, and he moved almost explosively, slamming his hand down on the counter hard enough to rattle the boxes full of kitchen utensils sitting nearby. "What do you want me to say?" he demanded in a loud voice.

Blake was unperturbed by the rare outburst. "If you'd told me, I wouldn't have asked him to help today," he said flatly. "I didn't even know anything was wrong until he told me. And who am I supposed to feel sorry for here, Jules? Did you finally give in and convince yourself he was better off without you?" he asked angrily.

The muscles of Julian's jaw jumped as he gritted his teeth. "No. He did. Any other questions?"

Blake's lips tightened, but he knew he'd pushed enough. Even Julian had his limit, and he'd obviously reached it very quickly. "No," he responded quietly, shaking his head.

Julian continued to look at him unflinchingly, his eyes turning hard and as black as obsidian. It was obvious that he was getting angrier even as he tried to calm himself. "Today was hard for him?" he asked in a low voice.

"I believe so," Blake answered, resting his elbows on the counter. "He was… distressed. Wanted to ask about you, I could tell."

Julian's eyes unfocused slightly, and he looked away, tapping his finger against the granite countertop. "I thought I'd prefer hearing that answer," he muttered. He stood and began moving toward a cooler where there were several beers waiting. "I was wrong," he admitted without looking back at Blake.

Blake frowned. "You want him to be miserable? Or at least, as unhappy as you?"

Julian shook his head. "I *want* to want him to be miserable," he clarified dejectedly. "I just can't bring myself to do it."

Blake would have laughed, but Julian was so obviously hurting he couldn't find it in himself to see much humor in it. "What happened, Julian? You both seemed… happy."

Julian fished a beer out of the cooler and let the lid fall shut, and then he straightened and turned to look at Blake, his eyes full of sadness. "I scared him," he explained with a helpless shrug. "And he sent me away."

Blake slumped a bit at the counter. "I'm sorry, Julian," he said, knowing full well it wouldn't help. "I really thought—"

"So did I," Julian whispered as he popped the top off the beer and downed a long drink of it.

"You know, normal people use bottle openers," Blake pointed out wryly as he looked at the bottle cap Julian had tossed on the counter.

"I have little use for normal people," Julian responded coldly as he stared at the countertop, not seeing it.

Blake sat silently as Julian continued to drink, keeping him company as the night stretched on.

TUESDAYS was about an hour from closing, and filled tables were few and far between. Cameron focused on cleaning up after a party that had stayed late. He stacked plates on his tray and slid glasses carefully onto the rolling cart nearby before glancing out the window.

Spring was in full swing outside, all signs of snow and ice gone. His mouth quirked. Most people figured that being "up north" meant Chicago had lovely springs and autumns. It did, he supposed, but surrounded by concrete, glass, and asphalt, he figured it might as well be June by now. But once outside when the sun set, a lovely crisp cool would blow in, circulating off the lake, and that seemed to bring the sleepy city back to life.

As Cameron returned his attention to cleaning the table, a man entered the restaurant and looked around quickly as he unwrapped the thin scarf from his neck. He wore a black pea-coat and his dark hair was unruly from the windy night. He stepped up to Keri at the hostess stand and requested a quiet table.

"Preferably in one of the alcoves," he added in a posh British accent.

Keri led him to a quiet table, leaving the menu and promising quick service. She got Cameron's attention, and he nodded. He walked back to the service area to wash his hands before heading back out to the table.

"Good evening, sir. My name is Cameron, and I'll be taking care of you tonight," he offered pleasantly. He rattled off the night's special and showed the man the other menus. "Would you like some time?" he asked after he was done.

"No, thank you," the man answered with a smile as he looked up at Cameron appraisingly. "I'll take the special and the house wine," he ordered, relaxed and smiling as he spoke.

Cameron blinked as the casual phrase struck a nerve. "Of course," he covered with just the slightest hitch. "I'll get that order in for you right away," he assured the man before turning to depart.

True to his words, Cameron returned within minutes with a fine crystal glass and a bottle of wine that he deftly opened. He poured a bit into the glass for the man to taste and waited, still musing over how one innocent phrase hit him so hard even after all the time that had passed.

The man tasted the wine and nodded his approval as he set the glass down and looked up at Cameron, measuring him silently.

"Are Tuesdays always this busy?" he asked finally.

"Busy?" Cameron picked up the glass to fill it halfway. "Early, usually. This time of night, not so much. If you want to eat earlier in the evenings, we do accept reservations."

The man smiled and laughed softly, a surprisingly deep, rich sound. "I always have reservations," he quipped.

Cameron frowned a bit and looked at the man directly. "I'm sorry. I don't think I've seen you in here before," he said apologetically.

The man looked up at him and snorted in amusement. "That joke must not translate across the pond," he said with a slight shrug. "No, I've only been in here a few times. Mostly private parties or in the bar for a quick bite," he added.

Cameron nodded briefly and set down the glass and bottle, though he took another look at the man to be sure. "Enjoy the wine. Your dinner should be out shortly," he said.

"Thank you," the man drawled as he watched Cameron's movements carefully. "Has Mr. Bailey come in tonight?" he asked casually.

Cameron stopped and turned back, his thoughts scurrying quickly. Bailey. He had heard that name somewhere before, hadn't he? He couldn't place it as a customer, though.

"I'm sorry. Can you describe him for me?" he asked politely.

The man looked up at him thoughtfully and then shook his head. "I must have you mistaken for someone else," he finally concluded in an easy drawl. "Mr. Bailey was well-known to the man I was thinking of. He visited him in hospital a while back." He narrowed his eyes, and Cameron was struck suddenly by how similar this man's eyes were to Julian's. They weren't even the same color, more a light brown or maybe hazel, but there was the same intelligent, calculating quality to them. "Perhaps you knew him as Julian?" the man said abruptly.

Cameron's stomach seemed to drop into his toes, and he prayed that his face didn't betray his physical reaction. He shook his head slowly. "I do know many of the repeat customers," he murmured, knowing he was a terrible liar. Cameron figured sticking to the truth was the best, if at all possible, but he didn't know what to think of this man. There was something slightly… hard-edged and predatory about him. "But I'm afraid neither name rings a bell," he added in the hope that the lie would go undetected.

The man looked up at him with a slight smile still on his lips and he nodded. "My mistake," he offered smoothly. "Suppose I'll just have to find him another way," he said almost happily.

With no verbal acknowledgment required, Cameron turned and walked back to the service area without slowing his pace. When he got out of sight, he leaned back against the wall and took a deep breath.

Even if the man was looking to find Julian, Cameron couldn't help him. Not now. He didn't know how to get in touch with him, and he couldn't have found the house again if his life depended on it. He sighed, pushing away the sudden, familiar pang of loneliness. He was surprised to find that he was slightly jealous as well. The man sitting out there was looking for his ex-lover, and Cameron knew nothing about him now. He closed his eyes, reminding himself yet again that it was no longer his business to know anything about Julian.

He delivered the meal not long after, setting it in front of the man with a minimum of fuss. "Please let me know if you need anything," Cameron told him softly.

"Oh, I certainly will," the man murmured in a low drawl, looking up at Cameron and smiling his charming smile.

Cameron suppressed the tiny flash of warmth he felt at someone—a handsome someone—smiling at him like that, despite how the man's very presence also bothered him. He had purposely avoided anything resembling a relationship since Julian had walked away. It was the first real attention he'd allowed himself to notice in months. That it didn't feel quite right spooked him.

He lifted the tray and folded the stand against his thigh, trying not to glance again at the man.

"Do you work here every night?" the man asked casually as he spread his napkin in his lap.

Warning bells went off in Cameron's head. The last time he'd answered questions like these, it had led him to Julian. And as wonderful as that had been, it had ended very badly. "I work a variable schedule," he answered. "That's the restaurant business for you," he added with a shrug. He stepped back to leave.

"Yeah, the restaurant business," the man echoed thoughtfully. "I hear it's a killer," he said slowly as he looked up at Cameron with his odd, sparkling eyes.

Cameron slowly looked up at the man and thought that maybe he now knew how other people felt when faced with Julian: intimidated and frightened by the dull grind of uncertainty and fear in his gut. How could someone be so polite and outwardly pleasant, but still cause that feeling? Was this how Julian operated with other people?

"It can be, sir," Cameron acknowledged with only the slightest waver in his voice. "Enjoy your meal," he forced out as he moved away, heading straight for the service area.

"He's kinda cute," one of the waitresses commented to him as soon as he stepped into the back. "Cam, why do you get all the hot, lone guys? Are they all gay?" she asked jokingly.

Startled, Cameron looked over at her with wide eyes. "Something's off about him, Sylvia," he said to her.

"What do you mean?" Sylvia asked in confusion as Miri stepped up beside Cameron and peered out the window into the dining room.

Cameron closed his eyes, unable to believe he was saying this. "He kinda scares me."

Miri and Sylvia both turned around to look at him incredulously.

"That guy?" Sylvia asked in disbelief as she looked back through the blinds. "He hasn't stopped smiling since he got in here!" she protested.

Cameron nodded slowly. "Yeah," he said. He rubbed his arms as if he were cold. "I don't know," he muttered.

"What'd he do?" Miri asked him as she stood on her toes and looked out the window again.

Cameron tipped his head and mentally arranged what he wanted to say. "He asked about another customer, but I guess that's not too out of line."

"And that scared you?" Miri asked doubtfully.

"Some of the things he said," Cameron murmured. He sighed and glanced to Miri. "He asked about Julian."

"What?" Miri asked in disbelief. She frowned and turned to look back at the man again. "Maybe he's… his brother?" she posed hopefully. "Kinda looks like him."

Cameron slanted her a sharp look, his jaw set. She shrugged and winced. Cameron rubbed a hand over his eyes. "All right," he said tiredly. "Go back to work," he told them with a frown. They both nodded as Sylvia risked one last glance at the man in the dining area. Cameron allowed himself a moment to openly hurt at the mere thought of Julian, and then he forced himself to get back to work as well. About fifteen minutes later, he made his way out with a water pitcher to freshen the man's glass.

"I hope your entrée pleased you," he murmured, having to say *something.*

"It was very good," the man answered in a low voice. He was watching Cameron in a way strikingly similar to how Julian had always followed his movements. There was definitely a predatory hint to it. But while with Julian's eyes following him Cameron had felt flattered and excited, now he just felt pinned and suffocated.

"Would you like to have dessert tonight?" Cameron asked after filling the water glass, trying to shake the discomfort.

The man smiled crookedly. It gave him a slightly rakish, almost mischievous air. "What are my choices?" he asked in a somewhat suggestive tone.

Cameron's back stiffened. He knew he wasn't misreading the man now. "English trifle with caramel, vanilla bean crème brûlée, Dutch chocolate pyramid, or strawberries and cream," he answered, telling himself to ignore what the man was suggesting.

The man's lips twitched in amusement. "Maybe another time," he decided softly. "I wouldn't want to keep you any later," he drawled as he nodded at the huge wrought-iron clock in the entryway of the restaurant.

His words struck Cameron just as hard as all his other actions had. It was almost the same thing Julian had said to him all those months ago.

Glancing toward the clock to dispel the feelings, Cameron saw it was almost eleven. Normally he'd have assured a customer that he could stay as long as he liked. But tonight…

"May I bring you the check?" he asked.

"Please," the man answered, his speculative eyes never leaving Cameron.

Cameron nodded and left, swallowing hard once he was turned away. This man really gave him a bad feeling. He wished he knew why; and he wished, not for the first time, that he could get in touch with Julian. He wanted that feeling of safety and security he'd experienced in Julian's arms.

He supposed, if it was a real emergency, he could contact Blake. But Blake was harder to reach than he had been six weeks ago. He didn't come to the restaurant anymore. He hadn't been there since the day he'd moved. He merely called occasionally to check in, never talking for more than a minute or two. Cameron had his number, but he felt stupid, going to all that trouble over a diner who was hitting on him.

Cameron pushed through the service area doors and called up and printed the check, his hands shaking the whole time. He was just being paranoid, he tried to tell himself. He was allowing his experience with Julian to get to him, still suffering from the barely healed wound to his heart. Now Cameron just wanted this man who'd brought up painful memories to go away.

He walked back to the table silently and set down the leather folder. The man immediately slid a credit card on top of it, his eyes on Cameron, who avoided them. Cameron took the folder and headed over to the bar to run the card and print the signature slip.

He wasn't really paying much attention, but when the confirmation flashed across the computer screen, the man's name caught his eye. Arlo Lancaster.

Lancaster.

Cameron swallowed hard. That was the man Miri talked about not too long ago. She'd said Blake warned Julian about him. Now truly upset, Cameron was thankful he'd kept his mouth shut. He'd hurt Julian enough as it was. He didn't need to be giving out information about him to people he needed to who made him need to "watch his back" as well.

He nearly crumpled the signature slip, but managed to get it into the folder with his trembling fingers. Cameron wanted—needed—to get this man out of the restaurant and call Blake. He took the leather folder over to the table and set it down along with an ink pen before stepping back to wait, hands clasped tightly behind his back.

Lancaster signed the slip, leaving a generous tip, one on the level of Julian's tips. He slid his card back into his wallet and then stood as he replaced his wallet under his jacket. A leather strap was clearly visible under the jacket, as was the hilt of the gun that rested in the holster. He wasn't a big man, wiry and perhaps the same height as Cameron, but despite his average size Cameron noted Lancaster exuded the same feeling Julian had.

But Lancaster truly scared him.

"Thank you for the dinner, Cameron," he offered as he readjusted his jacket and smiled.

Cameron went absolutely cold. It was all he could do to manage a polite nod.

Lancaster either didn't notice or didn't care about the effect his words and actions had, and he moved past Cameron as he walked toward the door. Cameron had the very terrifying thought that he had just dodged a bullet.

Once Lancaster was out the door, Cameron went to the front office, found Blake's new number, and called him at home.

"Yes?" Blake answered gruffly on the second ring.

"It's Cameron," Cameron said shakily.

"What's wrong?" Blake asked immediately, though his voice was still calm.

"Arlo Lancaster just had dinner."

Blake was silent for a long time, so long that Cameron thought the connection might have dropped. Then Blake cleared his throat. "I'm not going to ask why you felt the need to call me," he finally said. "Don't worry about it, Cameron," he ordered, though his voice was kind. "Just be alert walking home tonight."

"Alert?" Cameron asked in surprise. "You mean he—"

"Don't leave for another hour. But when you do, go straight home," Blake said, his tone stern. "And do it quickly when you go. No cabs. Walk like you usually do."

Cameron stared at the wall and bit his lip. "Okay," he said quietly.

"Good night, Cameron," Blake offered gently.

"Good night, Blake." Cameron hung up the receiver and looked at it for a long time as his mind raced in circles before leaving the office.

CAMERON left Tuesdays a little after midnight like Blake had instructed. It was amazing how such a short amount of time with Julian had made Cameron so paranoid. Even here in the city, he'd never been truly afraid, and he felt he was usually a confident man. But not now. Not in this situation. He was frightened and growing more so by the minute. He'd never been afraid for himself before now. Only for Julian.

He walked out of the building into the warm, slightly stuffy air and started walking home, just like he always did. It wasn't long before the rustle of soft footsteps accompanied his own.

The first time he noticed, Cameron thought he was hearing things. Echoes on a quiet night. The second time, he knew. He swallowed hard and stopped at the corner before chancing a look over his shoulder. A slim figure walked along the sidewalk at a casual pace, hands in pockets and head bowed against the warm wind that whipped between the tall buildings on either side of the street.

Cameron looked back at the street and jogged across it. He'd been out at this time of night hundreds of times. And here in the retail-driven city center, there was almost always at least a small amount of traffic on the streets. But for some reason, tonight there was nothing. His heart was beating hard as he started walking again, trying to keep it casual. The other person—man?—continued on his own path, seemingly oblivious to Cameron's change of direction until he reached a crosswalk. He looked both ways and then crossed the street, keeping up with Cameron in an alarmingly off-hand manner.

Cameron forced himself to remain calm. Or at least somewhat calm. Not visibly freaking out. His condo was only a block away. But if the man was indeed following him, there was no way Cameron could go there. Not safely. Behind him, his shadow picked up the pace and began to slowly close in on him.

Shivering as his nerves ramped up, a memory of Julian once saying he'd stopped Cameron from being mugged popped into his head. Maybe that was all this was. His hand strayed to his breastbone, touching the necklace hidden under his shirt. Before he could think about it, Cameron stopped and whirled around, determined to see what was coming.

The sidewalk behind him was empty, save for a newspaper rolling slowly across the street.

Cameron stared for a long moment, unnerved, his breathing jerky. The hair on the back of his neck was standing up. Julian had been able to disappear like that; this man was apparently cut from the same cloth, and Cameron was no longer entertaining thoughts of coincidences or possible muggings. He looked from side to side before slowly turning back to the direction he'd been walking. He walked more slowly, all his senses alert for the slightest hint of the man following him again. The rustle of a newspaper followed him, but he heard no more footsteps.

Letting out a shaky breath, Cameron again debated the wisdom of going home. He wasn't sure if he was letting the whole mess with Julian get to him. He shook his head and started walking faster again. He was almost home. If he could just get home behind the locked doors, he knew he'd be able to shake off the odd feelings.

As he made it to the door of his building, a low hissing sound met his ears. "Keep walking," a muffled voice said from the shadow of a decorative pillar. "Go around the corner and wait. Then come back and get inside."

Cameron stutter-stepped, but he distantly recognized what was going on, even if it scared the hell out of him. He made himself keep moving, right past his door and up to the corner, forcing himself not to look back. Once out of view he turned and ducked into the darkness. He took several more steps and stopped, leaning back against the brick wall. He was shaking all over, his breathing coming in tiny gasps as he strained to hear what was going on.

It was Julian. It *had* to be Julian.

Moments later he could hear the shuffle of feet and what sounded like a hard collision of bodies. "'Scuse me!" someone shouted drunkenly. "Hey! This here's *my* side a the road!" the drunk shouted belligerently. It was followed with the scuffling sound of a stumble, as if someone had been shoved.

"God!" he heard a frighteningly familiar British accent exclaim in disgust. "You smell like piss, mate."

Cameron's stomach plummeted.

"Piss? I'll show you piss!" the drunk cackled gleefully.

Moments later there was another muffled exclamation, and when Cameron cautiously peered around the corner at the street he could see Lancaster jogging to the other sidewalk. The man looked back over his shoulder as he walked quickly, and then he stopped and kicked at his shoe as if it had something on it. He looked around at the street ahead, hands fisting at his sides, and Cameron jerked back into the shadowed doorway where he was hiding. He felt choked with fright and squeezed his eyes shut for a moment. But he had to see, just in case Lancaster came his way.

"Bugger," Lancaster muttered as he looked out at the empty street. He turned and looked back over his shoulder, obviously searching for the drunk who had accosted him, and he shook his head in disgust when he found himself alone on the street. "Jules?" he called out in an almost amused voice. There was no response from the deserted streets. "That's a new one. I'll give you that much," he said into the silence and then cocked his head to await a response. None came.

Lancaster waited another few breaths, then turned and began to head back the way he'd come, swiftly moving out of sight.

Cameron waited until he couldn't see the man anymore before he walked cautiously back to the corner and peeked around it down the sidewalk to his building. A man appeared out of the alley along the other side of the building, dressed in tattered layers and holding a nearly empty bottle of liquor. He was looking the other way, making certain the man who'd been following Cameron was out of sight. As Cameron watched, he took a long swig of the bottle in his hand. He straightened and seemed to shake out his shoulders, growing taller and straighter, then he rolled his shoulders and hunched again. Cameron's first thought was that it was Julian in disguise. It had to be. His heart hammered as he took a step away from the corner.

The bum turned and looked back toward Cameron. He caught sight of Cameron and raised his bottle unsteadily in a silent salute before beginning to shuffle off the other way, weaving drunkenly and struggling clumsily with the fur-lined hat he wore to keep it out of his eyes. As the hat moved, Cameron caught a glimpse of Preston's shock of blond hair even in the low light of the street-lamps, and his heart sank briefly with a pang of confusing disappointment.

Coming around the corner, Cameron found it hard to breathe. It hadn't been Preston's voice that had warned him. And where Preston was, Julian was sure to be close. His hand again moved to his throat where the pendant still hung. It *was* Julian. Even after what Cameron had said to drive him away, Julian was still protecting him. He looked around the shadows, knowing instinctively that Julian was still there, somewhere, waiting and watching in case there was still danger.

"Julian?" he called softly, just as Lancaster had done. The name echoed through the empty streets until the distant sounds of traffic were once more the only sounds Cameron could hear.

"YOU can't protect everyone, sir," Preston advised in his customary soft, calm voice.

"I should be able to protect the people I care about," Julian argued as they sat in the massive kitchen of his home, sharing a drink at the kitchen table. "There aren't many," he pointed out as he rubbed his tired eyes.

Preston cocked his head, watching silently. It was early June, and they had been holing up for nearly three weeks. They could both smell the end coming; they just didn't know yet what form it would take.

"Arlo's not stupid," Julian continued gruffly. "He'll figure out how to get to us eventually."

"Perhaps sitting and waiting isn't the best way to go about this," Preston suggested. "Perhaps we should address the issue and move on?"

"Address the issue?" Julian asked bemusedly. "You mean go out and get shot at."

"It's always seemed to work in the past," Preston answered with a wry grin before taking another sip of his whiskey.

Julian breathed in deeply and looked into his glass as if he might find the answer in a bottle of Bushmills.

"If that's not appealing, perhaps you could retrieve those in danger and bring them here," Preston went on slowly.

Julian looked up at him with narrowed eyes.

"It is a fine defensive position," Preston pointed out knowingly.

"Blake would come easily enough. His wife is already in Paris with her mother. But bringing Cameron here would be the equivalent of kidnapping him," Julian told him dejectedly. "He wants nothing more to do with me, Preston."

"So leave him be," Preston responded with a careless shrug.

"What?" Julian asked in surprise.

"He wanted nothing to do with your protection then, why give it to him now?" Preston asked curiously. "We wouldn't be spread nearly so thin if we left him be."

Some of the color in Julian's face drained as he thought about leaving Cameron be, as Preston had suggested. God knew what Arlo would do to him.

"I can't do that, Preston," he whispered in a stricken voice. "I'm the reason he's in danger."

"If you say so, sir," Preston agreed amenably as he poured them both more whiskey.

Julian rubbed at the back of his neck as he watched his companion. He and Preston had been friends and colleagues for more than twenty years. He'd known the man longer and better than anyone else in his life. It was his job to be blunt.

He supposed it was fitting that it had come to this: the two of them sharing their last bottle of whiskey as they came to terms with being cornered.

"I never really liked him, anyway," Preston muttered as he filled his glass almost to the brim. "Can't we just kill him and move on?"

"Who?" Julian asked in horror. "Cameron?"

"No, sir," Preston answered drolly. "Arlo. We could find him easily enough. We know he's watching the restaurant."

"Arlo is not the only one who wants me dead. He's just the spearhead," Julian pointed out. "If we go after him prematurely, innocent people could be hurt."

"One innocent in particular, I assume?" Preston drawled as he watched the whiskey in his glass swirl.

"Yes," Julian answered testily.

"Well. Waiting and watching is getting us very little," Preston reminded. "Mr. Nichols has become a recluse. We're in hiding, which I believe I need to point out is not something we do well. This is not the way we're accustomed to operating, sir, and Lancaster knows it. He'll know he's found your weakness simply because he can't find you."

"I'm well aware of that," Julian murmured.

"If you kill the man sent to kill you, especially if that man is Arlo Lancaster, the odds of anyone else being willing to take the job are very slim," Preston continued reasonably. "It's my opinion, sir, that Arlo is the only person willing to do it at all. People have wanted to kill you for years, and none have come even close to succeeding. There's a reason it's only just now coming."

Julian looked up at him, his entire body flooding with dread. He knew Preston was right, and he knew what he was about to say. He didn't try to stop him, though.

"Letting the memory of what Mr. Jacobs was keep you from being what you are will get you killed eventually, sir," Preston told him in a flat, no-nonsense tone. "He's not here. He no longer wants to be here. He's not a part of this unless you make him one. We should meet Lancaster head on and make a dirty mess of it. For old time's sake, if nothing else," he said with an arched eyebrow as he continued to swirl his whiskey thoughtfully. "I owe him at least two bullets in the ass," he muttered under his breath.

"And Cameron?" Julian asked softly.

"Protecting him was a mistake," Preston ventured regretfully. "I fear we merely drew more of Lancaster's attention to him."

Julian tore his eyes away from his glass to look up and meet Preston's. He wished he could argue, but Preston was rarely wrong when it came to tactical matters.

Preston opened his mouth to continue, but the cell phone at Julian's elbow began chiming before he could speak. Both men looked down at the phone and then at each other in surprise. Julian could count on one hand the number of people who had that number, and he had made certain it wasn't easy to track down.

Julian turned his head to watch it ring. The caller ID displayed the number as private, but Julian knew instinctively who it was.

"You may as well answer him, sir," Preston whispered, his voice low as if the phone would overhear him. "If he knows enough to call when we're drunk, then we're in bigger trouble than we thought," he said before making a sarcastic toast in the air with his glass and taking another sip.

Julian gave a snort and reached for the phone. "Arlo," he answered in a low voice.

"Hullo, Julian," Arlo greeted cheerfully. "Nice accent."

"It gets the job done," Julian muttered.

"I liked your other one better. I have a proposal," he said, knowing Julian wasn't likely to speak again and merely delving right into it. "You see, I'm on a limited budget for this one. The people who hired me want you dead, but they don't want you dead badly enough to shell out what it actually costs to kill you. Follow?"

"I follow," Julian assured him. Arlo was supplementing this job with his own money. This was personal for him, and he would get it done no matter the cost. That was both good and bad.

"All this surveilling and whatnot, it's beginning to bore me. Cameron Jacobs has got to be the most plain, unremarkable man I've ever come across," Arlo said in annoyance. "He'd better be good in bed, Jules, that's all I've got to say. You did an impressive job of hiding Blake Nichols, though, I have to admit. Tell me, Julian, why hide your handler but not your lover?"

Julian gritted his teeth, remaining silent.

"Problems in paradise, hmm? I can solve that for you," Arlo continued in an amused voice.

"You said you had a proposal," Julian reminded him, slipping into the accent that came most naturally to him, a lilting gaelscoil Irish. There was no point in hiding it from Arlo or from anyone else anymore. It was almost a relief to speak it. "Or did you plan to kill me by boring me to death?" he asked in annoyance.

Arlo tutted at him. "Always were the wit, weren't you? All right, then, my proposal is this: Meet me at Blake's restaurant at your regular time. Just you. Tell Preston to bugger off somewhere. We'll settle this like gentlemen."

Julian was silent, wondering why the idea did actually appeal to him a little. Was he confident he could kill Arlo or was he just ready to die?

"Either you show up Tuesday night, Julian, or Cameron Jacobs doesn't make it home alive," Arlo promised softly before ending the call.

Julian closed the cell phone slowly and looked up to meet Preston's eyes. The man raised one eyebrow and tilted his head knowingly. "The only way to save the one you love is to die for him?" he ventured calmly, his own Irish accent flowing as if he'd never hidden it.

Julian nodded wordlessly, staring at the tabletop.

"It's very chivalrous, anyway," Preston commented offhandedly. "Shall I set up a sniper's nest somewhere devious?" he asked with a hint of anticipation.

"No," Julian answered softly. He looked up at Preston seriously and leaned forward. "Make me a promise, Preston," he requested.

"Of course, sir," Preston responded without hesitation.

"If I'm killed," Julian murmured, "you have to take care of Smith and Wesson."

Preston blinked rapidly, pressing his lips together to try to repress any emotion he might have wanted to display at the thought of taking on the care of Julian's two cats. Finally, he looked down at the table and frowned. "Could I just throw myself into the coffin with you instead?" he asked hopefully.

Julian smiled and shook his head.

"Damn," Preston muttered as he got up from the table and walked away.

CHAPTER 9

CAMERON was gathering goblets when Sylvia practically flew into the service area, catching everyone's attention. "Cam," she hissed. "He's back."

Cameron's chin snapped around, and he stared at her. "He?" His heart hammered in his chest.

"The scary guy," she answered breathlessly, getting Miri's attention as she walked by them.

Cameron's hand tightened on the crystal glass in his hand. "Are you sure?" he asked.

"Look," Sylvia whispered as she moved toward the door and its small window.

The past few weeks had marched by uneventfully with no sign of Arlo Lancaster, who had so unnerved him, and also no sign of Julian after he and Preston had run Lancaster off that night. Cameron's life had calmed and settled into a daily blur… until now.

They could barely see the man from their angle; Lancaster had requested the same quiet table he'd been given the first time, and he sat in the chair that allowed him to watch the door. As they peered at him, Keri led another man to the table to join him. A tall, dark, handsome man they all recognized.

Cameron's breath caught as he looked upon Julian for the first time in months. He slowly leaned forward, grasping the counter tightly as he looked out through the slats. His chest suddenly ached badly, so badly he could barely swallow.

Julian stood by the side of the table for a long moment, managing to look large and intimidating even in the finely tailored suit. Lancaster leaned back in his chair casually, looking up at Julian almost insolently before he stood, buttoned his suit jacket, and offered his hand with a few words in greeting. Julian looked down at the hand for a moment, and then he grasped it and shook it stiffly. He looked around, seeming almost uneasy, and he unbuttoned his jacket slowly as he sat opposite Lancaster.

They sat silently, staring at each other.

"This is not good," Sylvia whispered at Cameron's side. "What do we do?"

Cameron stared through the blinds, feeling his emotions drain away. He'd been too upset, too scared, too lonely, all for too long. It was too much to feel any of it right now, so he buried it deep down. "We do what we always do," he answered flatly, voice becoming more firm as he spoke. "This has nothing to do with us."

"What are you talking about?" Miri asked from Cameron's other side.

"We don't know them. We don't know them from any other customers," Cameron told them. Ignorance would keep them safe. Julian had taught him that.

The women nodded slowly, and they all looked back out at the two dangerous men.

They seemed to be complete opposites. Julian sat proper and tense, his face expressionless as he looked at the other man. Lancaster, though, sat slightly sideways with his elbow propped on the back of his chair, reclining casually with his ankle resting on his knee. He was grinning impishly and meeting Julian's eyes unflinchingly.

Cameron straightened and tugged at his collar before smoothing down the front of his shirt. He picked up the card listing the evening special and walked out of the service area.

How he found the determination, he didn't know. How he knew what was going down was wrong, he didn't know. All he could do was follow Julian's lead as he'd seen it before—do his job and pretend not to know the man who had been his lover.

When he got to the table, Lancaster had just begun to speak in a low voice. "You're a hard man to track," he said in amusement. "Hiding in your castle. Might as well be Bruce Wayne."

"Does that make you the Joker?" Julian asked flatly, clearly not amused.

Cameron paused a few feet away, completely taken aback by the sound of Julian's voice in a melodic Irish accent. It was right, but it wasn't. He'd never heard Julian use an accent. Maybe it was something he was doing with Lancaster? Something to hide his identity? If so, he was really good at it.

Lancaster laughed softly and nodded.

"Why are we here?" Julian asked with the barest hint of annoyance.

"I heard you like this place," Lancaster answered innocently. "The food is delicious. Although the service is somewhat lacking."

Julian was silent, staring at his companion blankly, and Cameron took that as his cue to approach the table. "Good evening, gentlemen," he greeted, trying desperately to keep his voice from wavering. "My name is Cameron, and I'll be your server tonight." His voice, thankfully, came out purely professional, as was his manner. He rattled off the night's special without looking at either man and then asked, "Would you like to start with some wine?" He couldn't bring himself to make eye contact, especially with Julian.

Lancaster looked up at Cameron with a large grin. "Wine sounds wonderful," he drawled happily. "Bring us your most expensive bottle," he requested as he looked back at Julian almost challengingly. "We're celebrating tonight."

From the corner of his eye, Cameron saw Julian's jaw clench.

Cameron tipped his head in a brief nod and set the specials card between them. "Right away, sir," he murmured before he strode away to get the wine and glasses.

Somewhere deep inside he reeled at being so close to Julian again and not being able to do anything about it. But he knew he couldn't let that little bit of himself out. He just *couldn't*. If he did, there would be no reining it in again. That fear he'd always felt on Julian's behalf, the fear that his lover would be hurt or even killed, was back full force. As Cameron re-entered the service area, he realized that he felt it even though he wasn't with Julian anymore—and that he'd much rather feel it being *with* Julian.

"What are they saying?" Miri demanded in a hushed whisper as she and Sylvia crowded around him.

"You should be working," Cameron said sharply as he walked to the fine wines cabinet and pulled out the best wine the restaurant offered. He carefully wiped down the bottle and picked up two glasses and set it all on the tray. But he had to pause as his hands shook enough that the classes touched together with a quiet chime.

"Jesus," Sylvia muttered as she looked at the expensive wine. "What, are they on a date?" she added distractedly.

"Don't ask," Cameron muttered darkly.

"I hope you know what you're doing," Miri said to him in a hushed voice. "You can *see* the tension over there. I could cut it with one of Jean-Michel's knives!"

Cameron picked up the tray, righting the slight bobble and then pausing for a steadying breath. "They're just customers," he said, reminding himself as well as them. He left the girls behind and carried the tray to the table, setting it on the nearby stand before presenting the linen-wrapped bottle.

Lancaster looked down at it and nodded his head at Julian. "Let him try it, if you please," he requested.

Julian continued to stare at him wordlessly. Both of his hands were resting on the table in front of him; Cameron knew he usually kept at least one of them in his lap when he ate. He also knew why, but he didn't want to think about that right now. Lancaster sat with both of his hands above the table as well. They reminded Cameron of Old West poker players, always keeping their hands in sight. Miri was right; the tension was palpable.

Cameron set down the bottle as he pulled out the corkscrew. He opened the bottle efficiently, surprised his hands weren't shaking anymore, let it air for a moment, and then poured a couple sips' worth into one of the glasses before offering it to Julian without a word. Cameron finally let his eyes settle on his ex-lover, and he felt a pang of longing so strong it almost doubled him over.

Julian still stared at Lancaster intently, his entire body coiled and tense. Finally, he dragged his eyes away and took the glass. He looked up to Cameron, and in his dark eyes there was a spark of something Cameron had never seen there.

It might have been… fear.

Julian sipped at the wine and nodded his silent approval. Cameron couldn't do anything but stand there, the bottle clutched in one hand, after he saw that look in Julian's eyes. He wondered if it was a reaction to his presence or to Lancaster's. Cameron made himself look over to the other man and offer the wine bottle.

Lancaster nodded without looking at him, waving his hand through the air as he smirked at Julian. "So, what will it be, Julian?" he asked smoothly. "The special?" he asked sarcastically.

Cameron took up the empty glass silently and filled it just over halfway before setting it down in front of Lancaster carefully. Lancaster's words and tone scared him—the man had obviously researched Julian somehow. He seemed to know him well. Cameron swallowed and tried not to flinch.

Lancaster took the glass and held it up, as if ready to make a toast. He smiled at Julian, his eyes warm and friendly even though Cameron instinctively knew it was a mask.

"What was that toast you taught me, Jules?" Lancaster asked Julian with a smile. "Something very Irish," he mused as he tried to remember it.

Julian stared at him, obviously having no intention of answering. Cameron glanced at Julian carefully as he lifted Julian's glass, filled it as well, set it down along with the bottle, and waited silently, although he edged away from the table. He had taught this man toasts? Picturing Julian with a boisterous crowd of drunks, reciting "very Irish" toasts didn't seem right to Cameron. Had he truly known his lover even a little bit? He moved a half-step backward.

"May those who love us love us," Lancaster said suddenly as he held up his wine. "And those that don't love us, may God turn their hearts. And if He doesn't turn their hearts, may He turn their ankles, so we'll know them by their limping."

Julian pursed his lips, leaning forward slowly and finally resting his elbows on the table as he looked across at the other man. His dinner companion leaned forward to meet him with relish.

"You really think this is how it works?" Julian asked in a low, dangerous voice. The Irish accent sent a shiver through Cameron's body, and he couldn't help but stare at Julian, wondering how many other things he had never known about the man. "You think you can come into my city without retribution?" Julian continued. "You think you'll make it to dessert?" he practically snarled.

Lancaster's smile vanished, and he gave one quick nod of his head. "You should have thought of that before you taught me everything you knew," he murmured in a voice to match. "The special?" he asked in a completely different tone as he sat back. He nodded again. "We'll both have the special," he told Cameron with a smug, satisfied smile.

Cameron's eyes bounced back and forth between them, and he could only nod jerkily. "The salad will be out shortly," he said. It came out weak to his ears. He collected the menus and turned away. As he did so, he saw Julian raise his own wine-glass and hold it up to Lancaster. "To your limp, Arlo," he said solemnly.

Behind him, a small clank and a grunt of pain signified that one of the men he'd left behind had just kicked the other under the table.

If he hadn't been so terrified, Cameron might have laughed.

"WHY are you here?" Julian asked through gritted teeth.

"Because your time has run out," Arlo answered bluntly. "You've been doing the wrong work for the wrong people, mate. Informing for the police? Sound familiar?" he asked cheekily.

"We all do what we have to," Julian responded in a low voice. Arlo knew more than even Julian had suspected he would.

"But you didn't have to, Jules," Arlo argued, the smile still on his face. "You don't need the money. You don't even need the work anymore. The only reason you still do it is because you enjoy it," he accused knowingly.

Julian gritted his teeth harder and lowered his head slightly, refusing to look away.

"You enjoy the stalking. The fear. You enjoy the killing, and you always will. You're not one of the fucking good guys, so why try to tell yourself you are?"

Julian sat back slightly, taking in a deep breath. The hell of it was that Arlo was right. He enjoyed what he did. He was good at it and always had been. He had, in the end, been given a choice. Remain one of the bad guys or be loved. And he had walked away from love. He'd chosen to be a killer rather than to be with Cameron.

"Were you behind the big fucking dog?" he finally asked Arlo.

Arlo actually laughed. "No," he answered with a gleeful shake of his head. "But I heard about it." He practically giggled. "Juvenile, but still slightly brilliant."

Julian sighed and took a long sip of wine.

"If I don't take you, someone else will," Arlo told him, suddenly serious again. "It's just a matter of time."

Julian met his eyes and nodded. "Someone else," he repeated grimly. "The man who hired you. Tell me who he is," he demanded. "You know I can get to him. You won't have to do this."

Arlo responded with a slow, wicked grin. "What makes you think I don't want to?" he asked.

TWENTY minutes after taking their orders, Cameron arrived at the table with the two entrées. The mood at the table had gone steadily downhill, but somehow it helped Cameron maintain his distance. It was like a husband and wife squabbling. He wouldn't get involved then, and he wouldn't get involved now. But he still had to listen.

He lifted the two covered plates and approached the table. When he set the dinners in front of them, Lancaster gave it a sniff and quirked an eyebrow. "What is this, exactly?" he asked Julian.

"Shut up and enjoy it," Julian snarled.

Lancaster looked from him to Cameron. "What is this?"

Cameron blinked at him for a moment before answering. "Snapping turtle soufflé and Southern red-eye gravy with pommes frites."

"Jesus Christ, Jules," Lancaster groaned as he sat back and glared.

"You want to go into tonight with nothing but a few hundred dollars of wine in you, be my fucking guest," Julian muttered.

"I can get you another entrée," Cameron felt compelled to offer.

Lancaster was watching as Julian started to eat, and he wrinkled his nose distastefully. "This is fine," he muttered. "Thank you," he gritted out.

"This was always your problem, you know that?" Julian said to him heatedly as he dropped his fork onto his plate with a clatter. Cameron had rarely seen this level of emotion from him, especially in public. "You were all show and no real substance. You never fucking did your research."

"I found you, didn't I?" Lancaster shot back.

Cameron withdrew without his usual reminder to flag him down if they needed anything. No way was he interfering in that conversation.

"Eat your fucking dinner," he heard Julian snarl again as he left.

It would have been comical if Julian hadn't sounded so furious. Cameron tended to his other tables and kept an eye on that one, just in case violence erupted. He didn't think it would—he thought Julian had nearly limitless control—but tonight it seemed like Julian's anger bordered on rage.

When Cameron glanced back several minutes later, he saw Lancaster upend the wine bottle over his glass and shake it. He dreaded going back to the table, but he knew he had no choice.

"More wine?" he asked quietly as he stepped up beside the table.

Both men answered at the same time, Julian with a resounding "No" and Lancaster with a cheerful "Please!"

The waiter raised a doubtful eyebrow, suddenly seeing the morbid humor of the situation. It wasn't at all funny. These two men were at each other's throats, but there was an element to it that made him want to laugh hysterically. "How about I take your plates while you decide?" he offered tentatively.

Julian sat back and crossed his arms over his chest, watching Lancaster through narrowed eyes. Lancaster mirrored him and cocked his head to the side. "Dessert?" he asked with a smirk.

"Go fuck yourself," Julian answered calmly.

Cameron had no idea what to say and wished he could just walk away. Instead he started picking up both plates and soufflé ramekins.

Lancaster glanced up at him and narrowed his eyes. "You're the bloke who claimed he didn't know Julian," he said. "'Never heard of him'. Funny that, because my sources told me you two were a bit of a thing," he continued as he leaned more across the table toward Julian and grinned. "That research thing again," he mused with a shake of his head.

Cameron couldn't stop himself from glancing at Julian. He willed Julian to believe that he hadn't told Lancaster anything. God, if Julian thought he'd betrayed him on top of everything else…

"I don't know what you're talking about, sir," Cameron managed to get out.

"Yeah, I can tell," Lancaster laughed wryly. "Don't worry about it, mate," he sighed as Julian remained tense and silent. "He doesn't really care what you do anymore," he announced as he met Julian's eyes. "I've been stalking you for weeks, and Jules here hasn't said word one about it. You've got new things going, don't you, Jules?" he asked maliciously. "No need to bother with the cast-offs."

Cameron flinched before he could stop himself. Julian, stone-faced as ever, glared at Lancaster without ever bothering to look at Cameron.

"Come on, Jules," Lancaster invited, still smiling the same charming, almost boyish smile even though his eyes glinted dangerously. "Tell him about it. Tell him about what and who you were doing. Why you never saw him on Sundays and Thursdays. Where you went on Saturday nights after you left him."

"We'll take the check," Julian responded through gritted teeth.

Cameron fled immediately. Once he made it to the service area, he set down the dishes with a clatter and leaned against the counter, shaking and biting his lip hard, trying not to let the tears that threatened loose.

Miri came over and took his arm. "Cam? What do you want us to do?"

He forced himself to straighten and rub his eyes while he took several deep breaths. "You're staying here, and I'm delivering this check. And hopefully, they're leaving Tuesdays and not coming back."

Inside, Cameron was a mess. He'd trusted that there hadn't been any others while Julian was with him, and he still believed that, perhaps naïvely so. The man was just trying to get a reaction from him. But he didn't want to think about who might have come *after* him. A man like Julian could have anything and anyone he wanted. And that, more than anything, was what hurt. That after he'd driven Julian away, he could have been so easily replaced.

Trying to shore up what courage he had left, Cameron collected the ticket, slid it into a leather folder, and went to get rid of them. He needed them gone so he could go find somewhere to fall apart again, worrying about the man he'd given up the right to love.

When Cameron returned to his customers, Lancaster was still leaning over the table, looking at Julian intently. "So," he was saying in a low voice, "who gets to leave first, eh? Do you want the advantage of time, possibility of losing me and running back to that hidden fortress of yours? Or would you rather I go first, give you the rush of wondering if there's an ambush waiting?" he asked with relish. "So many ways to die tonight," he mused almost serenely.

"You shouldn't enjoy what you do too much," Julian advised. "It makes you stupid."

Lancaster threw his head back and laughed.

Cameron slid the leather folder onto the table, collected the other plates and flatware, and stepped away from the table, trying his best to keep his eyes off both men and avoid their attention as he placed the dishes on a waiting tray.

Lancaster sat back and put his hands behind his head, watching Cameron in amusement. "I'll go first then," he decided after a moment, still looking at Cameron speculatively. "You'll want to say goodbye, after all," he said as he stood and buttoned his suit jacket. He smirked down at Julian, who sat unmoving, watching him. "This was fun," he announced. "I'll let word get around," he promised in a lower voice, leaning over Julian and placing a hand on his shoulder as he spoke into his ear. "They'll know you were man enough to pay for your own last meal."

Julian nodded slightly. "You do that," he muttered.

Lancaster took a step away from the table, stopped short, and put his hand on Cameron's arm. Cameron flinched. "My condolences for your loss," Lancaster offered seriously, ignoring Cameron's reaction, and then he turned and began walking away.

Cameron didn't move as he watched him leave the restaurant. He wasn't sure what to think anymore, except that Julian was in a hell of a lot of trouble. Visibly shaken, he turned to face Julian.

Julian was shaking his head as he stood and pulled his black leather billfold out from his breast pocket. "Fucking wine," he whispered, still in the Irish accent. Cameron was beginning to think it was real. He'd never seen Julian quite so unraveled.

He met Cameron's eyes briefly before looking back at the money in his hands. "He was lying," he added as he began counting out the money to pay the bill.

Cameron watched him, aware of the longing and upset in his expression and not caring about hiding it anymore. "Lying about what?" he asked in a pained voice.

Julian looked up at him as if surprised that he'd actually spoken. "There being anyone other than you," he answered bluntly.

Cameron inhaled sharply and wrapped his arms around his middle, his eyes remaining locked on Julian the whole time. He had to step back, or he'd never be able to look away. And he realized with a painful jolt that this just might be his last chance. "I'm sorry," he said abruptly. "For what I said."

Julian looked at him closely and gave a slight jerk of his head to the side in response before looking back down at the money he was counting. "Is that because I'm about to die?" he asked calmly.

Cameron couldn't stop the soft whimper this time. "No. Because I was afraid. Because you didn't deserve it," he said pleadingly, willing Julian to understand.

"Yes, I did," Julian assured him with a small nod. He placed the rest of the bills on the table and then looked up as he buttoned his jacket. He looked heartbreakingly sad, which scared Cameron even more. "Will you tell Blake something for me?" he asked softly.

Cameron gave a small nod.

"Tell him to run like hell if I don't come back."

Cameron swallowed on the knot in his throat and nodded again. "He'll be waiting for you, won't he? Lancaster. He wants to kill you."

Julian nodded minutely. "Tell Blake I'll come here if I'm able," he requested hoarsely.

Cameron could see the tangible defeat on Julian's shoulders, and it made him angry. Julian had always been strong and stoic, and this ghost of who he had been was wrong. So very wrong.

"You've given up," he said accusingly. "What happened to 'I'm good at what I do'?" he demanded.

"He's good at what he does as well," Julian responded calmly. "There's a price that comes with doing what I do," he explained distantly. "We all pay it in the end. Just tell Blake," he requested, barely able to say the words.

Cameron was struck speechless by the mixture of defeat and longing and fear in the black depths of Julian's eyes. His heart broke with an almost physical pain as he realized what he had truly done to the man, a man who had once been so magnificent. It had never been Julian who'd been capable of breaking anything in their relationship, Cameron realized. He'd had all the power all along.

Julian opened his mouth as if to say something more, but then he bowed his head slightly and turned, walking out of the restaurant without a backward glance.

Cameron stared at the glass doors where Julian had exited until Blake appeared shortly thereafter, obviously having been forewarned that this little meeting was going to be taking place. Cameron realized his boss had been hiding all these months, and he had no reason to hide now that Lancaster had somehow found Julian.

"Cameron?" Blake murmured to him.

The waiter turned to look at Blake. "He said he'd come back here if he was able," he said woodenly. "He said if he didn't that you should run like hell."

Blake nodded, looking pale and drawn, and he looked at the door as if he could somehow see what was happening somewhere out in the city through the glass. He looked back at Cameron and let out a slow, shaky breath. "Did he say anything else?" he asked worriedly.

Cameron's reply was a bare whisper. "He said he was about to die."

BLAKE saw the last guests out just after midnight, not much later than usual. Leaving the cleanup to the other employees for once, Cameron joined him at the bar.

"Are you waiting for him?" he asked shakily.

Blake nodded as he wiped down the bar. He looked up at Cameron and nodded again. "If he said he'd come here, then he will. And if he doesn't, it'll be Lancaster coming after me. If he wants me, he'll have to walk through a double barrel to get to me," he said determinedly, and Cameron noticed the shotgun leaning against the bar. He was surprised by its sudden appearance, but he told himself that after Julian, nothing should really shock him anymore. "Julian didn't run like I begged him to," Blake said grimly. "I won't either."

Cameron stared at him in stunned silence for several moments as he came to a decision. "Can I wait with you?" he finally asked.

Blake looked up at Cameron sadly. "It won't be pretty, no matter who comes back," he warned. "He might kill you, too, if he has the chance."

Cameron merely nodded in return. That scenario was out of his hands, and he knew it. If Arlo wanted him dead, there was nothing he could do to stop him.

As it got later and later, Cameron became more and more worried despite telling himself that everything would work out. Julian would take care of Lancaster and come back, he told himself. What happened after that, Cameron didn't know. But there was no way he was letting Julian go without a fight. He had to convince Julian that he knew now that what they had was worth it. Worth anything. They'd figure something out. They had to.

He realized now that Julian had been *what* he was because of *who* he was, not the other way around. And by asking him to change, Cameron had hurt him more than any bullet or broken foot or dog bite ever could have. He'd hurt himself too, depriving himself of the only man he'd ever truly loved.

Blake wasn't much comfort as they waited together. The man was almost as worried as Cameron, and he obviously wasn't the type who was used to sitting around and waiting for the other shoe to drop. He paced and fidgeted, cleaned glasses that were already clean, peeled the label off a bottle of Bushmills whiskey, sat on the stool next to Cameron and spun it back and forth, then got up and paced again. Cameron simply kept checking the clock.

Blake finally opened the whiskey and poured, setting one glass in front of Cameron. "Drink it. You look like you need it. Lord knows I do," he muttered. Confirming his words, Blake poured a glass for himself and took an unusually deep drink.

Cameron sipped at the Irish whiskey, just then seeing the irony in it. "Is Julian really Irish?" he asked Blake as he looked down at the drink.

"I have no fucking idea," Blake answered in frustration. "I've never heard him use that one. I've heard British, Boston, Spanish, Kurdish, French, Texan, and surfer dude, but never Irish. Might mean it's the real one, if he never used it," he said in a distant, rambling tone.

Cameron blinked at him. "Surfer… dude?"

Blake waved his hand around. "You know, 'Chillax, bra, we just gotta harvest some dead presidents' kind of shit." His voice had parodied the SoCal accent he was aiming for. "He only used it on the phone because he couldn't pull it off in person."

Cameron nodded, wide-eyed, wondering if there was anyone who truly knew Julian. "I guess it explains some of the weird phrases he used, anyway. Got his accents confused." He laughed brokenly.

Blake smiled slightly, but didn't reply.

They sat silently for a full half-hour before Cameron looked up at his boss again worriedly. "How long does it take, Blake?" he rasped. "How long does it take to… kill a man?"

The older man studied him as he shifted his glass back and forth on the polished bar. "With Julian, I'd say not long," he finally answered. "But Lancaster is different."

"He said Julian trained him."

"From what he's told me, yes. They both know the other's strengths and weaknesses. They think the same," Blake tried to explain hesitantly. "They're like… waves crashing against each other." He peered at Cameron, trying to gauge how he would react. "For whatever reason, someone has decided that Julian needs to be taken out of the business. And anyone *in* the business knows that the only man who can do that is either very, very lucky or knows how Julian thinks. Arlo is, unfortunately, both."

"And Julian?" Cameron asked. His voice was a mere thread.

"Hard to say," Blake answered. "If he met Arlo here, it means Arlo couldn't find him physically. He got a message to him somehow, and God knows what he threatened him with," he mused. "Whatever it was, it hit Julian's buttons. That's the only reason he would have come out tonight. He was backed into a corner."

Cameron swallowed down on the knot of misery and dread. Could the something Lancaster threatened have been him?

"He's protecting his territory," Blake continued, putting his hand on the bar in front of Cameron and meeting his eyes. "His reputation, his contacts, his home. And, I believe, he's protecting *you*, kiddo. Or at least the idea of you. The idea that he can have something normal without it being in danger."

Cameron nodded slowly. "I know," he said hoarsely, raising his hand to cover his upper chest where he could feel the warrior's cross warm against his skin. "I hurt him badly, didn't I?" he asked regretfully.

"Yes," Blake answered bluntly. "The whole time I was worried about you, but… maybe you'll get the chance to make it up to him," he offered as condolence.

Shortly after, Preston knocked gently at the glass doors of the restaurant, and Blake hurried to let him in.

"Do you have him?" Blake demanded excitedly.

Preston merely shook his head as he unbuttoned his coat.

"I lost them both, sir," he said in sorrow as he followed Blake back to the bar. "He's on his own now," he told them as he sat and poured himself a glass of whiskey.

Blake sighed and looked at the clock. It was four a.m. He inhaled deeply and let out the breath in a thin, slow exhale. All they could do now was wait.

THE city lay dark and relatively silent in the muggy night. To the casual observer, there was no hint of the deadly game of cat and mouse that had been played in the streets. The sirens of police cars being called to investigate shots fired and the occasional broken window or unexplained alarm were nothing unusual.

Julian walked slowly along the sidewalk, his head down and his eyes focused solely on the next step. He understood why Arlo had made it a game. Julian had trained him, taught him almost everything he knew. They'd worked together. They'd been friends, as close as brothers. Tonight was Arlo's version of poetic justice. Julian had tossed him out when he became too reckless, something Arlo had never forgiven him for. When Arlo received the contract for Julian's head, he'd obviously seen the opportunity to prove to Julian just how good he was.

And Julian had to admit, the kid was good. There had been an odd sort of battlefield respect to their war games tonight. Certainly neither wanted to shoot the other in the back. Julian knew Arlo had held off on several killing shots because they hadn't been… honorable. And, God help him, he'd done the same. But when it came down to it, he'd been forced to take the last shot. It was truly kill or be killed.

He stopped and leaned against a decorative column for protection, shivering as he tried to dispel his morbid thoughts. The shot had been taken; there was no use lingering over it. He looked up and down the road, knowing that Arlo might still be out there. Julian thought he'd killed him. He was pretty sure. But he, of all people, knew that unless he carried his enemy's body parts with him when he left, the enemy might still be out there.

Julian pushed away from the wall and kept moving. After what seemed an eternity of slow, slightly dragging steps, he came within sight of the high-rise that hosted Tuesdays on its top floor. Julian stared at it gratefully for a long moment before soldiering on. He slid in through the revolving glass doors and stumbled to the elevators. He was relieved to find that they were still on and working even though it was late, and he leaned against the inside of the car as it soared upward.

When the elevator stopped with a jolt, Julian lurched and groaned with the sudden change of motion. He was exhausted, almost physically unable to put one foot in front of the other. The doors opened silently, and Julian stood staring at the floor blankly. Finally, he pushed away from the mirrored wall of the elevator car and began walking toward the glass doors of the restaurant.

"IS HE really Irish, Preston?" Cameron asked tentatively as they sat at the bar and waited.

"He is today," Preston answered wryly before taking a small sip of the whiskey in his hand.

Cameron sighed and let it drop. Preston obviously had the same theory as Julian when it came to straight answers. They answered your question, but not in any useful way.

They were managing to make conversation, though. Nothing important or heavy, just idle discussion, anything to force the time to pass. Cameron was hard-pressed not to ask Preston more questions he knew the man wouldn't answer.

But the later time the clock displayed, the more frightened Cameron got. Julian had seemed to have no confidence in his ability to make it through the night, and Blake and Preston were both somber and worried. Cameron didn't know anything about Julian's abilities; he was forced to take his cues from the men who did.

He was taking a drink of water when Blake raised his head and half-stood to look out the glass front of the restaurant. Cameron turned, dropping his glass of water on the floor in his haste, where it shattered and sent pieces skittering across the marble floor.

Julian wasn't walking quickly as he headed for the doors. It was obvious he could see them through the glass, but he didn't even raise a hand to acknowledge them. He merely kept his head down, his left leg dragging a little as he limped gamely toward the doors.

Cameron almost fell over as he stood from the stool to get a better look. Julian reached out and put his hand on the locked glass door, like a little kid peering through a storefront window at a coveted toy. Cameron stepped away from the chair and moved toward the door,

Preston and Blake both at his heels, heading toward the foyer to unlock the doors. Julian's hand slid down the glass as they came closer, leaving behind it a smeared streak of blood in the shape of his palm. He took an unsteady step away from the glass, reached out again as if trying to steady himself, and then crumpled to the ground.

Cameron froze in horror as Julian collapsed, and then he ran—ran across the foyer and skidded into the glass door just as Blake unlocked it. He yanked it open and tore around the corner. "Julian!" He dropped to his knees at the man's side and reached out to touch his shoulder. "Julian?"

Julian's head lolled to the side as Blake joined them on the ground. His eyes didn't even flutter in response to Cameron's voice. Blake pawed gently at his chest, his hands coming away wet with blood.

"Fuck!" he hissed as he pushed Julian's dark suit coat aside and yanked open the shirt underneath, looking for the source. Buttons went flying and a soaked handkerchief dislodged from a spot low on Julian's abdomen. Blood began streaming from the wound out over Julian's exposed skin.

Cameron couldn't catch his breath as he watched helplessly, horrified by all the blood. He bent over and pressed a soft, shaky kiss to the corner of Julian's mouth. "Julian, please talk to me," he begged. "Please."

Julian groaned in response as Blake pushed up and went running back into the restaurant. Preston had disappeared.

"Cameron," Julian whispered hoarsely.

Trying to hold back the tears that were suddenly clogging his throat, Cameron leaned to press his forehead to Julian's. "I'm here," he managed to get out fairly evenly.

"He got me," Julian murmured with a shuddering gasp of air. It seemed like a silly thing to say as he lay there bleeding. It was obviously the only thing his mind could form.

"Blake's going to help you," Cameron promised before he choked back a soft sob. He brushed his fingers through Julian's damp hair, searching in vain for some way to comfort him.

Blake was back just as quickly as he'd left, talking on the phone at his ear and bringing with him a stack of clean rags from behind the bar. "Where else are you hit?" he demanded of Julian in a no-nonsense tone.

"Where there's blood," Julian grumbled weakly as he closed his eyes again.

Blake glared at him and put the phone to his mouth again. "He's still a jackass, if that helps."

Cameron didn't stop stroking Julian's cheek, and he was trying hard to keep it together. Julian didn't need him to fall apart right now. He could do this. "Is there anything I can do?" he asked, surprised that his voice came out fairly steady.

Neither man answered him. Julian's eyes remained closed as Blake spoke rapidly on the phone and then tossed it away to work on Julian's bloody abdomen. Julian reached blindly for Cameron's hand and gripped it weakly. Cameron laced their fingers together and squeezed reassuringly.

"I'm sorry," Julian whispered just before Blake found the wound low in his abdomen again. He pressed a cloth into it to curb the bleeding. Julian's body curled, and he cried out in pain.

Cameron gasped for breath and clutched at Julian's shoulder, trying to hold him still. His eyes were drawn to the ugly-looking wound. "Jesus," he whispered, shocked by all the blood and overwhelmed by the level of agony Julian had to be in to actually cry out.

"Did you get him?" Blake demanded of Julian as he worked. Julian was panting for breath, unconsciously squeezing Cameron's hand with the pain, and Blake leaned closer to him. "Did you kill him?" he repeated forcefully.

"I don't know," Julian gasped as he opened his eyes once more and stared up at the glass atrium above. "He fell into the lake," he managed to tell them hoarsely.

"Fuck," Blake hissed angrily as he reached under Julian to check if the bullet had gone all the way through. His hand came away bloody, and he reached for another towel to press to the exit wound. Julian cried out again and struggled to get away from the pain, kicking at the marble tile and trying to slide away and curl in on himself as he writhed.

Cameron grappled to keep him from moving too much. “Please, Julian, try to lie still,” he begged.

Julian growled softly, the sound turning into something like a wounded animal whining. His struggling slowed, though, and Cameron feared it was more from exhaustion and loss of blood than cooperation.

“I’ve got paramedics on the way, Jules,” Blake told him softly. “This is beyond me,” he explained in a pained voice. He glanced at Cameron worriedly. “He’ll be safe at the hospital,” he told him, “until we can confirm the hit. Hell, if he fell into Lake Michigan, the infections alone will kill him.”

Cameron nodded jerkily, and his entire body tingled with the knowledge that Lancaster might still be out there. Maybe not far away. Maybe coming to finish the job. His breathing got short and shallow as he looked around the foyer. They were completely unprotected, weren’t they? What would happen if the man attacked them here? Even as he asked himself the question, he realized that Preston must have left in order to cover Julian’s back. He couldn’t imagine the man would leave Julian in this state unless it was to protect him.

Cameron was doing well not to gasp for breath as he tried to remain calm. The pain Julian was in was tearing him up. “Julian,” he whispered pleadingly. “Please don’t leave me.”

Julian’s grip on Cameron’s hand was becoming painful. He tried his best not to move as Blake applied pressure to the wound, but he was still writhing and bleeding on the expensive marble as his eyes began to glaze over.

He looked up at Cameron, and his eyes caught on the battered gold and garnet necklace hanging from Cameron’s neck, swinging back and forth like a pendulum. When he looked at Cameron a few moments later, it was with clear regret and resignation. “I’m sorry,” he gasped again.

Cameron’s face crumpled as Julian apologized again, and he gently kissed Julian’s lips then his forehead as his tears fell against

Julian's cheek. "You can't leave me," he whispered desperately. "Who's going to protect me from the fuzzballs?"

Julian was silent in his struggle against the pain, but he turned his face up to Cameron's and tried to meet the gentle brushes of his lips, searching for the comfort of contact. His grip on Cameron's hand was weakening at an alarming rate.

"Get… a cat," he finally panted in a voice so weak it was barely audible.

Cameron gasped out a small laugh despite himself, and he shook his head and ran his free hand through Julian's hair again.

"Hold on, kiddo," Blake urged as he applied pressure to the bleeding wound and watched the elevators impatiently for the paramedics he'd called.

"I'm sorry," Julian managed as his eyes closed against his will.

"Julian! Please. Oh God. Julian, please…," Cameron begged miserably, holding Julian's hand tight and pressing his lips to his forehead between choking breaths. Julian didn't respond as the fingers held in Cameron's hand finally loosened and went limp.

Cameron clung to his hand even when he wasn't holding on anymore, whispering in his ear as Blake hovered, keeping pressure on the wound and cursing emphatically until the EMTs finally showed up and pushed them both out of the way.

Cameron crawled backward to lean against the glass doors, eyes wide and wet as he watched, struggling to get enough air in as he tried equally hard not to scream out all the terror.

THE day was a beautiful one, even if it was scorching hot. The trees were green and full, and the ground steamed with waves of heat from the summer sun high in the blue sky. The world seemed calm and at ease, lethargic in the heat.

The group of mourners was small, but larger than anyone present had expected. Julian Cross' passing had come and gone with nothing more than a whisper. No official announcement had been made. No family had been contacted. No telephone calls had been exchanged to let mutual friends know he had died. None of his acquaintances had known one another. But word had got around. There were politicians and prominent businessmen mingling solemnly with humble workmen and shady criminals, all of them thinking they'd known the man.

On the morning of the funeral, the crowd had to negotiate the beautiful and haunting ground of Forest Park, forced to stand around the variety of monuments in order to get close to the grave-site.

Miri had taken Cameron shopping to get him some clothes she deemed worthy of the funeral. He ended up in all black, an ironic fact not lost on him. Black suit, black shoes, black shirt with the tiniest gray pinstripe.

Black for secrets. Black for shadows. Black for sorrow. He blended in with the rest of the crowd, but he felt absolutely and totally alone.

Blake had taken him home from the hospital that night after the doctors pronounced the time of death, and he had stayed with him all night. They'd sat in silence on the couch together, neither capable of saying anything, until they fell into fitful sleep.

Cameron had almost totally withdrawn in the three days since Julian lost all that blood just outside Tuesdays. It wasn't something he'd be able to get over, he knew, holding his lover's hand and watching him die. Hearing an apology as Julian's last words, when it had been Cameron who'd needed to say it.

It had done something to Cameron. Changed him somehow. He couldn't feel anything but the awful ache and piercing loneliness, and he wasn't sure he ever would.

Standing here in the midst of the peaceful glen, quiet despite the crowd, it suddenly became all too real. Cameron would never see him again. He would never be able to tell Julian the things he wanted to say. That he was sorry. That he was a fool. That he'd face any danger if he could just be with him.

He staggered from where he stood with Blake and several of the other servers from Tuesdays and pushed his way out of the group to walk across the path to a marble mausoleum. Stepping behind it, he slowly slid down the wall until he sat on the ground and pressed the heels of his hands to his eyes, trying to stop the tears. He hadn't cried since that night, since they'd pushed him away from Julian's side.

Now the agony swelled so painfully that he thought it might choke him. But the exhaustion meant he couldn't gasp, he couldn't wail. He could only sit, quiet and heartbroken, while the tears streamed down his face.

CHAPTER 10

THE sun shining down on the city made the snow-covered sidewalk in the distance glitter, and the glare swirled up in shimmering trails. Downtown Chicago was a concrete and metal maze that held in all the cold like an icebox, and just like it would roast you alive in the summer if you let it, it would freeze you solid when the wind blew. The wind off the lake was the worst, its frigid gusts enough to freeze standing water in bare minutes.

Cameron walked along the street in his heavy wool coat, duffel bag over one shoulder, cell phone in his opposite hand. "No, I don't think so," he was saying. "I've been out all day, and with this cold weather, I need a damn break!"

"Well, you should come for dinner soon. Jean-Michel is afraid you don't like his food anymore," Blake told him over the phone.

"He should know better," Cameron said drolly. "Okay. Thursday. How about that?"

"Sounds good. I'll reserve a table for us," Blake responded happily. "How's work going?"

"Pretty good, I guess. No complaints," Cameron answered vaguely.

"I understand. We can talk about it at dinner," Blake offered.

"I guess I should visit the restaurant more often," Cameron responded, his tone gone distant and flat.

"You do what you need to do, kiddo. I'll talk to you tomorrow."

"I'll be there. Now get back to work," Cameron said, some smile back in his voice.

"Will do."

Cameron closed his cell phone and slid it into his pocket. He shook his head. After nearly six months, Blake was still taking care of him. Or at least trying to. Cameron had finally started rebelling in early fall.

The first few weeks had been horrible. Cameron could barely stand to be awake, much less up and moving around, and he stayed closeted in his apartment, just trying to wrap his brain around what had happened.

Two weeks after the funeral, while feeding the dogs, he suddenly remembered Smith and Wesson. A phone call to Blake revealed that the house had been emptied and sold at auction not long after Julian's death, bought by a man overseas who had yet to arrive and claim it. Blake himself had attempted to find the two cats, going to Julian's house the day after his death, but he'd searched the house from end to end with no avail, and none of the staff knew anything about their whereabouts.

Preston had disappeared the night Julian was killed, and no sign of him or the cats ever surfaced. Cameron was devastated. He knew Julian had loved those cats. They were absolute monsters, so why else keep them if he didn't love them?

He could only hope Preston had taken them with him.

After a month, Blake came and banged on his door and told him that if he refused to work at Tuesdays, then he had another job for him. With Blake's guidance, Cameron became a relay contact. All he did was answer a cell phone, take the message—often in code he didn't understand—and call someone else to relay the information. He was accurate, fast, and most importantly, kept his mouth shut about it.

After the first few insanely large under-the-table payments, Cameron repainted his apartment, remodeled the kitchen, and bought new furniture for the first time in his life. He bought a new, nicer wardrobe that Miri helped him pick out. She wanted him to socialize more. He decidedly didn't, but after a couple months, he started going out with her and some friends just to get her to leave him alone about it. He found the distraction really did help sometimes.

After summer passed, he realized that he didn't sit on his hands well, and he joined a nearby gym. Finding it another welcome distraction, he went religiously, and to his surprise, toned up his wiry muscles quite a bit. He also ran a couple miles on the treadmill each time he was there. The changes in his body made him feel like a different person, one that he liked, and when Blake suggested he take a kickboxing class, he went along amiably.

After a week of the class, he realized that his lie about Julian's bruises coming from kickboxing had been pretty well-crafted after all.

Cameron hadn't wanted to go back to Tuesdays. Ever. It had taken three months before Blake even got him up there. The foyer was the worst. The marble had soaked up the blood and been stained beyond any hope of cleaning. It had been replaced, but the new tiles were slightly whiter than the ones that surrounded it, and so they had created a decorative medallion on the floor instead.

It bore a remarkable resemblance to the warrior's cross Cameron still wore around his neck, and it reminded Cameron of the tombs of knights laid to rest in churches in Europe.

Cameron could still see Julian lying there, though, and the bloody smear down the glass door. After he got past it and got inside the restaurant, things were a little better, but it still shook him so badly that he avoided the place unless Blake insisted.

Finally, after nearly half a year, Cameron felt almost like his ordinary self. He still lived alone in the remodeled condo with his four dogs, who each stood about nine inches high, fully grown. He still read a lot and listened to jazz on an Internet radio station. He still cooked for himself and watched DVDs and liked to dress sloppily and sit around the apartment.

It was only sometimes that he couldn't handle being alone and had to call a friend for company to get his mind off what he'd lost. That friend was usually Blake, because he knew what Cameron was going through. Julian Cross had been a hard man to find and an even harder man to lose.

THERE was a soft knock on the door, almost drowned out by the noise inside the apartment. The only reason Cameron heard it was because the dogs suddenly careened out of the kitchen toward the door.

With a soft, inquisitive grunt, Cameron set the pork chops he'd pulled out of the fridge in the sink and headed to the door. Out of long habit he looked through the peep-hole first. There was no one in the view, but another soft knock followed as he peered out.

Cameron frowned as he pulled back from the door. He wasn't sure he liked this. Why wouldn't someone stand in front of the door? Sometimes he could be too paranoid, he told himself. The building had security, after all. Shaking his head, he flipped the deadlock and opened the door a bit, standing half behind it.

"Hello, Cameron," a soft, accented voice greeted from beside the door, its source still out of sight.

A breath caught in Cameron's throat, and his fingers clenched on the edge of the door. That voice. It was so close to….

How could someone be so cruel? Anger flaring, Cameron threw the door open so hard it slammed against the wall as he stepped out into the hall to see who was deliberately yanking his chain. "Who the hell do you think…?"

Arlo Lancaster leaned against the wall next to the door, hands stuffed into the pockets of his pea-coat as he watched Cameron with dark eyes. He had an ugly scar along his left eye; it had to be the shot Julian had taken that he'd hoped killed him. He smiled wickedly when he met Cameron's eyes.

Fear made Cameron go cold all over. This was a nightmare he'd tried very hard not to think about. He couldn't even manage to protest when Arlo ushered him back inside his apartment.

"You've changed things since the last time I was here," Lancaster murmured from behind him as he closed the door.

That statement chilled Cameron to the bone all over again, and he was sure it showed, because he could feel the blood drain from his face. He shifted uncomfortably and took a few wooden steps away from the other man. "New paint," he said as his mind started scrambling. What was he supposed to do? There was no one to help him, and no one to miss him for at least two days, when he was supposed to show up at Tuesdays for dinner with Blake.

Lancaster nodded and grinned. "Where is he?" he asked politely.

Cameron's mouth went dry and pain shot through him like lightning. "He's dead," he answered in a choked voice.

Lancaster's lips curved into a slight, almost fond smile as he nodded his head thoughtfully. "Hasn't contacted you after all, has he?" he murmured almost to himself. "Good thing I have a Plan B," he told Cameron with a wry grin. "I'll take you with me, anyway. My bet is he was just done with you, but you know. Can't be too careful. Would you care to put food out for the animals before we go?" he offered in amusement. "You may be gone quite a while," he added dryly.

Cameron's stomach twisted. "What for?" he asked. As he started thinking about it, the hair on the back of his neck prickled. Could Julian really be alive?

Lancaster's smile melted away, leaving him looking hard and dangerous, even more so when a gun appeared in his hand. "I don't care if your animals starve," he snarled. "Move."

Cameron nodded slowly, clenching his hands when they started to shake. "The food's in the kitchen," he said, gesturing slightly before he started moving, watching Lancaster. "Should I pack a bag?" he asked as he poured out extra food and water.

Lancaster gave a derogatory laugh. "We'll buy you a toothbrush," he drawled as he kept the silenced gun trained on Cameron. "Now assume the position, my friend," he ordered with a wave of his free hand at the nearest wall.

Cameron's shoulders snapped back. "Excuse me?"

"Hands flat on the wall, feet apart," Lancaster barked impatiently. "Get moving, Jacobs."

Keeping his eyes on the gun, Cameron moved as instructed, though his chin stayed turned to watch Lancaster as his palms settled against the wall, and he widened his stance carefully.

Lancaster placed his gun in the back of his waistband and moved behind Cameron. "Move and I'll snap your neck," he assured Cameron as he put his hand on the back of Cameron's head and pushed it to lower it. He began to slide his hands down the sides of Cameron's body, then one palm moved to his chest and the other to his spine as he patted him down.

Letting his head fall forward, Cameron kept his back rigid, eyes closing as he realized what Lancaster was doing.

"Hiding anything?" Lancaster asked him in a sarcastic, teasing tone.

Cameron grimaced. He almost wished he was. "No," he answered truthfully.

"Forgive me if I don't believe you," Lancaster drawled politely as he continued with the pat-down. A little bit of Julian's professional manner showed in his protégé as Lancaster searched Cameron thoroughly and quickly.

Somewhat relieved by the clinical touches, Cameron nonetheless frowned at the wall. Lancaster stood again and backed away when he was done, giving Cameron a pat on the back to let him know he could relax.

"Lead on," he ordered as he gestured to the door. Cameron hesitated, but the gun at his back was reason enough to make his feet start moving. When Cameron got to the door, Lancaster murmured, "Try anything, and the dogs are the first to be shot."

Cameron shot a look of pure loathing over his shoulder as he opened the door. "You really think he's still alive?" he asked. "If he was he'd have… contacted me," he told Lancaster shakily.

"Oh, yeah?" Lancaster responded knowingly. "What makes you say that?"

"He loved me," Cameron insisted in a rough whisper. "He would have let me know he was alive."

"Oh, I don't know," Lancaster drawled with a slow, malicious smirk. "Love is just a word most of the time," he claimed as he shoved

Cameron out into the hall. "If you were one of us, you'd know that already."

ARLO LANCASTER roughly yanked the blindfold off Cameron's head, and Cameron blinked in the low light, trying to get his eyes to adjust to his new surroundings. After getting into the back of a van with no windows, Lancaster had tied the piece of cloth over his eyes and trussed him up like a Christmas tree. Then they'd driven for what seemed like forever. Cameron had lost count of the turns and stops. For all he knew, Lancaster had merely driven around the block fifty times and they were still in his neighborhood. Or they could be in Milwaukee.

They were definitely in a large building, though, one with few windows and a lot of dust. It appeared to be a warehouse, long abandoned. And it was cold. Cameron hadn't been given the option of grabbing his coat, and he was already chilled from riding in the van. It was settling into his bones, making him shiver.

The huge room was full of wooden crates, and the floor was littered with wooden shavings used for packaging. In the back there was an office, illuminated by a weak light. Lancaster shoved at Cameron's back and started him walking toward it.

As they got closer, Cameron realized that someone else was already in the office. His breath caught painfully in his chest when he met Blake Nichols' eyes.

Blake growled softly, tugging at the ties that bound him to the metal chair in which he sat, and he glared past Cameron's shoulder at Lancaster. "I told you," he said in a rough voice. "Cameron had nothing to do with any of this."

"Well, he does now," Lancaster answered cheerfully. He gave Cameron another rough shove between the shoulder blades, pushing him into the office. "You know how to use those?" he asked tauntingly as he nodded at a pile of opaque plastic strips that sat on the chair beside Blake.

"Yeah," Cameron muttered. "They're zip ties."

"Very good," Lancaster laughed. "Use them," he ordered.

Cameron bristled. "You want me to zip-tie *myself* to the chair."

"Yes, darling, and be quick about it, hmm?" Lancaster cooed. "I'm sure we'll have company soon enough."

Cameron reluctantly walked over to the chair and picked up the zip ties. "What do you want tied down?" he asked, resentment clear in his voice.

"Ankles to the chair legs, wrists to the arms," Lancaster ordered seriously. "Be speedy about it."

Cameron frowned but sat down with a thump and zip-tied his ankles over his jeans. He took another strap and laid it over his left wrist and pulled it closed enough that his hand could move but not pull out of the plastic loop. "Sorry," he said unrepentantly. "I'm out of hands."

"Cross' loss," Lancaster responded as he walked over and zip-tied Cameron's other hand, tight enough that it cut into Cameron's wrist.

"Goddammit!" Cameron hissed, his fingers going rigid with the pressure.

"Quit whining," Lancaster huffed as he stood again and backhanded Cameron.

Cameron yelped in pain as his head snapped to the side with the force of the blow. When he looked back, there was a trickle of blood trailing from the corner of his mouth.

"Leave him the fuck alone," Blake snarled.

"You should have kept Julian away from him," Lancaster chastised as he moved away.

Blake's dirt-streaked face reddened slightly, and he looked at Cameron guiltily. "You really think Julian's still alive?" he asked Lancaster disbelievingly. "You don't think he'd have shown up by now?" he practically shouted.

"I think neither one of you knew him half as well as you thought you did," Lancaster answered as he threw himself into an old desk chair, causing it to slide and spin slightly. He pulled out his gun and began idly checking it over.

"He was my best friend," Blake argued in a pained voice.

"Yeah?" Lancaster asked tauntingly. "Mine too," he responded coldly as the smile on his face dropped suddenly. He stood and began pacing back and forth slowly. "You even know his real name?" he challenged. "Where he's really from? Hmm?"

Blake swallowed with difficulty and glanced at Cameron, and then he lowered his eyes instead of answering. Finally, he just shook his head.

"Yeah," Lancaster agreed. "No one does, Nichols. No one but Preston. And no one else will," he claimed simply. "When I met him, he was living in London, and he was speaking German with a perfect accent," he told them in amusement. "Finally, he came out with this random Irish one day and told me he was tired. The only person he'll ever really give a damn about is Preston. Remember that."

He stopped suddenly and cocked his head at Cameron, then lurched out of his chair and took an alarmingly quick couple of steps and bent closer, grabbing at the necklace around Cameron's neck.

Cameron's eyes widened in fear as he felt the yank on the chain around his neck. "No. Don't…."

Lancaster looked up at him as he held the trinket in the palm of his hand, his dark eyes masked by the low light. He gave the chain a yank and snapped the clasp.

"Dammit!" Cameron hissed as the chain cut into his neck painfully, and then the comforting weight of the pendant was gone and in Lancaster's hand. Cameron stared at it. He'd not taken it off, not once. Ever. Even after he'd pushed Julian away. Even after he'd watched them bury him.

Lancaster straightened and took a few steps away, closer to the light, as he looked at the pendant. He looked up at him again, anger flaring in his eyes as he clenched it in his fist. "Do you have any idea what this is?" he asked with a snarl.

Cameron flinched and stared at Lancaster's hand. His eyes darted up to face the anger in the other man's eyes. He didn't understand it, but it frightened him more than any emotion Julian had ever displayed. "Julian gave it to me," he answered in a whisper.

"No shit," Lancaster snapped as he took the pendant and held his hand up as if he wanted to throw it out the door into the empty warehouse. The emotions warred briefly on his face, but in the end he couldn't do it like he so obviously wanted to. Instead, he looked back down at it and then tossed it into Cameron's lap disgustedly as he turned away.

Letting out a shaky breath, Cameron looked down at the necklace that lay draped precariously over his thigh. Without thinking he strained to reach it with one hand, but there was no way to touch it. He closed his eyes and tried to calm down.

"What the hell did Jules see in someone like you?" Lancaster wondered quietly to himself as he walked away, looking out at the quiet warehouse with a shake of his head.

Cameron pulled up his head to watch the other man, who had no way of knowing Cameron still asked himself the same question, even now after Julian had been gone for so long.

"What is it?" he asked thickly, looking back down at the necklace. He wasn't sure he wanted to know, not from Lancaster. But to this point he'd thought it meant something only to Julian.

Lancaster turned slightly and looked back at him with obvious contempt. He looked away again, as if answering the question while looking at Cameron was just too much for him. "The stone is to be given from one warrior to another," he answered bitterly. "It's called a warrior's cross. Symbolizes the fucking bond between us, and the cross we all have to bear for being what we are."

Cameron's brow wrinkled. He wasn't a warrior. Not even close. "He said it was worn for protection," he objected.

"Yeah?" Lancaster asked through gritted teeth. "That's what I told him when I gave it to him."

Cameron's head snapped up and he stared at Lancaster in disbelief. Lancaster stood with his back to Cameron, staring out over the darkened warehouse.

"Now I won't feel too guilty killing the bastard," he murmured.

Cameron knew he was trembling just as much from fear as from the cold. He swallowed thickly, tasting blood, and he glanced at Blake fearfully. Blake was watching him, and when Cameron met his eyes, Blake merely shook his head dejectedly. They were bait, pure and simple. Bait for a fish that had already been caught.

"I found Smith and Wesson," Blake finally murmured to Cameron with a nod of his head to the corner of the office.

Cameron's eyes trailed to the corner to see a large cage, filled and covered with blankets to protect it from the cold of the warehouse. Through a part in two of the blankets, Cameron could clearly see long, orange fur. As if on cue, a low, throaty meow emitted from the cage, followed by another.

"He may not come for you two," Lancaster told them grimly as he stood in the doorway with his back to them. "But he won't leave those beasts behind," he wagered with confidence.

"How did you find them? Where were they?" Cameron blurted.

"Preston had them," Lancaster answered after a moment of thought. "He was easier to find than Julian," he explained.

"Yeah?" Blake asked wryly. "Funny that, since Julian's *dead*!" he shouted in frustration.

"Where Preston is, Julian isn't far behind. I found Preston," Lancaster continued as if he hadn't heard Blake's words. "I followed him. I tried to kill him, but the fucker got away," he practically snarled. "But I did find the cats."

"How did you know about them?" Cameron questioned. "Are they okay?" he asked worriedly, his mind grasping for something to think about that didn't include any form of death.

"They're fine," Lancaster answered as he rubbed at the scratches on his cheek. "I was with Julian when he first found them," he added as he turned around and cocked his head at Cameron and Blake. "Found them in a ditch one night. So tiny they still had blue eyes. Had to be bottle-fed. Julian saw their ears as we were driving by. He stopped in the middle of a goddamned multimillion-pound arms deal to rescue those damn cats," he said with a sigh. "Did not make our buyer happy," he mused. "Those cats were the reason we had to leave Ireland. It was almost worth it to watch him feed them," he mused distantly.

Blake snorted in apparent amusement, and he was shaking his head when Cameron looked back at him. "At least we know he never changed anything but his name," he muttered.

Cameron's throat tightened as he thought of Julian. There seemed to be two entirely different people inside the man he had called his lover. Lancaster and Blake both talked about a killer, a man who was brutal and relentless and possibly downright cruel. They spoke of him with both respect for his abilities and perhaps a hint of fear of what he might have been capable of doing.

But Cameron had seen a different man. A man who was afraid of handling Cameron's puppies because they were so tiny. A man who enjoyed pretending he couldn't tie his tie correctly because he liked to have Cameron do it for him. A man who loved those two damn cats so much, who loved *him* so much it nearly destroyed him when Cameron stupidly pushed him away.

"You really think he's still alive?" Cameron found himself asking Lancaster hopefully. "Do you know for sure?" he asked in a whisper.

"I haven't seen him," Lancaster answered honestly, a smile pulling at his lips. "But I've felt his eyes on me," he claimed confidently. "Haven't you?" he asked tauntingly, obviously knowing the answer was no.

IT SEEMED like they sat in that office forever before there was a sound that echoed in the warehouse. Lancaster was immediately standing once more, tense and coiled as he peered out into the darkness.

“Not exactly high ground,” Blake chastised in a wry tone. “Only light in the damn place, and you’re sitting in front of it,” he said with a cluck of his tongue. “If that’s Preston out there, you’re dead already. He was a sniper before he took to driving that Lexus, you know.”

“I’m well aware of the type of people Julian surrounds himself with,” Lancaster murmured in response. He didn’t sound at all nervous. In fact, he sounded almost excited. “Julian won’t let him shoot me. He’s got unfinished business to tend to first.”

“Damnit!” Blake exclaimed suddenly. “Julian is dead!” he shouted again, his voice nearly cracking with the pain of saying it. “We watched him die!”

“Did you, now?” Lancaster asked in a soft, distracted voice as his eyes scanned the warehouse. He looked like a ferret, low and tense and twitchy. “You sure about that?” he murmured with an obvious smile. “You saw him bleeding. You saw him taken away in an ambulance. One that was driven by Preston, by the way.”

“What?” Cameron blurted in confusion. Blake sat staring at Lancaster’s back stupidly, a look of what might have been hope beginning to form on his face.

“Did you see the doctor who worked on him? Did you see his body after they said he was dead?” Lancaster continued. “No, because they patched him up, hid him in intensive care under a string of false names, and carted him off to somewhere else when he was able to be moved.”

“How do you know this?” Blake asked tentatively.

“It’s my job to know these things,” Lancaster answered softly as he began to relax once more, obviously having decided the noise was nothing. “I traced him as far as I could, but that doctor didn’t know where they’d taken him. I can tell you one thing,” he went on with a cocky grin as he checked his gun for perhaps the fifth time. “Julian Cross did not die the night you thought he did. He lived at least another three weeks, even if he was mostly on his back and immobile. Whether he made it past the move to wherever, I don’t know. The doctor—before he died mysteriously in a wreck last month—told me that moving him might have killed him,” he said thoughtfully as he spun back and forth slowly in the old chair. "I guess we'll see," he crooned happily.

There was a loud bang in the darkness, and Lancaster was once again on his feet, standing in the doorway. He was purposefully silhouetting himself in the dim light, and Cameron couldn't understand why.

"Julian," Lancaster said softly into the dark.

"Where are they?" a deep Irish-accented voice suddenly demanded in response.

Cameron gasped when he heard him. Julian's voice was shockingly close, seemingly just outside the circle of light cast from the office. It came from everywhere and nowhere, aided by the echoing quality of the cavernous warehouse. It sent chills up Cameron's already frozen back, and he started shaking even more.

"What, no hello?" Lancaster asked Julian coldly as he remained in the doorway. Then he shook his head and sighed. "Tell me something, Cross. What did you see in this kid that I don't?"

"This is beyond the bounds," Julian responded calmly, the disembodied voice low and barely controlled.

Lancaster's body went rigid. "There's no out of bounds in this game," he snarled in return. His head tipped, and he moved his gun to the side, pointing it into the corner. "Make a move and the kitties get it," he warned in a flat, slightly wry voice.

"You have no idea what you're doing," Julian growled in a low, dangerous voice. Cameron squeezed his eyes shut against the tears that threatened. He had never heard that level of anger in Julian's voice before, not even that last night at the restaurant. Even so shocked to hear the voice of a dead man, he was frightened by the emotion.

Lancaster's hand tightened on the gun he held level at the cage in the corner, and then he moved his aim until the gun was trained on Cameron. "Did he really deserve a warrior's cross, Julian?" he asked in a voice that was close to hurt.

Cameron looked at the gun, his breaths harsh as he trembled and tears blurred his vision.

The darkness didn't respond.

Lancaster cocked the gun.

Without a sound of warning, a heavy block of scrap wood flew out of the darkness and smacked against Lancaster's bicep with a dull thump. Lancaster jerked away from the doorway, and the gun went off, the bullet noisily hitting the concrete near Cameron's side and ricocheting away as Lancaster grunted in surprise and pain, stumbling back and losing his hold on the weapon, which clattered to the floor.

Blake began to struggle with the zip ties that held him. "Get down, kid," he grunted as he pushed his metal chair toward the far wall of the office. "Get down and stay down," he ordered through gritted teeth as he tried to rock his own chair and tip it over.

Lancaster righted himself with a curse and turned to face the doorway as he pulled another gun and aimed it. Cameron gasped when Julian appeared in the doorway. He was dressed all in black, and his angry eyes shone like polished black marble. He was like a ghost, materializing out of the gloom. He stood in the doorway, angry and massive and *alive*.

Lancaster fired, hitting Julian square in the chest. Cameron and Blake both shouted wordlessly, but the shot merely caused Julian to stumble backward. Lancaster stared at him in obvious surprise. Julian smiled slowly as he cocked his head at the man and stepped closer.

"You wore a vest?" Lancaster asked in an offended voice as he lowered his weapon slightly. "Cheater."

"Next time try the head shot," Julian advised.

Cameron stared at Julian in utter shock. It didn't feel real, hearing him. Much less hearing him speak in that beautiful, accented voice.

Lancaster raised the gun again, but Julian lunged at him in a movement that was so sudden and fierce that Cameron flinched away from it as well. He had never seen anyone move like that. It was like a lion attacking.

Julian shoved Lancaster into the back wall of the little office, cracking the cheap drywall and sending dust and plaster flying into the air. Cameron tried desperately to tip his own chair over like Blake had told him, but he couldn't drag his eyes away. The battle between the two men wasn't graceful like fights he'd seen in movies. It wasn't precise and silent. It was fast and ugly and chaotic and loud.

Every time a man landed a blow there was a sickening thud of flesh on flesh. It was brutal, making it difficult for Cameron even to listen to, much less watch. He couldn't believe that the man who'd been so gentle with him was capable of such frightening strength and violence.

Cameron closed his eyes when he felt his chair tipping, and he crashed to the ground with a grunt as pain lanced through his shoulder and arm. He had no sooner hit the ground than he saw Lancaster catch Julian's arm in mid-swing. He heard the snap of bone breaking as Lancaster put pressure on both sides of Julian's arm.

Julian didn't shout in pain; he wrapped his other arm around his opponent and turned them both bodily, picking Lancaster up and swinging him, tossing him through the glass window of the office. The action didn't even look to have caused him much effort.

There was a crash from the darkness outside, followed by a wordless shout of pain and anger. Julian pulled his own gun and fired repeatedly into the darkness until the chamber clicked empty. He dropped the gun and extracted a long black dagger as he turned on Cameron.

Julian bent over him, grabbing for the arm of the chair and slicing at Cameron's wrist hastily. He ripped the zip tie away and leaned over Cameron to cut the other one. A shot rang out, and Julian gave a low oomph as he fell into Cameron and rolled slightly.

"How's that one?" Lancaster called from somewhere in the darkness. "That one work better with that vest?" he spat sarcastically.

Cameron grasped at Julian as the other man lurched against him and the knife went skittering across the floor. He could see the outline of Lancaster's body moving toward them.

"Julian," he breathed in warning. "Julian, he's coming." He pushed at Julian with his free hand, which came away wet with a stream of blood.

Julian slid to the floor, his arm bleeding freely and leaving smudges of blood on the concrete as he scrambled for his backup gun. Lancaster broke into a run, bursting through the office door to knock the weapon out of Julian's hand. Julian rolled and kicked at his leg, sending Lancaster crashing into the old desk against the wall. He slid to the floor as the desk splintered beneath him.

Julian was on his feet even as Lancaster fell and tried to get back up, and he tackled him as soon as he got to his knees, grappling for the weapon.

As the two men rolled around, Blake writhed in his chair, trying in vain to get loose. His wrists were bleeding from the effort, but he didn't stop. Cameron turned his chin to try to find the knife in the dim light. He caught sight of it about five feet away, near the back wall of the office, half-hidden under an old filing cabinet.

He started scooting toward the knife, using his free arm to drag himself and the chair forward, glancing back at the two killers as they fought.

Julian was bigger and stronger than Lancaster, but Julian was wounded and bleeding freely and Lancaster was all wiry muscle and grit. And he played dirty. As Cameron watched, he pulled a knife from a sheath at his ankle and sank it into Julian's side, sliding the blade under his arm, above the vest he wore. Julian howled in pain, his back arching as he fell to the side. Lancaster pounced him, pinning him to the ground with one hand as he used the other to push the gun they grappled over toward his face. Julian grunted in pain and tried to guide it away with the hand of his broken arm.

"Hit me with a goddamned piece of wood," Lancaster said through gritted teeth as they struggled.

The gun went off again, causing both men to jerk and roll away from each other in a momentary truce as their ears rang. Cameron pushed himself closer to the knife, reaching for it desperately even as he tried to watch the two men. Lancaster jumped Julian again as Julian contorted, trying to yank the knife out of his side, and he hit him hard across the face with the butt of the gun. Cameron winced and looked away. His fingers just barely slid over the blade of the knife as he heard the solid thump of Lancaster hitting Julian again.

Cameron cursed and stretched until his entire body screamed with the effort, and he managed to knock the blade sideways, spinning the knife until he could grasp the handle without risking it sliding under the cabinet. He finally got it in hand and quickly used it to cut the zip tie restraining his other hand and his ankles.

When he was free of the chair, Cameron scuttled across the dusty floor toward Blake, the knife still in his right hand. But his eyes were fastened on the two men fighting just feet away. Lancaster straddled Julian as the bigger man held the gun in both hands, pushing it away from his head as Lancaster tried with all his strength to aim it. He had Julian pinned beneath him. If Julian used any energy to dislodge him, Lancaster would be able to fire the gun and finish him.

The gun fired again, hitting the concrete beside Julian's head and sending shards of concrete everywhere. Cameron covered his head, and Blake flinched away. Julian shouted in rage and pain and tried again to swing at Lancaster, only to catch his hands just in time to prevent the gun being aimed at his head once more. Cameron swiftly cut through the ties that bound Blake's hands, and Blake took the knife from his shaking fingers and went to work on his own ankles.

The strength of Julian's injured arms began to give out, and Lancaster pressed down on him, turning the gun slowly toward his forehead. Julian gritted his teeth and closed his eyes, trying to find the strength to fight back.

"Help him!" Blake shouted as he struggled to cut through the last zip tie.

Cameron looked desperately around the office for something, anything, to use as a weapon. Before he could move, though, Lancaster grunted in pain and went rolling off Julian's body, landing spread-eagled on his back beside Julian on the cold concrete. Cameron had no idea what had happened, and from the stunned look on Julian's face as he lay on the ground, he wasn't quite sure, either.

Lancaster rolled to his knees, doubled up and obviously hurt. He grunted as he stared out the door of the office, and as he crouched and held his hand to his shoulder, the filing cabinet near Lancaster's head burst open with a crash and rattle as the silenced round hit.

A hail of bullets followed, the silenced pops making little sound in the cavernous warehouse, but the sound of the barrage in the office bounced off the corrugated tin of the roof and walls and rang in Cameron's ears. His instinctive reaction was to duck and cover his head as he stumbled a few steps away into the corner of the room. Lancaster ducked as well, and Blake tackled Cameron to the ground and shielded him as the room exploded around them.

When the assault ended, no one in the ruined office moved.

An eerie silence fell in the warehouse, and when Blake finally raised his head to allow Cameron to look around, dust and bits of shredded paper and cardboard were just beginning to settle.

The adrenaline began to leak away as Cameron stared, and the cold seeped in again. He started shaking as Blake helped him off the ground, and they surveyed the damage together.

Lancaster lay on his back, bleeding and staring at the ceiling unblinkingly. Preston stood in the doorway, calmly reloading what appeared to be a high-powered rifle with a scope. Julian lay at his feet, still covering his head and curled protectively as bits of shredded newspaper floated down around him.

"You could have given me a better shot, sir," Preston told Julian calmly.

"Sorry," Julian groaned weakly as he uncovered his head and let his arms fall to his chest. "Is he dead?" he asked with a hint of dread in his voice.

Cameron's eyes tracked to Lancaster's body, and his eyes widened. Lancaster certainly looked dead. Cameron looked back at Preston just in time to see the man cock his head and heft the rifle off his shoulder, pointing it at Lancaster with one hand. Then he pulled the trigger, letting off a short burst of silenced rounds. Lancaster's lifeless body jumped as the bullets hit home, and Cameron jumped as well with a torn gasp.

"He is now," Preston answered succinctly as he re-shouldered the rifle and smiled.

"Thank you for being thorough," Julian grunted as he rolled onto his side and clutched at his ribs.

"As ever, sir," Preston responded politely before setting the rifle against the doorframe and kneeling next to Julian. He gripped the knife handle that stuck out of Julian's side and gave it a wicked yank.

Julian cursed weakly and lowered his head as Preston stuffed a handkerchief under the vest to stop the bleeding. Preston stood once more, turning to look at Blake and Cameron and nodding at them as if greeting someone in the park. He then turned his attention to the cage in the corner, where Smith and Wesson were making a cacophony of horrible sounds.

"Jesus Christ!" Blake breathed in horror as he stood. "Preston, what the hell?"

"There comes a time in this job where being honorable has no place," Preston announced as he carefully stepped over the debris on the floor. "That's why he needs me," he told them with an evil smirk as he stepped over Julian toward the cage.

Blake stared at both men for a long moment and then moved to help Julian to his feet. As soon as Julian was standing, Blake grabbed him by the shoulders to look at him. "You son of a bitch," he snapped, and then he swung at him, sending him reeling backward through the darkened doorway. "I'll kill you myself!" Blake shouted as he grabbed at Julian's black shirt and made to hit him again.

"No! Blake!" Cameron cried out in surprise. Hadn't they had enough violence for one night?

Julian wasn't even able to put up a hand to defend himself. He weaved dangerously and collapsed backward. Blake stopped his swing, moving to catch the bigger man as he fell.

"Damnit," Blake muttered as he lowered Julian's unconscious body to the ground. "How does he always manage to avoid the second hit?" he asked Preston in annoyance.

"Loss of blood, sir," Preston answered calmly as he released Smith and Wesson from their cage.

BLAKE and Preston got Julian sitting on the bed so they could carefully remove his boots. The hospital had given him scrubs to wear home, draping a couple blankets over his shoulders to keep him warm as he moved from hospital to vehicle and vehicle to apartment. His chest was otherwise bare, due to the bulky sling on his arm and the bandages wrapped high around his ribs to cover the wound on the opposite side. His arm was broken, but it wasn't a bad break. The bullet that had hit him had gone through the meat of his upper arm; it was painful, but it wasn't a bad wound either.

The stab wound in his side had been the real worry. He had lost a lot of blood, and the knife had done damage not only to the soft tissue, but to the ribs as well. He was just lucky the blade had missed his lungs. It hurt him to breathe and move, but he would certainly live.

Cameron had come out of the terrifying evening with a wide assortment of bruises, a split lip, lacerations on the wrist that was attached to the chair while he struggled to reach the knife, and a real after-the-fact nervous breakdown.

But now he was mostly calm and numb, having cried himself out at the hospital and finally getting somewhat warm. He watched Julian as the other men stepped back, and he tried to resist the urge to step closer. Instead he just stood back and watched as Julian stared blankly. The other man had half-drowsed, half-stared on the way home from the hospital. Possibly shock, the doctor had said. Definitely morphine.

He'd yet to say a word to any of them or even look at Cameron.

"I'm going to get the stuff from the hospital," Blake said quietly, and he left the room. He was still angry, Cameron could tell. He had been moving and speaking gently ever since hitting Julian at the warehouse, trying not to display any more of the anger, but the restraint merely served to make it more obvious.

Cameron could hardly blame him. Now that he was at least partially past being scared to death, he couldn't look at Julian without wanting to throttle him, without remembering all the pain his loss had caused. Or without wanting to curl up beside him and simply be relieved that he was alive.

Julian seemed to make a massive effort to focus his eyes, and he looked up at Cameron blankly. Cameron wanted to yell at him to snap out of it. He couldn't ask him all the questions he wanted to ask or kick him in the shin until Julian was once again healthy and in his right mind. Instead of shouting, he stepped closer and slid his hand behind Julian's good shoulder. "Careful," he warned softly as he guided Julian to lie back against the pillows.

Julian reached up slowly and gripped Cameron's wrist. He looked up into Cameron's eyes, still slightly distant but obviously attempting to fight the remainder of the morphine he had been given. "I missed you," he stated softly.

A bolt shot through his chest, and Cameron bit his lip against a pained moan. Searching Julian's eyes before answering, he slowly nodded. After several moments of staring into Julian's dark eyes, he finally realized that he didn't *know* what to say.

Julian breathed out raggedly and looked down at Cameron's hand. He pulled it closer and slid his lips along the inside of Cameron's wrist before he pushed his face into Cameron's palm and closed his eyes again.

Cameron squeezed his eyes shut as he cupped Julian's cheek, stroking the stubbled skin with his fingertips. He'd missed Julian so much he hadn't been able to breathe without it hurting. Cameron didn't want to hurt anymore. He didn't want either of them to be in pain.

"You need to rest," he urged softly. But he couldn't force himself to move his hand away.

Julian nodded and lowered his head dejectedly, and then he moved gingerly to lie down.

"Are you hurting?" Cameron asked as he carefully placed his hand at Julian's forehead, afraid the painkillers had worn off already.

"No," Julian answered weakly as he released Cameron's hand and slid down to lay on his back. It was the first time Cameron had heard him lie and not put any effort into making it believable. He stared at the ceiling for a long moment and then closed his eyes slowly.

"I'll be out in the living room if you need anything," Cameron told him, unable to be in the same room any longer.

Julian merely nodded to let Cameron know he had heard. He kept his eyes closed, and finally he rolled onto his side, despite the obvious pain, and curled slowly. Smith and Wesson were immediately beside him, curling against him and purring loudly.

Exhausted, Cameron let Julian move as he wanted and left the bedroom, closing the door behind him before he had to stop and pinch the bridge of his nose.

"Are you okay?" Blake asked pointedly, noticeably inquiring after Cameron instead of Julian.

After a long moment, Cameron dropped his hand. "I don't know," he said quietly. He trudged toward the kitchen where Preston sat at the kitchen table, calmly drinking a cup of coffee. Cameron thought this was Preston's apartment. Cameron was afraid to ask if Julian had been living here. It wasn't far from Cameron's own.

Blake watched Cameron for a long moment before moving slowly to sit across from Preston. "You'll feel better once you hit him," he murmured sympathetically.

Cameron's jaw clenched, and he practically collapsed into the chair at the head of the table. Blake glanced at him and sighed softly.

"I'm not judging you, son," Blake assured him. "I missed him like hell, and I barely like the bastard," he said with a nod of his head at the closed bedroom doors.

Cameron's nose wrinkled. "He's only a bastard some of the time," he defended.

Blake gave a snort and shook his head. "Expect it to get worse. He's not good at being hurt."

"Did you see him the time he was wearing the sling and still came to the restaurant to eat?" Cameron asked abruptly. "He told me later it was because he'd missed the week before. It was before I really realized why he was there every Tuesday. He'd been shot two weeks before—and he still came to dinner."

Blake nodded his head slowly. "I didn't mean hurt physically," he said softly. "Although he *is* a horrible patient. Did you serve him one night in late November, when he ordered an extra glass of wine?"

Cameron tipped his head to one side. "Yeah, I did," he said. "That was when it started. He asked me if I liked my job."

Blake looked over at Cameron thoughtfully and then huffed softy. "Well. That extra glass of wine? That was Arlo's. It was the anniversary of the day Julian tossed him out on his ass. Every year, Julian would order him a glass of wine, regret who he was and what he did, and usually end up too drunk to stand."

Cameron frowned. "He didn't stay. I remember thinking it was a very odd night. Two glasses of wine, didn't even touch his dinner… and he left me a two-hundred-dollar tip."

Blake nodded. "I know," he said with a sigh. "I called him on a job that night. I remember being afraid I hadn't caught him in time, that he'd be too drunk to do it. That was where the shot in the arm came from. My point, though, is that he regretted the way he and Arlo parted. I think, deep down, Julian didn't mind dying if it was Arlo doing it."

"So why did that change? Why did Julian start trying to kill him?" Cameron asked.

Blake shrugged. "That, you'll have to ask him. Julian's mind doesn't work like a normal person's."

Cameron inhaled deeply. He'd wondered—feared—that he was the reason for Julian's change of heart. He pushed the thought away.

Preston glanced over at them and cleared his throat. "He loved you, Mr. Jacobs," he stated evenly. "In his way. He loved Mr. Lancaster too."

"I know he loved me," Cameron said in a small voice, surprised that Preston had spoken at all. Pain lanced through him as he looked back at the bedroom doors. "But I threw it away."

"Cam, I've never seen him like he is with you," Blake said. "He's… a totally different man. Maybe who he would have been, if life were different. Even after you broke it off, he still loved you."

"He didn't love me enough to let me know he was still alive," Cameron whispered.

Preston was silent, his eyes on Cameron, who looked back at him expectantly.

"Why didn't he try?" Cameron demanded, anger coming to the fore. After tonight, his nerves and control were shot, and he didn't have the fortitude or the desire to hold anything back.

Preston responded to the anger by merely blinking and meeting Cameron's eyes expressionlessly.

Cameron turned his chin sharply toward Blake. "You said he still loves me, even after what I did. Then why didn't he tell me?"

"Cam, it's not that simple," Blake began.

"You're pissed at him too! He left us thinking all this time that he was *dead*!" Cameron continued, his voice rising and his face flushing as he stood up and started pacing.

"I know, but, Cam—"

"No. No buts, Blake. One phone call. One e-mail. One something to let me know he was still breathing. If he forgives me, if he cares for me so much, why leave me to suffer all this time?" Cameron spit out, trembling as his emotions got the better of him.

"That, I don't know, sir," Preston answered calmly, as if Cameron had asked about the weather. "Mr. Cross has a reason for everything he does or doesn't do. That doesn't mean I always understand."

Cameron swallowed hard and looked at Blake for an answer. Blake met his eyes, and then he closed his own and shook his head. Cameron turned on his heel, grabbed the jacket Preston had laid out for him, and left the apartment.

ROUGHLY a week after his ordeal, Cameron still refused to answer the door or the telephone. He stayed in his apartment with his dogs, stewing angrily over Julian's deception and throwing things when he thought about how many times he'd dreamed about Julian coming back to him.

It wasn't fair, to know he was alive and yet be so angry at him. And it was worse than that if what Blake said about Julian still loving him was true.

Cameron was sitting on his couch, staring out the window blearily when the buzzer rang. He didn't move, letting it ring again. It continued to ring demandingly until Cameron turned his head slowly to glare at it. Finally, he got up and dragged across the hardwood floor in his bare feet to punch at the button.

"What?" he snapped. Last time it had been Miri, trying to deliver a care package from the restaurant.

"Let me in, Cameron," Julian's soft voice demanded in a no-nonsense tone.

Cameron pushed the button without even thinking about it, and then he shook his head in exasperation at how automatic it was to just do as Julian said. Knowing he was coming, Cameron unlocked the door and moved away, sighing as he headed back for the couch. He was beginning to tremble as he sat and wrapped himself up in a throw blanket.

Why was Julian here?

When the knob turned, Cameron caught his breath. He could only stare and try not to shake as Julian stepped into the apartment. He shrugged out of his coat and hung it on one of the hooks beside the door, and he cocked his head and looked at Cameron, not coming further into the apartment. Cameron was surprised to see that he was wearing his sling. He must have been in a lot of pain to deal with the cumbersome thing, and he still moved slowly as if he hurt all over.

Cameron stared at him, unable to think of a single, solitary thing to say.

"Hello, Cameron," Julian murmured softly, the Irish accent still seeming unusual and foreign out of his mouth.

Cameron blinked and opened his mouth to say something, but just as quickly closed it and shook his head. He swallowed with difficulty, allowing himself to look at his erstwhile lover. He was wearing jeans, boots, and a plain blue T-shirt. Cameron had never seen him in anything but an expensive suit or… nothing at all. It was disconcerting.

"Hi," he finally whispered.

"You look well," Julian observed after a moment of silence.

At that moment, the dogs came stumbling out of the bedroom area where they'd been napping in front of the fireplace and scampered toward the entry to swarm Julian's ankles.

"Blake's been taking care of you?" Julian asked as the dogs latched onto his shoelaces and the hems of his jeans. He didn't look away from Cameron as they cavorted around him. "May I come in?" he asked when Cameron didn't answer.

Cameron was too dazed to do anything but nod. He didn't want to look away, even for a second. As angry as he was, he thought he would have been able to remain composed in Julian's presence, but seeing him again, here in his own home, was both painful and wonderful. What… why… how… questions swirled in his head, and there was no way he could pick just one, so he shut his mouth and climbed off the couch. He met Julian's eyes deliberately and walked the several steps forward to stand more than an arm's length away from the other man.

"You look really good," Julian whispered appraisingly as he watched Cameron.

Some of the shock ebbed, replaced by a terribly painful ache Cameron thought he'd gotten over. "Thank you," he murmured.

"I'm sorry for what I've done," Julian offered regretfully.

Cameron sighed heavily and looked up at Julian, his eyes intent on the other man. He stepped a little closer, a couple feet away, and reached out to ghost his fingers over Julian's cheek. When Cameron pulled his hand away, Julian closed his eyes and lowered his head.

He never saw Cameron's fist coming.

Julian staggered back a step and shook his head, putting his hand to his lip as it seeped blood. He huffed slightly and looked down at

Cameron with a little nod. "I was sort of expecting that earlier," he admitted.

"You son of a bitch," Cameron bit off, wincing and shaking his hand out at his side. "What the *fuck*?"

"I'm sorry," Julian offered softly. "I had to disappear if I wanted to live."

"Live? *Live*?" Cameron asked incredulously. "But you're *dead*!"

"In theory," Julian agreed with a wince.

"A theory I've had to live with for six months!" Cameron said sharply as his hand curled back into a fist.

Julian's eyes darted to the clenched fist warily, and he lowered his chin. "I know," he said curtly. He didn't offer another apology.

The tone of Julian's voice cut Cameron deeply, and the upset overwhelmed the anger, for the moment. "Where have you been?" he asked brokenly.

"Trying to bury myself," Julian said in answer.

Cameron couldn't keep back the torn scoff. "Good luck with that, 'cause it's already been done!" he snapped. He ran his hand through his hair and took a steadying breath as he stared toward the kitchen. He knew if he continued to look at Julian, he'd have an absolute fit. "Did Blake know?" he asked in a dark, angry voice.

"No," Julian answered with another wince. "I spoke to him this morning," he added. "He hit me again. Twice."

Cameron had to laugh, but it was a soft, broken sound. "Pretty deserved, if you ask me." He looked back at Julian and narrowed his eyes. "I don't know what to say, Julian," he whispered. "You were out there, alive and well, and you never once tried to tell me. Never once tried to let me know you were okay."

Julian bowed his head and slid his hands slowly into his pockets.

"How did you do it?" Cameron demanded.

Julian winced and looked up at him again. "Preston bribed the doctors, told them to declare me dead and hide me under false names.

They kept me there until I could move on my own. I was on my back for three weeks, recovering for another six," he told Cameron softly. "When I was sure I could handle myself once more, I had to make certain Arlo wasn't out there, waiting. I couldn't contact you. I didn't want to see you in danger again because of me."

It made sense, but that didn't make it hurt an iota less. Cameron was a different man because of having Julian in his life, because of the love, the fear, the pain, *and* the danger. "And now?" he asked shakily.

Julian gave a slightly self-conscious shrug. "There's no more contract because I'm dead. He's gone. And I'm back."

"You're back," Cameron repeated softly, everything, everywhere hurting. He wanted so badly to reach out and curl around Julian to try to make himself believe he was really here and forget all the pain. "But nothing's changed. There's more like him still out there still looking to hurt you. It's still just as dangerous as it was two weeks ago when I thought you were dead and you were too much of a coward to come tell me you weren't!"

"That's true, yes," Julian affirmed, his normally impassive face displaying a hint of pain at Cameron's words.

Cameron's fingers dug into his own arms. "So, what now? Why are you here? Would you have ever come back?" he asked painfully. "If he hadn't shown himself? Would you ever have come back to me?"

Julian was silent as he turned his head and studied Cameron. "Last I heard, you wanted me gone," he finally reminded softly. "It wasn't my right, to show up here and beg you to take me back."

Cameron blinked at him stupidly.

"But now?" Julian continued calmly. "I don't care if I have the right or not. I was hoping that after the anger had passed, you might want me to stick around."

Cameron exhaled shakily, and he raised both hands to rub at his face before dropping them again to return Julian's even gaze. "And how long do you think that will take? For the anger to pass? Because I'll tell you right now I have no idea how to deal with this."

Julian shrugged uncomfortably. "I suppose it will take a while," he nearly mumbled.

Letting out a strangled sound of frustration, Cameron turned and clenched his fists. "It's not going to be easy," he said hoarsely.

"Not if you're angry," Julian agreed. "Not if you can't forgive me."

"I fell apart when you were gone, and it took all this time to put myself back together," Cameron said, voice choking on pent-up anger and pain. "And now… Julian, Christ." He squeezed his eyes shut and dropped his head, fighting for control.

Julian was silent. They both knew how hollow the words "I'm sorry" could sound. Cameron was sorely tempted to tell him to leave just to get this source of pain out of his life. But he knew if he refused Julian today, he would never see the man again, and that idea hurt even more.

Cameron managed to hold it together and opened his eyes to look at Julian as he edged away. It broke his heart all over again, to see that look on Julian's face. "Please," he croaked. "Don't leave. Not again."

"I never left," Julian insisted quietly with a shake of his head.

Cameron studied Julian for a long moment as his heartbeat thumped in his throat. Then he nodded slowly. Trying to regain some measure of composure, Cameron glanced to the kitchen. "I need a drink. You want a drink? I'm getting a drink." He walked off to the kitchen without waiting for a response.

"Good," Julian muttered. "Drink mine too, will you? I remember you being easier to deal with when you're drunk."

Letting out a short bark of laughter, Cameron stepped to the refrigerator and pulled out his last bottle of wine. "It takes more than it used to," he told Julian ruefully, setting down the bottle and snagging two glasses from the cabinet.

Julian remained silent as he watched.

Cameron poured the two glasses and set the bottle aside, pushing one glass toward the other side of the bar before taking a long sip of his own and holding the chilled glass to his forehead as he closed his eyes. This roller-coaster ride of emotions was exhausting, and he wanted to get off before he fell apart again.

"What's with the accent?" he asked abruptly.

Julian blinked at him, nonplussed. "What, you don't like it?" he asked defensively.

Cameron frowned slightly. "Actually, I do. A lot. I just want to know where it came from. And if it's really yours."

Julian blushed heavily and cleared his throat. "It's mine. I was born in Dublin," he answered uncomfortably.

"Dublin, Kansas," Cameron stated with the slightest touch of bitter humor in his voice.

Julian shrugged guiltily. "It's close," he mumbled.

Cameron's lips twitched. "Uh-huh." He shook his head. "What about the other things you told me that night?"

Julian shifted uneasily. "I lied to you," he admitted. "I lied about a lot of things. But never because I wanted to or wanted to hurt you."

"What should I believe now?" Cameron asked pointedly. Then, surprisingly, a slight laugh broke free. "Because, you know, you tell me something using that damn accent, and I might just be putty in your hands."

Julian blinked at him in surprise. "I missed you," he answered softly as he watched Cameron raptly.

"I should hope so," Cameron said, eyebrows raised in expectation of more information forthcoming.

Julian's lips twitched. "And I love you," he added obediently.

Cameron nodded, tilting his head and waiting, still expectant, though now he was smiling again, this time even wider. He felt disgustingly giddy, which was terrible when he knew he should really still be angry.

Julian bit his lower lip thoughtfully and lowered his head just slightly, still looking at Cameron unerringly. He thought for a minute and then inclined his head again. "And I like the color paint you chose?" he tried hopefully.

Cameron couldn't hold back the laugh. "You're an asshole, you know that?" he accused.

"Yes," Julian answered obediently.

"Is Julian Cross your real name?" Cameron asked with a touch of dread. He didn't know that he could think of the man as anything other than Julian.

"Mostly," Julian answered with a wince. "Julian is my given name. Cross… isn't," he offered with an apologetic shrug.

Cameron nodded in relief. "As long as you're Julian, I think I can deal with that," he admitted tentatively.

"I am," Julian affirmed hopefully. "And I'm possibly in need of an ice cube," he added as he licked at his bleeding lip.

"No kidding," Cameron responded. "Blake warned me it would hurt, but you know, it was a spur-of-the-moment thing."

"I would advise you not to shake it," Julian muttered dryly. "First time I hit someone I broke my finger," he added with a smirk.

"I think I avoided that," Cameron said, looking at his hand. The knuckles were already darkening to bruises. He sighed and paused, just to look at Julian, soak him in. "I couldn't stop thinking about you," he admitted softly, most of the harsh emotions finally draining away. "Everything I did, every change I made, I wondered… what would you have thought?"

Julian was silent, looking at Cameron closely across the kitchen counter. Finally, he reached across the counter and took Cameron's chin in his hand. "The only thing that matters is you," he claimed. "If you're happy."

Cameron found his breath hard to catch as Julian's fingers brushed against his skin. He reached up to grab Julian's wrist so he wouldn't pull away.

"Can you forgive me?" Julian asked worriedly.

Cameron's shoulders slumped, and his hand tightened on Julian's wrist. "Maybe," he whispered honestly. "I just don't know, Julian. I still hurt. I still want to be angry."

Julian let out a pent-up breath and nodded. "I can live with maybe for now," he whispered unsteadily, a mix of relief and pain clear in his voice.

Cameron's heart thumped as his eyes scanned him over, truly looking at Julian for the first time in so long. He looked tired and worried, worn out and completely spent. His eyes weren't the same sharp obsidian Cameron remembered in his dreams. He realized that all this time, Julian must have been living on a high wire.

"You haven't been taking care of yourself," he accused softly.

"No," Julian agreed unrepentantly. "You were right. I need someone to do it for me."

Cameron licked his lips slowly, a frown creasing his brow as he nodded. He looked Julian over, feeling guilty already for the bloody lip he himself had given the man. "What do you need?" he asked softly.

Julian dug into the pocket of his jeans and extracted a bottle of prescription pills. "I need a glass of water," Julian answered miserably.

"Okay," Cameron said, trying not to be amused as he turned and retrieved a glass to fill.

Julian took the water with a mumbled thanks. He swallowed the pills with one gulp and then drank down the rest of the water. He didn't meet Cameron's eyes until he handed the glass back to him.

Cameron accepted it as he looked over Julian's flushed face. "Want some more to drink?" he asked quietly as he reached up and smoothed down the ruffled hair around Julian's ear.

Julian shook his head in answer. "How are you?" he asked softly. "Aside from angry?"

Cameron sighed and shook his head slightly. "Hurting," he murmured. He turned to lift his shirt and show Julian the vivid black-and-blue bruise that ran from his shoulder down to his elbow.

Julian frowned and looked at it in confusion. "What's that from?" he asked softly.

"When I tipped myself over in that damn chair," Cameron said, still inspecting the bruises that were just now starting to fade.

Julian reached out with his good hand and slid his fingers gently down Cameron's arm. "I'm sorry you were hurt," he murmured.

A frown creased Cameron's forehead as he watched Julian's unreadable eyes. "Did you ever plan to really kill him?" he asked curiously.

Julian looked up to meet his eyes and smiled sadly. "Yeah," he answered. "I've been trying to kill him for five years," he admitted. "There's a reason I've never really succeeded."

Cameron didn't understand and couldn't begin to. He bit his lip and curled his fingers loosely around Julian's wrist, allowing himself to touch more than he had ever thought he would again. "Blake said you were… together once," he ventured hesitantly.

Julian's head jerked slightly, and then he closed his eyes as he shook his head. "No," he answered softly. "Not like that. I loved that bastard like a brother," he told Cameron as his voice hardened. "But he got reckless. Put us in danger. I couldn't have that."

Cameron released Julian's hand and began to move, pacing away from the kitchen. "It hurts to lose someone you love," he whispered as he turned around to look at Julian again.

Julian nodded, turning his head slightly to watch Cameron as he moved. "It hurt more when it was you," he whispered suddenly.

Cameron stayed quiet for a long moment, warring within himself. He wanted to wrap around the other man and let himself sink into the comfort of what they had once had. But the mention of Lancaster reminded him that he also wanted answers. "Why did you give me the necklace?" he asked softly. "You said it had meaning to you, but you never told me why."

Julian flinched and backed away a step, head lowered and eyes closed. "It did have meaning," he muttered in answer. "It was special to me. It was a symbol of protection, of brotherhood and loyalty. It was a symbol of the only kind of love I knew before you," he said quickly as he looked up at Cameron sadly. "The only time I could look at it and not remember how angry I'd been was when I saw you wearing it."

"He betrayed you," Cameron said softly. He looked up at Julian, his own face pained. "I betrayed you too."

Julian met his eyes briefly before a shiver ran through him, and his eyes flickered away. He didn't say anything in response.

Cameron bit his lip. "It's gone," he whispered.

"What is?" Julian asked hoarsely as he turned his head again, almost meeting Cameron's eyes.

"The necklace."

Julian tilted his head, his brow knitting as he reached out with his good hand and slid his fingers under the collar of Cameron's shirt. "Good," he finally said curtly.

Cameron jerked his chin up in surprise. "Good?"

Julian nodded wordlessly, his jaw set stubbornly. "Good," he repeated as he reached up and slid his hand along the side of Cameron's neck, letting his thumb run along the top of Cameron's collarbone. "One less thing hanging between us," he said as he met Cameron's eyes steadily.

Cameron found himself getting lost in the emotion in those eyes, and he knew if he didn't back away now he would be lost for good. He took a slight step back, forcing Julian's hand to slide away.

Julian remained where he was, watching him silently. "Loving each other isn't enough now, is it?" he asked, his voice flat and lifeless.

When Cameron looked back at Julian, he couldn't keep the pain out of his eyes. "I'm afraid it's too much," he said, voice breaking. "There's still danger, isn't there? To both of us. What if I lose you again?"

"Then you'll hurt again," Julian answered bluntly. "And finally move on just as you were the first time."

Cameron swallowed hard on the gorge that rose into his throat. "I don't want that to happen," he whispered, looking up into Julian's eyes.

Julian tipped his head to one side, pursing his lips as he considered his answer. "I lost you before because I lied to you," he pointed out. "I could tell you nothing would ever happen again, that we'll always be together and safe, but…." He shrugged helplessly and shook his head. "You're the one who said you could be hit by a car on the way to the grocery store."

Cameron nodded slowly as he closed his arms around Julian's waist. "I'd rather be scared with you than without you. Being afraid when I knew I could have been with you was terrifying."

Julian nodded solemnly as he slid his good arm around Cameron's shoulders and pulled him close. He set his chin on the crown of Cameron's head as Cameron embraced him. "I've found that having someone to watch your back helps you face down the terror," he said softly.

"Yeah," Cameron whispered. He closed his eyes and turned his head to press his ear against Julian's chest so he could hear the thumping heartbeat.

"Preferably with a sniper rifle," Julian couldn't help but add under his breath.

Cameron snorted and shook his head. Then he tipped his head back. "Julian, since you're… dead… will you still be doing… that job?"

Julian inhaled slowly and took a small step back, raising his chin to look over Cameron's head. "I have no reason to," he finally answered. "The game's changed, anyway," he mumbled as he looked back down at Cameron.

"Changed?" Cameron echoed.

"No honor in it," Julian answered, almost embarrassed as he spoke.

Cameron slowly smiled. "I knew there was a little bit of a white knight hiding under all that black armor," he teased gently.

"Don't kid yourself, now," Julian warned with a hint of a blush.

Cameron smiled before going on tiptoe to kiss Julian gently.

Julian tensed against him, his lips parting against the kiss. "Does this mean I get a second chance?" he asked breathlessly.

"Yes," Cameron whispered in between kisses.

Julian seemed to deflate against him, the relief obvious as he pulled Cameron closer with one arm and hugged him hard. "You'll stay with me?" he asked uncertainly.

"Would you please not die again?" Cameron said against his chest.

Julian sighed and rested his chin on Cameron's head again. "If that's the caveat I'm afraid I won't be able to comply," he said wryly. "I promise to try very hard not to," he added seriously.

"That's what's important," Cameron said. He closed his eyes and inhaled deeply. "I love you, Julian. I know I broke both our hearts when I sent you away. But I never stopped loving you."

Julian nodded and looked down at Cameron sadly. Suddenly his dark eyes lit up, and he broke into a smile. "Have you ever been to Ireland?" he asked with a hint of mischief in his voice.

"Ireland?" Cameron said, leaning back to look up at Julian, surprised by the non sequitur. "I've never been out of the Midwest, much less overseas."

"Oh, we'll fix that," Julian promised as he slid one arm around Cameron and began trying to work his way out of his sling.

Frowning, Cameron tried to hunch close. "Don't hurt yourself," he cautioned. "So you want to take me to Ireland?" he asked, his voice a little dubious.

Julian finally freed himself of the sling and took Cameron's face in both hands, heedless of the pain it must have caused him to move. "I want to take you anywhere you want to go," he told Cameron in a low murmur before kissing him possessively.

Cameron felt dizzy when Julian finally let him breathe. "As long as I'm with you, I don't care," he murmured as he moved one hand to cup Julian's cheek.

"I love you, Cameron," Julian whispered as he held Cameron to him tightly. "Please don't ever doubt it again."

Cameron tipped his head back, looking into his lover's eyes and whispering, "I promise."

MADELEINE URBAN is a down-home Kentucky girl who's been writing since she could hold a crayon. Although she has written and published on her own, she truly excels when writing with co-authors. She lives with her husband, who is very supportive of her work, and two canine kids who only allow her to hug them when she has food. She wants to live at Disney World, the home of fairy dust, because she believes that with hard work, a little luck, and beloved family and friends, dreams really can come true.

Email Madeleine at mrs.madeleine.urban@gmail.com.
Visit Madeleine's blog at http://madeleineurban.livejournal.com/.

⌘

ABIGAIL ROUX was born and raised in North Carolina. A past volleyball star who specializes in pratfalls and sarcasm, she currently spends her time coaching middle school volleyball and softball and dreading the day when her little girl hits that age. Abigail has a loving husband, a baby girl they call Boomer, four cats, three dogs, a crazyass extended family, and a cast of thousands in her head.

Visit Abigail's blog at http://abigail-roux.livejournal.com/.

Other Titles from Madeleine Urban & Abigail Roux…

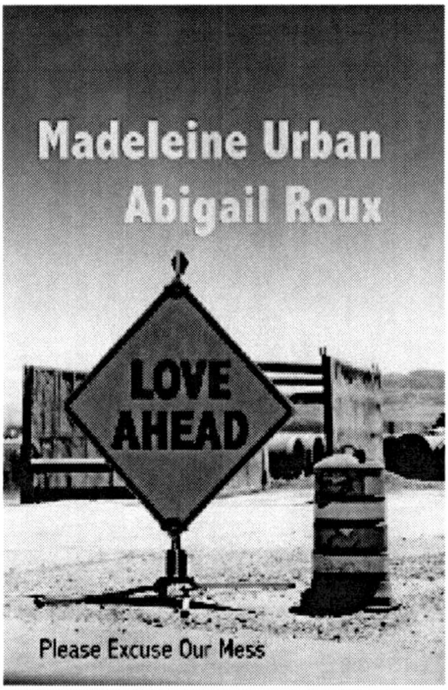

LaVergne, TN USA
28 October 2009

162284LV00005B/24/P

9 781615 810291